COLD TRAIN

THROUGH HELL

JEREMY FULMORE

COLD TRAIN THROUGH HELL

iUniverse books may be ordered through booksellers or by contacting:

iUniverse
1663 Liberty Drive
Bloomington, IN 47403
www.iuniverse.com
844-349-9409

Because of the dynamic nature of the Internet, any web addresses or links contained in this book may have changed since publication and may no longer be valid. The views expressed in this work are solely those of the author and do not necessarily reflect the views of the publisher, and the publisher hereby disclaims any responsibility for them.

Any people depicted in stock imagery provided by Getty Images are models, and such images are being used for illustrative purposes only. Certain stock imagery © Getty Images.

ISBN: 978-1-6632-3992-1 (sc)
ISBN: 978-1-6632-6489-3 (hc)
ISBN: 978-1-6632-3987-7 (e)

Library of Congress Control Number: 2022909146

Print information available on the last page.

iUniverse rev. date: 07/10/2024

CHAPTER 1

He inserted the keycard into his hotel room door and pulled it out briskly. A small green light by the card reader flashed and blipped, and he pushed the handle down. That was when he sensed it. Something was wrong. Call it awareness, perception, or instinct. Whatever it was had triggered a warning.

He pushed the door open with his right hand, paused, and took a step inside. He scanned the room from left to right. A dark polished wood table with a lamp stood by the entrance. A tan love seat sat under the window with thick gold curtains, next to an accompanying tan couch. An area rug covered rich hardwood floors. A large flat-screen television was mounted on the wall between two ornate windows. Another matching tan chair completed the living room set with a glass table centerpiece. The bookshelf on the far wall displayed random vases and trinkets. Double sliding doors led to the first bedroom. A painting of a bridge, black and white, hung next to the second bedroom door, also with double doors that opened inward. The adjacent wall bore an upscale bar and a small sink. All seemed to be in place.

Jake placed the keycard on the table beside him and stood still, ears straining over the sound of the air conditioner. The city blustered far below. Roaring engines and blaring horns were nothing more than background noise for people accustomed to city life. Barely noticeable. Other than that, the room was quiet. Perfectly still.

He took a few more steps past the dining room. Six heavy chairs encircled a dark wood table with a mirror-like gloss under a chandelier.

A single ivory candle rested in the center of the table. None of the chairs seemed out of place.

He was beginning to wonder if his imagination was running wild with conspiracies when he heard a creak. It sounded like it was coming from the bedroom. The apprehension in his gut shot straight to his chest. It froze him in place and he laughed at himself as if he were losing it. Then he heard it again, a distinct shifting of pressure on the floor, like someone moving across the carpet.

The doorknob clicked, and the bedroom door in front of him slowly opened. An unnerving sensation tugged at his innards, tingling dreadfully. His knees buckled, but he stood firm, ready for what came next. He clenched his fists and thrust out his chest.

There could be an easy explanation, he thought, like a maid replacing the lotions and soap he'd used earlier. Perhaps the manager was checking in, seeing if everything was satisfactory since he was paying top dollar for this penthouse suite. Or maybe another guest was given the wrong key. Mistakes happened.

Jake braced himself as a well-dressed man stepped out of the bedroom. He was tall and good-looking in a navy blue suit jacket and slacks, tie, and black shoes polished to a shine. His thick black hair was neatly slicked back to the nape of his neck. His hands were empty. A good sign.

The unpalatable sting in his throat only intensified when Jake realized he was in the presence of Jericho Black, billionaire. A man with his hands in many pots. Financiers all over the world knew him by first name basis. And Jake had been extensively checking into his history and business connections. The distasteful realization of getting caught was nauseating.

"What are you doing here?" asked Jake as if he had no clue.

Jericho motioned to the bar. "May I?" he asked. He made his way to the display and helped himself to the top-shelf alcohol behind the bar. He held up and admired a bottle of Pappy Van Winkle's 20 Year Family Reserve bourbon. After placing a tumbler on the counter, he poured himself half a glass.

Jake scrutinized Jericho while trying to maintain an air of calmness. This was Jericho Black, after all. Jake hoped he came across as intrepid and defiant, despite his legs feeling like rubber. Rather than chance a moment of looking foolish to the infamous man, he opted to stand perfectly still.

Jericho Black took a sip from the $3,000 bottle of whiskey Jake had sent to his room after spotting it in the hotel bar the night before. He'd savored the opportunity to taste something so rare. Now he wondered if he'd ever get the chance.

Jericho tipped the glass back, almost emptying it with one swallow. He gently placed the tumbler on the bar and stared at Jake, saying nothing. He barely even blinked. Jericho's silent regard raised Jake's pulse, and his ears reddened like a furnace was blowing heat on the back of his neck. A tacky coat of sweat formed on his skin.

The billionaire stood solid and imposing. He gripped the bar with both hands, wide fingers spread. At six feet two, and although Jake was several inches taller, Jericho's gaze was quite intimidating.

"$375,466,212 with all the transactions tallied," said Jericho. "No one except the people in this room knows that you took it." Jericho glanced back to the partially open bedroom door, and another man emerged. He was much bigger and rougher looking in a black suit, no tie. His cheap suit gave the impression that expensive outfits were often ruined because of his line of work.

CHAPTER 2

The nefarious aura of the new intruder had Jake looking for a chair. The guy was big and ugly. Large, plump hands with thick fingers. Scruffy looking. An unrestrained and uncompromising nature about him. The animus for Jake was apparent in the flare-up of his upper lip. He plopped down in the tan recliner facing his unwelcomed guests. He thought it best to talk and talk fast. Jake looked at the Goliath first, then Jericho.

"I took it as leverage," said Jake. He turned his attention to the large man. "I have a tumor. A brain tumor. Noncancerous. Benign. I've had seizures for most of my life. Been in a coma three times. One time for two months. The growth remained the size of a quarter for most of my life, but for the past year it's been steadily growing, about a quarter millimeter a month."

"You stole millions of dollars to pay medical bills?" asked Jericho. "Come on, Jake. You have to do better than that."

Jake struggled with the right words. "I stole the money because I have less than three months to live, and I need a cure."

Jericho and the big guy laughed. "Cute. Stumbling on words in an effort to get the story straight," said Jericho. He circled Jake's chair. "You wanted to live it up, didn't you, Jake? Go out with a bang! Rent this fancy hotel room. Order this fine bourbon. Your story should touch me, but it doesn't."

"I'm dying," Jake said. "It's the truth."

Jericho shrugged his shoulders. "Just because you're going to die, you should be given a pass?" He winked at his henchman. "I mean, what are the consequences, right? If you get caught, three months and you're dead anyway. I get it. However, the people you stole from will still be here, alive and pissed. What about that?"

Jake took a deep breath. "I was trying to buy a cure. Not blow the cash. I thought I could make it up to them some other way."

Jericho scoffed. "Nearly 400 million dollars is a lot to owe, Jake. What kind of cure are you looking for?"

"A miracle," said Jake. "Like the one Roland Stark used to perform."

Jericho flinched ever so slightly. "What about him?" he asked.

"I found him," said Jake. "I know where he is."

The preacher and miracle healer Roland Stark had a close business relationship with Jericho many years ago but hadn't been seen in decades. Rumors said he went off to some remote region of the world and disappeared. His social security number hadn't come up in any database; no credit cards, loans, bank accounts, or other credit in his name. Most assumed Stark was dead and had been for a long time.

"He lives in Florida," said Jake. "New name and identity. Witness protection or something similar. I didn't pry any further."

Jericho shrugged his shoulders again. "As far as I know, you found some bum who claims he's Roland Stark. You have to do better than that."

"What he told me should be proof enough," said Jake. "I tracked him down and told him my problem. He said if I wanted a cure, to find you. He said you could cure me, just like you cured all those other people and made it look like it was the work of God."

Jericho chuckled and tapped his glass of bourbon with his index finger. "You call that proof? Any bum could've told you that. You're making things up as you go along. Roland Stark is dead."

Jake shook his head. "That little glare in your eyes tells me that contrary to popular belief, you didn't have him killed, and you're hoping what I'm saying is true . . . and it is. Roland claims you're the one behind everything. You cured those people. I went to work, checked out his story, and saw your dealings with Ribel Pharmaceutical. You transferred a large amount of money to the CEO. I thought maybe Ribel was the source of your cures. That's when I decided to steal the money—to get your attention since you never accepted my requests for a meeting."

Jericho and the big guy exchanged glances, eyebrows raised. "You just up and stole the money to get my attention?" asked Jericho. "How does that make any sense?"

Jake's heart raced faster than ever. *Just tell them*, he thought. "I'm a computer programmer. A hacker in my spare time. I tracked the movements of Kyle Shubert, the CEO of Ribel Pharmaceutical, followed the stream of transfers from you to him and intercepted the funds before it could get there."

"Why?" said Jericho.

"It was just to get your attention, not keep it."

"And then?" asked Jericho.

"I guess . . ." Jake fiddled with his fingers. "Return the money in exchange for you to heal me?"

Jericho accepted Jake's explanation with a single nod. "Clever man, I will say that. My office is bombarded daily with all sorts of nobodies wanting to earn a minute of my time. This scheme takes the cake. Top of the list!"

"A fucking genius," said the big man. Jake couldn't quite place his accent.

"Well, you have my attention," said Jericho. "My full and undivided attention. Unfortunately, you also have the attention of a few other folks. In specific, certain Russian oligarchs. And in case you didn't know, with powerful oligarchs comes the Russian mob." Jericho motioned toward his big friend. "That's who this gentleman here represents. Think of him as the Cyber and Intellectual Property Crimes department of the Russian mob."

Jake looked at the big guy and then at Jericho. "I thought it was your money," said Jake.

"Nope," said Jericho. "I'm purely an intermediary."

Jake talked even faster. "I intended to—there was a memo that questioned the investment dollars and transfer—and I saw that he had foreign accounts . . . transfers, you know . . . and . . ."

Jake frantically pled his argument directly to the big guy. "I was going off the data from company reports. The money earmarked for research and development was going to be transferred into offshore accounts!"

"That's how dirty money gets clean, dumbass!" Exclaimed Jericho. "Too bad you were too caught up in your brilliance to see you were pissing on the wrong tree."

"But I thought, what was the harm in stealing money that was going to be stolen anyway," said Jake.

There were two taps at the door, followed by the sound of a keycard unlocking the door. Jericho adjusted his tie and took another sip of bourbon, unfazed by the disturbance.

Two more men in suits entered, a wide-bodied Hispanic male and a redheaded brawler with a beard. They were big men. Hard men. Men who looked like they broke and buried things and made all traces of other men disappear. They carried black duffle bags large enough to hold a body. If that body was cut in half.

Jake wished he could vanish and transport himself to a beach in the Caribbean, safe and sipping mai tais. The two men strode past him, dissolving his beach fantasy, practically kicking sand in his face. They went straight to the bedroom door. Each grabbed a handle and slid them open. Inside, a young girl sat in the center of the queen-size bed.

She was a teenager, no more than about sixteen. She had black hair with bangs that came past the eyebrows. Her skin was tanned, unusual for the early spring when a chill was still present in the air. She wore black-rimmed glasses and a blue jacket with an emblem, a white shirt, and a skirt in matching plaid—a school uniform. Private or Catholic, he couldn't tell. She sat cross-legged with a laptop on her thighs. She looked up and gazed steadily at Jake. Then she returned her attention to the computer screen, her face aglow with a soft blue light. Before Jake could say anything, the doors slid shut.

CHAPTER 3

Cardigan Paige sat comfortably on the bed of the hotel suite. She'd entered Jake Coltrane's personal information into a simple password cracking program she'd developed, to no avail. That stuff usually worked on private computers owned by the average user, but not so successful on a fellow computer guru. Every safeguard imaginable was set up on Jake's laptop, including an eighteen-character password.

Frustrated with her progress, Cardigan closed the laptop and took a moment to appreciate her lush surroundings. Oriental rugs, white oak floors, thick gold drape . . . and then there was the bathroom with white marble floors and Jacuzzi tub. A 20-jet spray extravaganza, massaging skin every which way! Maybe Jericho would let her try it out before they left. Her mom definitely wouldn't. She'd say something like, you never knew who was in that tub last or what they did in it. What a prude.

Speaking of who was doing what and where, she wouldn't mind knowing more about Jake Coltrane. She'd been tracking his movements for the last few days, and all she knew so far was that he stole a lot of money, and Jericho wanted her to get it back. The money didn't even belong to Jericho to begin with. He was just passing it along. It was the Russian's problem. They should be taking care of it. She looked up at the textured ceiling and sighed.

Cardigan knew Jericho wanted to be someone the Russians could trust. She rolled her eyes. Even though he was a stone-cold criminal. In any case, getting to cut school was fine with her. He had permission from mom whenever he needed her, which turned out to be a sweet deal. Anything to get her out of Sister Mary Catherine Spalding High.

Jericho could be a twerp, a dick, and an asshole, but he paid well. Also enrolled her in prep school. And fabricated a résumé touting all sorts of charity work. And practically guaranteed her an acceptance to a major university. Even cleaned up that damn probation issue with the FBI a few years back. That last feat was probably why her mom let her get involved with Jericho.

Maybe mom wished that Jericho would fall in love with her and propose. She flipped the laptop back open and frowned. From all indications, Jericho wasn't interested. Getting her out of that foul trouble with the government would have to do for now. Still though, what she was doing was borderline criminal, right? Taking money that a guy stole from a corporate account and putting it back? Maybe not. Maybe she'd be viewed as a younger, cuter Robin Hood or something. Wait, Robin Hood was a criminal.

Cardigan checked the time. What was taking so long, anyway? Maybe they'd take her to get some pizza after. She was delighted with the possibility. Pizza was the best.

She hoped Jake looked as good in real life as he did in his pictures. If he turned out to be some sloppy, catfishing computer geek, she might leave a trace on his computer so that he'd get caught the next time he tried to steal money.

The door opened, and Cardigan peeked up from the screen. Jericho's goons obscured the entryway as they shoved their way in, but behind them, she glimpsed a tall, lean man with light brown skin, short curly hair, and dreamy eyes, sitting in a chair, staring right at her.

The doors closed again, and she smiled.

CHAPTER 4

"Time's running out, Jake."

Jericho squatted, getting eye level with Jake. An inquisitive look animated his face. "You have no history as a criminal. You're not even a real hacker. Sure, you know your way around the computer, but you've never so much as planted a virus or taken over someone's hard drive. So why go to such extremes?"

"A cure for an inoperable tumor isn't enough motivation?" asked Jake. That brought about a chuckle from the big guy. "You want to check my medical records?" Jake continued. "It's all there. I know you can cure me. I'm positive you can."

"Are you one of those conspiracy nuts?" asked Jericho. "Do you believe in the Illuminati? Aliens and Area 51? Do you think rich people are hiding the cure for cancer and AIDS? Yeah. Just because I'm rich, I must be hiding the cure to life's ailments from poor schmucks like you."

"He might be playing stupid," said the big man, speaking clearly for the first time. Heavy accent. Russian. "Get us to entrap ourselves."

"He's not playing stupid," said Jericho, "he is stupid. Don't worry, my big Russian friend. He's working alone. No connections with other organizations or the government. Just one big dumbass looking to score millions because he found someone careless with his money. You need to pay Shubert a visit. Scare the piss outta him for being so careless with his passwords. As for this guy, you can do whatever you want with him."

Jericho pulled his cellphone out of his pocket and peeked at the screen. It made an audible click when he pushed the button to put it back to sleep. He looked at the big man who smiled and made his way towards Jake.

"Wait," said Jake, raising his hands to keep the Russian at bay. "Roland Stark said you have a substance you add to water, just a drop or so. He saw it in your jacket pocket, a little tube you carry around with you. He says you never let it out of your sight." The Russian goon gaped at Jake, then Jericho, unsure. Jake took a chance. "You saved a woman with a fatal bullet wound by using this stuff," he said, voice low and firm. "Then you continued to let Stark 'cure' people through God because it made so much money."

"What the fuck is this guy going on about, Jericho?" asked the Russian.

"Ancient history," said Jericho. "I'm tired of hearing his mouth."

Jake pulled the smartphone from his pants pocket and quickly swiped until he found the image. He waved the phone in the air, pointing the screen at Jericho.

"See this?" said Jake. "This is how I know what he said is true."

An old black-and-white photo tinted yellow with age filled the screen. It appeared to be a log cabin at a civil war work camp. Several soldiers posed within the picture. One grasped a shovel. Three loitered on the side of the cabin. Another stood stony-faced in the doorway. And three more hung out along the makeshift log path that led from the front door to somewhere outside the frame. One curtainless window faced the camera, just left of the door. Jake directed Jericho's attention to the window. A shadowed face gazed out from the darkened pane, its faint features almost recognizable.

"I designed a program that can find anyone anywhere, at any time and place," said Jake. "I used this program to find Roland Stark, and I also used it to find this photo."

Jericho Black squinted as he moved his head forward to focus on the image. His jaw dropped ever so slightly. "Son of a bitch!"

CHAPTER 5

The bedroom doors slid open. The same teenager sat in the center of the bed, but now cables connected the laptop to other computers—powerful processing stuff, including custom-built water-cooling towers, routers, Ethernet hubs, and Wi-Fi repeaters. Thug number one busily took direction from the girl as to what went where. Thug number two held the doors open; eyes narrowed on Jake.

"Looks like they're all set in the other room," said the Russian. He cleared his throat. "What're you looking at on that phone? Do we have problem?"

"No," said Jericho, studying the image a bit longer. "No problem at all."

"Is this program that finds people an even bigger problem?" asked the Russian.

Jericho scrunched his face. "Maybe, in the future. Right now, we have this wide-eyed fool who thinks this is me." Jericho handed the Russian the phone.

The Russian twisted the phone this way and that. The seven-inch screen looked like a matchbox toy car in his massive hands. "You can't see anything. Too dark. Your fancy program says this is Jericho Black, and you believe it?" the Russian asked Jake. "This picture is from over a hundred years ago. And probably photoshopped. You're one of those smart people with no common sense, aren't you?"

The redheaded brawler came from the other room and reached out to Jake. "Passcode," he said. "Your computer and the bank accounts."

Jake looked at Jericho, who raised his eyebrows.

"A sign of good faith," said Jericho.

"You prefer I use the tools I brought along with me?" asked the Russian. He handed the phone back to Jericho and flexed his arms. "You would be saving yourself some unnecessary pain and suffering by telling him the password."

Jake sensed his options slipping away. The money was the only leverage he had left. Stealing from the Russians was not like stealing from a crooked CEO, but giving up the money without a fight left him nothing to bargain with. His survival odds might improve if he alluded to working with someone else. Maybe the government. He could at least threaten prison if anything bad happened to him. Jake silently rebuked himself. Why hadn't he thought of that sooner?

"Write it down on this," said Jericho.

Jake took the slip of paper Jericho produced from an inner pocket and looked over to his left to eyeball the Russian. The Russian was going to be a problem. He rocked on his heels, alert and ready for Jake to refuse the passcodes.

"Step one in our negotiations," said Jericho, extending a pen toward Jake.

"Please," said the Russian. "Show me you have zero common sense. I am getting bored out of my mind standing here listening to your bullshit."

Jake accepted the pen and placed the paper down on his thigh. He paused, frozen for a few seconds. Then he wrote down the passcode to his laptop. He removed another slip from his pants pocket with the codes of all the other accounts where he'd hidden the money. He passed the papers to the brawler, who grabbed them in a tightened fist and rushed back to the bedroom. The doors swooshed close behind him, but not before Jake saw the girl take the slips of paper and start tapping away on the laptop.

A lump formed in his throat. "What now?" he asked.

"We wait," said Jericho. "It shouldn't take too long. We'll make sure the money is transferred."

"I thought you were leaving?" said the Russian to Jericho.

"No," said Jericho. "I need to stay a bit longer."

The strained silence played hell on Jake's nerves. He kept his eyes on the Russian, who was grew impatient as the seconds stretched. Malice oozed from the Russian's pores. Jake was pretty sure that once Jericho left the room, Jake was as good as dead. His only option was to keep Jericho in the room somehow. Keep him talking.

"The girl on the bed. She's one of your hackers, isn't she?" asked Jake.

"She is my best," said Jericho. "Good kid."

"How old is she?"

"She's sixteen. Half your age, Jake."

"How is a sixteen-year-old working for you? How does that happen?"

The Russian shifted his footing and caught Jericho's attention. He looked at the Russian through lowered eyelids as if disturbed by a sudden, distasteful thought. "If you mean to imply that I use underage kids to do the dirty work because they won't get the same jail time as an adult, don't be silly," said Jericho to Jake. "She's legit. One of the most gifted hackers out there. The FBI caught her a few years ago hacking into one of their tree-hugging databases. I pulled a few favors and got her charges reduced to probation. Now she works for me, and it's the best thing that could've happened to her." Jericho smiled to himself and shook his head. "Kid was out to save the world. I quickly taught her that saving the world doesn't make you rich. Doesn't even make you famous. You want to save the trees? Make enough money, and you can buy the land yourself. Then no one can fuck with it." He scowled and pointed a meaty finger at Jake. "But get the money the right way. Not stealing it like you. That was stupid."

"Stupid is an understatement," said the Russian. "Moron is more like it. You steal the money because you believe Jericho can give you formula to live hundreds of years? You seem like smart guy. This program you write to look at face, why could it not be wrong? Are you that arrogant?" He paced back and forth, agitated.

"There's zero chance the photo is fake," said Jake, snapping his head in the Russian's direction. "I inspected it myself. My program is foolproof. It starts by using my facial recognition program. The cheap versions, the ones popping up at stores and malls and airports? They just scan faces and compare them to existing pictures to find a match. A person can disguise things like changing their hair, nose, eyes, lips, and skin color. You can fool the eyes so well that even your mother won't recognize you.

"But there's a limit to what you can alter," Jake continued. "Like the space between your eyes or their size. Same with the distances between your eyes and ears or the outside corners of your mouth to the center of your pupil. You might have a disguise for your chin, but once you speak, the angle of your real jawline reveals itself. The distance from the center of the bridge of your nose to your inner ear opening will always be the same."

The Russian was detached and bored; curling the corner of his lip wishing the babble would end. Jericho however seemed interested. Mulling over the details. It gave Jake confidence to continue. Shifting his body in the chair, he focused all of his energy towards Jericho.

"The software considers lighting and shades to calculate angles to render a three-dimensional image for analysis. It takes into account plastic surgery, like if your lips are injected with Botox or your skin has been lightened or darkened or if you've had a nose job. Collected data is recalculated to scale and adjusted. But here is what's best about the program." Jake leaned forward and slowed his speech down, so Jericho and the Russian heard the next part. "It analyzes details down to a skeletal level. The same way facial reconstruction can be performed using technology while simply starting with a skull, this program can take a face and design the base image of that person's skull. The result is detection that renders disguises useless. Then the program hacks into every public and private camera it can find. It scans countless images on the internet." He leaned back, hands raised with palms forward, almost as if apologizing. "It's also fast. Super-fast. And practically infallible."

"Except for one time," said the Russian. He paused, savoring the punchline. "It said the man in the photo was Jericho Black, which clearly it is not. Jericho . . . say something to this fuck."

Jericho had remained unnaturally still during Jake's explanation. Now he rested his hand under his chin, thinking. "Not now," he said. He paced in front of Jake, deep in thought. "That picture of my likeness was on the internet. Was Roland Stark on the internet?"

"No," said Jake. "The program I developed is a hacker's dream designed to find people. It can access millions of cameras worldwide. Even the stuff on personal phones if the security is not set up correctly. Also, anything that works off Wi-Fi. Think of all the images appearing via live cameras. Think of the cameras at the malls, ATMs, or street cameras in the cities."

"Sounds dangerous," said the Russian.

"Sounds valuable to me," said Jericho. Jake could almost hear the wheels turning in his head. "Can this software run automated?"

"That's the way it was designed. Ease for the operator. Just plug in a face, and it does the rest."

"Have you deleted the search for my image?" asked Jericho.

"What is happening?" said the Russian. "What are you getting at?"

Jericho shook his head and glared while Jake fought off the urge to smirk.

CHAPTER 6

Cardigan took the slips of paper with the passwords and went right to work. Her light pink gel nails sped across the keys as she scanned the screen. She logged into the three accounts, each on a different browser. The IP address wasn't an issue since it was generated from Jake's computer. Any additional security questions wouldn't impede her access.

Jake had set up the dummy accounts and performed a direct transfer from CEO Kyle Shubert's main account. The name Jake used was fake, or was it? Was Julie Shubert a real person or an alias? Maybe it was an anagram, something personal that Kyle would see as a snub if he were to figure it out in time.

It was a stretch. Maybe Julie was just Julie. Cardigan opened another web page and searched to confirm her hunch. Bastard, she thought with a smile. Julie was Kyle's ex-wife. Over 300 million dollars into three accounts bearing Julie's name. Freaking genius. She spied something else. An execute file was attached to one of the account files and linked to Kyle's email. Curious, she thought, and clicked it.

What an asshole, she thought again, grin widening. Her face glowed, not just from the soft blue lighting of the computer screen. A letter was set to be sent to the ex-wife in thirty-five hours and counting. Cardigan greedily digested its contents.

I have a guilty conscience. The way I treated you and the girls during the divorce eats away at my soul. The truth is, I hid money, and I'm ashamed. Let's not make a big production about it—I don't want to get in trouble with your lawyers. Therefore, I'm giving you your fair amount. I set up three bank accounts in your name. Please, let's keep this quiet and just between us. I beg you. You were my wife of twenty-five years, and I know I can trust you. Thank you for your understanding and forgiveness.

Yours Truly,

Kyle

Cardigan chuckled softly. Of course, Julie would say something to Kyle. Anything too good to be true had to be bogus. She'd question him, and he'd freak out, then ask for the money back. Then the real fun would begin. Cardigan tucked a strand of hair behind her ear and appreciated the cleverness of Jake's trap. A cute game he was playing, she thought, tapping her nail against the screen.

Enough admiration, there was work to do. Cardigan went right to it, setting up the money transfers back into Kyle's main account. It'd take a while. Transfers of this size had to be verified. The second slip of paper Jake turned over had codes and security questions and answers for each account so she'd be ready. He'd also installed a phone card on his computer so that when the bank called to verify, a text message would pop up, and she'd be able to respond directly. Jake was organized and efficient, and she liked that.

Still, this would take some time.

She opened the C drive to see what Jake had been doing with his time. Nothing too interesting, except one program was running in the background, demanding an insane amount of bandwidth. Curious, she opened the file and the screen flooded with images. At first, she thought Jake must've installed an emergency virus to keep people from snooping around, but it seemed careless, even for a hacker. Who'd set up booby traps on their own machine? That was just insane. No, it had to be something else. A valid program. She pushed her face close to the screen, absentmindedly chewing on a pinky nail, to scrutinize the images. Her mouth slowly opened into a look of shock and she turned to Ronaldo who was standing in the corner with his arms crossed as usual.

"Jericho needs to know about this, Ronaldo," she said, motioning him to take a look.

He leaned in, eyebrows furrowing at the familiar face. "Damn!"

CHAPTER 7

The double doors slid open, and out came the wide-bodied goon spotting Jericho standing beside the Russian on the left side of the room. He motioned for a sidebar with Jericho and whispered urgently, occasionally glancing at Jake. Then he backed away, and Jericho nodded in acceptance.

"What is going on?" asked the Russian. "Talk to me!"

Jericho Black urged the Russian to follow him off to the side near the dining room entrance. They turned their backs on Jake to exchange words. Jake strained to listen but couldn't make out anything coherent. They were speaking in Russian, he decided. The big guy gestured adamantly, his grimace conveying objections to Jericho's much more calm and assured demeanor. Finally, the Russian conceded, and they turned back toward Jake, who'd taken the reprieve from constant surveillance to stretch his arms and legs. The Russian returned to his position by the bedroom doors, clearly aggravated. Jericho sauntered over to the bar for another bourbon, face unreadable.

"Cardigan just verified the images you have of me walking into the hotel with my large friend here," said Jericho. "Your program seems to be legit. Pretty ingenious. Just as I thought. I'm guessing everything's being recorded on a server of some sort. Your program must require a hellacious amount of bandwidth. Maybe even multiple servers."

"If I go missing, I'm sure that someone will find those recordings useful." Jake kept his tone neutral, his goal to threaten but not instigate. "It won't take investigators long to put two and two together."

"Did you know we were on to you?" asked Jericho.

Jake was clueless as to how they found him so quickly. He figured

Jericho's people would be scratching their heads in confusion and swept up in finger-pointing for days before Jake could waltz in and play hero. Four days, he'd estimated. It'd only taken them twenty-four hours.

Tracking Jericho's movements were simply part of the plan. But Jake had gotten lucky. It'd impressed Jericho.

Just like Roland Stark said it would.

"Look," said Jake, feeling more optimistic. "Since we're all crooks here, I suggest we walk away and pretend none of these unpleasantries ever happened."

"You think this program can save you?" asked the Russian. "We have so many people on the payroll in NYPD that those images can easily be mysteriously deleted. We have unlimited funds to make it all go away. If not police, then politicians. There is always someone higher up the chain who will take the money. Who do you think you are fucking with? An amateur?"

The Russian scoffed and aimed a menacing fist at Jake. "Make no mistake. I came here to kill you." His eyes widened into angry orbs of danger. "We will take the money and dispose of you permanently."

"But this guy," he said, pointing his fat finger at Jericho, "he likes to watch. He has cameras everywhere; wants to know what everyone is doing. He sits and watches for hours, waiting for someone to sneak up on him. He's kind of paranoid. Or maybe it's a fetish; what do I know about these things? He is a weird one, this one," the Russian sighed and forced his arms back down to his side. "He asked me something ridiculous back there. He wants a trade. Unbelievable."

Jericho gulped his bourbon down and poured himself a fresh glass. "I want access to that program, Jake."

Jake almost cracked a smile. His original plan was back on track. Steal the money, meet with Jericho, show him the program that Roland Stark was confident Jericho would pay any price for, and get the cure for his tumor.

On the other hand, the big Russian was a problem. His appetite for slaughter was as stubborn as the benign tumor at the base of Jake's neck. "What guarantee would I have after the program is handed over?" asked Jake.

The Russian took a deep breath and peered down his nose at Jake. "No guarantee at all!"

"You have my word," said Jericho.

"Not good enough," Jake replied.

"What guarantee would you like?" asked Jericho.

"Protection after I'm cured," said Jake. "That's all I want."

The Russian's face contorted with fury, and he muttered in his native tongue. Jake didn't need to speak Russian to know it was nasty and vile. Acrimonious. His dramatic gestures suggested a man intent on mutilation. Jericho spoke to him in Russian, trying to get him to calm down.

"Nyet! Nyet! Nyet!" said the Russian.

Jericho Black reached into his jacket pocket and pulled out a phial of blue-tinted liquid. There was no more than an ounce in it. He placed it on the bar next to his glass.

"I agree to your terms," said Jericho. "This is the cure. After you take it, the tumor should be no more."

The Russian paced furiously. "How can you be such a huge moron, *mudak*?" he yelled at Jake. "This is the twenty-first century. Science and technology rule. You are a master of this technology. Yet you obsess over a fairytale like an ignorant, illiterate bumpkin from the dark age. Jericho Black is a man like everyone else. He will live a good life and die like everyone else. You find nonsense and convince yourself it is real because you are afraid of dying." He whipped out his pistol, stomped over to Jake, and shoved it under his chin. "Here, let me help you. I have the only true cure for fear of dying. It is called death. Rest in peace. After being dead, you will no longer be afraid of dying!"

Jake gripped the sides of his chair. Sweat sprouted from his forehead and rolled down his temples. The metal of the pistol was cool on his skin. The bedroom doors swung open. Jericho's men strode out with the young girl following closely behind. "It's done," said the brawler.

Jake's eyes went to the young girl gazing at him and smiling. She was just over five feet two and willow-thin. Just a typical teenaged girl, who also happened to be an accomplished hacker working for dangerous men.

"The equipment is yours," she said to Jake. "I have better stuff at home. And I love your program. I'd love to steal it. You have a real gem there." She eyeballed the Russian's pistol against Jake's jaw. "So, what's going on here?"

"Jericho is about to give this *mudak* the fountain of youth," said the Russian. He removed the gun from Jake's chin to gesture at Jake's chest.

Jake slumped in relief. "Make his body brand-new and full of life. If you believe in that sort of thing. He will be young forever!"

"Interesting! What's a *mudak*?" Cardigan asked.

"Asshole, scumbag, shithead, take your pick," said the Russian.

She looked at the phial sitting on the bar. "Can I get some too?"

"No!" said Jericho.

"Why not?"

"You're too young."

"Is stupidity part of being a hacker?" asked the Russian of the room. "I can't fucking believe this!"

"You can't have any, Cardigan," said Jericho. "Do you want to be an underdeveloped teen your whole life? Think about it. You still have a chance to fill out some. And you're still a virgin, for goodness' sake. At least you should be."

She looked down at her body with her mouth wide open. "You're such a . . . *mudak,* Jericho!"

"I'm just being truthful, sweetheart. Hey, Ronaldo, take the girl home. I don't want her mother calling me tonight, cursing me out for taking her out of school again and keeping her all night. And don't tell your mother about the stuff on the counter, Cardigan, or else she'll curse me out for not curing her goddamn wrinkles. Go to the pizza shop on the corner and get a whole pie. That should make everybody happy. And great job, Cardigan. Now get!"

They paraded past Jake one by one, led by the guy Jericho called Ronaldo in a black suit, followed by tiny Cardigan in her blue uniform, followed by the redheaded brawler in another black suit.

"I love the letter you wrote for the ex-wife," Cardigan told Jake as she passed him, tousling his hair like he was a toddler in time-out. "Nice touch. I'll send you a message later. I know where to find you."

"You're only sixteen, so you won't send anything to this grown man!" Jericho shouted as she walked out the door, the scent of cherry blossom lingering behind her.

The compliment touched Jake, but he hadn't written a letter to the ex-wife. What else had Cardigan discovered?

"The child is gone now," said the Russian. "Only the three of us left."

CHAPTER 8

———◆———

"Let us finish this." The Russian raised his pistol.

Jericho nodded. "Yes, Jake. Explain how you'll get this program to me."

"That'll be complicated," said Jake, straightening in his chair. His throat hurt, and he'd love a glass of water but decided against asking. "I designed the program at work and stored it on the mainframe. It was the only place where I could access massive processing power. Then there's the difficulty of transferring that much data without arousing suspicion. It's going to take some time to pull off."

The Russian laughed. "This guy," he said, waving his gun at Jake. "Still don't know what is going on, do you?"

"We are negotiating for the software," snapped Jericho to the Russian. "It seems like you're the one who doesn't understand."

The Russian's chest swelled. He lowered his pistol in disbelief. "I was sent here to make sure the mess gets cleaned up, Jericho. No deals for this program. Period."

"What if I offered to pay for his life?" asked Jericho.

"Have you lost your mind?" said the Russian.

"How about the same amount he stole? You double your money right here, right now. Go call your people."

The Russian shrugged his shoulders rapidly three or four times and bobbed his head from left to right. His facial muscles tightened, and his chin wrinkled like fingertips in water too long. His weight shifted from his left foot to his right foot. "I was thinking that is not enough," he huffed, moving his hand as if he were tossing coins into a fountain. Short,

23

JEREMY FULMORE

combative breaths shot out of his mouth. "That is not why I was brought here, Jericho. I have a job to do." Malevolence crept into his voice. "This guy here fucked up by stealing from us. Put us all at risk. Letting him go for some shit program is unacceptable. The hacker must be taught a lesson."

Jericho and the Russian stared at the other in silence. Then Jericho turned to Jake and said, "Stand up."

Jake's knees wobbled, but he stood as instructed.

"How long will it take to get me that software?" asked Jericho.

"Two weeks," said Jake.

"Are you listening to me, Jericho?" said the Russian.

Jericho downed the rest of his whiskey in one take. He walked to the sink, rinsed out his glass, and filled it halfway with water. He returned to the bar and placed the glass on the counter, then opened the small cap on the phial and let a single drop fall into the water. He put the phial next to the glass and walked over to Jake.

He brought a switchblade out from his pants pocket, and Jake tensed. Jericho ran a finger along the black pearl handle until he found the button and pressed. Out sprang a long, narrow, double-sided blade. He put out a hand. "For the formula to work, we'll need a small amount of your blood. Give me your finger."

Jake stared at the blade and then the Russian, who mean-mugged him with a vicious glare. Jake wasn't sure what he'd gotten himself into and had no idea how to get himself back out of it. Things had taken a peculiar turn. He swayed on his feet. So thirsty.

"What I'm giving you can't be replicated in a lab because it's not synthetic," said Jericho. "It's alive. And it must be accepted. Once introduced to the source of human life—blood—it can then adapt to its new host, enter the cells, and revitalize the body."

"What is it?" asked Jake, feeling faint. A rush of anxiety sent chills up his neck.

"You'll have to trust me on this," said Jericho. "Just a prick."

Jake extended the index finger on his left hand, palm side up. Jericho Black held it firm with two fingers and steadied the knife. "Remember, I want that program delivered in two weeks. That's our deal."

24

Jake looked over at the glass of blue-tinted water, then the phial, and nodded. "You have my word."

"Good."

Jericho squeezed his finger so tight that Jake's first reaction was to pull away, but he couldn't, as Jericho's firm grip had paralyzed his arm. Jake was so focused on the pressure building in his finger that the sound of the first pop startled him. With the second pop, it wasn't just the sound that caused him to flinch; it was the pain. Only after the fifth pop did Jake realize the knife was plunging into his torso.

Jake went to scream, but the large Russian appeared behind him, one arm around his neck and the other clamping his mouth shut. Jericho Black went into a stabbing frenzy, thrusting the blade in and out of Jake's body with ferocity. The hilt of the blade slammed into his body when it could go no deeper. More than twenty stab wounds blossomed on Jake's torso.

Jake's body grew limp, and the Russian released his grip, letting him drop to the ground. Blood pooled around his spasming body. His eyes rolled into his head.

"Damn," said the Russian. "You make a fucking mess, Jericho."

"What are you complaining about?" said Jericho. "This is what you wanted, right?"

Jake lay on his side, enveloped in pain. He couldn't think or breathe. Images of Jericho thrusting the blade in and out replayed in his mind. The detached look on Jericho's blood-splattered face had terrified him. No hint of remorse, no anger, no feeling. He was like a demon.

Jake remained as still as he could. Every rise and fall of his chest brought about a new convulsion. His eyes fluttered and fixated on the Russian, who had removed his bloody shoes and was looking for something to clean them. Nothing worse than leaving bloody footprints, Jake dimly thought.

He shifted his weakening attention to Jericho calmly checking his jacket for blood at the bar. There was plenty of it. His white shirt was splattered with red spots.

The Russian erupted with a sharp chuckle. He shook his finger at Jericho as if he had figured out something. "You are a slick one, Jericho Black. I was not expecting this. This was genius." He wiped a smear of blood from his arm. "They say when pigs are led to the slaughterhouse, they scream something terrible. They sense what is coming. I was worried about you and that shit about the stupid program." He stared in surprise as Jericho poured the rest of the phial's contents into the water. "Hey, what are you doing?"

Jericho swirled the bloody blade in the water, turning it cloudy gray. He stirred until the water was clear again.

"Why are you doing this?" asked the Russian.

"He's thirsty," said Jericho. "Does this settle things with your people?"

The Russian looked down at Jake's crumpled body. "Yes, we are satisfied. But what about this?" He swept his arms around the room. "There is blood everywhere. It can be easily cleaned off the hardwood floor, but the rug is ruined. And what about the body? We can't leave it here. You should have thought this through."

"Not a problem," said Jericho. "I have a change of clothes in the next room. We can freshen up before we leave the hotel. Then we can get some dinner. My guys will come back and take care of the body. But first, let me finish this."

"That would be the decent thing to do," the Russian agreed.

Jericho took the knife and the glass of water and crouched before Jake. "You know what I want, right?" he murmured.

Jake's lips trembled. He struggled to speak. "The program," he whispered.

Jericho cradled Jake's head and the glass of water to his lips. Jake drank as best he could. Thoughts struggled to the surface of his foggy mind, a memory of Roland Stark telling him about a woman shot during a live telecast. Jericho had given him a glass of water for the wounded woman. She drank it and was instantly healed. The raw footage still lived on the internet, along with all the other footage of Roland Stark healing people. Jake had researched it himself.

"I think I feel something," said Jake.

"Good." Jericho Black shoved the blade into the center of Jake's heart. The pressure against his chest was impossibly heavy. A warm flow of blood pooled beneath him. Thoughts raced through his head. None of them good.

With his last bit of strength, he grabbed Jericho's arm and held on as tight as he could while looking into Jericho's eyes. Jericho deserved to feel guilty about what he had done. Jake hoped his face would haunt Jericho for the rest of his life.

He was denied that bit of solace. Not an ounce of remorse lived in those eyes. Jericho may as well have been smashing a cockroach. It meant nothing to him. Jake felt his strength fading, and he let out one long breath.

CHAPTER 9

I t was pitch black. Jake was in a railcar, moving fast. Iron wheels hit the railroad ties with a *ka-chunk,* and a hard clank rang out every few seconds. He rocked back and forth, swaying with the movement. He didn't remember how he got on the train, why he was naked, or why the other people riding with him were naked. They were going somewhere. That was all he knew.

Random flashes of light streaked through the window and revealed how many people rode with him. There were many. He stood in the aisle, holding on to the metal handle hanging down from the bar above. The car reminded him of an old New York railcar from the late sixties or early seventies.

The floor was caked in grime and strewed with trash. Vulgar graffiti covered the walls and windows. A particular stench wafted through the corridor—a commingling of unbathed bodies, the pungent odor of armpits, the rank aroma of piss, and the sour whiff of excessive sweat. It was hot, humid, and unbearable.

Someone bumped into his shoulder. Their flesh came in contact with Jake's, causing an intense burning sensation accompanied by a sizzling sound. Jake flinched and moved away fast. The other person grunted as well. Sizzling and grunting echoed throughout the packed railcar. No more than an inch or two existed between each person.

The car jolted and lurched, every so often dropping like an elevator, giving Jake a distressing sensation of free-falling. Another clank of the rail and a shoulder bumped into the center of his back. He gasped at the molten pain. The woman who had bumped into him yelped. Jake turned his head instinctively. She was in her midfifties, with wild hair and dirt encrusted on her face. Her despondent blue eyes looked up at him.

"Why are we here?" she asked.

"I have no idea," said Jake. "I don't know how I got here."

"We died, you stupid son of a bitch!" said an overweight man on Jake's right. He had a white mustache and beard, and his accent was from one of the southern states. He turned away. Embarrassed or ashamed, Jake couldn't tell.

"Fuck you," said another. He stood near the southern man. Jake could see his head moving as he talked, but his face was hidden. He appeared to be White, in his late forties or early fifties. Light blond or gray hair, it was hard to tell. "I was watching television. Real Housewives. I fell asleep. Someone must've drugged me and brought me here, like in those fucking movies, the ones where you have to figure out how to get out, or you die. There must be traps here, and they'll make us choose between saving someone else or saving our own lives." The man hacked and spat on the ground. "That's what this is. Some rich asshole's way of entertaining himself. We let the wrong people take over the government, and this is what happens. This is what you get. Big tech controls our lives now. Are you happy, all you people blind to the truth? Now you'll see what your ignorance caused."

"I said we're dead, you ignorant, conspiracy-loving son of a bitch!" said the southerner. "I fucking remember! I was . . ." He didn't want to say it. He'd finally worked up the nerve to rob a home, invasion style, and he'd never been more excited. There was a family; husband, wife, and teenage girl, and he had his shotgun.

He kicked down the door, and it was quick. Boom. There went the father. He never even got out of his chair in front of the television. The mother grabbed the daughter's hand and ran for the bathroom. He took off running right behind her, shoved the shotgun barrel into her back, and pulled the trigger. Boom. There went the mother, the top half of her tumbling into the bathtub.

He grabbed the teenager by the arm, his breath hot with excitement. She screamed frantically. In the heat of the moment, the truth behind his actions slapped him in the face. He wasn't interested in the money; it wasn't the robbery that made his blood boil. His goal was to cause terror.

He dragged the girl past her father's bloody corpse, preoccupied with the things he would do to her young, innocent flesh. He pictured her terrorized face as he pleased himself and how such utter domination would keep him satisfied for at least the next month. He didn't notice when another man crept out from one of the other rooms. The crunch of a shell loading into the chamber shocked him, and he turned around. The unexpected guest held a shotgun. Boom. There he went. Next thing, he found himself packed in a smelly railcar heading toward who knew where. "This is hell, you dumbshit."

"No," said the middle-aged woman next to Jake. "That can't be right."

"Oh, I believe it," said another man facing Jake. One hand held the metal pole running from the ceiling to the floor. The other hand rested by his side. Tattoos of eagles and lightning bolts climbed up one arm, across his chest, and down the other arm. He was bald with a long goatee tied by a rubber band. On his stomach were the numbers 14 and 23. "Look at this fucking tall brown bastard here," he said, speaking directly to Jake.

Jake looked him up and down. "Fuck off."

The man pointed to the 14 on his stomach. "'We must secure the existence of our people and a future for White children,'" He recited while smiling. "You're a mixed-race abomination of nature. That's why you're going to hell!"

"Is this the time for that shit, whacko?" said the woman by Jake. "I don't think this is hell. It can't be."

His grin widened. "What lady, don't think you deserve to be here? Well, I know why I'm here. Someone's got to teach these animals their place." He looked Jake up and down. "The outside world thinks the guards run the show in prison. Uh-uh! The inmates run the asylum. Most frightening thing you ever heard is in the blackness of night, a grown man screaming for help at the top of his lungs. You know what's happening. You know that poor son of a bitch is screaming for help that ain't ever coming. You can only put the pillow over your ears and try to drown out the sound, thinking next time it might be you. You hear those screams, boy?"

Jake did hear screaming, piercing shrills far off in the distance, beyond the screech of the railcar. Endless cries for help echoed through the darkness. He shuddered.

"No. That can't be what this is," said Jake.

"Why? Because you are a believer?"

Jake didn't answer, but it was what he was thinking.

"Let me explain something to you," said the man with the goatee. "That religion ain't for your kind. We let you adopt it." He chuckled, showing off plaque-coated teeth. "Cruel, I know, making your kind think you deserved the same salvation. Haven't you figured out why all that praying never helped you?"

"Shut up, asshole," said the woman.

"You monkeys may know how to read, but you still don't understand the meaning," he continued. "The Old Testament mentions Adam, but that wasn't his original name. The Jews changed the code to cover up the truth. The Jews aren't God's people. The original pronunciation of Adam is Audom, which in the ancient language, before the Masoretic codex interpretation, means, *he who shows blood in the face.*"

He slapped his cheek and turned to show the redness in his skin. "Only white can show blood in the face. Ever wonder why in the Bible, after Cain was cast out of the Garden of Eden, it says that he went with these other people? Those were the people of other races, dumbass. That's why it doesn't make sense to you, but it makes perfect sense to me."

"It doesn't say White people in the Bible, jackass!" said another person, somewhere in the crowd.

"That's because, like this monkey, you never learned how to read. The Bible is constantly referring to 'my people.' God said, 'my people.' Reread it, dumbass. 'My people' doesn't mean everybody. It's specific. It means people made in the image of God, which is White people. Others were not made in God's image and therefore are animals, like every other animal on this planet." He turned his attention to Jake once more. "All those dumb bastards in church have no clue. You can't be saved, boy. Neither can that Indian or that chink or that spic over there. The rest of you Whites are here because you were too stupid to see the truth. Jews wanted so badly for 'my people' to mean them that they cut the foreskin off their peckers. But that ain't good enough, either. And you," He said, jutting his jaw at Jake. "Just because some White man defiled your great-grandmamma doesn't make you qualify as God's people either."

"Then why is your White ass here, shit for brains?" said Jake.

He smiled again. "To make you scream, boy. I'm a soldier of the truth. It's my birthright."

Jake shook his head in disgust. "White supremacists are in a race against others who are not interested in racing!"

"What the fuck is that supposed to mean?"

Jake said, "There are tens of thousands of White supremacists groups, but I bet you couldn't name five supremacy groups from all the other races combined. No other race thinks it's important. Sure, there are racists in every race. But you bastards are the only ones who form hate groups with laws and doctrines, putting numbers and symbols on your fucking body to symbolize your allegiance. No other race takes hate to the extreme because no other race gives a fuck about being the number one race! Only you guys. The rest of us are trying to be happy."

The man shook his head. "Turd boy you are so ignorant," he said. "You ain't in no race. You're in a war. Dumbasses who don't know they are in a war get slaughtered and enslaved, shit stain!"

The train bumped, and its iron wheels screeched as the brakes were applied. Everyone in the cab lurched in unison. Jake struggled to see what was going on. The train drifted to a squealing stop. There was a tone and the doors opened, but the station was completely black. Roasting-hot air rushed into the car. Everyone remained still. Quiet.

"Where the hell are we?" asked someone.

The racist snickered. "He made a funny. 'Where the hell are we?' We are in hell, kind sir." He focused on Jake. "Time for everybody to get the fuck out and prepare yourself for the pain!"

CHAPTER 10

Alexei Voznesensky's massive frame dominated the plane's center aisle as he made his way toward the back. His hips bumped against the aisle seats on the left and the right. He noted the worried looks of those already seated, each concerned the huge man was going to squeeze into their precious space and sandwich them against his thick shoulders for ten hours. They needn't have worried; Alexei preferred comfort just as they did, which was why he always bought two tickets. Two seats in coach were cheaper than one business class ticket from Domodedovo Airport in Russia to New York. Then, after a two-hour layover, he was off to California.

Alexei approached his seat, aware of a pair of green eyes contemplating him. She was in an aisle seat, the one next to her empty. He checked his ticket. His seats were directly across from her. He smiled, raised the armrest between the two chairs, and shifted his mass downward, grunting as he lowered himself into the cozy space and strapped in. He glanced across the aisle. She was blonde, with a beauty mark above her lip. Attractive, like a model. Her right arm exhibited a tangle of tattoos down to her fingers.

"Nice artwork," he said.

"Thanks," she replied. Clearly from the United States.

She regarded the tattooed letters on the back of Alexei's hand. OMYT, an understated tattoo compared to her artwork.

"It means 'water hole' in Russian," he said.

She smiled pleasantly. Not understanding the significance.

It was a remnant of the old system and his youth, translated as *water hole* but representing something much darker. Simply put, Alexei was a person hard to get away from. After thirty years in the *Vory V Zakone*,

33

Alexei had many tattoos but none for her to examine for artistic value. They told a story. A record of his deeds. His résumé. When Alexei Voznesensky walked into the room, those in the life saw the OMYT on the back of his clenched fist and prayed he wasn't coming for them.

The steady pitch of the plane's air-conditioning flooded his ears as Alexei settled in. He thought back to his meeting in Russia. They'd met at a small restaurant, nothing fancy, with twelve tables in the main dining area and ivory vinyl floors, the kind that had to be buffed to a shine with a machine. Red tablecloths draped the tables, each encircled by four wooden chairs. A brown door in the left rear corner near the restrooms led to an old part of the kitchen no longer used for food preparation. The stainless steel preparation table, used as a bar top, had four high back barstools set up around it. A gray, windowed swinging door led to the functioning kitchen and another entrance, where the servers could move freely back and forth to the dining area.

The meeting was highly unusual. People like Alexei weren't allowed to meet with the boss directly for the risk of being implicated. Specific layers of protection existed between who called the shots and who pulled the trigger. Yet the *pakhan* wanted to talk with him personally, and two others of high importance had been called to the meeting.

The restaurant belonged to Sergei Bolshov, the *pakhan*—the boss. Sergei sat to Alexei's right, bald up top and gray on the sides. He kept the sides short like a crew cut and wore black-rimmed glasses, a light blue collared shirt, and black slacks. A woman sat across from Alexei on the short side of the prep table wearing a brown blouse and tan Capris. Alexei knew her as Natalia Makarova, a big-shot lawyer with power in underworld activities and connections to the Kremlin, making her presence even more intriguing. She was middle-aged, with brown hair and a medium build. She was wanted by many men, not because of her beauty but because of her power. Then finally, to Alexei's right was Turgenev, a filthy rich oligarch whose fortunes were tied with natural resources. He was slightly older than Alexei, tall, good-looking, and in shape, with salt-and-pepper hair. His crisp white shirt fit him to a tee. Alexei guessed he never wore the same shirt twice.

Plates and silverware clanked beyond the swinging door as the cooks and servers prepared dinner service. A light gauze of smoke circulated in the air from Natalia's cigarette. She puffed away, flicking the ashes in a tray in front of her. Shooting glances at Alexei as if he kicked her cat or something.

Despite being in his seventies, Sergei was still a hard man. A bit on the small side, but no one had joked about his height since he'd been a teenager. Alexei once heard Sergei bit off a man's nose in the *gulag* for making fun of his size. Sergei was respected above all because he was wise. A true leader. And legendary in the *Vory*. He'd survived the mob wars in the early nineties to consolidate his power and expand the Odessa mob to where it is now.

Sergei took a sip of Turkish tea from the traditional glass on the table in front of him. "Everyone here is highly appreciative of what you have done," said Sergei to Alexei. "These two would like to know how it went and find out a little more about this hacker who stole the money. In specific, was he working with anyone else?"

"This is sensitive information," added Natalia, exhaling a plume of smoke. "The operation was one we had not taken in a while. Cleaning our money in the world market is important to us. Having a stable connection that we can trust helps us avoid detection by serious government entities in the US. Did you ask the questions we presented to you?"

Alexei's massive hands were folded across his midsection. His thumbs gently thumped on his belly as he often did whenever he was irritated. "No SEC," said Alexei. "He was working alone."

"How did he come to target the Ribel accounts? Was he tipped off in any way?"

"I don't know what you mean," said Alexei.

"Of all the companies in the world, he happened to find the one we funneled money into. You are talking about hundreds of thousands of possible targets, yet he found us instantly and siphoned the money right away."

"He was lucky. He was monitoring Jericho Black when he stumbled upon it."

"Really?" asked Natalia. "Why was he after Jericho Black?"

"I feel so stupid having to repeat this out loud. He was looking for a cure for himself. He thought Jericho had a miracle potion that would heal the tumor in his head. The tumor made him stupid. He thinks this program of his found Jericho's face in a picture from a war over 150 years ago. Silly man. At first, Jericho offered to pay the $400 million to spare his life."

Natalia and Turgenev exchanged glances. Alexei immediately began explaining.

"But then Jericho killed him, personally. He was bluffing," Alexei explained in a rush. He didn't want the ire of those two raised. "The hacker merely stumbled onto the exchange of funds while watching Jericho Black and thought Jericho would appreciate the gesture of him returning the money, enough to share the cure with him. Fantasy stuff. The acts of a desperate man looking to prolong his life. Unfortunately, it ended it for him right there."

"Good," said Sergei. "Alexei has a reputation for getting all he can out of his victims before finishing the job. I trust that he properly interrogated the victim."

Turgenev asked, "What was this money that Jericho offered for his man's life and why?"

"He thought the hacker's program was valuable. It can find and track people and such."

"How good is this program?" asked Natalia.

"I told you, Jericho was bluffing. He had no intention to pay for the program."

There was quiet. Natalia and Turgenev seemed lost in thought.

Turgenev was the first to snap out of his trance. His chest heaved up and down like a child about to throw a tantrum. Natalia attempted to place her hand on his to calm him. He withdrew his hand from the table quickly making for an awkward situation. "I would like for you to kill the CEO Kyle Shubert and his wife. I would like this done immediately. I want the house burned down and everything destroyed. Take no chances with this. I want them reduced to ashes. Nothing left."

"Take a breath, Turgenev," said Sergei. "You don't give orders here." Sergei could see the sweat soaking into the shirt under Turgenev's armpits as well as on the collar. His face reddened. "We have an arrangement," Sergei continued. "A working relationship. But we are *Vory*, and you are not. We appreciate your money, but as far as giving orders, your money does not buy that."

Turgenev's jaw muscles flexed and tightened. "I am putting in my request now, Sergei. No disrespect."

Sergei sat for a moment to stare across the table at Turgenev. "I will put in the word to take care of your problem. Does that sound reasonable?"

"Alexei will do the job," said Turgenev.

Sergei rose from his chair in anger. "You do not give orders, Turgenev. I do not wish to remind you a third time."

Natalia gaped at how quickly the tension escalated and took action. "We don't want anyone else unnecessarily involved in this, Sergei. You understand. As few people as possible."

Seconds passed in silence before Sergei eased back into his chair. "What do you think, Alexei?" He glared across the table at Turgenev, waiting for Alexei to answer.

Alexei felt at ease. As if all the tension had shifted to Turgenev. "I can do it," said Alexei. "California? I always wanted to spend some time there."

"Take a few days to settle," said Sergei. "At Mr. Turgenev's expense."

Turgenev nodded in acceptance.

"It is settled then," said Natalia, rising to her feet. It took a few more seconds for Turgenev to stand. Alexei imagined Turgenev didn't want to appear weak with Sergei still staring him down. Perhaps it was why Turgenev said nothing on his way out. No nod or gesture paying respect. He was not standing as erect as he did upon entering. Not as proud or confident. Natalia ushered him through the swinging door and out the back entrance of the restaurant in silence.

"Can you believe that shit?" said Sergei once the door stilled. "I remember this bastard, Turgenev. He got his start by taking subsidies from Gosplan to pay teachers and other government workers. He put the money in his private bank account while playing the American markets. When the workers demanded their pay, he hired us to stand with machine guns and tell them to back away from the buildings. He made a fortune. When voucher privatization came along, he had enough cabbage to gobble up numerous companies. We ran the security for him. He hired us to take care of all the ugly details of the fight to control the country's assets after entrepreneurism was no longer illegal. We were partners during the Yeltsin years. When Putin came into power and decided to clean up, he turned his back on us. Putin's approval legitimized him, so he no longer needed us. Left us to fend for ourselves. Don't think that I forgot this, Alexei. You will do this job in California, but I have another job for you. Find out what has him so spooked. It has nothing to do with the SEC. He is afraid of something else."

The roar of the airplane engines throttling up to full power brought Alexei back to the present. The plane launched down the runway, pinning him to the back of the seat. He pulled out his phone to make a call. Zachary Nemtsov answered after a few rings.

"How was the meeting?" said Zak.

"Good."

A stewardess walked by, and she and Alexei made eye contact. She started to ask him to put his phone away, but something about the look on Alexei's face changed her mind. She closed her mouth and took a seat behind him. Gears whirred, and the plane shuddered as they quickly gained altitude.

"Zak, I need to go to Los Angeles after arriving in JFK. Urgent stuff. I should be back in a few days. Until then, keep an eye on the girls. I hear one of them is making trouble."

CHAPTER 11

F lashes of light in the darkness. Like when lightning illuminated the clouds during a storm. Jake could make out the silhouette of jagged mountains slicing into the horizon but nothing else. They could be anywhere. People crowded the door, some peeking out, but no one could muster the courage to step off the railcar. Others chose to huddle in the darkness of the graffitied corridor, keeping far enough away from each other to avoid the burn of skin touching skin.

Ding-dong

The tone rang again. The doors stayed wide open. Air hissed as the brakes released, but the train didn't move.

"This is our stop," said the racist. "Time for us to depart."

"Leave then, if you're so brave," yelled a young teen. She faced the open door, staring out into the darkness.

"I would if the rest of you'd get out of my way," said the racist.

"Getting out of the way means going out there," said someone else. "I'm not fucking going out there."

The wild-haired woman behind Jake asked, "Would you stay with me once we leave here? I prefer not to be wandering in the darkness alone."

Jake shuffled in a half-circle to study the woman. She had the jitters, but so did he. The distress of going into the unknown alone weighed on him. It was best to pair with someone who had his back. He nodded assent when the teenage girl at the door broke out into a horrible scream. The crowd stirred, moving as one to create distance from her screams, and the sizzling sound of flesh touching flesh filled the area, followed by painful grunts.

"Time to get off the train!" the racist repeated, grimacing as someone bumped against him.

"There's something out there," intoned the teenager, shaking her head as if she had seen something she couldn't believe.

"I saw it too," someone else declared from inside the car. "Eyes. Big ones. Like the eyes of a giant."

"A giant?" asked another man. "Are you out of your fucking mind?"

"This is hell!" said the man who remembered being killed. "It's fitting, right? Our torture begins."

"Get out of the car!" shouted the racist. "I don't feel like standing here for all eternity getting burned by you spineless twits."

"He's right," a man murmured. "Standing here until we get tired and collapse on each other seems stupid. The doors are open. Let's get out of here."

"Fuck that!" said another. "We stay right here until we know what's out there."

"Great, just fucking great," said the racist. He was breathing heavily. "I'm in hell with a bunch of cowards." He closed his eyes and gritted his teeth.

"Why are you so sure this is hell, asshole?" asked Jake.

There was movement as someone tried to push their way out. The sound of searing flesh reminded Jake of a steak hitting the grill at 700 degrees. Several people shrieked. The car filled with smoke. The smell of burning flesh invaded his nostrils, and his stomach muscles weakened.

A man a few bodies removed from the door tried to shove his way past. The harder he pressed his flesh against someone else, the quicker and more severely they burned. His skin blistered and charred as he shouldered a woman trapped by a body on the floor, her arm bursting open to reveal pink meat and bone.

The putrid smell had everyone gagging. Someone puked on those around him, making the smell even worse.

"Oh god, it's horrible," screeched a woman, backing herself into a crusty wall. "There's no circulation in here."

"Just move," said someone else. "It has to start with you people by the door. Just get out!"

The lurching gargle of someone puking was followed by the sound of splattering vomit on another's back. "Sorry," said the southerner, gagging. "It's awful in here. I need to get out."

"Fuck you," said another by the door. "I can't see shit."

"I'll start," offered a Middle Eastern woman in her midthirties. "We can't stand here all day figuring out what to do." She faced the door shoulder to shoulder with the man who'd claimed he'd seen giant eyes. She took a deep breath and gingerly extended a foot forward until she touched solid ground. She shifted her weight and moved her other foot outside. "The ground is hot but tolerable," she said. She took two more steps away from the railcar, sliding her feet forward to check the footing instead of taking bold steps. "It seems pretty solid."

All eyes were trained in the woman's direction, so when the giant opened his eyes, everyone saw it. Except for her. A pair of eyes gleamed in the middle-distance, level with their vision, each eye as large as the railcar. If a giant owned those eyes, he was lying on his stomach, like a cat patiently waiting by a hole in the wall.

She took a deep breath to speak, a smile forming on her lips, when the sharp thud of a hand snatched her. Steaming air shot into the car, blasting everyone's face. Far away, Jake heard the muffled sound of a scream, then the crunch of bones and flesh being popped and grinded. The crunching continued for several seconds. Then silence.

The people stood frozen in the car, speechless.

The racist's wheezy laughter broke the silence. "Oh . . . that was so cool! It snatched her ass so fast, if you blinked, you missed it." He howled and hooted, puked a little and then started laughing again.

The obnoxious pissant spewing nonsense made it impossible to think. His knees wanted to buckle in fear but he dared not move. Yet he knew the time would come where they all had to run.

"What the fuck was that?" a scared voice asked.

"We're screwed if we go out there," said another.

"No, no," said the racist, calming his laughter. "Don't sweat it. She was a raghead. All you good White people have nothing to worry about. Go ahead and walk out. You're all safe. It's this shit stain here that has to worry. Along with the Jews, the chinks, and the spics."

Jake wanted to scream, but he could not let this asshole think he was getting into Jake's head. He steered his focus off the jerk and back into the situation they all faced. What the fuck was that out there?

A flurry of people flinched, bumped into each other, and looked down toward the ground.

"Something ran into me," said a man at the center. "A couple of things. I felt them run past me."

"Me too."

"I felt it too."

Jake felt it as well. What now?

"Ahhhh . . ." a woman yelped. "They're all gathering by my feet."

"Shit," said a man. "OUCH! One bit me."

"Rats!" someone cried. "They're after the fucking puke. They're eating it."

A rat bit Jake on his big toe. It throbbed, and the blood that trickled out attracted more of them. They flurried toward Jake, nipping away at the open wound. His chest heaved, but he showed no pain. Through the chaos, the racist observed him. Watching to see if he flinched. Jake didn't think the racist was getting bit like everyone else. He glowered at the racist, refusing to drop his eyes.

"Ahh!" the people shouted and cried.

The rats grew violent as they amassed, climbing on top of each other and biting anything that moved. The car filled up like a pool. Jake felt them all around his ankles. Then his calves. They needed to get out of there.

The eyes of the giant opened, its pupils dilated.

"Run everybody, run!" said the racist.

Everybody ran. Those by the door took off first, followed by the others. Jake felt the wave of people trying to escape, but he stubbornly stood and endured the crowd of hungry rats picking at his flesh. Still, the racist watched. Waited.

He suffered three more bites before giving in. He kicked at them, sending a flurry of rodents down the aisle. Another kick cleared a path to the door, with the wild-haired woman fleeing right behind him. The racist ran out afterward. He flipped Jake the bird before taking off in the other direction. People were screaming and running in droves. More eyes opened. Jake watched as immense hands snatched up swaths of naked bodies. A piercing flash of light blinded him a moment, but not before revealing that the mountains he'd seen previously were not mountains at all but giants laying around on scorched earth like sunbathing alligators. They moved on all fours, awkwardly, like people pretending to be animals, toward a feast of frantic people fleeing the cars.

Jake ran down the endless row of railcars. Thousands of people poured forth, only to find themselves on the feeding platform of the giants. He felt the incredible thrust of steaming wind as swiping hands carried away fistfuls of screaming people. Every so often, he checked to see if the wild-haired woman he befriended in the car was still there.

"I see something up ahead," said Jake.

The endless stream of railcars and people veered left, and Jake spied an opening off to the right. A way out. "Not too much further."

He turned around to encourage the wild-haired woman, but she was gone. He had no choice but to keep going. The screams behind him reached a crescendo as he kept running until he heard nothing at all.

CHAPTER 12

The darkness around Jake narrowed into a passageway and then expanded back to what felt like a vast space. It was still dark. The ground under his feet changed from hot concrete to a gritty, earthy texture. Everything sweltered; the air, the ground, his bare feet, his skin. Relentless sweat rolled down his body. He searched for the horizon and saw no forms like giants. No hills or mountains. It was flatlands.

Jake trudged forward. His body wanted to collapse in a heap and fall into a sweaty sleep. Occasionally, something ran by and nipped at his feet. The sharp, stinging pain reminded him he had to keep moving. If this truly were hell, his torment would be unyielding. Walking through the flatlands was preferable to what he'd escaped. And he needed time to figure out where he was and how he got there.

Jake plodded for what felt like miles. The longer he walked, the more the igneous heat beneath his soles increased with intensity. Each step scorched more than the last. Blisters bubbled up and popped, only to be replaced by even bigger blisters. He awkwardly skipped along, trying to limit the time his feet touched the ground. He danced and he shuffled. The creative footwork provided no relief. There had to be something that would alleviate this discomfort. He looked around three hundred and sixty degrees. Tiny legs pattered on the ground and quickly ran up on him and stung his pinky toe, shooting darts of fire up his calf. He flinched and cursed and took off running, picking up his feet and putting them down as fast as he could.

The pattering behind him grew louder as if whatever had helped itself to his toe was in pursuit of a more substantial meal. The darkness lightened some, and off on the horizon, Jake made out the outline of a building. He ran toward it. A crescendo of pattering legs gave chase behind him. The ground heat intensified. His feet sizzled with each step, his little toe swollen and numb and inflamed all at the same time. But he kept running. If he lost his footing, the creatures would engulf him, bringing broiling pain all over his body.

He had to make it to that building.

A wrought iron fence with an opening between two pillars surrounded the building. At the pillars, the dirt ended, and a concrete path began. His feet hit the concrete with minor relief, although it was still hot. He heard the creatures swarming behind him. They sounded hard like they had exoskeletons, probably some sort of insect with multiple legs. He reached the front doors of the building, which were open, and without missing a stride, ran in and down a long hallway. Perhaps he could lock himself in a room and wait. It was his only hope.

He spotted a doorway nearby on his left. He turned the knob and crashed his shoulder into the door, swinging it open violently. It hit the doorstop and bounced back with a loud bang. Jake spun on his heels as best he could and grabbed the edge of the door, managing to close and lock it with a deadbolt before the creatures crashed into the other side. Their tiny stiff legs scraped at the frame, trying to get in. With the door at his back, he gulped the fetid air into his heaving chest. He slid down to the floor and tried to catch his breath. The room floor was warm, not scalding hot like everywhere else. Still, a steady stream of sweat dripped down his body while he waited for the little creatures to give up.

The clawing at the door stopped. As his eyes adjusted to the dimness of the interior, he realized he wasn't in a room at all; he'd gone from one hallway to another. It stretched about thirty feet before disappearing into impenetrable blackness, with doorways on each side. Dirt and blood caked the floor and grime blackened the base of the walls. Squawks and moans and soft whimpers echoed down the hallway.

Jake wasn't alone. He got to his feet and staggered, almost falling. The pressure on his big toe from the rats and his little toe from the creatures made it hard to keep his balance. He rested against the door, took a couple of deep breaths, and willed himself to move. Jake slowly limped along, his hands raised and poised like a black belt ready for action. He didn't know karate or even how to fight, for that matter, but the pose made him feel better.

He edged up to the first pair of doors, straining his neck to see what lay inside before he got there. The first door revealed a classroom with vintage wood chair-desk combos, with a metal bin under the chair for storing books. The second door revealed the same. Jake poked his head inside each, peering into the corners for hidden shapes. He flipped the light switch to see if anything would light up in the strange, Gothic schoolhouse he'd found himself in. No such luck.

He inched down the hallway, carefully checking each room as he passed. They were all classrooms. Old worn wooden floors with school desks throughout. He imagined the desks were in neat rows at one point. Now they were scattered haphazardly. Faint whimpers were ever-present, like background music. He opened one classroom door and was hit with the sound of intense screaming. His instinct was to run until he saw a man on the floor with no one else around. He was writing in pain in a fetal position. His arms wrapped around his torso. Screaming incessantly. Horrified, Jake closed the door and kept moving.

Jake limped down to the next door. A school lab room. He cocked his head, trying to figure out what was different. Then it came to him; the room sat in silence. No sound reverberated from the hallway. No whimpering. It was like a dead zone of quiet. Perhaps something in the lab could be used to tend to his toe: peroxide or a soothing balm to quell the pain. Even a flashlight would do. He hadn't had a chance to get a good look at his toes. He wondered if it looked as gnarly as it felt.

Jake crept inside. He spied a storage cabinet and quietly limped over to see what he could find. As he reached for the cabinet doors, he glanced to his right. A pair of eyes watched him. Jake jerked backward. A man was pinned to the wall, hanging like a living replica of da Vinci's Vitruvian Man. His arms fully extended from his body, and his legs spread apart in an upside-down V. Stakes penetrated his wrists and ankles, fixing him in place. There were two more bolts through his cheeks, stretching the skin outward from his face and pinned to the wall.

"Mercy," a faint voice said. The man was still alive. "Mercy," he implored. The skin of his cheeks stretched out like taffy making it difficult to close his mouth or even speak.

Jake nodded. "Okay, okay. Hold on." He doubted he possessed the strength to remove the bolts on the wrists and ankles, however his stretched face bothered Jake the most. He reached for the bolts at the cheeks.

"Don't touch that! What's wrong with you?"

Jake spun around, hands raised. He did not expect anyone else to be there. A naked man stood in the middle of the room. Asian, average height, stocky build.

"Mercy . . . mercy," pled the tortured man.

"Someone's coming back for him. They'll be here soon."

"I was just going to take out the ones on his face," said Jake.

"Do you want to end up like him? You touch him, and we're fucked." He nudged his head for Jake to follow, then hunched over and ducked out of the classroom and across the hall into the next. Jake crept behind him. They entered at the back and walked past a wall of lockers. The front of the classroom had a large teacher's desk and a chalkboard. Grimy windows dotted the other wall. Jake wiped a corner of the closest window with his palm to look outside and was rewarded with a scene from an apocalypse movie. Blackened tree trunks sprouted broken, leafless branches. Scorched earth and gray dust swirled everywhere. Storm clouds floated eerily above like a roiling ocean. It was the most detail he had seen of the outside world since he'd arrived.

Jake's new friend sat with his back to the lockers and took a breath. He motioned for Jake to sit beside him, so he did.

"The name is Zhiqiang," he said, running a hand through fine black hair.

"I'm Jake." Jake offered a hand and then withdrew it when Zhiqiang stared.

"Are you trying to turn me into one of the Contretemps?" said Zhiqiang.

"Contretemps?" said Jake, crinkling his forehead.

"The people cursed for touching. They needed to touch another so badly that they ignored the pain of contact. They held on too long and now their skin burns forever. Despite letting go."

The screaming in the background rang in Jake's ears. People wailing constantly. Echoing throughout the halls. It was maddening. So that is what happened to the guy on the floor in the classroom. "Contretemps, you called them?"

Zhiqiang nodded and looked around the room. "I haven't been to this place before. Any clues about how to get through this?"

"No. I don't even know what this place is, Gee . . . Geuh . . ."

"Call me Zee. It's much easier that way."

"Okay, Zee," said Jake. "You obviously know more than I do. I started on a train with a bunch of strangers. Then there were giants eating people. Then I got stung or bit by something, and it hurts like fuck. Some asshole on the train kept insisting we're in literal hell, but I can't be in hell."

Zee shifted his eyes suspiciously toward Jake, then back ahead, then back to Jake, this time turning his whole head. "You just got here? Aw fuck! A virgin. Damn, you're not going to be much help."

"Help? With what?"

"With getting out of here, dumbass!" Zee shook his head in disbelief. "You people from that region are all mixed up."

"Hold up," said Jake. "What exactly do you mean by 'you people'?"

"Christians. That's what you are, right?" Zee sighed. "I keep meeting you people here and having to explain things to you so you won't end up like that poor bastard back there, pinned to the wall. This *is* hell! Got it? Everyone goes to *Diyu,* but your time here is not indefinite. Your sins determine how long you're here. When you go through your trials, you'll be reincarnated. For now, you must accept that you are in Diyu. This is one of the Eighteen Hells."

"Eighteen?"

"Yep. Eighteen. The Hell of Boulder Crushing, the Hell of Scissors, Hell of Disembowelment, Hell of Steaming, Hell of Pounding, Hell of Oil Cauldrons, Hell of Grinding, Hell of Mountain Fire, Hell of Sawing..."

"Stop!" Jake said as Zee raised his tenth finger. "Sounds interesting, but you're talking nonsense. I'm a Christian. I was baptized. I took communion and everything."

"Yeah, yeah, and that was supposed to guarantee you from going to hell . . . yadda, yadda. I heard it all before, thank you. I bet most of you end up here because you're meant to experience the Hell of Tongue Ripping for believing that simply following your God makes you better than everyone else."

Jake shook his head. "No. I can't believe this is happening. It's a mistake."

"Yet here you are," said Zee. "It's best to go through like everyone else. Pay your debt for your sins and be reincarnated."

"There is no reincarnation, Zee."

"Isn't your God supposed to come back and raise everyone from the dead? That's reincarnation."

"It's not reincarnation. It's spiritual."

"Won't you have new bodies?" asked Zee. "New bodies mean reincarnation."

"You think you know what I'm talking about, but you don't. Trust me. It's not reincarnation, and I can't be in hell."

Zee shrugged and swept his arms around, inviting Jake to use his eyes. "Time to cleanse your soul and become worthy of being reincarnated."

"Listen, if you die and go to hell, that's it. You're there forever. If you die and go to heaven, you'll be happy for all eternity. No reincarnation. No second chances."

"Isn't the earth supposed to be made new, and all the worthy souls live there with your savior for a thousand years?"

"Yes."

"So they live on earth with an earthly body for millennia?" asked Zee.

"Yes."

"Sounds a lot like being reincarnated to me."

"But . . ."

"Yes, yes," said Zee, waving away Jake's protestations. "I'm too stupid to get it. I know. I butted heads with you stubborn Christians before. Yet here you are. Right here with me anyway."

"This is a mistake," said Jake. He looked above. "What have I done wrong?"

Zee slapped Jake. His face sizzled from the reprimand.

"Are you one of those people who sit around crying about your predicament or are you going to fight your way through this? Wise up. I'm telling you there's a way out. Serve your punishment through hell and hope you have atoned enough to be reincarnated. Or resurrected. Whatever the hell you believe." Zee pointed his finger at Jake. "You never give up. Understand? Giving up means ending up like that bastard on that wall. He could get out if he wanted. He could resign his soul, and he'd start over at the beginning of his trials. But he pities his situation. That's why he's stuck there." He lowered his finger and looked around. "We need to move on and get out here. On to the next hell."

Jake thought about the blow delivered to his cheek. His mind swam with thoughts. He'd always considered himself a survivor. He looked out the window into the wasteland. "If what you say is true, what hell are we in now?"

"I don't know. Probably the Hell of Skinning, based on that poor sap back there. I can't tell from the surroundings. This is some strange ritualistic place I've never seen before."

Jake looked askance at Zee. "This is a classroom."

"Is that what this is called?" said Zee. "Does it serve some kind of ritualistic function?"

"It's a school," said Jake. "A place of learning. You've never seen one before? Wait . . ."

Jake thought back to the beginning of their conversation. Zee had said he ran into Christians many times and knew the religion. He referred to Jake as from a region and not a country. Why wouldn't he know what a school was? In addition, when he spoke, his mouth moved, but he wasn't speaking English. Yet Jake understood him perfectly and vice versa.

"Where are you from, and what year were you born?" asked Jake.

"Year?"

"Yes, Year. 2010, 1917, 1452 . . ."

"Ah," said Zee. "I remember someone asked me this before. Some means of counting the changing seasons. We didn't give a damn about such things where I am from."

Jake rested his back against the lockers. "You have no clue how long you've been here, do you?"

"I don't know the numbers you are referring to. And I don't care. The only numbers we keep track of here are the numbers on your back."

"What numbers?"

Zee showed Jake his back. Hundreds of markings, some darker and some lighter, sprawled across his shoulders and spilled down to his coccyx. More than half of them were darker. The lighter ones were on his lower back. It was as if they were inked in sequential order.

"When you're caught and tortured by one of Hell's Apostles, you're marked. Then you go back to the beginning of hell, where you first started. For you, that's the Hell of Beasts, where you encountered the giants."

"You mean you can go back?" asked Jake.

"My number is 17,214. You don't have to see the numbers on your back to know what it is. When Tartarus catches you, he'll mark on you the number of times he's willing to let you travel through his hells."

"Tartarus? Who is he?"

"One of the Hell's Apostles. That's what I call him. He's very painful. He looks through your emotions, all the pain and fear and sorrow, and pretends to be concerned. Asks your permission to be looked at by him. I don't know what would happen if you said no. In any case, most people say yes. Then he brands you with a number. Once you use up your chances, you get trapped in hell's belly."

"I thought you said it wasn't forever!" said Jake. "Being trapped in hell's belly sounds like forever to me!"

"I didn't want to scare you. Hey!" he said, remembering something. "Did you touch that pin back there?"

"Why?"

"It's like a tracking device. Whoever did that to the guy will know where you are and come looking for you. Did you touch it?"

Jake got nervous. His breathing quickened. He had touched it—grazed it, just as Zee yelled for him not to.

The hairs stiffened on the back of Jake's neck. A tingling tickled the surface of his skin like static electricity. He opened his mouth to describe the sensation when Zhiqiang leaped to his feet and stuffed himself into one of the lockers behind them. Jake took it as a hint and followed course. He opened the locker nearest him and tried to back inside it. His bare feet squished something soft, like raw sausages. He slid across one and almost came out of the locker but caught himself before he fell. He stepped back inside and kicked what was down there to make room for his feet. It was a tight fit. His shoulders pressed against the walls, and his knees bent at an awkward angle but Jake finally managed to get the door closed.

A sharp bang came from the hallway, and he heard the frantic slapping of bare feet running. Jake peeked through the tiny vents to see what was happening. His heart thumping so loud the muffled sound pulsated the walls of the locker. A man ran into the classroom, knocking aside a row of chairs, desperately fleeing the larger, purple-skinned man right behind him. The purple fellow grabbed the fleeing man by the back of the neck and pinned him to the desk at the front of the room. Jake gasped as the purple guy looked as much as seven feet tall and four feet wide. His entire body was thick and massive—all muscle, no fat anywhere. A giant bull tong hung from his nose and over his lips. He licked at it from time to time, raising it with each swipe of the tongue. A large cleaver lay ready in his other hand.

"Please, Gaap," cried the man. "I don't have many chances left!" The pleading man cried into the desk, his body pale and frail under the imposing Gaap. He held his hands out in an open posture. Surrendering.

"You know my name?" said the purple one in a deep, threatening baritone. "How many do you have left?" Gaap examined the man's back. "Just two more times? You're screwed. So much that it does not matter. Give me what I want."

Gaap plucked the man up with one hand by the nape of his neck. Jake gawked at the forceful flex of his cleaver arm. The frail man swung in Gaap's powerful clutch, his feet barely touching the ground.

"No, please!" the man rasped, raking his fingers against his neck, trying to pry himself from Gaap's grasp.

The cleaver rose fast as the beast carefully maneuvered the man's body until his manhood rested on the desk. Gaap sent the cleaver crashing down in one swift swing. The sharp thud shook Jake to his core as he gasped. It was over before he'd even known what happened.

Gaap threw the man to the floor and wiggled the cleaver free from the desk. The victim writhed in agony and sputtered long wails of pain, both hands holding the hole where his penis once was.

"Oh, that pain is nothing," boomed Gaap. "What about the pain of being born without one?"

Jake searched between Gaap's legs to verify. Indeed, the beast did not have a member.

"I need to find one that fits," said Gaap. He swiped the penis from the table, spit on the severed end, and fixed it to his pelvis. It stuck there, and he moved his head left and right to see how it looked.

Jake placed his face in his hands and choked down bile while Gaap admired his new appendage. A noise came from the hall. What next, Jake thought? He peered through the locker vent wishing they would all go away.

"Wall," said Gaap. "What are you doing here?"

Another walked into the classroom. "Someone touched one of my tools," said Wall. "He's in here."

Wall had the look of a man, except his skin was extremely yellow, and his fingers were long and gnarled. He was wearing clothes. The first person Jake saw with clothes on.

Wall looked at Gaap modeling his new penis. "Doesn't work," he said. "Looks like a jellybean stuck to your crotch."

"Ha, ha, asshole." Gaap snatched the penis off his pelvis and threw it against the wall with a wet plop.

"Don't leave it there," admonished Wall. "No one will stay and hide here believing it is safe if you leave body parts scattered all over the floor. Put it away properly."

Gaap sighed in frustration. He picked up the limp bundle of flesh and headed straight towards Jake. Jake shuddered with each step. He squeezed his hand over his mouth tighter as Gaap reached for the handle. Gaap opened the locker and threw the severed penis inside, hitting Jake in the knees. Sausages, Jake thought in disbelief. He thought those were sausages at his feet. He was too afraid of what came next to look away. He was scared stiff. Gaap turned as if he did not see Jake, but that was just a tease.

He spun back and leaned down slowly, putting his head inches from the locker. "Check out this guy's," said Gaap. "This looks proportional enough, don't it?"

Wall came over and stood beside Gaap to study Jake's crotch. "Way too big for that guy, but for you, it's perfect. You'd look cool with that penis."

Jake blacked out. His last thought was how much he loved his penis.

CHAPTER 13

Screaming. Was the suffering so intense that he had an out of body experience and now he could hear himself? The screaming was ear-splittingly loud. It sounded higher in pitch. Now he was babbling something. What was he saying? Was he the one screaming?

His heart jolted, and he shot upright. Dear god, did he still have his Johnson?

Jake found himself in a seated position in a hotel room. He saw a half-empty bottle of Pappy Van Winkle on the bar and an empty tumbler resting beside it. The muffled screams grew quieter and settled into frantic breathing. An open door showed a cleaning cart parked in the hallway.

Behind him, on the same chair where Jake told Jericho his story, sat a fair-skinned housekeeper. She wiped at the tears running down her red cheeks and then covered her mouth in shock, her ponytail swinging in dismay. She appeared to be in her midforties, brown-eyed and petite, wearing burgundy pants and a V-neck short sleeve shirt with white sneakers. The nametag said, Rose.

"You're okay? Thank god," she said in a shaken voice. "You have no idea. I thought I was seeing my first dead body."

Jake looked at his clothes. Blue jeans and a crisp blue shirt with white stripes. Black socks. His shoes, blue Clarks Wallabee high-tops, sat neatly by the door. He felt clean and showered. His hands were soft, and his nails trimmed. They smelled of expensive floral lotions or oils.

"Why am I here?" asked Jake, bewildered.

"Exactly," said Rose. "You were supposed to be checked out already, so I came in to clean, and I saw you lying there. I thought you were drunk from the night before, sleeping it off on the floor, so I tried to wake you up, but you didn't move or respond." She shuddered. "And you were cold. I tried to call the manager, but I was shaking so bad my fingers kept hitting the wrong buttons on my cellphone. Then you got up. Just like that, you sat up. You scared me half to death."

"I'm sorry," said Jake. His head was foggy. "I don't know what happened. I'm a little confused."

"I knocked on the door to see if anyone was inside, and I got no answer, so I came in," she repeated. "Christ. You gave me a heart attack."

Jake sat there for a moment. It was all coming back in flashes. She mentioned something about checking out. He'd booked the room for four days. Jake reached in his pocket for his phone. Not there. He pulled himself to his feet. His legs wobbled, and he stopped to gather himself, uneasy. He spied his phone on the bar counter and went to check it. The time was slightly after 9 a.m. An automated reminder said it was checkout day.

"This can't be right," said Jake. "I had the room for four days."

"Yes. And today is Monday. Most people who put up the 'do not disturb' sign leave the room in a mess, so I figured I'd better get started early when I saw the sign no longer on the door."

"I took the sign off?"

"Probably last night when you were drinking."

"I wasn't drinking. I didn't even have a drop."

Rose eyed the bottle of Van Winkle. "Then it must be something else because you were out cold. By something else, I mean drugs."

"No drugs." Jake cleared his throat. "I do have a condition, but it hasn't happened in years."

She made the sign of the cross. "Thank goodness you came out of it. I don't know what I would've done." She remained in the chair pressing her hand against her chest as if willing her panic-stricken heart to calm itself. Then she stood up and exhaled. It was time to get to work.

But Jake's unease intensified. Things weren't adding up. The image of Jericho Black stabbing him rushed into his mind, and he had to grip the counter not to fall. What about all the weird things that followed? They'd been just as real and intense. Was any of it factual, or was it the final stages of his growing tumor wreaking havoc on his memories?

He needed to figure it out. And to figure it out, he needed his computer. Jake went to search the bedroom but couldn't find his laptop. He packed up his things as best he could and went back to the main room. Rose jumped when he entered.

"Has anyone else been in the room?" he asked.

She gripped the edge of the bar tightly for support. "The door was locked when I got here, and no one can enter without a keycard. The ones we use are coded each day and are only good for our shift." She moved behind the bar to stash the bourbon and wash the tumblers in the tiny sink.

All those people coming in and out of his room with their own keycards—how likely was that? He must have imagined it all. Jake took one last look around, then slung his gray backpack over his shoulder. He checked the time. If it was Monday, he was late for work.

CHAPTER 14

On several occasions during his youth, Jake's tumor caused seizures. Advances in medicine brought those seizures to a halt many years ago; however, he remembered one time when a fall gave him a concussion.

When Jake experienced a seizure, his body didn't crumple like in the movies, so gentle and slow that someone could catch him. He'd go down like a tree, stiff and straight. It was especially dangerous among strangers, as they tended to move out of the way as he fell. The several knots on the back of Jake's head could attest to that. Paired with the tumor at the base of the spine, he was lucky his brain wasn't permanently scrambled.

Awaking from a concussion always felt to Jake like time had been stolen from him. People would report on everything they had done while Jake was out; going to work, watching a movie, playing video games. In Jake's timeline, he'd be doing one thing and suddenly be in a completely different scene. To him, it was instantaneous, like a jump cut. He wouldn't even know it happened unless someone told him that several days had passed.

The ding of the elevator brought him out of his trance. That must be the explanation. A seizure to make him lose consciousness and then a concussion from the fall. Those weird dreams that followed were new.

Jake went to the front desk, turned in the keycard, and stepped outside into the warm sun. A bracing wind whipped through the city as if to remind everyone that winter hadn't given up just yet. Manhattan functioned as it always did; noise, cars, crowded streets, and everyone in a hurry. He zipped up his jacket and steered his still-weakened body through the ambivalent masses, trying to piece together his thoughts.

He crossed the street and kept walking, passing a couple of hot dog and pretzel stands. A vendor opened the warming cart and released a luscious and savory aroma. When had he eaten last? He passed a pizza shop opening for lunch. The delightful scent of crispy baked crust and melted mozzarella atop a zesty sauce filled his nostrils. His stomach rumbled. Then he spotted a place on the corner that looked like an old diner. Pat's Diner. A car wash bustled with business right behind it. Busy place, good food, or so he'd heard. The heavenly, mouthwatering smell of classic cuisine wafted through the air and urged him on. His stomach and nose seemed to tell him that this was the place, so he went inside.

Pat's Diner had a classic old diner feel. Red vinyl booths complemented the chrome tables and barstools. Mini jukeboxes, no more than a foot tall, sat ready to take quarters in return for some old favorites. Round swivel barstools accompanied the main counter, complete with a view into the kitchen. It wasn't crowded. Two men hung out by the register, talking up a server. A few couples resided in the booths to the right while another woman swiped at her phone in the corner. Just after ten in the morning—post-breakfast and too early for the lunch crowd—it was the perfect time to get something fast.

Jake made his way to one of the booths and slid inside. He had a view of the street. A laminated menu card nestled between the salt and pepper shaker and the small Splenda container. He flipped it over a few times and waited to order.

The friendly server, a toned, brown-skinned woman in her early thirties dressed in black shirt and slacks walked up with a kind of playful look about her. She fanned her extra-long, fake eyelashes a few times before speaking.

"Good morning, my name is Lisa. I'll be your server today." She took the napkin-rolled silverware out of her waist apron and placed it on the table. "Would you like to start with something to drink?"

"Anything that gets free refills," said Jake. "And I know what I want."

She smiled, pen poised above her order pad.

"Give me the Royal Breakfast combo," said Jake. "Make that two of them."

She placed a hand on her hip and paused to make sure she heard him right. "The one with four eggs, four slices of bacon, hash browns, and three biscuits with gravy? You want two of them?"

"And the pancake breakfast as well," Jake added.

"The one with three eggs and sausage?" She shrugged her shoulders and nodded. "Okay. Big eater, huh? You must be an athlete. Do you play basketball? You're not playing against the Knicks, are you?"

Jake smiled graciously Being six feet seven and Black, he always heard basketball comments. But Jake was all thumbs and elbows when it came to sports. "No basketball. Just a computer geek," he said.

"It's all good," said Lisa, with an extra flutter. "You sure you can put all of that away?"

"I don't see why not," said Jake.

"Okay, I'll put it in just as you asked," said Lisa.

"Thanks," said Jake and smiled.

She was nice. Pleasant. She had a great personality and a lovely smile. Attractive, courteous, and ingratiating. Everything he looked for in a woman. And he sensed the potential of reciprocity behind those long lashes. Then again, he may have just been hungry. And her opinion of him could very well change once all that food was spread out on the table. He knew he was curious as to how he was going to finish it all. Had he ever been so hungry before?

She returned with coffee and poured him a cup, leaning over the table ever so slightly. She smelled amazing. "I put a rush on the order," she said. "Just for you . . . since you're so hungry."

She spun on the heels of her black flats and pranced away, holding the carafe away from her body with one hand. She passed by a man sitting at the counter, and Jake did a double take. This guy was 1970's Ron O'Neal straight out of *Superfly*. A light-skinned Black man, like Jake, but dressed flamboyantly, with hair down to his shoulders and slightly curled out at the end. His muttonchops stopped an inch short of the corner of his mouth. A white mink coat covered a bare chest. The outfit was complete with white gabardine bellbottom slacks and matching white alligator shoes. A white hat with a black band and feather sat next to him. He was pint-sized with a face that looked just like Katt Williams. Was the comedian in town for a show? Jake looked around for cameras, chuckled and took a sip of coffee.

The headache of having to show up at work physically invaded his thoughts. It was silly. With more than half of the IT industry working from home, his boss still felt the need to have everyone come to the office. He was the kind of prick who felt production increased under his watchful eye when really he was an imbecile who ignored facts and hard data because he thought he was smarter. The only thing keeping the birdbrain's business afloat was his daddy's money.

The phone buzzed in his pocket, and Jake looked to see who had sent the message. It was Ryan Compton.

Sometimes he swears he is psychic.

Ryan Compton, his boss, sent a long, wordy text asking Jake if he was coming in to work. Blah-blahing about meeting deadlines and commitment to excellence. As a boss, Ryan was a joke. Management via throwing fits and threats to fire everyone. A childlike impression of what it meant to be in charge. Jake despised the simpleton but going to work for someone else was not an option. Jake's creation, the advanced tracking software using facial recognition, was perfected on the company's dime. Technically, it belonged to Ryan.

The detestable taste of his work situation vanished with the graceful entrance of Lisa carrying his food, her arms full of plates. The cook came out and dropped off the pancakes. He shook his head after looking at Jake. Probably expected to see a 500 lbs. mammoth sitting there. Lisa leaned in close, spreading the plates out on the table.

"Enjoy," she said.

"Thanks," said Jake. The smell of freshly cooked bacon flowed from the plate to his nostrils. Heavenly. He dug in with both hands, starting with the first plate of eggs and bacon. Gobbled it up within a minute. He smeared butter and grape jelly on the biscuits and munched them down. Then he started on the next plate with the hash browns. Eggs and biscuits went as quickly as the first batch. He turned to the pancakes, loaded them with extra butter and syrup, then cut through the fluffy cakes with his fork and shoveled them down along with the remaining bacon. He stacked the plates as he went, piling them up one after another until it was eight plates tall.

"I think you should take a look out the window, hoss. Those fellows in the black Escalade are thinking about coming in here and fucking you up."

Jake looked up from his plate and found that while his attention had been diverted, the Katt Williams look-alike had situated himself in the opposite booth. He rolled a toothpick in the corner of his mouth and stared at the Escalade. "Those boys are hungry for blood," he commented. He had a slight drawl in his voice.

"Take a look out the window," he said again. "Don't stare at me. Look out the window. Thrust your chest out. Do something to show these motherfuckers you're not to be fucked with."

Jake glanced out the window but was more concerned about the immediate invasion of his privacy with this pint-sized pimp interrupting his breakfast.

"I said look nigga, not glance!" said the pimp. "Stare those boys down. Don't look at me!"

"What the hell are you doing here?" asked Jake.

"Sorry," Lisa interrupted, pouring Jake another cup.

"Forgive me, sister," said Jake. "I wasn't talking to you. I'm being harassed over here to look out the window."

Lisa pointed her chin at the Escalade. "Do you know those dudes?" she asked. "They've been parked there the whole time, staring into the diner."

"That's what I been telling this motherfucker," said the pimp. "But he actin' like a little bitch!"

"Screw you," said Jake. "Maybe you're trying to start some shit."

"Maybe they're looking for a punk-bitch eating pancakes." said the pimp.

"You're the bitch. Bitch!"

"Excuse me?" said Lisa.

"Not you, sister," said Jake. He looked across the table. "I think it's about time you get the fuck up out of here." He pointed to the entrance, and Lisa began walking away. "Wait, Lisa," called Jake. "I'm sorry you got caught in the crossfire, but some people have no respect for others. Can you believe this guy just sat down here while I'm eating?"

She turned around. "What guy?"

"Him!" said Jake, pointing across the table.

Lisa looked at Jake and then dug in her apron for the check. She slapped it on the table, turned on her heels, and stormed off.

"Now I lost my appetite," said Jake. "You can't afford to pay for a meal, so you thought you could grab some of mine since I have so much of it. Is that it? Is this some hustle? Do you take me for a sucker? Can't pimp hoes, so you're pimping for pancakes now. Pathetic."

"Don't believe me," shrugged the pimp. "It's your funeral."

Jake snatched the bill off the table and slid out of the booth.

"Finish those pancakes," said the pimp. "You'll need the energy."

The register was off to the right, at the opposite end of the counter. He passed the patrons seated near the kitchen entrance. In the middle of the kitchen, he could see Lisa. He waved to her to see if everything was okay. She was talking to another man, a big guy of Mediterranean descent. The manager, Jake guessed. Lisa saw him wave and folded her arms tight across her chest.

Another server, a young girl with brown hair and blue eyes, stepped up to the register to take his money.

"How was everything today?" she asked.

"Food was good," said Jake. "I'm annoyed you let people hustle food at someone else's table."

The waitress shook her head. "Someone was at your table?"

"Yeah, that little pint-sized asshole right there." Jake turned and pointed to where he was seated, but no one was there. "He must've gone to the bathroom or something. He walked over and sat down in the booth while I was eating."

"What did he look like?" she asked.

"He looked like Katt Williams," said Jake. "He was sitting at the counter when I walked in."

"The comedian?" one of the guys sitting by the register asked. He was fifty years old, Hispanic, a little on the heavy side. His words slurred as if he was still recovering from a night of drinking. "I love me some Katt Williams. You say he's in the bathroom?"

Jake hesitated. His head felt foggy again. "Well, I guess he is."

The kitchen door burst open, and the large man stomped toward Jake, followed by Lisa. He glared at Jake like he was going to do something violent.

"I hear you called this woman a bitch," he said.

Jake balked. "What? No. She got it wrong." He attempted a smile at Lisa. "I wasn't talking to you."

"That's what I thought," huffed the manager. "Changing your tune when you see me. I don't care how tall you are. I will still kick your ass if you talk to anyone that works here like that."

Jake shook his head. "Listen," he said, appealing to Lisa. She refused to meet his eye. "I apologize if you thought I was talking to you."

"Yeah, yeah," said the manager. "It's about time you leave."

"I was talking to that other asshole who sat down at my table," continued Jake.

"It was Katt Williams," said the drunk by the counter. "He's in the bathroom now. You can get an autographed picture put up on the wall that says 'Katt Williams took a shit here!'"

"Enough, Julio," said the manager, still raging at Jake. "I don't ever want to see you in here again. You're not welcome. You hear me?"

Jake left the diner fuming. As he adjusted the backpack over his shoulder, his eyes encountered the Escalade. Steam rolled out of the idling tailpipe. Jake squinted and tried to make out the driver when the vehicle backed up in a hurry and drove away.

CHAPTER 15

Maxim liked to wear the modern version of traditional suits. Jackets tapered at the waist. Slim-fit pants tailored to end at the ankles. Expensive Italian shoes and big, gaudy watches. No ties, but he loved his fedoras. Flashy fedoras in bold yet tasteful colors. He sat upright in the back of the Escalade, watching Jake Coltrane eat his breakfast as he rubbed the small patch of blond hair on his chin. He enjoyed the bristly scratching sound; it served as a distraction while he thought.

Maxim had seen the hacker lying on the floor dead no more than three hours ago. As a member of the *Vory*, Maxim was no stranger to death. He'd seen many in his lifetime and expected to see many more.

A talent for quickly determining the time of a person's death came in handy when one often found oneself opening doors and finding lifeless bodies. Maxim had memorized the stages. There were four. First was pallor mortis, simply a paleness in the face and surface of the skin within the first two hours of death. Then came algor mortis. Without circulation, a body began to cool to the ambient temperature, dropping an average of 0.8 degrees Celsius per hour for the first twelve hours. Next was rigor mortis, the "stiffness in death" that most people recognized. Chemical changes in the muscles postmortem caused muscles and joints to stiffen. The cornea dried out, giving the eyes a milky, hazy appearance. Rigor mortis began around two hours after death and lasted as long as two days in some cases. Last was the fourth stage of death: livor mortis, where blood was at the mercy of gravity and collected at the lowest point of the body.

Three hours ago, Jake Coltrane's body was in livor mortis. Understandable, considering he was reported dead by Alexei three days ago.

Now he was eating breakfast.

"Are you sure he's the one that was in the hotel room?" said Oleg, the stocky driver. Oleg was loyal, dependable, and loved to drive. His green eyes peered at Maxim through the rearview mirror.

"It's him," said Maxim. "He is wearing the same clothes. No wounds, no blood anywhere, but he was surely dead. At least I thought he was."

A call to Maxim the day prior intimated that someone would pay for the hacker's laptop if it were turned over to them, no questions asked. One hundred thousand in American dollars. The call came from Leonid Semenov, a financial gopher for the oligarchs. He typically took half, which meant the oligarchs offered two hundred thousand for the laptop. Usually Maxim would agree to such a deal immediately; however, he heard other things from other sources.

Anyone who had the talent to intercept financial transactions, like the hacker, would be valuable to the *Vor*. Even better, he probably had other accounts on the take. Maybe he'd parlayed those monies into cryptocurrency or some other untraceable currency. In any case, a whole slew of possibilities opened to make extra cash, and Alexei chose to leave those potential earnings lifeless on the hotel room floor. The sadistic maniac was always too quick to kill.

Nonetheless, the conundrum didn't end there. Jericho Black offered Alexei millions to spare the hacker's life for a program. The oligarchs didn't want the program; they wanted the computer, which Jericho left in the hotel room. Maxim was betting it was worth more than one hundred grand if the oligarchs were after something other than the program.

"What should we do, Maxim?" asked Dimitri, his loyal comrade. Dimitri's dark hair hung over flinty brown eyes, and he slouched impatiently in the front passenger's seat, busted knuckles curled on thick thighs. Maxim sensed his desire to jump out of the car and fold the hacker up like a suitcase.

"Easy," said Maxim. "Let me think." He'd asked Leonid of the potential complications of making additional money from resources taken from Alexei's kill. Leonid assured him not to worry: Alexei wouldn't be a problem to anyone.

Another dangerous web, he thought to himself. Maxim and Alexei were *Vory*, and although intimately entwined with the oligarchs, they were two separate entities. *Vory* gave orders to *Vory*: thieves ordering other thieves. Oligarchs were part of the financial economy who benefited from the work of the *Vor*. The separation provided protection and profit both ways. When it came to *Vory* business, the oligarchs had no say.

Clearly they were having a say now.

"The proper thing is to tell Alexei that the hacker is alive," said Oleg. "Give him a chance to fix his mistake."

"Alive, as in attacked and survived?" asked Dimitri, shaking his shaggy hair. "He doesn't have a scratch on him. No limp, no broken bones, no indication of any internal injuries. He is perfectly fine. Alexei let him go, plain and simple."

"You know Alexei," said Oleg. "When has he ever let someone go?"

"The real problem is, we know he's still alive," said Maxim, "and if Sergei finds out that we know and said nothing, we'll be the ones to pay for it."

"So, what is the plan?" asked Dimitri.

Maxim sighed and scratched the hairs on his chin. He was running out of time. If his hunch was correct, there'd be major repercussions when Alexei was killed. Any chance at making some real money had to happen before the underground felt the inevitable shockwaves. "I say the hacker being alive is a bonus for us. He has a system. He can teach our people how to intercept financial transactions within companies and transfer them to our chosen accounts. When we are finished with the hacker, we will kill him ourselves. We'll look like geniuses, siphoning money from businesses at our leisure." And Maxim could turn the computer over to the oligarchs and collect the other hundred grand with none the wiser.

"Do we take him now?" asked Oleg.

Maxim peeked out the window. Jake Coltrane stomped out of the restaurant and into the crowded sidewalk, glaring at the vehicle. A stream of people flowed back and forth. Construction workers milled on the potholed road, some repairing a patch of asphalt. A delivery truck backed up to one of the store fronts. Bicycles whizzed by cars inching up the street.

"No," said Maxim. "We have his laptop and password. We can find out enough about him to take him later, somewhere with fewer eyes."

Maxim waved his hand, and Oleg put the vehicle in drive. They spun around and headed down the street, leaving Jake Coltrane behind. Maxim flipped open the laptop. On the screen was a Post-it with the username and password. He typed in the information and soaked in as much as possible about its owner and his secrets.

CHAPTER 16

Ryan Compton sat behind a big oak desk in his office twiddling a pen between his fingers. His chair was leaned back in a leisure position. His head twisted slightly to the side estimating Jake. "Glad to see you could make it into work today, Jake," said Ryan. "I'm being facetious. You know that, right? When someone is flippant as opposed to being serious?"

Jake rolled his eyes, peeved at the mere sound of Ryan's high-pitched voice and even more annoyed that Ryan had a rubber ball in his office that others had to sit on when speaking to him. His idea of no one getting too comfortable in his presence.

"Now that you are here, I want to discuss the project with you," said Ryan. "Everyone's waiting on your latest inputs. I mean, this is a team, and you're part of it. Show some appreciation for me putting together this great team to reach maximum productivity. And all I expect for my efforts? Progress, Jake. You seem to be stymying the efforts here. Is that right, Jake? Are you a *stymier*?"

Jake studied Ryan's long pale face and red cheeks, his gel-plastered hair and waxed eyebrows, his pencil neck, and his frail frame. He resisted the urge to kick the ergonomically correct rubber ball right in his face. "No," said Jake. "Not a *stymier*."

"Good," said Ryan. "And the team?"

"I'm part of the team, Ryan. Give me a few minutes, and I'll brief the team on the progress of the latest additions." Jake strained a false smile to the point where his lips felt as if they were going to crack.

"Very well, Jake." Ryan checked his watch, a shiny Bulgari. "Go ahead and start the meeting without me and fill me in later. I have an appointment."

Sure, Jake thought, *see you tomorrow.* "Okay," said Jake. "I'll send you the details by email."

Jake used the bouncy red ball to spring himself upright. He exited Ryan's office and went down the hallway to his cubicle. He liked to keep it neat. Three monitors, one keyboard, one mouse and a tower under the desk. He had no books, papers or pictures. Everything he needed was stored digitally. His only frustration with cubicle décor was that damn rubber ball Ryan insisted everyone have.

Before Jake could sit down, he spied Ryan strutting to the elevator. He checked his watch, and pressed the button to take him to the parking garage. Jake felt the dark storm cloud hovering above the office leave as Ryan entered the elevator. After the doors closed, the room erupted in a collective sigh of relief.

One by one, the six other developers popped their heads above their cubicles. He saw the glances of four men and two women directed right at him.

"Have you figured it out?" asked Dana who was closest to him. "You said that you needed time off to think and when you came back you would have the program working."

Dana was in her midtwenties, short black hair and bright blue eyes. For some reason, she liked wearing tracksuits. Not spandex—the old school tracksuits; sweatpants with a matching jacket. Despite her fashion taste, Jake saw her running her own team someday. She was extremely talented.

He didn't have the heart to tell her the program was fully functional since he was using it to help cure his tumor. And steal millions of dollars for that same cause. "Really close to getting it working," said Jake. "Let's meet in the conference room in about an hour. I have a few things to take care of first and then I will share my new ideas with everyone." Namely, figuring out what he might've been up to the past few days since he could not remember.

He took a seat on the bouncy ball and fired up his computer. It booted up within seconds. He went to work, plugging away at the keys. The main server for the facial recognition software and the search program he developed explicitly for tracking Jericho Black was a few rooms away in a temperature and humidity-controlled space. The doors were locked and secured, with all the bells and whistles, like motion detectors and heat sensors.

Ryan may not have known much about software design and implementation, but he did have enough resources to buy the best. The computing power of this mainframe was state of the art. Jake was free to exercise the full extent of its computing power without causing a drain on the system.

He accessed his program and searched for any images of himself caught on camera during the last four days. Nothing. As far as he could tell, he'd never left the hotel room. Next he searched for Jericho Black and his current location. Nothing came up. He looked for the site that had the Civil War photo. It had been taken down. He then tried to hack into Kyle Shubert's computer, but couldn't gain access. The password he'd used had been changed.

Jake looked for the stolen money he'd transferred into private accounts. Each account was deleted. Strange, he thought. An image of Jericho drinking his bourbon flashed in his mind, the Pappy that Jake had purchased from the bar downstairs.

"Enjoy your vacation?"

Jake spun around on his ball to find fellow developer Chet Osterman looking over his cubicle wall with a coffee cup in hand. He was a bright and cheery guy, talkative. Something Jake was not in the mood for.

"It was good," said Jake, quickly shutting his screen down.

"Where did you go?" asked Chet.

"Stayed local. In the city. Nothing big."

"What did you do?"

"Caught a show. Did some bike riding. A spa. Stuff like that."

"Cycling? You should've gone somewhere else for that. Plenty of places upstate with awesome trails. What kind of bike do you have?"

"I need to get back to this before I forget. Got an idea about how to fix the bugs in the latest revision, and I need to jot it all out before the meeting."

"I can help you out with that."

"No. No. It's better if I do it. Flows out smoother that way."

"Sure, sure. Well, we were all racking our brains while you were gone and came up with some ideas."

"Good. Maybe we came up with the same thing. Now, I need to finish this."

"Okay, got it. I'll be at my desk if you need me. Just let me know."

Chet lingered by the front of the cubicle before slowly walking away. Jake sighed and turned the monitor back on.

No laptop, no accounts, and no money. No trace he'd ever stolen anything. No police looking for him, and no evidence that he'd ever met Jericho Black. Jake rolled his thighs along the ball, thinking. How much of what he remembered was real and how much was linked to that crazy dream about hell that he had? Did the dream include him meeting Jericho Black? Did it go as far back as him stealing the money?

Jake stood and faltered. He felt a bit woozy. A pit in his stomach, like he was coming down with something, or something was coming up . . . like breakfast. He clutched his gut and lumbered down the aisle of cubicles to the main hallway. His work shared public space with three businesses: a medical lab, an insurance company, and a real estate company. He made his way to the public bathroom halfway down the hall. Newly renovated gray slate tiles on the floor and new stalls greeted him. If he had to pray to the porcelain god, better to pray to new porcelain.

Two sinks with mirrors flanked the entrance. Jake went to one and ran the cold water. He splashed some onto his face and the back of his neck. Then he leaned down to look under the stalls to see if anyone else was there. Alone.

Jake studied the mirror, checking his face for signs of twitching eyelids or spasms in his jaw muscles. He looked fine, but for how long? His life was ending. He was a genius when it came to programming, but no one would remember him in a few months.

The world wasn't fair.

"I wouldn't worry so much. The stress is doing a number on you."

The Katt Williams look-alike hovered behind Jake, wearing a lavender silk shirt with almond-colored bell-bottoms. Jake spun around and nearly lost his balance. He gripped the side of the sink to steady himself. Not this guy, again.

"Are you stalking me?" asked Jake.

71

"Stalking? Nah, brah. I'm trying to help. But if you don't want my help, I'm cool with that."

"I don't need your help, brother," said Jake. "What I do need is to call security for your ass."

"It's like that, huh? Fuck you then, nigga!"

"What do you think you're doing, following me here to my work?" said Jake. "I see you again, and I might put a hole in you."

"You can try, motherfucker. It won't be as easy as you think."

"Wait right there, son of a bitch." Jake stormed out of the bathroom and to his office.

Dana saw Jake march in and grew concerned over the look on his face. "Is everything okay?" she asked.

"I have a stalker!" said Jake. "Can you believe that?" He grabbed the nearest phone and dialed for security. It was answered on the first ring. "There's an unauthorized person up here I would like removed from the premises," said Jake. He listened to the voice on the phone, suddenly dizzy. "Huh? What does he look like? He looks like Katt—" Jake shook his head. His thoughts scrambled. He ran to a trashcan and puked.

CHAPTER 17

A gentle breeze came off the Santa Barbara coast. Ocean waves crashed along sparkling sand. Seagulls squawked. People were everywhere. It was like the movies: sun, fancy cars, bikini-clad women. People surfing and sunbathing in perfect weather. Living as if their lives were one big vacation.

How cute, he thought. Shakhty, where he was raised, was nothing like this. The former coal-mining town was now one of the major producers of tiles. The surrounding areas were seedy and perilous. It was also cold. Very cold. A stark contrast to life on the American coast.

Alexei took a seat at an outdoor restaurant overlooking the beach at a table with a large white umbrella that could be hand-cranked open. He waved a waiter over and ordered an espresso. Double. Next to him, a couple of blonde women with round sunglasses and sun hats sat and gossiped. Their tropical skirts had slits going all the way to their hips, barely covering the bikinis underneath. Vibrantly tanned tourists with cosmetically enhanced boobs and lips occupied every table around him. He listened in on the nearest conversation. Not too hard, considering how loudly they spoke.

"So, how is the new nanny working out with the kids?" asked the one on the right.

"Terrible," said the other. "Last week, Tommy started talking back to me rudely, and she didn't correct him."

The other one gasped, and so did Alexei, but for different reasons. He couldn't fathom a parent who didn't feel responsible for the actions of their children.

"I let Gary know right away," the woman continued. "He spoke to her about it. At least he said he did. I never can tell. Sometimes he takes her side in these things. I think he's screwing her."

Alexei sniffed. Who were these people? Was life here so glamorous that they'd lost touch with reality? Even the privileged oligarchs of his homeland were never so disillusioned by wealth as to not know what ordinary life was all about. Many of them had hard lives as children. They knew what it was like to go days without food. These people looked down on the hardworking backbone of society, Alexei decided. They saw themselves as royalty, without the burden that came with it.

Alexei checked his wristwatch and chugged down the last of his espresso. He slapped down a ten-dollar bill on the table and went to stand. From the corner of his eye, he saw someone watching him. He knew that there were all types of men who lived here. Specifically, the type of men who loved other men. Alexei was one of them. He was open about it. Never once tried to hide it. Even when he was young. Yet he tended not to put out those signals, so it surprised him that someone might take an interest in him that way.

The man sat confidently alone at a nearby table, wearing a white polo shirt and blue slacks. He had black hair with glasses, about five feet seven, firm and fit. As Alexei turned to get a better look, the man pretended to fixate on his phone. Alexei considered starting a conversation, but he had a job to do. Playtime would have to wait.

He got inside the rented black Lincoln Continental and fired up the engine. It was roomy. Plenty of space for his barrel chest and gut. He put the car in gear, and the tires chirped as he took off down the interstate. The Pacific Ocean sparkled in the distance to his left, littered with surfers, jet skiers, sailboats, and yachts. Alexei continued northbound. He turned right when he saw his route and headed into the hills.

Alexei drove for another half an hour, careful not to take too direct a route. He made his last turn and accelerated uphill until the modern, picture-windowed home came into view. Columns supported it in the front to counteract the hillside on which the back half sat. A deck went around the first level of the six-bedroom, seven-bathroom house. Alexei pulled between the columns below the deck. He exited the car and headed up the stairs. The best thing about the property was the privacy. Technically out in the open with neighbors all around, but concealed from prying eyes by the large grove of trees and substantial hillside.

Alexei walked through the door and onto the shiny, bright white ceramic tiles of a spacious chef's kitchen. He entered the walk-in stainless steel refrigerator and took an Italian ice off one of the shelves. Cherry. He grabbed a spoon and scraped off a few layers to taste it. The soft, tart ice stuck to the spoon. He pulled it off with his tongue. It was good. He took it with him to the den, scraping off another layer of cherry as he walked.

Kyle Shubert, a sixty-something White male with salt-and-pepper hair and slim build, sat gagged and bound to a chair in the middle of the floor, just where Alexei left him four hours ago. He still loved his family, Alexei noted, based on the pictures scattered about the den, even though he and his wife had separated.

Alexei put down his Italian ice and ripped the duct tape from Kyle's his mouth. A bloody rag had been shoved inside prior so he still could not speak. Kyle's lower lip puffed out from his chin, swollen and bloody. His eyes and nose looked just as bad. Plastic zip ties bound him to a metal chair taken from the kitchen. Alexei looked at his watch. He had about ten minutes to spare. The restraints on Kyle's wrists cut deep when Alexei gave each one an extra pull. Three drops of dark red blood fell onto the white tiles. The contrast stunned him. Artsy almost, Alexei mused.

Alexei removed the bloody rag from Kyle's mouth. Sergei's instructions were clear: find out what he could.

"Listen," said Kyle, in a fluttering voice. "I have money."

Alexei looked around the room. "Of course, you do," said Alexei. "Save your breath. I have heard that countless times. People with no money and people like you, with all the money. Always thinking paying me off will save them. Fat chance. However, I will make it easy on you if you cooperate. Tell me what I need to know."

"Why?" asked Kyle. "We had an arrangement. An agreement. We kept our end of the deal, and you paid us. Why kill us after you gave us the money?"

"Good question," said Alexei. A deal had been made between Kyle and Turgenev. The hacker may have gotten things off course, but everything was back on schedule. So why order their execution now? Curiously, Alexei noted Kyle said why kill *us*, which meant that ordering the wife to be killed was not an afterthought but part of the compact.

Alexei took the blood-splotched, gray rag and stuffed it back into Kyle's mouth. Kyle twisted and fought, so Alexei shoved harder until Kyle's head was pinned against the back of the chair. He pushed once more for good measure before releasing. Kyle managed a muffled grunt.

"Is your ex-wife going to be on time?" asked Alexei.

From the pictures, she appeared to be twenty years younger than Kyle. They had two children in their teens: a boy and a girl. The ex-wife was beautiful, of course. Men with money and beautiful young women always seemed to be a match. Funny how beautiful young women didn't seem to fall in love with poor old men as much, Alexei thought, picking up his melting Italian ice for another bite. To be fair, the men didn't try to hide the nature of the arrangement one bit. *She is beautiful, and she wants my money. Luckily, I come with the perks.*

The Shubert home was mostly made of glass, so Alexei saw the red Mercedes as it made the last turn and dipped under the balcony to park next to his car. Kyle saw the vehicle as well, and flinched against his restraints.

"Calm down," said Alexei. "In the text, I said that she should come alone. Things to discuss in private, away from the kids. If she listened, they will not be in the car with her. If she did not . . ." he raised a hand like, *whaddya gonna do?*

A tall, shapely woman in her early forties got out of the car. She wore a stylish red blouse and an elegant matching skirt that accentuated her smooth, toned legs. An expensive handbag tucked neatly under her arm. She was alone.

Alexei picked up one of the photographs to ensure she was the right one and noticed something in the background. He made out familiar writing on some of the businesses behind her. Russian. The photo was taken in Russia.

Many beautiful Russian women came as brides to America after the fall of the Soviet Union. Julie was one of them. Before the fall, Russian women were depicted as thick, masculine, and unappealing, with fine whiskers on their chin and bulky arms strong enough to beat anyone at arm wrestling. In the nineties, when American men saw what real Russian women looked like—beautiful, thin, and shapely women willing to do anything for a Visa—they went out of their minds, like finding stacks of money behind the walls of a new home.

Alexei approached the door and opened it as Julie grabbed the handle. Her startling blue eyes widened, and perfectly red lips tightened to pose a question when Alexei grabbed her by her long blonde hair and threw her inside, sending her sprawling across the floor.

Alexei grabbed another chair from the kitchen. He wasn't worried about her running or doing something equally as stupid. He recognized the look in her eyes when she saw the tattoos on his arm. She'd probably made someone in the *Vor* a small fortune by coming to America to be with Kyle.

Alexei spoke to her in Russian. "Sit down."

She sat down in the chair as instructed. He bound her arms to the chair with two thick plastic ties. He wrenched them down good and tight.

"What do you want?" she asked in Russian.

"There was a hacker who stole money from your husband's account," said Alexei. "You probably don't know about it because we caught it and put it back before anyone noticed. This hacker caused quite a storm that is coming back to haunt you. We were curious about the origins of this storm."

"We?" asked Julie. Mascara-streaked tears dripped down her cheek. "Who are you?"

"I represent people who had a deal with your husband. Certain monies were deposited into the company account on their behalf. I was under the impression that it was simply money laundering. Yet, I was told to include the wife when the order was given to me. That doesn't happen often. My guess is you are guilty of something."

"I'm the *ex*-wife," said Julie. "Married for twenty-two years. We have two children."

"I know about the children," said Alexei. "This is why I told you to come alone. What are their ages?"

"Thirteen and fifteen," said Julie.

"They are growing fast. Was this the home they were first brought to from the hospital when they were born? The only home they have ever known." He glared at Kyle. "Shame on you, Kyle, keeping the home for yourself. You must treat your offspring with respect. How can you call yourself a man?" He realized he'd spoken in Russian, so Kyle hadn't understood a word.

"And what about you?" asked Julie. "How can you be so cold as to take a mother from her children? If this is about money, then take it back."

Alexei picked up a picture from the office table. A family photo taken maybe three years ago when the teenagers were still children. They were on a sailboat, the younger girl at the helm. Kyle at her side, immersed in instructing her on how to navigate. The older girl posed as captain, ordering the quartermaster straight ahead. And Julie being Julie, sunbathing on the deck in a red one-piece, martini in hand, and not a care in the world.

"Why did the two of you divorce?" asked Alexei. "You seem like such a nice couple."

"He was never here," said Julie in Russian. "What are you? A marriage counselor or something? You son of a bitch."

"I am trying to figure out how you're mixed up in this," said Alexei. "Kyle keeps saying the same thing, that there was a deal to launder money through the company, but clearly you know about it. Probably going to get a good portion of that cash, am I right?"

"He is a generous man," said Julie.

"Why would a man do such a thing for an ex-wife?"

"Guilt," said Julie. "Deep down, he still loves me."

"I thought you would feed me some bullshit like that," said Alexei. "It makes me feel less guilty about killing you. I saw how you looked at the markings on my hand when I opened the door. You know them. You have seen them before. You seemed less surprised than Kyle did. This whole endeavor revolves around you somehow. But you want to play dumb blonde, so okay. It's over for you."

Julie laughed. Not surprising because, in Alexei's experience, people who faced death laugh from time to time. A kind of nervous reaction of the body. Except, this was different. Her laughter was haughty. Pompous and portentous.

"You are a dog doing what you are told for treats. Arrp . . . Arrp!" she barked like a tiny Chihuahua. "Kill me because that is what you love to do, but don't pretend that you are interested in power deals involving real money. You are way below that."

The scared, beautiful model of a housewife was gone, and in her place was the real Julie Shubert: shrewd and determined. The fight in her piercing blue eyes was nothing like that of her husband. These were the eyes of a woman who had seen her fair share of suffering. She came from the hardest parts of Russia. Someone scraped the dirt and grit off this one to discover she was beautiful and then sold her.

Alexei spoke in Russian. *Vory* slang. Something only those in the *Vor* would know. He asked her what her association was.

"My brother," said Julie. "He worked this out for me long ago."

Alexei nodded. This was how she came to be Kyle Shubert's bride. He understood. "What is this all about?" he asked.

"That bastard Piotr Turgenev needs to pay," she hissed, with a neurotic nodding of her head. Stray blonde hairs danced in front of her face. "For his treachery, Piotr will be put to the knife, and there is nothing you can do to stop it. I have protections in place." She spat at Alexei's feet. "You will be going to hell too, you monster!"

Alexei looked down at the thick glob of spit on the top of his shoe and back up at the couple, whose eyes focused somewhere behind him. Some cheap barroom trick, he thought, to get him to turn his head. Then again, they were tied up. What could they possibly do?

He scanned each large windowpane until he caught the reflection of a man approaching. He held what looked like a stun gun. Alexei rotated swiftly out of the way as the electrodes flew past him, snapping violently with a sharp burst of high voltage. He grabbed the assailant's arm and came down with an elbow to the top of his head.

The stun gun clattered to the floor, and Alexei scrambled toward it. From one knee, the assailant drew a Glock from his holster. He fired two sharp bursts, but Alexei stepped forward and had his hand around the assailant's wrists before he fired a third, pushing the barrel away from his body.

Blood sprayed the back of Alexei's hand. He twisted his body, shifting momentum back toward the assailant to deliver another elbow to the chin. The impact shook his entire body, and the assailant fell limply to the ground—three seconds of fighting from beginning to end.

Alexei leaned forward and recovered the stun gun. During the assault, he'd felt no pain, yet bending over to pick up the weapon proved to be a chore. His assailant was the good-looking man from the beach restaurant.

He'd been taking pictures not out of desire but to make sure he had the right target.

That he could be a mark hadn't crossed Alexei's mind at the time. Who else knew he was there? Alexei turned to ask Julie. Her head hung at an odd angle against the back of the chair. She'd caught both slugs, one in her neck and the other below the nose. Dead center.

"What is going on here?" asked Alexei.

Kyle's face was covered with the blood of his ex-wife. No muffled screams emitted through the gray rag stuffed in his mouth. His eyes stared off into the distance, unblinking. He did not turn his head. He was in shock.

So was Alexei.

The assailant moaned and wriggled like an inch worm along the floor. Alexei took the baton-style stun gun and zapped him a few times behind the back of the neck. If the guy was a professional, he wouldn't talk, so it was useless to ask him anything. However, he might have backup. Alexei made his way to the front door, carefully avoiding the giant windows, just in case someone out in the woods waited with a rifle. He used the cover of the doorframe to peek out and survey the area. There was a blue five-gallon jug by the door. He picked it up and made his way back inside.

Alexei moved back through the house and to the kitchen, hiding from the outside by the center island. Then he opened the five-gallon jug and smelled it. Kerosene. Perfect. It would serve as a distraction if anyone else was out there waiting for him.

Alexei went on the move again, staying low, with the jug in his hand. He poured the kerosene along the wooden floors, the expansive area rugs, and along the baseboards. He soaked the drapery, the couches, and chairs, leaving a trail of kerosene leading through the kitchen. Then he grabbed his would-be assassin by the legs and dragged him toward the back entrance, dousing him with the remaining bit of kerosene as he went.

It was decision time. Staying inside the house while the fire was burning was too risky. He had to take a chance. Alexei opened the sliding glass door and stepped outside. He took the stun gun, aimed for the kerosene and pressed the button. Flames erupted immediately, engulfing the body and everything else in its wake.

The body screamed and writhed as the flames shocked him into consciousness. He stumbled to his feet, saw Alexei, and ran toward him. Alexei slammed the door and pressed his full weight on the handle to keep it shut. If there was someone else outside waiting for him, this was when he was most likely to take a bullet to the back of the head.

Alexei held on tight as the enflamed assassin pounded on the thick glass. The assassin turned and stumbled toward the front door, collapsing before he could get there.

Black smoke obscured Alexei's vision. Heat radiated through the glass. He let go of the door handle and found his way down the stairs at the back of the house. He went around to the front, where his car was parked. Black plumes of smoke barreled out from the roof, and a window shattered.

Why did that attacker bring kerosene with him? He must have planned on burning the house to the ground. Didn't Turgenev say burn the house and everything in it? Yet, the attacker was gunning for him. No question about that. Before he reported this to Sergei he'd better have proof. And the only proof he had at the moment was being reduced to ash.

CHAPTER 18

Jake had a 5:30 p.m. appointment at the hospital near his apartment in New Jersey. His neurologist had demanded he come in for testing after Jake described what had happened. Four days unconscious was the textbook example of a coma, the Doc had reprimanded, and added that Jake might be terminal, but for the time being he was still Dr. Chadha's patient, and he was going to fight for Jake until his last breath.

Jake smiled. It was nice to know some doctors cared and weren't just going through patients as fast as possible. That's why he went to St. James Hospital and checked himself in for an MRI. The routine was as common for Jake as tying shoelaces. He undressed down to underwear and socks and put on the flimsy gown that tied up in the back.

The last time Jake was in the hospital, it was to visit his sister right before she died. Her life ended faster than anyone expected. She felt a lump in her breast one morning, got the confirmation it was cancer a week later and was dead within three months. It was extremely hard on Jake. He was always the sick one. Jenny was fit and healthy yet she died before him. She was not even thirty years old. Chalk it up as the Coltrane curse. They all die young.

A nurse came by and told him to sit in the wheelchair. The exposed part of his back hit the cold vinyl giving him goosebumps. She wheeled him through the hallway to the Magnetic Resonance Imaging room. The room was cold and pastel white with a few tables and chairs. The tunnel of vibrating doom crouched in the center of the room, preparing to spin up as if it were going to launch Jake into hyperspace.

Everyone smiled cordially, trying to make him feel as comfortable as possible. He humored them. He already knew his fate—there would be no shocking results, therefore no need to reassure him anymore. Still, he appreciated it. They questioned him as they started the IV, asking him his name and what he was there for several times. He answered calmly, smiling back at them, waiting for the next step to take place.

Finally, the technician came out in a lab coat and introduced himself. He was a strong-looking guy with the belly of a man who had a hard time pushing away from the dinner table. Jake recognized a Haitian accent when he spoke.

"Mr. Coltrane, I'm Robert, and I'll be taking you through the imaging today." His voice was so jovial he was practically laughing every time he spoke. "You may have gone through this many times, but not by me, so I have to ask you the same stuff I ask everyone. Okay. Do you have any metal on your body that we should know about? Anything from previous surgeries or any piercings?"

"Nothing but two nipple rings and a Prince Albert," said Jake.

Robert laughed. "Maybe the Prince Albert is far enough away, as only your big head will be going under the magnet, but you never know. Is there anything else?"

"Hell no," said Jake. "Not even that. You think I'm going to let someone pierce my Johnson? No, I got nothing. I'm clean. Fire away."

More laughing. "Okay, Mr. Coltrane. We are going to slide you in there. Keep your hands and legs in tight, close to your body as possible, and try not to move. After a while, you will feel something come into your arm through the IV. Don't be alarmed. This is the dye that helps us see the imaging a little clearer."

"Got it," said Jake.

"Are you claustrophobic?" he asked.

"No," said Jake.

"Okay, well, in your left hand we'll put this little button right here. You just need to push it if you start freaking out in there. We'll be out here monitoring your breathing and heart rate, just in case. Are you ready, Mr. Coltrane?"

Jake gave him the thumbs-up. Robert joyfully walked out of the lab and situated himself behind the glass of the control room.

"How are you doing in there, Mr. Coltrane?" His voice crackled through the loudspeakers.

"I'm good," said Jake.

"Okay. Let's get started."

Jake could see them off to his left, checking monitors and plugging away on keyboards, getting ready for the test. He turned toward the soft white light of the ceiling, thinking how he always felt that the question of claustrophobia was misleading. He wasn't afraid of small spaces. He could get into the trunk of an automobile, close it, and feel perfectly fine.

The MRI was entirely different. It slid his body into a narrow tubular opening that whirred and shook like something out of control. The tube was so tight he doubted he could reach a button on his shirt if he tried. Anyone certain they weren't claustrophobic would have their convictions tested after a few minutes.

He felt the cold dye pumping into his arm. The machine spun at its maximum rpm.

"We will have you out of there as soon as possible, Mr. Coltrane," said Robert.

Suddenly, Jake wasn't feeling so well. He began sweating, and his stomach twisted. He felt dizzy and confused, like what had happened at work earlier in the day. His breath was slow and harsh like someone was standing on his chest.

"How are you doing in there, Mr. Coltrane?" crackled Robert through the speaker.

"Not so good, I think," Jake responded.

"It's almost over," said Robert. "Just another minute or so."

"I'm getting out now!" panted Jake. He attempted to push his body up and out but could barely bend his elbows for position to gain leverage. His hands slid fruitlessly along the inside of the tube, squeaking against the plastic.

"Calm down, Mr. Coltrane," said Robert. "I'm pulling you out now."

Jake couldn't wait for the conveyor belt to pull him out. He tried to wriggle down the structure on his back like a snake. He was almost out when everything went dark. A deep emptiness rose around him. Sticky heat crawled up his legs, then his midsection.

Jake reached for the panic button, but it wasn't in his hand. He wasn't even lying on his back anymore; rather, he found himself naked inside a locker, looking out toward the front of a dark classroom. A sizable purple beast-man had Zee by the back of the neck, dangling him over the teacher's desk. He raised his cleaver high. Jake saw the sharp edge glisten. Then the chopper came down and whacked Zee's penis off his body.

Zee screamed as Gaap tossed him into the corner of the classroom like a banana peel.

The jaundiced demon Wall snorted at his partner. "What the hell are you going to do with that?"

"Nothing!" snapped Gaap. "I'm just mad that . . ."

Jake's foot hit the locker door with a tiny clang. They turned to Jake at the same time.

"He's back!" said Wall. "Where did he disappear to the first time?"

"I have no fucking idea, but he's still got what I want," said Gaap. "It's so big I can see it from space!"

Gaap faced Jake from thirty feet away. Every fiber in Jake's being screamed for him to run, but he resisted. He eased himself out slowly, avoiding any sudden movements, pushing aside the severed and discarded penises at the bottom of the locker.

"He's about to make a run for it!" said Wall.

"Fuck that!" Gaap screamed. He slid his cleaver across the top of the desk and flung Zee's severed penis toward Jake. Jake thrust his legs forward, used his hands to grip the outside edges of the locker, and propelled himself across the floor. The penis whizzed over his head and slammed into the metal with a thud. He skidded toward the rear entrance as Gaap kicked chairs in his direction. They tumbled and broke apart all around him, but none hit Jake. He shot through the door.

Jake ran down the darkened hallway, the sound of crashing chairs and breaking debris echoing behind him. The rumbling stomps of a seven-foot beast vibrated the ground. Several people Jake couldn't see screamed in the darkness, afraid the roaring beast was coming for them. He fled to the door at the end of the corridor leading to the hallway and outside. The ground grew slick, and he crashed into the door. He pulled on it frantically, then remembered that he'd locked it earlier. Jake twisted the lock and slipped through the door as Gaap appeared. Gaap slid across the floor as well and crashed into the door, slamming it shut and shoving

Jake down the hallway. It gave Jake a few extra seconds, and he used it to run toward the exit.

Where those creatures that chased him into the building might be waiting.

If they were still outside, they'd eat him alive; he was sure of it. He didn't have time to consider it. He had to keep moving. He wasn't willing to chance the doors. Some of them might contain beasts worse than Gaap. A distant sound caught his attention. He heard the shrill of the creatures outside.

Jake dared not look behind him. The thunderous footsteps were enough to know Gaap was closing in. He had no other options. Jake spotted a door on the left and went for it, throwing his shoulder into the door at full speed, only to bounce against the hard wood. His heart jolted with dread before noticing the door had a knob. His shaky hands fumbled with the knob until it opened. He slipped through the door and slammed it shut, then ran his hand across the wood, looking for a lock that didn't materialize. He stood on soft, scalding hot sand.

"Run, you son of a bitch!" snarled Gaap from the other side. He pounded on the door. "I will track you down. You're my new pet, asshole! Whatever hell you go to, I'll find you!"

Jake shook his head. It was impossible. He couldn't be in hell. It was a trick. No—this was the coma. Something happened again that triggered the coma. It had to be.

Jake took a few steps backward and bumped into something. He turned quickly, not knowing what to expect. No one. He searched left, then right. Nothing but a vast expanse of sand and a faint light over the horizon.

"Who is there?" said a voice.

Out of nothing, teeth appeared into a devilish grin.

"Don't be startled," said the creature. The grinning teeth formed an arc around eighteen inches long. "No need to run from me. I want to talk. Have we met?"

Jake didn't see a body or a face attached to the grin, just a pair of white gloves whose fingers moved impatiently.

"You must speak up," said the creature. "I cannot see you."

"We uh, have not met," said Jake.

"I am Tartarus."

"Jake. Jake Coltrane."

Jake heard a whistling in the air. High in the blackened-gray sky, lightning flashed in dark clouds, allowing him a glimpse of something flying off in the distance, sweeping back and forth.

"I have had strange visits lately. Perhaps it's a sign," Tartarus mused. The hovering grin seemed to refocus on Jake. "People cannot leave one hell and enter another until an apostle is done with you," he explained. "One of the silly rules set in place long ago. Yet somehow, you defy these rules." The gloves pointed to the winged creature flying overhead.

"I ran," said Jake. "Nothing special about that."

"Everyone runs, Jake Coltrane. The difference is that you were able to get away. That door back there opened for you. It's not supposed to open. You're not supposed to be able to come through it until an apostle allows you to leave his hell."

"It's because I don't belong here," said Jake. "I'm not in hell, nor am I dead. This is a dream."

"I see," said Tartarus. "Everyone believes this is a bad dream when they first arrive. But believe me. You never wake from this."

The grinning teeth moved upward as if Tartarus had stood. Jake realized if he squinted, he could see the outline of the apostle's body, like a silhouette of a void. Darker than what surrounded him and empty. Tartarus's profile suggested the shape of a tall, slim man with over-long limbs ending in expressive white gloves. They moved like a conductor for an orchestra.

"What are your thoughts about hell so far, Jake Coltrane?"

"It sucks."

"That's the point, isn't it?"

"Am I going to be tortured for all eternity?"

"Why not? It kills the boredom."

The flying creature grew closer. Sweeping left and right.

"You could choose not to do that, you know," said Jake. "Torture me."

"Don't be foolish." The pointy-toothed grin laughed. "Wishing you were in heaven, are you? Sorry, but things did not turn out that way for you, Jake Coltrane. It's okay to be angry about it but hoping to avoid strife is pointless."

"Hell does not have to be this way. People like you can change it. No more fear or anxiety. No terror. No more suffering."

"I'm not a person," said Tartarus. "I am a being."

"An apostle of hell, from the looks of it," said Jake. "With a sense of civility."

He sighed. "That sounds boring to me, Jake Coltrane," said Tartarus, his gloved fingers wagging a reprimand. "Have you ever thought about what heaven would be like if you got there?"

Jake gaped. "Paradise," he said plainly.

"Paradise is but an idea. I'm asking if you've ever thought about what you would do in heaven. Be with your family and friends? Party? Play games and entertain? What?"

"I'd enjoy it," said Jake, unsure. He'd never pondered the question before. He shook away the doubt. "It'd be the greatest feeling ever."

"And what exactly would you *feel*, considering you no longer have human needs?" Tartarus chuckled. "When all the earthly pleasures are no longer required, the adjectives quickly come to an end trying to describe what paradise is like. *You feel good all the time*." Tartarus chuckled again, and the grin leered.

"It's better than this place," said Jake, insulted and bitter.

"Really?" said Tartarus. "How about this? He wants you on your knees, grateful for being in his presence, day after day after day. When you're finished being grateful, you can give thanks for being created to serve him. Then you know what? You can sing his praise. Day after day, forever. Does that seem like paradise, Jake Coltrane? Is it everything you dreamed of for all eternity?"

"And what about here?" said Jake.

"After going through that hell, this one is more to my liking, Jake Coltrane."

Jake looked up. The flying creature circled above him. It was Wall, in black pants and an unbuttoned white shirt that flapped in the wind. His arms were swept back and stiff, like the wings of an airplane. His long curly hair fluttered around his head as he glided on a dark, puffy cloud. He cackled when he spotted Jake.

"He is looking for you, I presume," said Tartarus.

"Who the hell travels from hell to hell without paying his taxes and then disappears?" called Wall from above.

"Disappears?" asked Tartarus. The grin tightened in disapproval. "Jake Coltrane, you didn't tell me that you can also disappear. Where do you go, Jake Coltrane?"

"Back to my body. I told you that this is a dream."

"Nonsense," said Tartarus.

"Trap him now, Tartarus," said Wall. "He mocks us."

"I must agree with Wall, Jake Coltrane. You mock us. I am going to look upon you. Then I will decide how many chances you get before you enter eternal damnation."

Jake scoffed. "I thought you said this was hell. I'm already in eternal damnation. You mean to tell me there is another one?"

"Feeling brave, are you?" asked Tartarus.

"Braver than ever," said Jake. "I told you, this is a dream."

"Okay, Jake Coltrane. I will look upon you now. Prepare yourself."

"I thought you said you can't see me," said Jake.

"You misunderstand. I simply had my eyes closed."

Tartarus opened his eyes, and Jake instantly felt the weight of gravity upon him. It was as if every negative feeling that he'd ever felt in his life weighed down his soul. Like building blocks stacked on top of each other. Tartarus's amber irises encased large, black pupils, and the longer his gleaming eyes were upon Jake, the worse Jake felt. It was impossible to stand. He fell to his knees. Despair swallowed him. Deep-seated pain and sorrow gripped every fiber of his being. He wanted to die and begged for the end. Everything went dark.

The sound of alarmed voices penetrated the darkness. He heard people loudly speaking all around him. The darkness ebbed. Jake opened his eyes to find himself in the emergency room.

"Unplug the machine!" said someone. "Unplug it!"

Sensors stuck to his skin and monitored his heart rate, blood pressure, and oxygen level. The IV in his arm dripped fluids slowly into his vein. The mask covering his nose and mouth provided oxygen, but the emergency was not over.

Five people crowded the room, some wearing blue scrubs and others wearing green scrubs. No one paid attention to Jake. Instead, they were working on someone, a bespectacled woman in her thirties, on the floor beside him. Her scrubs were pulled up to her chest, and Jake could see a defibrillator stuck against her abdomen. Her body pulsated and convulsed. Burns accumulated around the paddles as she clutched them tight, shrieking.

Another nurse cradled her head, tears streaming down her face. The others fought to hold her down but were afraid to move her hands, as the paddles seemed to be melted into her flesh, and she wasn't relinquishing her grip. A man came through with a needle and injected something into her arm. After a few seconds, the shrieking turned to a whimper and then a low moan. Jake looked down at her red face from his bed. He could see the fear ingrained in her gaze as her eyes, unaware of anyone in the room, finally closed.

CHAPTER 19

The cold space in the emergency room recovery area had curtains drawn around him. Jake could hear the busy nursing staff roaming about and whispering things after passing his bed. Every so often, someone came to check on him. A doctor, a nurse, a specialist of some sort, then it was back to the sounds of the hospital.

A complete battery of tests was ordered on Jake due to an apparent heart failure. His bed was wheeled from lab to lab in an effort to understand what happened during the MRI. Wires, sensors, and monitors rolled with him. He had sticky tape glued to his skin where sensors had been removed. IVs were inserted into each arm, the left dedicated to hourly bloodwork and the right to administer drugs. He attempted to get feedback, but no one was talking to him. They seemed spooked. All he knew was that he had died, suddenly and mysteriously. And then he came back.

By the early evening, his bed had taken its last trip through the hospital's hallways, and he was brought upstairs and given a room. It had a small bathroom, a draw curtain for privacy, and a television mounted on the wall. The little remote control had a speaker, so he didn't have to blast the volume. He picked his way through the channels but couldn't find anything that held his interest. The boredom of being stuck in a hospital with no one to talk to made him stir-crazy. Then someone called to him.

"Jake?" a woman called from behind his privacy curtain. Jake sat up in his bed. He could smell her sweet perfume.

"Catalina?" His heart filled with delight upon sight of the tall, olive-skinned Brazilian woman who got darker in the sunlight. Her long eyelashes fluttered over the corner-winged eyeliner look that he loved. She wore a blouse with vest and slacks as if she'd come straight from her work in the city at a hotel front desk.

She leaned over and hugged him. "What the fuck happened to you, Jake?" she said, in her pronounced Portuguese accent. "You had me so worried."

"It's great to see you," he said, squeezing her tightly. "But how did you know I was here? I didn't . . ." He paused, almost saying something that would get him in trouble.

She looked over at his cellphone on the desk beside the bed. "No, you weren't going to call," she said. "Were you?"

"I thought about it." Knowing that he'd had no intention of doing so.

"I'm listed as your emergency contact, Fofo," said Catalina. "The hospital called me and told me what happened. Good thing they did. I have a feeling I would've never known if they didn't."

"I thought . . ."

No, not thought. Afraid. Afraid that she'd moved on and forgotten about him. Even though that was what he wanted her to do. Now that she was there, he regretted cutting her out of his life. She had been his life partner and best friend. But he couldn't stomach knowing that she'd wake one day and find him lying next to her dead or come home and find him on the toilet dead, or anything else as gruesome. When he'd found out that his days were numbered, he quickly gathered his things and moved to his own place. It'd been three months since he left her, but now it felt like no time had passed at all.

"I would still do anything for you, Jake. You know that, right?"

He nodded, more ashamed than anything else. "This is hard enough for me alone," he admitted. "I mean, it's already starting. They told me my heart stopped while I was getting the MRI. Then they moved me to the emergency room because there was still some electrical activity . . . my heart needed to get back in sync. Imagine if you'd been there with me and that happened. I don't want you to go through that. It's been three months since—"

"Since you left me, Jake." She looked down. "You didn't move out. You left. Abandoned me."

"I was hoping that you moved on."

"I have, Jake."

It stung. The deep pang resonated down to his core. Fitting, he guessed. He got what he asked for.

"I watched my sister wither away to nothing," said Jake. "It's not easy. I wish that on no one. It's tough to deal with."

"I'll never know. You took it right out of my hands. Running away when I wanted to be there for you, leaving someone else to console me while you're still alive." Her eyes probed his for answers.

The reality of her absence in his life tormented his heart. But he'd brought this upon himself; there was no way around it. He had believed it a good decision to give her space to move on when he was gone. The unrelenting twinge in his soul said otherwise.

"Is he a good guy?" asked Jake, not knowing what else to say.

"I don't want to talk about him. You don't deserve to know about him. You don't deserve to know about my life. Let's focus on you. I haven't heard from you in months. I want to know what you've been doing. I want to know how you are and how you've been dealing with this."

"Have a seat," said Jake. "I'll fill you in."

She pulled up a chair and sat down next to his bed. She kicked off her shoes and stretched her heels out over the bed, then unclipped her hair, letting it flow over the back of her chair. She listened to Jake's story, long eyelashes blinking incessantly.

"And now you're seeing things?" she said. "When did that start?"

"A week ago. Maybe two. I have no idea what's real and what's not. I have these dreams when I am passed out. When I'm not dreaming, I see Katt Williams."

"What?"

"Katt Williams is stalking me."

"You're shitting me," she said and giggled.

"Nope. I saw him in this hospital. They carted me to one of the other labs for testing, and there was Katt Williams in one of the chairs outside Radiation. Sitting there with his legs crossed, shaking his head at me like I was fucking up or something."

"In full pimp costume?"

"Yep. Just like in the movie *Friday 2* when he owned that store in the strip mall."

"Unreal, Jake. The crazy part is you thought you stole money from the Russian mob and that they killed you for it."

"No. I stole money from a crooked CEO, and it turned out to be mob money."

"Jake, you're too good to do something like that. You're not a criminal. Something like that takes balls."

"Technically, it's a matter of principle, not balls. Then there is the thought of going to prison."

"What changed then, smart-ass?"

"When you're facing death, the fear of being in prison for the rest of your life doesn't have much bite."

She sighed. "I still think you'd never do something like that. It had to be one of the things you dreamed while in a coma. Does it check out on your computer?"

"I don't know where the damn thing is," said Jake. "Can't find it."

She lifted her foot and brought it down on his thigh hard, digging her heel into his quads.

"Ow. What was that for?"

"I could've been there for you, Jake. Now you're having to figure this out all by yourself. *Idiota*!"

They talked a few hours more, laughing, joking, and passing the time. He watched her fall asleep in the chair beside him, hoping she might crawl up next to him. But deep down, he knew that part of their relationship had passed. She'd moved on from being his girlfriend, but not his friend. After staring at her for about an hour, he finally fell asleep.

He awoke to the curtains being drawn open and sunlight streaming through the window. He looked over at the chair where Catalina had been sleeping. She was gone.

Another nurse walked around the room, different from the one that had taken care of him the previous evening. She had brown hair and wore blue scrubs. She walked with quick, tiny steps to the whiteboard and wrote her name. Tracy.

"Good news," she said. "Looks like you'll be going home this morning. Your neurologist signed off on your release. He will be in soon to talk to you, okay? Your clothes are in the closet."

Jake climbed out of bed, took a shower, got dressed, and waited for the doctor to arrive. Forty-five minutes later, Dr. Chadha walked into the room. He was a thin, short man of Indian descent, with a mat of shiny black hair on the top of his head. He was usually smiling and cheerful, but his mood was somber as he shook Jake's hand.

"That bad?" Jake asked.

"Not so much with your condition. We simply confirmed everything we already knew."

"What's the bad news then?"

"It's the young intern from yesterday in the ER."

"I was wondering what happened there. Everyone seemed to clam up about it."

"She's dead, Jake. Killed herself early this morning. Jumped out of her apartment window before sunrise. Her boyfriend was sleeping in bed and had no clue until the police knocked on the door. A tragedy."

"She had the paddles adhered to her stomach when I came to," said Jake. "They unplugged the machine. She had a nervous breakdown or something."

"The paddles were for you. To restart your heart. She never got the chance to use them. Your arrhythmia corrected itself. Before anyone could celebrate, she discharged the paddles on herself. Ten seconds later, she did it again. She was trying to kill herself, and she finally succeeded."

"That's terrible," said Jake.

Dr. Chadha shook it off. "Do you have anyone here to pick you up?" he asked.

"Nope, just me."

"You didn't drive here, did you?"

"You always ask me that. You know I can't have a driver's license because of my condition. I never even attempted to learn."

"Good man. Just checking. I also thought I would ask, as you now suffer from a heart condition, would you consider getting a pacemaker?"

Jake scoffed. "What's the point in that?"

"The point is that it is tough to watch a seemingly healthy thirty-two-year-old male patiently wait to die. But you've had your whole life to make peace with this, I guess."

"I was a ticking time bomb from the time I was twelve, Doc. I'm used to it."

"I want you to continue to fight, Jake. Not get used to it."

Fighting is what he thought he was doing when he stole that money in order to meet Jericho Black. As it turns out, it was just a manifestation of his deepest desires. Preparing for the end may be the only thing he has left.

CHAPTER 20

A lexei's plane touched down in New York City after leaving LAX six hours prior. At the sound of the tone, most everyone on the plane rose to their feet and began sifting through overhead bins and pulling items from beneath their seats to disembark. It never made much sense to Alexei, especially since he always sat near the back of the airplane. No one was going anywhere anytime soon, so they might as well relax.

A young man across from him, wearing those god-awful hiking sandals, stood with his backpack on his back like he was ready to dart to the front of the plane. At least a hundred people stood in front of him. Where did he think he was going?

Ridiculous humans, thought Alexei.

He unbuckled his belt and switched off airplane mode on his phone. Messages poured in—seven in total. Three personal contacts wondered if he was back in New York. He opened the message from Sergei in Russia telling Alexei to contact him immediately. He wanted word on how things went in California. With all the people around, that conversation would have to wait.

Next message was from someone in the Odessa family. Most likely they needed a person tracked down. Or possibly eliminated. Again, his priority was Sergei, so that mission would have to wait. The third message requested Alexei attend a mediation. Interesting. The *Vory* had rules that had to be strictly adhered to. If any member broke one, or if a dispute rose between *Vory,* then mediation was sought to work out the details and issue punishment, if needed. Alexei was the type of man who loved doling out punishment during mediation. Unfortunately, he would have to pass on this.

Julie Shubert's bullet-ridden face was still on his mind. Why did Turgenev hire someone else?

Alexei checked the next message. Another text from his associate in the Bronx. More problems. One of the customers had asked for a buyout of one of the girls. It was getting exhausting. These women constantly had issues. It was never-ending. He decided to ignore that one as well.

Finally, he got to the message Zachary had sent. It said to call when he landed so Zachary could meet him at the gate. Alexei made the call.

"I am still on the plane," said Alexei. "Are you at the terminal?"

"No, in the car," said Zachary. "I will park in the lot closest to the baggage pickup and meet you. What is the flight number?"

"869. United. It should not take long. I believe I heard the door open."

"Meet you there in a few minutes."

Alexei was the last to leave the plane. He walked through the tunnel and into the central part of the airport. The terminal was swarming with worn-out travelers. It took him about ten minutes to make his way down the escalator to the congested carousel where his luggage was located. He spotted his bag and worked his way through the scrum to snatch it off the belt, rubbing shoulders with others eager to grab and go. When he finally made it outside and into the cool spring air, Zachary had already spotted him and raised his hand.

Zachary was slightly taller than Alexei, around six foot three. He had dark curly hair and shadow of beard stubble. His light brown eyes were like an eerie contrast to the rest of him.

"Hey, boss," said Zachary. "I have something important to discuss."

"Make yourself useful and take the other bag," said Alexei. "It has the wheels that you can roll along while we talk."

They strode past the long-term parking buses, past the sea of cabs, and past the car rental booths. The pedestrian crossing led them right to the short-term parking lot. Zachary spoke as they got deeper into the parking garage, and the crowds thinned.

"We have a development with one of the escorts," he said. "It appears that a customer wishes to purchase her freedom."

Alexei scoffed. "From whore to housewife. These assholes let pussy blind them. Who is it?"

"Tatiana."

Alexei clenched his jaw tight before answering. "Tell that asshole that the price is $250K. That should wither his pecker. Enough of this boring talk about whores. I need to call Sergei. Do you have the phone?"

Zachary reached into his coat and pulled out a thick, black military-grade phone.

"Sergei, this is Alexei."

"What have you found out?" asked Sergei.

"The wife was blackmailing Turgenev. The money was for her. Not for laundering."

"What does she have on him?"

"I don't know." He kept the part about the assassin to himself. "What I can't figure out is why Turgenev ordered her killed after he paid her off? Something must have spooked him."

"Do you think it was the hacker's interference?" asked Sergei.

"Had to be."

"If I am to pay for silence and then change my mind and kill the ones I made a deal with, it means my confidence has wavered."

"Your thoughts as to why?" asked Alexei.

"The hacker stole whatever information was supposed to be exchanged along with the money," said Sergei.

"Makes perfect sense," said Alexei.

"Where is the computer the hacker used?"

"We left in in the hotel room."

"It's probably gone. My guess is that other systems in his possession have the same information on them. Hackers are notorious for making backups of everything. If we are to learn what they had on Turgenev, we need to grab all the hacker's computers and go through them."

"I understand," said Alexei.

CHAPTER 21

Finally, Maxim's opportunity came to grab Jake Coltrane. He was sitting in the back of the limousine waiting on Oleg and Dimitri to give the all clear before executing the plan. Jake's laptop was beside him on the black leather seat. It was worthless without the architect behind the keyboard. In order to capitalize on its full potential they needed Jake Coltrane.

They'd followed Jake to work the day prior and waited, hoping he'd put in a late night and leave when few people were on the street. That did not happen. He left work early and went to the hospital. So they split up and covered the hospital's exits, waiting for him to leave. At nightfall, Dimitri went inside and was told that Jake had been admitted.

Oleg and Dimitri took turns monitoring the hospital throughout the evening. The next morning, Jake was pushed to the curb in a wheelchair, and he left via bus. They followed, mirroring the bus route, expecting Jake to get off near his home, and he did.

They watched him go inside and checked the area before they moved in, allowing Jake a chance to settle, kick off his shoes, and feel safe in his routine. It was better that way. People put up less of a fight when caught completely by surprise.

Oleg stood watch on the street in front of the building. Dimitri went to the fourth floor to check for other occupants. He sent a text to Maxim. *No one roaming.*

Maxim put the phone down and stared out the window of the Escalade. The streets weren't currently busy, but plenty of watchful eyes were still about. It was late morning and taking a person against their will required some massaging. Some savvy. Some cunning. He'd thought about it for a while and came up with the idea of using the laptop. Jake would recognize it and open the door. From there, they'd explain the situation and emphasize that if he didn't come quietly, they'd drug him and drag him out after the sun went down.

If he continued to resist, Maxim would use the threat of violence against a loved one. The pictures he'd downloaded from Jake's phone contained a flurry of images of one woman in particular, Catalina. If push came to shove, he'd threaten Jake through her. That usually did the trick.

Oleg approached the car and tapped on the window. "All clear," said Oleg.

Maxim got out of the car, and together they crossed the street. The large, brick apartment building had six floors. It wasn't the type of building where they packed them in like sardines, but it wasn't precisely upscale, either.

They squeezed between parked cars and stepped onto the curb. Maxim had the slim, silver laptop in his hand. He walked down the sidewalk with his eyes focused straight ahead, as any ordinary citizen would. Then he saw something that could be worrisome. He slowed and double-checked, to be sure. It was a familiar Suburban. Zachary and Alexei occupied the front seats. Maxim checked the light: red. The intersecting street's pedestrian counter was at nine seconds. When the light turned green, the Suburban would catch up to them before they reached Jake's apartment building.

Maxim tucked Jake's laptop under his armpit. He couldn't chance Alexei recognizing the computer, and he was too far away from the Escalade to make it back to the vehicle in time. Alexei wasn't particularly bright, but he was extraordinarily brutal. Maxim was fucked.

Where could he place it where no one would find it? Beneath a parked car? Too risky. Among the towering bags of trash on the curb? Too dirty. Five seconds left. Maxim looked around in desperation. He caught sight of a familiar-looking woman walking down the street behind him. The hacker's girlfriend, Catalina, in a thin white jacket over a black tee shirt with blue jeans. A tidy ponytail swayed behind her as she walked. She held a cloth shopping bag full of groceries. Catalina glanced at her phone as if she'd received a message.

Maxim approached quickly and started a conversation. "Hi, you're Jake's friend, aren't you?"

She stopped, caught off guard. "Yes, I am. You know Jake?"

"Of course, I know Jake! The last time I saw him, he left this at my place. I wanted to return it, but I'm late for work. I don't want to go all the way up there, so if you could . . ." He shoved the laptop into the grocery bag, pushing it down so it wouldn't stick out.

"Oh, he was looking for that," said Catalina. "He'll be so glad when he gets it back. It is going to answer a ton of questions. Did you hear what happened in the hospital?"

"No, what?"

"His heart stopped. Luckily, they brought him back, and I'm so grateful that they did. Jake's an exceptional person. He has no idea what he brings to the table. That's the sad part of it all. He thinks that when he dies, no one will remember him."

"Yeah, that's not true." Maxim was running out of time. Alexei and Zachary will be on him any minute. "Well, I'm glad he is okay and now that I got his computer back to him . . . I would love to chat but I have to go to work now. Tell Jake I said hi."

"Who . . .? You never said your name. Do you work with him? He tries not to make any new friends because he, well . . . you know about his condition. Where did you guys—? Hold on, he sent me a text."

"Gotta go now."

Maxim turned toward the street and saw Zachary's Suburban stopped in the middle of the block. Oleg stood at an opened window, talking to them. Through the darkened cabin, Alexei and Zachary examined Oleg skeptically. He slipped back through the parked cars and crossed the street. A car honked as they went around the Suburban and nearly hit him. Maxim flipped off the driver and stood next to Oleg.

"Da," said Maxim.

"This bumbling fool here does not know anything, so I am asking you," said Alexei. "What the fuck are you two doing here?"

"We heard about the hacker that stole the money," said Maxim. "We heard that you disposed of him. I am here because I wondered if there was something valuable we might find in his apartment. We tried to contact you, but you were away in Russia. My apologies for not talking to you first."

Alexei listened, then nodded when Maxim finished. The man was hard to read. He gazed silently at Maxim with the same unchanging expression. Maxim had seen the resolve of many men crack under the weight of his silence.

"Someone tried to kill me while I was away in California," said Alexei.

More pressure on Maxim. He'd been told that Alexei wouldn't be returning from California. If Maxim gave him the slightest hint of being aware of the plot, it would be Maxim getting tortured in that stash house, not Jake. Luckily for Maxim, he knew Alexei was feeling him out.

"Was it on the highway?" said Maxim. "I hear they shoot you for not knowing how to drive there. I've ridden with you before."

The uncomfortable silence grew strained. Finally, Alexei cracked a smile and laughed, with Zachary and Oleg following.

"I have run many assholes off the road," said Alexei. "This is why Zachary drives everywhere."

Maxim had to placate Alexei and get him out of there if he'd have any chance of surviving. "If I find something on the hacker's computers, I will make sure you are covered monetarily," offered Maxim.

"How much?" asked Alexei.

Maxim smiled behind clenched teeth. "Twenty percent is customary commission for something like this."

"I would like that deal, but not this time, Maxim. Sergei wants information on Turgenev."

Alexei stopped abruptly as if he could sense Maxim's heart skip when he mentioned Turgenev. The weight of his gaze doubled, and Maxim squirmed under the pressure.

"You understand that I am talking about Sergei, right?" said Alexei. "Turgenev came to Sergei demanding that he take action against the CEO after a deal was struck, and then I arrived and nearly burned alive. The ex-wife had something over Turgenev. He insisted I go there, and since I was nearly killed, I am just as interested in getting dirt on Turgenev as Sergei. Anyone who knows anything about Turgenev and this arrangement he had with Julie Shubert had better speak now or forever hold his peace."

Maxim smiled inwardly. Alexei's explanation could be used to his advantage. Sergei was after information on that laptop, and Turgenev's people knew it was there. All Maxim had to do now was find that information and use it against Turgenev. He'd be sure to cut Sergei in on the deal, but not Alexei, and Sergei would protect him from the monster if he succeeded.

"Now that we have an understanding, we can go into the hacker's place and take whatever it is he has lying around," said Alexei. "Anything that relates to Turgenev is mine, understand? You can have everything else." Alexei reached for the door handle.

"Wait," said Maxim. "I came from his apartment. There is a small group of people there. Maybe they wonder where the hacker is since they have not seen him in several days, or maybe his body turned up somewhere, and they are mourning. Our presence might arise suspicion. It is best that we wait. Come back another time. Tonight, or maybe tomorrow."

"Tomorrow at the latest," said Alexei. "We don't have time to wait. You will get me the information on Kyle and Julie Shubert. Remember that name. Do I have to write it down for you?"

"No," said Maxim. "I remember. No worries."

Alexei nodded his head. "It has been a long trip. I need to go home and get some rest. I expect a call from you tomorrow. I know you have competent hackers working for you, but I want to use my people for the search. Understood?"

Maxim smiled. "No problem, Alexei."

CHAPTER 22

———◆—●—◆———

Jake exited the bus at the corner and looked up at his apartment building near the middle of the block. He lived in a humble one-bedroom apartment on the fourth floor, with a small kitchen and even smaller living space. Yet, he was excited to get home. Catalina had messaged to say she'd be there.

Her text said she took the day off to look after him. She was making him breakfast, and she needed to show him something. He imagined sexy Catalina standing over the stove, cooking for him. He'd sit on his brown couch, prop his feet up on the ottoman, and text his boss that he is not coming in to work today.

He missed her sense of humor and the sound of her voice. He missed her soft buttery skin and her caress. Maybe she'd sit next to him on the couch after breakfast. Perhaps breakfast would lead to something else. His bedroom was big enough for a full-sized bed, but not much room left to walk around it. Computer parts cluttered the corner and far wall. They'd have to navigate around his side of the bed, but once they were on it, all cares would melt away.

His pace quickened as he approached the front of the building, trucked up the concrete stairs and through the entrance. He turned left to the elevator and pushed the button to the fourth floor. The doors opened and he went straight to his apartment. Outside the door, he heard movement inside and smelled the scent of Catalina's perfume. He turned the key in the lock, ready to rush into the kitchen and soak in her beauty.

Jake rushed through the door and found a man sitting on his couch in front of the television.

She'd said she'd needed to show him something.

What she meant was she wanted him to *meet* someone.

When he searched his feelings, he had to admit that what he wanted was a sympathy fuck. It was utterly selfish, with no regard for what emotions the encounter might stir within her.

Nevertheless, karma was a bitch. Jealous and despondent, Jake snapped at the strange man on his couch. "Where is Catalina?"

The man spun his head around and it was Jericho Black. A bodyguard walked up behind Jake and folded his arms, ready to subdue Jake if need be.

"I got a phone call a few hours ago asking for the address to this place," said Jericho. "I wondered what the sudden interest was until I saw this report on television." He gestured toward the muted TV.

A news channel flashed images of a tragedy in Los Angeles. The two news anchors discussed it with expressions of concern blanketing their faces. A chyron scrolled on the bottom of the video: *Kyle Shubert, CEO of Ribel Pharmaceutical, dies in house fire with ex-wife, Julie. Arson suspected.*

"You appear to have stirred a hornet's nest," said Jericho. "What else did you steal on that computer besides the money?"

Jake was speechless. He had no idea what to say. He thought the tumor had been distorting his sense of reality. Yet Jericho Black and his bodyguard were now in his apartment. He called out to the only person who could help verify if what he was seeing was real or not. "Catalina?"

"She left about five minutes ago," Jericho said. "She went out to get some groceries to make you something to eat. She said she had something important to share with you. She your girlfriend?"

"I, uh . . . ex-girlfriend," said Jake. He watched the news replay images of a fire-ravaged estate. "We met before?" asked Jake. "Really met, like we talked and everything."

Jericho stared blankly, then grinned. "Sorry. I was supposed to be there when you woke up and explain everything. You were out longer than expected, and I had other business to take care of."

"In the hotel room," said Jake. His mind quickly went over the things he could remember and placed them into reality. Yet, something did not fit. "You stabbed me with a knife. That can't be right."

"Oh, it's right," said Jericho. "I stabbed you to death. Dead. That was the only way the big Russian would leave the room. After he left, I came back and tried several things to revive you. Nothing kick-started your healing, so I went to plan B. It was tricky, but it worked. I left you there to rest and placed word at the hotel lobby to notify me when you checked out."

". . . I thought you stabbed me but . . ." Jake lifted his shirt. His skin was perfect. Not a mark or blemish anywhere. Thoughts of the railcar rumbled through his head; him naked, in that suffocating heat, with those hideous rats and people barfing everywhere. How one asshole kept insisting they were dead and in hell. "Wait a minute. I need a drink."

Jake went into the kitchen and opened the cabinet where he kept his Bib & Tucker bourbon. He poured himself a small glass. "You're a bourbon guy," he recalled, offering it to Jericho. "How about a glass?"

"After the Pappy Van Winkle? Please!"

Another verification that what he remembered was real. Jake offered the bottle of Bib & Tucker to Jericho's large bodyguard, who refused. Jake shook his head and took a sip. His thoughts floated in the glass of amber liquor. He watched the liquid move and shimmer in the light. Jericho Black, the money, the cure . . . but coming back from the dead was outlandish and inconceivable.

Jake placed the glass on the counter. "Explain it again. I went to you for a cure for my tumor, and the cure brought me back from the dead. How is that possible?"

"Your program found an image of me from the Civil War," said Jericho. "You stole hundreds of millions of dollars to find out if I've been alive for over a hundred years. Now you question it? You're cured, Jake, so cured you can't even die."

Jake laughed. It started as a chuckle but quickly turned hysterical. "That's ridiculous," sputtered Jake. "What you are saying is crazy." He turned to the bodyguard for a sanity check. The bodyguard remained expressionless, seemingly oblivious to the conversation. "You can't cure death. Death is not a disease."

"In a sense, you're right," said Jericho. "It's not permanent. You will die eventually. Just not anytime soon."

Jake took a big swig of bourbon. Felt the burn in his chest. Put a hand on his face to feel how real it was as if touching himself would separate dream from reality.

Jericho reached over to the next seat and grabbed the jacket he'd folded over the top of the couch. He placed his hand in the inside pocket and removed several phials. "I keep these for special situations," he said. "They save the lives of humans who have value to me. Everything from gunshot wounds to cancer. Your instincts served you well on this one. I was the person who could cure you. Unfortunately, we had the situation with the Russian who wanted you dead. So, I was forced to use the parasite to bring you back to life."

"Parasite?" asked Jake, shuddering. He poured himself another glass and drank it all in one swig. "I remember thinking you had somehow created the philosopher's stone," said Jake.

"The mystical philosopher's stone," said Jericho. "An elixir learned by Adam from God and passed down through the patriarchs which gave them the ability to live many hundreds of years as stated in the Old Testament. Adam lived 930 years. Seth 912 years. Methuselah 969 years. Noah 950 years. Abraham 175 years. Isaac 180 years and Jacob 147 years. Funny how people seek to explain what can't be explained by creating other myths. It's a parasite. No magic formula."

"Tell me about this parasite," said Jake. "How is it that no one has ever heard of a parasite that brings people back from the dead?"

"Ancient Chinese secret, my friend." Jericho laughed. "You don't need to know where it came from. Just know it's in you now, and since you're standing here talking, it works."

"I'm speechless," said Jake.

"Don't be. It comes with a price. Do you remember what that is?"

Jake nodded. "I'll get you the software, as promised."

"Great," said Jericho. "Now here's the problem. The Russians are on their way here to grab your computer. The program isn't on any of these computers, is it?"

"No, this is all my spare stuff. My backups."

"What about your laptop?" said Jericho. "Where is that?"

"I don't have it," said Jake. "Don't you?"

"I left it in the hotel room like I said I would."

"It wasn't in there when I came to."

Jericho nodded, thinking. "Finding you here, alive, would only complicate things. You need to go. Leave. Hide out for a few days until things settle. After that, you come back and finish our arrangement."

"Okay," said Jake, striding toward his bedroom. "I will pack a few things and leave town. Oh, wait." He stopped. "Catalina."

"No time for her, Jake," said Jericho. "We're leaving right now. Text her and tell her you won't be home anytime soon."

"I can't leave now," said Jake, his heart beating wildly with a sudden realization. "I want to explain to her how everything about us has changed."

"What are you talking about?" asked Jericho.

"I'm cured! We can build a life together."

Jericho chuckled and stared at Jake as if he were unhinged. "What life are you talking about?" asked Jericho. "The one where you live for 200 years, maybe 300? How well do you think that's going to go over?"

Jake let the implications sink in. His jaw tightened. "I only asked for a cure."

"Well, you've been cured," said Jericho. He checked his watch. "Now, send her the text. Tell her not to come here. Tell her not to come looking for you. Tell her you will never see her again because those Russians won't give a damn about her cooking when they get here, and unlike you, I have no reason to save her life."

Jake quickly sent the text. *Had to run. Work emergency. Won't be home anytime soon.*

Jericho put his jacket on. His bodyguard moved toward the door. Jake's phone rang. Catalina. He stared at the screen, wondering what to say. Jericho grabbed Jake's phone and pushed the Reject button. He tossed the phone back to Jake.

"You can't have a relationship," he said. "That part of your life is over!"

Jake's world went from hopeful to crushed. The purpose of being cured was to have a life not just be alive. Life meant Catalina. She was his life.

"Let's go Jake," said Jericho waving him through the door.

Jake blindly followed them. His mind in a despondent fog heading towards the stairs. When he heard the latch of his apartment door click shut behind him, it felt like the end of a chapter in his life.

CHAPTER 23

They went down the concrete stairs, around the landing, and down more stairs in a cascade of shuffling feet, Jake sandwiched between the bodyguard Ronaldo and Jericho Black. His mind swirled with thoughts of a new life. Where would he go? What would he do? How would he survive? If he had to run, he would much rather do it with Catalina by his side. That visit in the hospital sparked up old feelings. Feelings for her he thought would go away.

They exited the back entrance and ran across the lot to where a black Lincoln Navigator waited with a driver behind the wheel. The bodyguard grabbed the handle of the rear door and held it open. Jericho and Jake got into the backseat and strapped in. The bodyguard jumped into the passenger's seat, and the vehicle pulled out onto the street and turned right. They traveled through the intersection, and all heads turned right.

"There they are," said the bodyguard. A Suburban idled in the middle of the street, and two people stood outside it. They both watched as the Lincoln sped past.

Jake's phone buzzed, and he looked at the screen. Catalina, again.

"Don't answer it," said Jericho. "If you have feelings for this girl, the best thing you can do for her is lock them away."

Jake hesitated. "Look. There is no real purpose for living if I can't be with the people I love. I care about Catalina."

"Then don't put her in danger, Jake. The Russians want to grab your gear from the apartment. It won't be good for her if she's there when they show up. Text her and tell her you're with your new girlfriend."

Jake's heart took a jolt. "No!" He slumped into his seat. "In any case, she told me she had another man in her life."

"Then you should have no problem sending that text to her."

Jake clutched the phone. "I didn't ask to live for 300 years! I only wanted to be cured."

"Send the text," said Jericho.

City streets sped by outside the window as he sat in the quiet cabin of the SUV. He never felt so alone. Jake wrote what Jericho suggested and pressed Send. Jericho patted him on the shoulder. Then he took Jake's phone.

"You did the right thing, Jake." Jericho rolled down the window and hurled the phone upward. The glass phone shattered into tiny pieces after Jake spun his head around to watch it hit the pavement. "Buy a burner," said Jericho. "And here." Jericho reached in his coat pocket and pulled out a credit card. A black card. He gave it to Jake. "Use this. I don't want people tracking you through your accounts."

Jake flipped it around and stared at the back. He'd only heard of these mythical black credit cards mentioned in movies and rap songs. Never actually saw one.

"Don't get stupid with that," said Jericho. "I'll rip your fucking eyes out."

Jake nodded and slid the card into his front pants pocket for safekeeping.

The Lincoln neared Newark Penn Station and maneuvered through traffic to get closer. Vehicles crowded the roundabout. They pulled up tight behind a small brown compact, so close that Jake could only see the top of the car. The bodyguard opened his door and stepped out onto the street, giving the crowd the once over, looking for anything suspicious.

"Are we taking the train?" asked Jake.

"Can't get plane tickets," said Jericho. "It's easier for someone to track you by plane. Every name on every flight is recorded. This is the best way to do it. Nothing to trace here. Everyone is anonymous."

Jericho's bodyguard opened the back door. The bright sun outside penetrated the darkened cabin of the Lincoln. Jake's eyes momentarily burned when he stepped out. Jericho followed him. They slipped through the crowd and into the terminal. Jericho moved as if he had escaped from Russians via train a thousand times. He had a travel ticket that he slid through to open the turnstile. Jake used his monthly pass to enter. He followed Jericho and his bodyguard to Track M for the train into Lower Manhattan. The platform wasn't crowded, just a few people here and there looking to get into New York City.

"We're going to take this train to Grand Central Station," said Jericho.

Jake saw the reasoning behind that. From Grand Central he could go anywhere in the country. It would make it harder for anyone to pin down his location.

"Can I trust you, Jake?" asked Jericho.

"Sure. Why?" said Jake.

Jericho's tone was somber and slightly irritated. "I smashed your phone because you didn't send the text I told you to send to your girlfriend. You mentioned something about contacting her in a few hours."

Jake said nothing. He shuffled his feet impatiently. He didn't want to push Catalina away. She was the only person left on earth that he couldn't part with. And now they had a chance.

He felt the grit of concrete under the soles of his shoes. The tone of the oncoming train sounded. His hair seemed to stand on edge as it approached. Static crackled in the air. He didn't have to feel the rumble of the tracks to tell him it was close; he could feel the energy of the train. Down the tunnel, the light from the train came around the last turn and illuminated the tracks.

"Does your program work off an app?" asked Jericho.

Jake nodded. "Way too much data to be stored on any laptop or phone. I created an app to access the mainframe."

"I want that mainframe," said Jericho. "I want it all."

"That's why I need time to get it to you. I have it stored in sections at my place of work. It's going to take time to download, and you need to buy a mainframe powerful enough to run it."

"Fair enough," said Jericho.

"Here we go again," said a familiar voice. Jake looked to his right. Standing next to him on the platform was Katt Williams in a bright green jacket and matching bell-bottoms., his white shirt unbuttoned to the sternum. "You should have sent the fucking text."

"What the . . ." said Jake. He turned to Jericho and pointed at Katt.

Jericho took a deep breath. "Here comes the train," he said.

"This is crazy," said Jake. "Do you see him—this guy next to me?"

"Catalina shared something with me," said Jericho. "Something you can't handle right now. I can't trust you to stay hidden for a week. Therefore, I'm going to help you out."

Jake pointed at the little pimp standing next to him. "It's Katt—"

A sudden, violent shove struck the center of Jake's back. His head jerked backward while his body fell forward, and his feet flew off the ground. Everything slowed. He instinctively reached for something to hold on to, but nothing was there. Just air. He was helpless, airborne, elevated dead center above the middle of the tracks. The light from the train brightened. The horn sounded. Iron wheels screeched. He contorted his legs so his feet might hit the track, and then maybe he'd flip forward onto one of the other tracks before the train reached him. He ran the sequence through his mind over and over again.

It felt like it took forever. Three. Two. One.

Jake's feet touched down hard. His knees buckled, and his buttocks hit the back of his heels. However, he was balanced. He still had a chance. Jake squeezed his quads to propel his leap forward toward the other tracks. He didn't clear the center barrier. His feet clipped the rail, slowing him down enough for his head and upper part of his shoulder to sever when the train came through. The impact was so forceful that his head and shoulder shot across the tracks and landed between the rails.

His ears hummed, but he felt no pain. He tried to process how he had escaped death. It took him a few moments to realize there wasn't a body attached to his head. His eyes worked, and he could hear fine, so Jake opened his mouth to ask for help. With no lungs, it was impossible to muster a sound. Instead, his bloody tongue oozed out of his mouth until it rested on the rails. He heard people screaming, so he shifted his eyes upward.

Jake examined the frightened faces of those brave enough to look down from the platform. He spotted a young man in jeans, toting a backpack, making a live video, his eyes full of excitement. He held the phone up, angling the selfie to include Jake's head in the video.

A woman, a brunette with glasses, peered down at him from the platform's edge, her phone pressed to her ear. "You're never going to believe this. I'm on the platform of Penn Station in Newark, and this guy jumped out onto the tracks and killed himself. Seriously, I'm traumatized."

Just how traumatized are you that you can phone a friend?

"Oh my god, his mouth is moving. You should see it. He's looking right at me. He's trying to talk to me."

Yes! Hang up the phone and dial 911, you stupid bitch!

"I was right across from him when he jumped!"

I didn't jump. I was pushed!

"I'm going to be scarred for the rest of my life! How could he be so selfish? Kill yourself in the privacy of your own home or something. Thanks a lot, asshole! Starving for attention so much that you have to kill yourself in public and ruin my day."

Is your day ruined? I got hit by a train, you fucking cunt!

His vision faded to black, but he was still present. He could feel his body again, and he was naked. There was no mistaking it this time: Jake had died. Unlike the other times, he felt safe. He exhaled. This was different. A much better place.

A beautiful woman in a thin white dress walked seductively toward him, right out of the darkness. She was stunning. Silky black hair, brown eyes, and bronze skin. High cheekbones accentuating full lips. The thin material of her dress stuck to her skin, revealing a perfect figure.

"Are you here to meet the savior?" she asked.

She went to take his hand, and Jake flinched, remembering sizzling flesh. But her touch felt soft and pleasant.

"Come," she said with a bright smile. "Let me show you the way."

CHAPTER 24

---◆---

They walked across sand through the darkness, her holding Jake's hand as she led the way. They traveled for what seemed to be days. As time passed, the temperature beneath his feet cooled. Dark storm clouds gave way to a bright moonlit sky. He marveled at the dense concentration of stars. She turned around excitedly and smiled at him, perfect skin glistening in the starlight.

"It is not far from here," she said. She smelled of the most pleasant fragrances. "It's over the bridge up ahead. Do you see it?"

A thick and sturdy bridge made from mortared stone arched above a pit too dark to see into. The bridge went on for miles and disappeared in the darkness.

"Come," she said. "Let's hurry."

They stepped onto the bridge, and Jake enjoyed the solid texture of the stones beneath his feet, smooth enough for a pleasant walk with enough grit to avoid slips and tumbles. Up they walked, the woman's dainty feet light and energetic like a ballerina, prancing up the incline effortlessly. Jake found it more challenging to climb, but anticipation helped him keep pace with the beauty.

Jake thought back to when he'd met Zee, who'd told him about the eighteen hells from his culture. He'd said everyone had to go to hell. Jake wished he could go back and tell Zee he was wrong. Different beliefs or not, everyone deserved the chance at salvation. Zee was back in hell suffering. He felt a tiny knot of worry but pushed it away.

"You said we are going to meet the savior, right?" Jaked asked the beauty.

"Yes," she said with a smile. "That's right."

"Born of the Virgin Mary."

"Born of a virgin, yes."

"He will come again to judge the living and the dead, and his kingdom will have no end?"

"Yes. He will raise the dead and all that have ever lived for the final judgment. The truly wicked will be returned to hell to be purged of all bodily sin. The righteous will be made immortal, and the earth will be restored to its ultimate glory."

"I told Zee," said Jake, slapping a thigh. "I told him! We debated semantics about reincarnation. I should have told him the righteous shall be risen! Just what you said."

"Yes. You are fortunate."

Jake nodded. "I feel bad for the others, though. I mean, don't get me wrong, some people are bad and need to be there, but some never got to know Jesus because of where and when they lived."

She stopped at the top of the bridge. "The Saoshyant does not like to be called by another name. Especially that one."

"What other name did I use? I said Jesus."

Her pleasant fragrance dissipated like a song cut off mid-melody. "The prophecy of the Saoshyant existed long before there was a Jesus."

"Sorry. Different cultures must have different names. Only one man is born of a virgin, so we're talking about the same person. Forgive me."

"You are speaking of someone else," she said sternly. "The prophecy of the Saoshyant being born of a virgin impregnated by the seed of Zoroaster while bathing in a lake was foretold thousands of years before Jesus was born. Saoshyant is to raise the dead for final judgment. Saoshyant will restore the earth and allow the righteous to become immortal. For his story to be mimicked and warped to lift Christianity to a higher power is insulting to all Zoroastrians!"

Beneath his feet, Jake felt the bridge changing angles. They were no longer heading upward. Now it led down. She clutched Jake's hand tightly and pulled him along. He tried to resist, but she was overpowering. The bridge narrowed and transformed into no more than a yard-wide walkway. She hurried him downward, now emanating a wretched smell, which only intensified. With her free hand, she removed her gown so he could see her

116

nakedness. Scabby lumps coated her sagging skin. Boils of oozing puss and blood burst across her breasts and stomach. The foul smell emanated from between her legs, an odor so thick that he could see the air warping as it rose from her region. Jake gagged uncontrollably.

When she stopped abruptly and turned around, what stood before Jake was haggard and terrifying. Filthy eyes caked with yellow gunk goggled at him. She opened her mouth and revealed jagged, rotting stumps where teeth once grew. Maggots spilled from her cracked, bloody lips when she spoke to him. Jake backed away.

"You have been judged to be a dumb-ass believer in a stupid, made-up fantasy for ignorant grown people!" she shrieked and hurled him over the side of the bridge with one hand.

CHAPTER 25

———◆———

Jake hit the solid ground hard. No sand. No water. He bounced and tumbled, then sprung to his feet and began running. There were no screams. No thumps. No clacking, hammering, or sawing, but this was another hell. He wouldn't be fooled again. The dead silence was more unnerving than the screams.

Jake kept running while the landscape beneath his feet changed. He was heading downward, so he stopped. Down was bad. Up was good. He had no idea why it made a difference, but he reversed direction anyway.

He turned around and immediately bumped into something impeding his path. A wall. How could that be? He'd come from that very direction, running in full stride. Jake placed his hands on the wall and shimmied left and right. There had to be an opening. He felt around until his hand slid through an opening. He walked gingerly through a darkened space until he came upon another wall. His outstretched hands felt the coarse surface slide beneath his palms.

He repeated the motion, again and again, and realized he was in something like a maze. Jake had heard that to get through a maze, one had to place one hand on a wall and walk that wall all the way through. So that's what he did. Eventually, he came upon a section in which he could see. He stepped through the opening and found himself in a pink and white room decorated with plastic furniture. The window wasn't real. Neither was the mirror, which appeared to be made of reflective material. The entire space was missing a side.

It was a dollhouse. It was made for little kids. The floors and walls ended at the precipice of a dark abyss.

"Hello," said a female voice. "Aruru has been waiting for you."

A woman who sat in a chair in the corner of the room stood upon seeing him. She wore a long black latex coat with eight-inch black platform heels, bringing her to the same height as Jake. He recognized her as a version of the woman on the bridge wearing gaudy makeup.

Her nose was slightly upturned and pointed. Her puffy lips flaked with bright pink lipstick. Exaggerated circles of red rouge dotted each cheek, and her dark hair was tied in a bun so tight the outer corners of her eyes pulled upward slightly. Dark swaths of purple eye shadow caked under eyebrows drawn in large arcs like the golden arches of McDonald's.

"So you like little children do you?" she asked. She looked down between Jake's legs. "Your first punishment is for sticking that horrible thing inside little girls."

"What?" said Jake. "I just saw you. You were taking me over the bridge. Why would you suddenly think I would do that? No! Not me. Never children."

"You took advantage of innocence!" she yelled. She pulled off her coat to reveal a shiny black fourteen-inch strap-on. "It is your turn to be violated."

Jake flinched and tried to go back out the door, but his legs wouldn't move. His arms flung out from his sides and spread wide. A pink plastic table slid across the floor and hit him in the thighs. His body collapsed on top of it. His arms stretched forward, and straps fell from the air to lock them in place. More belts cinched his ankles to the table legs. He struggled against the restraints, eyes swinging around the room until he saw them: small, nearly-transparent gremlin-type creatures skittering in every direction. They'd orchestrated his submission, fastening the straps in place and then giggling as he fought. He tried to pull his arms back. There was no give. He was completely immobilized.

"I'm not a pedophile!" Jake screamed.

"Aruru knows you were a trickster and a deceiver. The type of man who made people feel good at first and then fucked them without warning. That is what you did on the bridge, after all. You fucked Aruru's innocence without warning."

"No. No. Not true, uh . . . Aruru. We simply had a religious misunderstanding," he clarified.

Aruru strutted around him, her foul stench pluming from between her legs. Her narrow waist and hips barely held the heft of the enormous strap-on. She made a complete circle and stopped before him, plastic dick bobbling at eye level. He turned his head.

"Not a pedophile?" she asked. "Once innocence is lost it is gone forever. Aruru was innocent and got fucked by you. Aruru only wanted to be your friend." She leaped behind him and slapped his buttocks vigorously. Tears sprouted from his eyes.

"I wasn't trying to screw you, Aruru," said Jake. "I've never heard of this Zoroastrian stuff. Please, don't do this."

"Would you prefer to be boiled until your flesh falls off the bone instead?" asked Aruru.

"No," said Jake.

"Then it's settled. Aruru will fuck you."

Jake wriggled on the table in disbelief. Aruru was not listening to what he was saying. Why was she twisting everything around? He panted in short anxious breaths before trying to yank his arms free. It didn't even budge. He was bent over at the waist and completely vulnerable. She headed over to a side table and dipped her fingers into an oily substance. She rubbed it all over the strap-on and stood in front of Jake to show it off. It was at eye level.

"Big bad man hurt Aruru when Aruru was innocent. Aruru was only looking for a friend," she said. "You tricked Aruru and fucked her silly."

Jake looked up into her eyes. "I apologize, Aruru!" Jake said. "I am your friend. I would never hurt you."

"That is what big bad men with big hard cocks always say!" said Aruru.

She walked back over to the side table and paused, waving her hand over a tray like a model on the *Price is Right*. "Have you seen *Bloodsport*?" she asked. "It's Aruru's favorite movie."

Broken glass lay on the tray. She took a hammer and smashed them into dust, then grabbed a fistful and applied it to the strap-on until it sparkled like diamonds.

"I doubt you buy your dates bling-bling like this," said Aruru. "You take them home and ram that disgusting rod into them against their wishes."

"No!" Jake screamed. He pulled and twisted against the restraints until it felt like his arms were going to come off. "I'm not like that. This is a mistake. Stop twisting everything around you demented clown-faced freak!"

It triggered *oh shit* moment of silence he wished he could take it back.

Aruru walked over to Jake and pressed her rough index finger against his lips. Her pouty, flaky lips *shooshed* him. "There is plenty of time for screaming pet names once Aruru gets started, sweetie. Saying such things before Aruru gets going is as depressing as premature ejaculation. You don't want me to cum before I get started, do you?"

Jake looked at the glistening phallus. "Cum how?"

She cackled. "Imagine juice from the hottest pepper in the world squirted directly up your bunghole." She leaned over him and slapped his ass so hard he winced. The dildo scraped his cheek drawing blood.

"Don't you dare put a scratch on that thang!" said a deep voice.

The shadow of a massive creature engulfed Jake and Aruru. Jake strained to look over his shoulder. His head collapsed onto the table in dread. It just got worse. The bull tong in Gaap's nose dangled in front of his purple lips. His cleaver gripped tightly in one hand.

"Hey!" Gaap boomed. "Looks like you're all tied up, big man." He stood with his arms folded, examining Jake's ass. "Aruru! Loosen these restraints a little," he said with his head twisted. "I can't get a clean whack at it from this angle. It's all squished up beneath him."

"He belongs to Aruru now," Aruru bellowed. "Get out, Gaap!"

"You can fuck his tiny asshole to shreds for all I care. I want to take his package. His penis is going to look good on me. Just loosen him a little bit. I can pull it out and hack it from the back."

"You'll get him when I'm finished," said Aruru.

He shook his head in disagreement, slinging snot from the giant bull tong in his nose. "Not a good idea to wait. He might leave at any moment."

"Leave where?" Aruru asked.

"Leave hell," said Gaap.

"You lie."

"No, it's true," said Gaap. He folded his arms. The cleaver visible under one of his armpits. "He left before Tartarus was finished with him. And Tartarus was looking right at him when he vanished."

"Tartarus looked at him, and he escaped?" she gasped. Her clownish makeup caked and crinkled atop of her astonished face. "Impossible. What kind of madness is this, young lover?" she asked Jake. "You want to run out on me before I have my fun?"

Aruru placed her hands on Jake's hips. Sandpaper palms gripped him firmly.

Jake tensed his entire body, waiting for the violent thrusts to come. Then, as if things could not get any worse, the air in the room thickened. He had felt this kind of pressure before outside the schoolhouse. It pushed him down against the table, making it difficult to breathe. Tartarus had arrived.

CHAPTER 26

The intense desire to kill himself was what Jake remembered from the previous encounter. Mouthing off to Aruru was one thing. Tartarus was completely different. He dared not even move. His haughty denial about being in hell and that this was just a dream must be fresh in Tartarus's mind. He might have come to finish his torture since Jake escaped by coming back to life. The entirety of his weight was pressed against the plastic table in Aruru's playhouse as Jake remained as still as he could. Jake could feel him hovering closely. An apology might deflect the situation.

"Please don't do it again," said Jake, straining against the crushing weight of Tartarus's presence. "I didn't know what was going on. I prefer you don't look at me if you don't mind."

Aruru put her rough palm on Jake's head stroking it like a kitten. "Aruru wants to know if my lover can leave hell whenever he wants," she said to Tartarus. She played with Jake's hair between her fingers. "This can't be true."

"It is," said Tartarus. The grin of his teeth widened. "Excuse me, but I would like to know how he does it."

"Simple." Jake sucked air in tiny gulps to inflate his lungs long enough to speak. "I go back to my body."

Aruru gasped, putting a hand over her mouth while the other hand stroked Jake's head. "You rise from the dead, like my precious Saoshyant?" she asked. "You just fucked Aruru a second time, lover. Blasphemy!"

"My body can fix itself," said Jake. The discussion gave him hope that he might be able to talk his way out of this. If he was not there for the

123

long term, there should be no purpose in torturing him. "I'm not really dead," he continued.

"But you are," said Tartarus, his hands moving like a magician. "Or else you would not be here. The soul cannot be released from the body until the body is dead. There must be some other explanation."

"I was told it was a because of a parasite," said Jake.

"What was that?" said Tartarus. Jake heard nothing but Tartarus's gloves froze in a mid-magic trick.

Dead silence. Tartarus flinched and it produced a scream like someone was hiding in the darkness and now they were discovered. Gaap spun the cleaver in his palm and immediately took off in chase. Aruru snared and pushed Jake's head down hard while propelling herself towards the door.

"Don't let them escape," Tartarus demanded. "Those assholes are a thorn in my side." He stepped over Jake with one long stride and disappeared out the door. Jake heard more screaming through the maze. People yelling and pleading for mercy. It sounded vicious and chaotic.

But he was alone. Jake fought against the restraints on his arms and legs. He pulled until he felt skin peeling from his wrists and ankles. Fresh wounds burned and bled as he squeezed his hand through the tight knot, to no avail. For the first time, he understood the mentality of an animal gnawing off its limb to escape.

He was desperate. He had no idea how far they'd gone. It was better to lose some skin than face those three when they returned. Jake strained his head to see if they were coming back. The sight of the room sickened him. It was made out to be some innocent room for little girls. Pink vanity and dressers. A canopy bed with a fluffy teal comforter with pink hearts. Yet piss and scum streaked the pink and white walls. He could see dried blood splotches on the floor beneath the table along with other swirled and disgusting colored fluids.

"Pst . . ."

Jake was startled. He wrenched his head around and saw movement in the shadows. A man emerged from the missing fourth wall, near the edge of what seemed to be a pit of nothingness.

He crept toward Jake on all fours, old and shrunken, moving slow and cautious. Markings covered his back, and he was bald with white hair around his ears. His body looked emaciated and radiated fatigue. A victim of Aruru, guessed Jake. He crept closer until he was within a few feet Jake's rape table.

"I made it," wheezed the man. "I've risked everything to follow you around since I first saw you. Is it true?" His weakened voice shook, barely audible over the maelstrom in the maze.

"Is what true?" Jake asked.

The man put his finger to his lips, urging Jake to speak quietly. "Can you leave hell?"

Jake wondered if he should answer honestly. He decided to tell the truth and nodded.

The old man gasped in gleeful surprise. He fidgeted with his fingers before continuing. "There is a way we can both escape this place."

"That is what I have been trying to do before those freaks come back."

"I mean the right way. By choosing the right path," rasped the old man.

"Here, help me remove these ropes," said Jake. He would possibly listen to this man's nonsense after he was free. For now, he was running out of time. Going back to his body was not an option this time. Not after being cut in two. He was trying to be encouraging to the old man in order to get free. "Help me get loose. I know the way back to the bridge. It looked promising before it transformed. Maybe if I say that I am this . . . Saoshyant . . . we can—"

"That's not how to get out," cried the old man. "I'm trying to show you the real way!" He bit at his lips, using his teeth to pull off a piece of skin before continuing. "We've all walked around in this wretched place searching for the means to escape. I now believe the need to search for a way out is nothing but the design of hell itself. The things we did on earth put us here, so the only true way to escape is to atone for our mistakes while alive. The best way to do that is to change the path of someone who's headed for hell."

"What do you mean, old man?"

"Think about it." He sat hunched over on the floor next to Jake. His eyes in a fog recalling some distant memory. "We're here because of what we have done to others. Plain and simple. If we change someone's course and save them from hell. And that will save our souls in the process."

Jake was not interested in any more lessons in Theology. "Right now,

I'm trying not to be fucked with busted glass. You can preach later!" Jake pled.

"You question it, don't you?" asked the old man. "Why are you here? You believe you don't deserve to be here. You wonder what you could have done to get here. The mass murderers, the pedophiles, the snakes . . . you're stuck down here with them, and what's your crime? You stole some bubblegum and picked the wrong faith? Punishment doesn't fit the crime, does it? Meanwhile some asshole who's been an asshole all his life prays to the right god and is awarded paradise. How is that justice? Isn't that how you feel? The difference is the asshole helped people avoid this place. That's how he got to heaven, and you didn't."

"Nonsense, old man," said Jake. "I've heard all the religious mumbo jumbo I can handle for one day. What faith are you referring to, huh? Where does it say that? Some mystic papyrus somewhere? I'm sick of this. Help me out of here."

"It came straight from the mouth of Tartarus," said the old man.

Couldn't be. He was the king of hell. Why would he give away such a secret? "Who did he tell that to?" asked Jake. "To you?"

"He said it to another demon. I overheard it. If we'd saved a soul from coming here, we wouldn't be here."

Jake tugged until shooting pain ran down his arms. "Save me right now by getting me out of these ropes!" said Jake.

"I said save someone from coming here," said the old man. "Believe me; I have someone in mind. Since my family is dear to my heart, you can start by saving my great-grandson. His name is Adonis Silver, and he's taken the wrong path. I know it. Save his soul from hell, and you'll be granted access to paradise."

Jake scoffed. "How does that help you, old man?"

"I told you how to do it," said the old man. "I told you how to save my great-grandson so I will be saved to."

"That simple. Really? What do I tell him? How am I supposed to save his soul?"

"It's easy. You need to take his eye."

"His eye?"

"Yes, his eye. Take them both if you have to."

"Just stop," said Jake, crushed by his stupidity. "Stop talking and help me out of here." Jake fought against his restraints as hard as he could. "Take an eye and go to heaven," he said to no one in particular. "Great. What absurd gibberish!"

"Mark 9:47: *And if your eye causes you to sin, gouge it out. It's better to enter the Kingdom of God with only one eye than to have two eyes and be thrown into hell*," quoted the old man. "Adonis has an eye that will lead him to hell. So long as he has this sight, he will be doomed. You must pluck it out . . . sacrifice him if you must, before he becomes impure."

"Now you want me to kill him?"

"I said sacrifice." He gave Jake a stern look. "Must you question everything?"

"Yes! Especially from anyone in this fucking place!"

"People all over the world make sacrifices to their god. Every religion, since the beginning of man. Abstinence, fasting, and yes, sometimes they take a life. Take my great-grandson's eye, and if he happens to die in the process, God will not look at you as a murderer. You'd be saving him from eternal damnation."

"Stop talking," said Jake, wishing he could cover his ears. He jerked his arm violently against his restraints. The old fool was lost in pipe dreams while precious time ticked by.

The old man reached up and slapped Jake briskly across the face. The searing burn of skin-to-skin contact was a vigorous shock to the senses. "My great-grandson's soul is on the line," he said to Jake. He thought a moment. "Maybe some suffering is what you need. You haven't felt what true pain is yet. You don't know what we endure here."

He glanced out into the maze. "Here they come," said the old man. Jake felt them returning as well. The pressure of Tartarus grew stronger.

"May you remember why killing him will be the least of his problems if you fail," said the old man. He crawled back to the edge of the giant dollhouse and with a scream, plunged into the abyss.

CHAPTER 27

The pressure grew. Fine hairs all over his body stood stiff. He was still trying to free himself from the restraints when Aruru came around to the front of the table, led by her glistening, shard-covered phallus. Her platform heels clicked with each step as she slowly circled his position. The tip of her finger traced along his back as she passed. It felt rough and dirty.

"You should've seen Tartarus back there," she said to Jake. "He was marvelous. He's still out there, feasting on the poor souls who thought themselves clever, following him around to obtain hell's secrets. How silly of them, thinking they could cheat their way past the master. But they are learning now. The master himself is instructing them. Did you see any of them?" she asked.

Aruru squatted. A ghastly smell came from between her legs, causing Jake to gag. Her pale, knotted fingers picked at the flayed flesh of his wrists. "Aruru has seen men pull their arms out of their sockets trying to escape," she murmured. "Deep down, you must want Aruru's love." She rubbed his head again affectionately. The scratching of those rough fingers on his skull sounded like white noise from a speaker.

Gaap entered, his clumsy feet slapping the ground, long thick arms dragging his trusty castration cleaver.

"I can't wait to get ahold of that penis," he boomed.

Aruru chuckled. "You're so gay," she said.

Gaap clicked his teeth. "You know what I mean, Aruru. Don't start with me!" He used a finger to poke Jake on the side of the head. "If you weren't tied up, would you laugh at Aruru's gay joke?"

Jake clamped his mouth shut. Hot breath from his nostrils fogged the table beneath him.

"Tartarus said to get started without him," said Gaap. "This one is in for a surprise. Everything is set."

"Excellent," said Aruru. "Let the fun begin."

Gaap grunted, ejecting phlegm and spit up through the middle of his bull tong. "I'll sit here in the corner until you're done," he said. "Then I will collect what I came for. Your butt-ramming better not damage the package." He rubbed his palms together. "Damn, I can't wait to get ahold of that thing!"

Gaap squeezed his hulking mass into a tiny pink chair. With a thud, he slammed his cleaver into the floor. "Let's get this going, Aruru. Time is wasting!"

"You are not going to leave me like you did Tartarus, are you lover?" said Aruru.

Fat chance of that happening, thought Jake. He'd been cut in two, severed by the speeding train. Jericho did that so he would be down for a week. Without a head it was more like forever.

Aruru maneuvered behind him, and once again her rough, clammy hands clamped onto his hips. She flexed her knees into Jake's legs, raising his rear ever so slightly. "You can start screaming now, Jake Coltrane."

A searing pain imprinted onto his back, starting at the left shoulder blade and traveling downward, ending at the bottom of his lung.

"Tartarus was right," exclaimed Gaap. "Quick. It's happening."

Aruru massaged the phallus against his sphincter and violently thrust her hips forward. Jake screamed.

His head flew upward and slammed against something that shut his jaws so hard he almost bit off his tongue. A plastic material shrouded his body. He explored with his hands until he discovered a zipper, pulled it down and sat up to look at what contained him. A body bag— inside the back of a van. The van skidded across traffic, horns honking. Jake patted down his body, and astonishingly, it was intact.

"I'm back in one piece!" he said.

Two sets of eyes stared at him from the front of the van. The driver's door clicked open, followed by a whoosh of cold air, then the disappearance of the driver. He'd jumped out. The van veered sharply to the right. The woman gawked at Jake, then shut her mouth, cursed, and clamored into the driver's seat to steer the top-heavy van through traffic. Tires squealed as she pulled off on a side street and placed the van into park.

It wasn't a trick. They were somewhere in Newark, New Jersey, early evening, that much Jake could see from the back of the van. The suffocating heat was gone, the sounds of the city were in full blare. It felt like home.

"It was his third day," said the woman, more to herself than Jake. "His mom made him take the job because she said city benefits are the best. He was going to settle for a job at the Post Office, but the Coroner's office called first." She glanced at Jake through the rearview mirror. He noticed long eyelashes and a petite, freckled face. She had long black curly hair and light brown skin, maybe in her late twenties or early thirties.

"I don't think he'll be back," she said. Her voice wavered. "My heart is racing so fast; I cannot even begin to tell you. I would've jumped out of the van if he hadn't beat me to it. But I thought, who would stop the van? It might crash into people, and then I'd have to pick them up later." She took a deep breath. "Sorry, I'm talking so fast. I always talk fast when I'm scared. We spent hours picking up pieces of you across the tracks and under the train and stuff. And here you are, like Humpty-Dumpty put back together again. Oh my god. I'm getting ready to scream, mister. Don't take this the wrong way, but how is it that you're put back together again?"

Right. Normal people back in the real world. He nervously stroked the back of his arm. "It's a long story. I kind of thought that it—"

"Your head, mister . . . your head . . . your head is in that container right there by your leg."

Jake looked where she pointed. His severed head and bloody tongue peeked out of a clear container by his left thigh. "Fuck!" Jake shouted and jumped to his feet so fast and hard he hit his head against the top of the van a second time. He scrambled as far away from his head as possible, which triggered a hysterical scream from the woman.

"Oh my god . . . Oh my god, you grew another fucking head! How the hell did you grow another fucking head?"

They froze when flashing lights filled the inside of the van. The blue and red strobe lights of the New Jersey police car darted across the woman's face as it pulled up in front of them, windshield to windshield. A young Black police officer got out of the vehicle and approached the van. He went to the driver's door and tapped on the window. The woman used her index finger to push the switch, and the window rolled down smoothly. Startled, Jake pulled the body bag back over his head and laid down, trying not to breathe.

"Is everything all right in there?" the officer asked, looking around the van.

"Everything's great," she chirped. "I had to pull over for a sec."

"You didn't hit anybody, did you?"

"Hit anyone? No, why would you ask that?"

"Call came in about a van like this one swerving through traffic and hitting a pedestrian. Maybe the guy tried to run across traffic and got hit. In any case, the guy reportedly got up and fled the scene. He must be in shock. That's why when I saw your van, I pulled up to take a look."

"Nope, I didn't hit anyone, Officer," she said.

"Are you sure? You seem kind of nervous."

"Hm-ahm . . ." She threw her hands in the air. "Stress! This is a stressful job. Guy in the back? Yikes. In a million pieces back there."

"The jumper?" said the officer. "Yeah, I heard about that this morning. Jumped in front of the train. I'll never understand what possesses somebody to take their own life. Last week a guy calls 911 then ties a string from the front door to the trigger of a shotgun pointed straight at his face. When the paramedics open the door, *boom*, shotgun goes off and splatters his brains all over the place. Nothing left of his head. I heard your guy's head came completely off, is that right?"

"Yep, yep. That's his head right there in the container by the gurney. See?"

Jake had covered his torso and face as best he could. But his leg poked out from under the body bag.

"Damn, that foot is huge," said the officer.

Flashes of light danced across his body and around the van.

"Gross!" said the officer. He clicked the flashlight off. "They didn't have you collect all the pieces by yourself, did they? Where's your partner?"

"Private vehicle," said the woman. "He went on ahead. Should be at the office by now. Maybe he ran into traffic."

"Okay, well, get going then. Don't want this guy getting ripe out here.

Get him on ice." He tapped on the side of the van twice and went back to his car.

Jake heard the police car back up and drive away, then felt the clunk of the van shifting into gear. Jake slowly lowered the body bag from his face until his eyes met his other eyes pressed tightly against the plastic container.

"A camera, right?" she said, glancing at him through the rearview mirror. "You're some famous magician performing the ultimate magic trick?" Her eyes looked bloodshot, and tears welled under her lashes. She suddenly slapped the steering wheel. "This van must be filled with cameras. Is my boss in on it? I bet he was in on it." She found his eyes again. "At least that's what I was hoping when the officer came up. That he'd reveal the trick, and I'd laugh and say, damn, you got me. But he drove off. So now it's your turn. Tell me how the whole thing was a prank so that I can laugh."

There was silence. Jake couldn't explain away the tiny vibration of fear and uncertainty tickling the bottom of her heart no more than he could alleviate his own. Her sense of reality had been turned upside down. It must've been what Jericho was talking about when he'd told Jake to disappear from the lives of everyone he loved.

"Take me home," said Jake. The most depressing part of his new life was that he could not even share it with anyone.

He gave her directions, and she silently drove while Jake searched through containers to find his belongings. His pants were still on, albeit ripped and bloody. Half his shirt had been chewed up from the skidding wheels of the train. His shoes were mauled, unfit to wear. He sighed in relief when he found the tub with his identification, keys, credit cards, and most importantly, the black card Jericho had given him. He shoved everything back into his blood-stained pockets and waited. The sights and sounds of his neighborhood soon came into view.

The woman went around and opened the back door. Jake towered over her as his bare feet touched down on the black asphalt.

"What's your name?" asked Jake.

"Carrie Blake," she said. "Dr. Carrie Blake."

"Carrie, I would appreciate it if you didn't tell anyone about this."

"Like anyone would believe me. I'm a medical examiner. That job is weird enough. What would they think if I told them that the decapitated corpse I picked up grew another head and went home to his apartment? It's not my goal to be locked up in a rubber room, so . . . you don't have to worry about me. I'll just have to try and explain how I left the scene with several body parts, and I'm returning with a head and an arm." She gaped. "Wait, you grew back an arm too?"

Jake didn't have to look back at the gurney to answer. "Yeah," he said sheepishly. "I saw that when I was checking my clothes."

Jake took a small white sheet he found in the back of the van and draped it over his shoulders. With his head down, he shamefully walked toward his apartment building.

CHAPTER 28

S ome of Jake's neighbors gave him strange looks when he entered the foyer, all tattered and blood-stained, with a sheet draped over his shoulders. His feet ached on the cold concrete, and he flexed his toes one by one inside the sticky elevator. He opened the door to his apartment and went inside. The sheet slipped off his body as the door closed, and Jake headed straight to the bathroom and turned on the hot water. As the steam fogged up the bathroom mirror, he examined his face. His new head, he reminded himself and shuddered. Jake leaned in close, scrutinizing the skin by his left eye.

At the age of ten, Jake experienced the first life-changing event of his young life: the passing of his mother. They lived in Jamaica, Queens, right across the street from a park. His mother was fixing lunch in the kitchen when a bullet hit her right below the chin. Jake was the first to find her. He'd wandered in to ask why lunch was so late, and there was his mother, on the floor in a pool of blood.

He'd been unable to move, unable to scream, unable to do anything. After several minutes he backed out the door until he stood outside. To this day, he had no idea why he'd returned to his friends and never said anything about what he'd seen. His younger sister went inside the house an hour later. Mrs. Billows from next door saw her screaming down the street and came to her aide.

When they told him what happened, he refused to cry because he was ashamed. Everyone feared Jake seeing his mother dead might trigger a seizure, so he never saw her again. Not even at her funeral.

Jake's lack of action festered deep in his gut. He'd been as helpless as everyone thought he was. When one of his friends overheard some older kids claiming to know who shot his mom, guilt spurred him into action. He retrieved the .38 special his father had hidden in a shoebox in the back of the closet. He loaded the weapon and went to the park to confront his mother's killer.

It was late summer, a warm early evening just after 7:00 p.m. The clouds over the horizon held an orange hue. Shade from nearby trees sheltered the park. Over by the basketball courts, Jake spotted the guy talking with friends. He walked up slowly, trying his best to control the shaking. The person in question, Greg Wilson, had his back turned. When the pistol came out, everyone else ran. Greg turned around slowly to examine Jake, who was a few inches shorter than him. He looked down at the gun in Jake's hand and back into Jake's eyes.

"What the fuck is this, little nigga? You grow some balls? Let me see what you got, then."

Jake raised the weapon and cocked back the hammer. He pointed the barrel straight at Greg's chin, right where the bullet had entered his mother.

"So what's up? Think you a man now? Fuck. You point that at someone, you best shoot to kill. Ain't no fucking games out here, son. Leave the job undone, and I'll come back and kill your whole family, nigga." Greg pounded his chest with one hand several times. "You got the heart, motherfucker? Let's see it, then."

Greg stepped closer to the barrel, daring Jake. The weight of the gun seemed to grow with each second. He would never forget those brown eyes peering down on him like a giant, daring him to pull the trigger, intimidating young Jake to the point where the gun became too heavy to hold upright.

"That's what I thought, motherfucker!" He took the pistol from Jake's hand. "Now, I can't let you get away with that shit, can I?"

Greg hit Jake across the face with the butt of the gun just under the left eye. The gash squirted blood into the air, and Greg took off, scared. Jake tried to stop the bleeding with his hands until a neighborhood teen offered his shirt and pressed it against Jake's head. A few kids walked him home to his father. It took twelve stitches.

Jake examined his face in the steam-covered mirror and rubbed his index finger along the skin where the scar should've been. Smooth as silk. No trace of that injury nor the mark under his chin from when he'd fallen so hard during a seizure, he knocked out three teeth. Jake had paid for teeth implants several years ago. He grinned into the mirror. All his, every one.

"What the fuck? This is unreal."

In the shower, the lull of hot water didn't stop his mind from reeling. He thought about what the old man in hell had asked of him, to take the eye of Adonis Silver to save his soul, and Jake would be rewarded with paradise. He scoffed. Jake couldn't even shoot the man responsible for murdering his mother. After being killed twice, he should feel like death was no big deal. So why did the idea of taking an eye to save his soul seem so wrong?

He dried off with a towel, wrapped it around his waist, and then paused. The hand that he used to wrap the towel, the arm, the shoulder—all the muscles attached, they were also new. Jake put his right hand on his left shoulder to check it for seams or scars or some indication that he'd been cut in half and felt a rough patch. Jake turned his back to the mirror, and his heart jolted. The markings of hell splayed across his upper back. Jake counted seven.

With new information to digest, Jake headed toward the kitchen in need of a drink to help it go down. He picked out a new bottle of bourbon, Angel's Envy Rye, and poured himself a glass. He raised it to his lips and noticed someone sitting on the couch. The glass slipped out of his hand and hit the counter hard, shattering it into pieces and sending the bourbon everywhere.

The pint-sized pimp spread himself on the couch where Jericho had sat the day before, waiting. Jake eyed the front door, which was closed and latched, and then took in the pimp. He sported a purple silk shirt with the first three buttons undone, black bell-bottoms, and white alligator shoes. Thick gold Cuban links chained around his neck and lightly tinted sunglasses nestled in his tight curls. He also had a drink in his hand, pinky finger out, flashing a gold ring. He sipped noisily, barely touching the alcohol to his lips.

"Surprise, motherfucker!" said Katt. "I'm back!"

Jake rubbed a hand on his cheek. *This guy.* "Are you real?"

"The fuck is wrong with you? Yes, I am real and here to help you, trifling bitch! Maybe this time, listen to me. It'll save you a whole lot of pain."

"How did you get in here?"

"Through the fucking door, dumbass."

"And you poured yourself a drink of my bourbon?" asked Jake.

"I enjoy a good drink now and then. So yes, I took some bourbon."

Jake was going to teach this guy a lesson. Stalking him at work and the hospital was one thing. Breaking into his house was another. It was time to make a stand. Jake wasn't someone he could fuck with. He charged forward with the intent of extreme violence. He gripped the towel around his waist and raised his right hand behind his ear, balling his fingers into a tight fist. The muscles in his arm tensed. A straight right to the side of the head should put this little punk-bitch out for the count.

Jake shifted his weight and put his legs into the punch. It was goodnight for little Katt Williams. The little guy sprang to his feet before impact and slapped Jake across the side of the face with an open palm. His hand came down with enough force to drop Jake to his knees, knocking the towel from his waist.

Jake held the side of his face, slack-jawed. Impossible. He was twice the size of the little twerp. How did he do that?

"Who the fuck do you think you're fucking with, nigga?" asked the pimp. He stood over Jake beside the couch with glass of bourbon in hand, pinky extended, and hadn't spilled a single drop. "Look here, nigga, I ain't got no time for your shit."

Jake got to his feet, refusing to acknowledge what happened. His manhood was at stake. The little ninny couldn't have knocked him to the ground; the pipsqueak still bought his underwear in the little boy's section. He was a runt. Jake should be scraping him off the bottom of his shoe.

The first punch had been telegraphed, Jake decided. The next would be pure instinct. He relaxed his muscles then twitched to build speed like snapping a wet towel at the pool. His quick right was on target to land on the bottom of the chin. Lights out. Adios, motherfucker!

Jake watched Katt dip below the punch and could do nothing as his counter went straight for the groin. He grabbed a fistful of Jake's genitals and did not let go.

"It's like dangling a string in front of a cat! Can't have something like this slinging around in a fight and not expect someone to grab the rope and pull!"

He used Jake's momentum to sweep him off his feet.

"Stay down, bitch," said the pimp. "Down! Stay down, ya big-dick motherfucker!"

With each tug, the pain grew until Jake had to admit defeat. "I give up! Let go, damn it."

Jake held his hands up in surrender, breathing heavily. His face and penis throbbed with waves of pain.

Katt Williams let go. He dusted off his shoulder with the back of his manicured fingers, then took a sip of bourbon with an exaggerated "Ahhh."

"Who the fuck are you?" asked Jake from the floor, cupping his genitals and his cheek.

"I've been trying to introduce myself for about a week now, bitch. But you continue to ignore me, so I had to do something about that. We are one. A team. It's about time you come to grips with it." He touched his pinky to the tip of his tongue and ran it along an eyebrow. "I ain't going anywhere anytime soon."

"We're . . . one?" Jake's face twisted as he struggled to find the sanity in what he was about to ask next. "The parasite? You're the parasite?"

CHAPTER 29

A parasite that could manifest as flesh and blood. Something he could see, touch, and communicate with. Responsible for reviving him after being murdered—twice—by the same asshole. Standing over him at that very moment, just as real as anyone.

Jake laughed hysterically. "This keeps getting better," he said to himself, then shouted, "How are you hitting me when you're inside me?"

"I'm connected to your nerve endings, idiot. If I can put you back together, causing you pain is a piece of cake."

Jake shook his head. He waved his hand in front of his face. "You're standing right in front of me."

"Am I, though? Think about it. How would you react if I started talking inside your head? You'd lose your shit!"

"I'm not losing my shit right now?"

"As I said, I'm connected to all your impulses and feelings, but you'd lose your shit worse than this if I didn't present myself as a person."

"Son of a bitch, I've been to hell. Three times! Easing me into the notion that you can materialize in front of me is the least of my problems." Jake stood and found his towel. He wrapped himself up as he paced back and forth, staring at his new friend. "You look like Katt Williams. Why?"

Katt Williams sat back down on the couch, drink in hand, pinky extended. He sneered. "It's not my fault. That's on you."

"Really?" Jake leaned against the kitchen counter with his arms folded. "Oh, I can't wait to hear this explanation."

"I'm conjured from your imagination. You're the one with these images floating around in your head. I merely accessed them. I looked for a being you'd relate to that made you feel good." He swept his hand down his chest. "This is what I found."

"He's a comedian," said Jake. "He's funny. You're not funny! And how are you speaking? Where did you learn English?."

Katt stared in disbelief. "From you, nigga. From your mind. From your brain. From your thoughts. I said to myself; I need to communicate with this stupid motherfucker to keep him from getting killed. Again!"

"So you started talking," Jake said and snapped his fingers. "Just like that!"

"What a big dummy I ended up in," Katt said, looking to the heavens for help. "There are hundreds of languages. How can all those different words for *dog* all mean the same thing? The mind identifies a particular being as a dog, with the characteristics that fit *dog*, and sends a signal of understanding that this is what a dog is. Get it? I'm communicating through the impulses of understanding."

"What?"

"Nigga, you're a little slow, ain't you?" He sighed in frustration. "Let's play a game. If I told you to explain what it means to be anxious but only use one word, and you said *nervous*, and I said I didn't know what nervous meant, use another word, what would you say?"

"Edgy," answered Jake.

"If I said I didn't know the meaning of that word, what would you say?"

Jake shrugged his shoulders. "Uneasy."

"If I didn't know the meaning of uneasy, apprehensive, fretful, or scared, what would you say? If you've never felt anxiety, you can't understand its meaning. It's the same way you don't understand a language foreign to you. The word and the experience have to merge in your mind as one. Babies learn to speak this way."

The parasite was just confusing him. He walked over to the refrigerator and opened the top to the freezer. The cold air hit his chest as he grabbed a handful of ice for his aching junk. He pressed it against the towel. "I was told, with babies, it takes time for the brain to form."

"It takes time for the brain to go through the experiences of pain, fright, hunger, anguish, joy, and triumph, and learn the difference between them and water and juice and soda and everything else. You have to experience something before you can put words to it to describe it. When

I say I'm speaking through your impulses of understanding, I mean that I'm communicating directly with your experiences. It's your brain that's putting words to what I communicate. That's why I don't have to learn English to talk to you, you primitive dummy!"

"Fuck you," said Jake. Katt the parasite was aggravating. He squeezed his package and slapped him hard across the cheek. Now he was trying to educate Jake on communication. "Is there somewhere you can go? Like, permanently? Just stay out of my head forever? I have a lot going on right now, and I don't need . . ." Jake waved his hand at the two of them. ". . . this! Like these types of conversations. I walked around telling people Katt Williams was following me. How am I going to explain that?"

"I get it. Your pea brain can't handle what's inside of you. Cool. But you keep dying, motherfucker, and putting unnecessary strain on my person." He sloshed the bourbon around his glass. "By the way, you can call me Sly."

"Sly? Like Sly and the Family Stone?"

"No. That's not from your thoughts, nigga. That's the name I picked out for myself! That's my style, nigga. Sly."

"Unbelievable." Jake let out a nervous snicker. He looked Sly up and down. The pretentious fuck. Maybe he could exchange Katt, er, *Sly* for another parasite with a different personality. He'd ask Jericho the next time he saw him. "If you're not going to go away, then sit there on that couch quietly, all right?"

"I'm not a fucking fish in a tank, motherfucker! I'm in your head. I'm not actually sitting on your couch, and I can't be ignored. Don't forget how I've healed you."

Jake sidestepped the broken glass on the floor between the kitchen and the hallway leading to his bedroom. "Hey. If I step on any glass and cut my foot, just fix it and don't talk."

"Hilarious, asshole."

Jake took a roll of paper towels from the cabinet and got on his knees. He cleaned up the broken glass, sopped up the alcohol on the ground and checked for fine shards he might have missed. He spied ever so often for his new friend, Sly, still occupying the couch. Sly was completely self-absorbed. Pretentious. Always straightening out something on his person. As if his imaginary clothing could wrinkle or be out of place. He was brushing off the top of his white shoes when Jake had enough. "Is there a reason you are still hanging around?"

"Great question, dickhead. I'll tell you why I'm here. During the evolution of your species, as you got so smart, you thought that you could take care of things your damn self. You all seemed to have lost the ability to sense danger. Situations where adrenaline and reaction times should be through the roof, your dumbass doesn't have a clue. Like when that guy shoved you in front of the train. I tried to warn you!"

Jake recalled a few incidents and felt startled when he saw the glimmer of truth in Sly's words. Katt appeared when the Escalade parked at the diner, then again when he was in the hospital, and still again before Jericho pushed Jake from the platform. Still, Jake wouldn't believe it. "What dangerous situation am I in right now?" he snapped.

"The same situation as when you were pushed in front of that train. That guy couldn't trust you to stay out of your apartment for a week. I revived you in the van, thinking you would come to your senses, but apparently you're a slow learner. You made a beeline right back here, first thing."

"Are you telling me the Russians are here?" asked Jake.

"Yes, ya big dummy! They're outside as we speak."

CHAPTER 30

Jake rushed over to the window and peeked through the blinds. A service worker in blue Dickies, construction hat, and tool belt approached. Jake traced the worker's path back to the street, where a white van was parked. The decal said something about a locksmith, but he couldn't make out the company's name. It was dark outside and the streetlamps didn't provide enough illumination. It didn't strike him as out of place, yet Sly's presence made him leery.

Earlier that day, Jericho had said the Russians were looking take his computer stuff, something they wanted copied from the CEO's computer. If there were questionable files, Jake snatched them, that was for sure. He took everything. He was sure it was on his laptop, but only on his laptop. He didn't use any other equipment while hacking. No backups. Easy to dispose if anyone sought prosecution. The hard drives piled in his bedroom were from random projects. No big loss if they took them.

Early evening was when the streets were scattered with people coming home from work. Plenty of curious eyes all around. So how might they get into his apartment? Kicking the door down would be senseless. Sending a locksmith would be less suspicious. This locksmith could pretend the building manager had ordered the locks changed for failure to pay rent. No one would question that. The new set of keys could be passed on to the Russians to enter anytime they wanted.

Jake focused on the Escalade parked on the opposite side of the street. Same one he saw outside the diner when Sly first appeared.

"Shit," said Jake.

"Now do you believe me?" said Sly, relaxing comfortably on the couch.

Jake ran to the bedroom and grabbed some clothes. Underwear, socks, shoes, jeans and a black tee shirt. His jacket, wallet, and keys were on the counter. He had less than ten seconds if the elevator was waiting on the first floor. Jake ran to the door with the towel still wrapped around his waist, clothes and wallet jumbled up in his arms. Jake sped down the hallway past the row of shiny brown doors.

"Not that way, dummy," said Sly, right behind him from out of nowhere.

Right. There were two stairwells, one to the left and one to the right. Each led to a different entrance, front and rear. Jake put his shoulder on the door leading to the front. Everyone knew that way into the building. If the Russians were waiting for the locksmith to finish, they'd most likely remain within eyesight of the work van. Only residents knew about the rear entrance. Jake swiveled and took two giant steps, then leaned into the access to the other stairwell as the elevator doors opened. He caught a glimpse of the locksmith entering his floor before Jake disappeared down the stairs.

He checked for people between the second and third floor, then pulled his underwear up under the towel wrapped around his waist. Next came his jeans and black tee shirt. Then he sat on the stairs and put on his socks and shoes. He filled his pockets with his keys, wallet, spare phone and threw on his jacket.

Sly looked up and down Jake's clothing with a look of disapproval. "Shit's all skintight." He pinched the edge of Jake's pants. "Nothing can breathe. And look at those pants. I can see your ankles. Those are Capris, nigga. A man's ankles should not be exposed like that, dog."

Jake ignored Sly and made his way down to the first floor. He peeked out the rear entrance door. All clear. He adjusted his jacket and strode outside. *Be cool, Jake.* The plan was to calmly walk as far away from his apartment as he could. The little guy, Sly, strutted next to him.

He knew it was petty, but Jake couldn't let it slide. The audacity of some parasite thinking he knew what style was when he was walking around in a Rudy Ray Moore pimp suit was too much. His focus should have been escaping the Russians, yet the irritation about wardrobe comparisons swelled in his chest. Jake spotted Sly adjusting the collar on his purple pimp shirt and erupted.

"The hell do you know about style," said Jake, snorting. "Your wardrobe is laughable."

"Oh, I am cool. Alligator skin shoes and silk shirts? That's cool. What you got on is three sizes too small. You like one of them niggas in the ballet. Shit going all up in your butt crack."

Jake listened for sounds in the stairwell. Above then below the third floor. No one there except for him. He went down the landing to the second floor and then the first. He paused to listen a second time. Sly stood across from Jake and pulled the front of his shirt near the waist to ensure the material was not bunched up from running down the stairs. But he was not running at all. Why was he thinking about this now? The Russians were his immediate threat. Sly was only in his head. In a quandary, Jake erupted again.

"Styles change," said Jake. "If you got your knowledge from my brain, then you'd know this look is in. Not that seventies pimp-shit you're wearing."

"See, that's your problem," said Sly. "You said this look is in, and another look is out."

"That's right! And I must be crazy arguing about this with a fucking parasite."

"You don't have to explain shit to me. I know what I like, but you're a bit confused. See, there's a lot of influence mixed in with what you like. You're busy fussing over what others are wearing while I'm free to look at things objectively and pick out what I like without social influence. Truth is, you're wearing that because other people think it's cool. You're trying to impress them, while I wear what I like. Deep down, you still don't know what you like. You only like 'what's good.'"

Jake was mortified. "I'm ashamed of myself for arguing with you."

Jake flung the door open and crossed the street headed for the bus station. He kept his head down and walked straight. Low profile. But the problem was his height. Wherever he went, he was typically head and shoulders above the average person. He boarded the bus to East Orange, about a ten-minute ride. Being close to the football stadium was his best option. His height would serve as a cover. People often assumed he was an athlete. If the Russians had their spies combing the city, he wouldn't stand out near the stadium.

He was angry and frustrated. Alive but on the run. In hiding until things settled down. He couldn't contact anyone, even to say he was okay. No work and no computer.

Jake got off the bus right near a small shopping center. Across the overpass, he could see the stadium in the distance. He was close to a cluster of hotels, a Walmart, a grocery store, and plenty of places to eat. Jake found a nice little restaurant that didn't appear too crowded and ducked inside. Mexican, his favorite.

A slim teenager with short brown hair and a piercing in his nose greeted Jake up front and swiped a menu. There were open tables but Jake asked for a booth in the back. When Jake slid in one side, Sly slid in on the other.

Jake rolled his eyes in his head. "What do you want?" asked Jake. "Is someone in the restaurant trying to kill me? You seem to pop up whenever I am eating."

"I want to talk," said Sly.

"Talk about what?" Jake snapped.

"Anything. You have all this, and you don't want to share it with me."

"All what?"

"A life with others," Sly explained. "I get lonely sometimes."

It surprised Jake. He didn't expect Sly to be sensitive. In a softer tone. "Well, you irritate me, and I look crazy talking to you since no one else can see you." Jake panned around at the tables of patrons that were visible. "Can't you talk to me in my mind?"

Sly sighed. "I said this before, if I talked to you using your neural pathways, how would you tell the difference between your thoughts and mine? You'd be confused."

"No. Whenever I would sound like a dick I would know it's you."

"Ah . . . my personality," said Sly, leaning back in his seat. "It offends you," he said with his eyes widening at *offends*.

"What do you know about personality, parasite?" Jake snapped.

"See, this is what happens when I try to be nice to a motherfucker. This is my personality, so get used to it. If you can't handle it, I suggest you drink heavily because I'm not going away, and I'm tired of staying quiet. The only time you won't see me is when I am sleeping or doing something else."

"You sleep?"

"Nigga, did I not say that I am alive? Did I not say that I am a living creature? Okay, well, living things go! To! Sleep!" he enunciated, clapping on the last three syllables. "They get rest. What planet are you from?"

Jake rubbed his head after pushing the menu across the table. Fuming once more. Sly sat with his arms crossed, uptight and offended. Sly fumbled with his collar, then sleeves and did the tip of the pinky to the eyebrows swipe, which infuriated Jake. No one else can see him!

The server, a Pacific Islander with hazel eyes and dark hair to her waist, came to the table just in time to break the uncomfortable silence. She placed a basket of chips with a cup of salsa on the table and introduced herself. Jake spied the menu earlier, so he rattled off his order.

"Two Jalisco burrito dinners, two enchiladas, two chicken fajitas, a #4, #12, a #14 with extra guacamole, one Mountain Dew, and keep the chips and salsa coming," said Jake.

She jotted it all down. "You must be working out hard at the gym," she said. "Need that protein for muscle mass."

"Yeah, carbs, sugars, all that stuff for energy," said Jake.

She smiled. "I'll put that in, and your food should be out shortly."

"You have no idea what the fuck you're talking about, do you?" said Sly.

He was like a gnat biting just hard enough to get you to smack yourself, only to fly away unharmed. He glared sideways at Sly and shook it off. Made no sense to give him any energy. He wanted to talk? Jake was going to give him the silent treatment.

The server walked away which gave Jake the opportunity to check her out. Being distracted by Sly when she approached the table, he did not get a chance to take it all in. She reminded him of Catalina. Something about how her hips swayed left to right, like a seductive dance. Catalina danced all the time. She used to snap those Brazilian hips in front of him while he plugged away on his laptop, trying to distract him. And he'd always get distracted.

"Mmm . . . Damn!" said Sly. He licked his lips. "Oh shit. What is this? I like this kinda party!"

"Stop it," said Jake. "What the fuck is wrong with you?"

"You looked at her, drifted off somewhere and—damn! That shit feels good."

"What?" He'd been picturing sliding his hand along Catalina's hip, down the outside of her thigh and back up the inside, all the way to . . . "Are you kidding me?"

An image of Sly hovering over him and moaning while Jake had sex was at the back of his brain. Was this how his future with women was going to be? Having sex with a peeping parasite in the closet?

"Ah, man," said Sly. "I can't wait to experience sex! It's one of the few things about you that I'm looking forward to. Hold up." Sly leaned in. "Your manhood shriveled. Are you ashamed of sex?"

"I am not ashamed of sex!" Jake shouted. A few customers looked his way. He shook his head, flustered, and whispered. "I'm not talking to you about this."

"Why the hell does talking about sex have you in a tizzy?" Sly barked, laughing. "Seems like a great thing. You should do it all the time. Why are you blushing like you want to curl up in a ball and hide?"

"I said, I'm not talking to you about this," said Jake through gritted teeth.

"Well, that's just crazy. Something gives you a great feeling, and you want to walk around bashful. What kind of species are you? Weak as hell, is what I say." Sly rested his arms on the back of the booth. A toothpick appeared in the corner of his mouth. He rolled it along his tongue. "Weak as fuck. No ability to detect danger. Embarrassed talking about sex. How the hell have you all survived for so long?"

The server came back with a tall glass of Mountain Dew. She bounced on the balls of her feet. "I brought an extra bowl of chips at your request." She placed it on the table next to his drink and gave him a great big smile. Her eyes gleamed. "Is there anything else I can get you?"

"Ask the girl if she wants to fuck!" suggested Sly. "We can tap that ass and then crash at her place for the week. No place else to go. Ask the girl, Jake."

Jake ignored him. "No, that's it," he said to the server. "Thanks."

"I heard that Asian va-jay-jay goes sideways!" said Sly.

"Where the fuck did you hear that, you damn parasite?" Jake stopped breathing and locked eyes with the server. They looked at each other mortified, each holding their breaths.

"That was weird, huh?" she finally said, exhaling and nodding for him to agree.

Jake mirrored her, then shook his head. "I'm sorry. It's—it's a steroid thing. It messes with the mind. Causes coprolalia."

"Did you just admit taking steroids?" she asked.

"What? No! Of course not. That's illegal. Don't mind me. I ramble."

"Part of your condition?" she asked, eyebrow arched.

Jake coughed. "Yep."

"What's that again? Coprolalia?"

"Shouting uncontrolled obscenities," Jake confirmed.

"I thought that was Tourette's," she said.

"Tourette's syndrome is often associated with uncontrolled obscenities because of *South Park*, but that's incorrect. Tourette's is primarily facial twitching."

"I see," she said.

"Boy, you killed that chemistry," remarked Sly. He'd been watching them with a smirk. "What a dork. She just put her panties back on. And we're homeless. Thanks a lot, Jake."

"I'm going to go back there and check on your food," she said, hurrying away.

"At least I can look forward to a good meal," said Sly. He slapped his hands together greedily. "Unless you want to fuck that up too."

They sat in silence until the food came. Another server delivered the stacks of plates. Once again, Sly's presence led to Jake inadvertently insulting another woman. He paused to give thanks and tore into his meal, barely coming up for a breath. Sly disappeared sometime during the meal, which was fine with Jake. His new friend was troublesome. Learning how to put him away would prove to be useful.

He was on his ninth cup of Mountain Dew when he decided that hanging around East Orange was a no-go. The exchange with the server convinced Jake that pretending to be a professional athlete wasn't a good idea. He couldn't bullshit his way through it, and he'd probably gotten the athletes at the facility some mandatory steroid testing. He needed a better cover and time to think things over.

CHAPTER 31

A lexei's small efficiency apartment had little in the way of furniture. The walls were bare, but several brown water stains decorated the ceiling. The varnish on the faded wooden floor creaked when he walked across it. The kitchen was tiny—just an old, dirty yellow gas stove with missing knobs and a stained porcelain sink. He cooked his food in a microwave, which sat on a dingy, white Formica countertop, warped and bowed from water damage. A bed, a nightstand, a small desk, and a chair completed the dismal scene. That was it. Visitors sat on the bed—if it was made. Most of the time, it was not.

He laid in bed while the sun crept through the closed blinds and listened to the sounds of people outside his apartment. He hadn't slept all night; his mind was preoccupied with being pegged for murder. Not in California, but local.

Last night, Zachary told him that a Newark coroner had picked up Jake Coltrane's body. Jake Coltrane, who was not chopped up and dumped in the river. He was not burned beyond recognition or loaded into a 55-gallon drum and filled with battery acid. No, Jake Coltrane had been pushed in front of a speeding train.

Complete bullshit.

Alexei was a bit worried. Only a single fiber of hair was needed to link Alexei to that body. And cameras surely had recorded him outside Jake's hotel room. Jericho could buy his way out of incrimination, but Alexei wouldn't be as fortunate.

He should've never trusted Jericho to clean it up.

Alexei stared up at the cracked and stained ceiling from his bed. His phone buzzed on the nightstand, and he reached over and unplugged it from the charger. His thick index finger swiped the screen. A message from Zachary. It was time to have a visit with the coroner.

He messaged Zachary to come and pick him up, then walked through the kitchen to the cramped bathroom. One step across the white octagonal-tiled floor, and he was standing in the shower. He pulled the moldy plastic shower curtain shut and faced the grime that streaked from the base of the nozzle to the floor of the stall. Then he relieved himself down the shower drain. After a few quick turns of the knob, water sprang from the limescale-encrusted showerhead. It took a few seconds for the water to warm, and he stood beneath it as it went from ice-cold to scalding hot.

After the shower, he dressed in his signature black ensemble. Some compared him to a cheap imitation of *Men in Black*, but the movie wasn't where he'd gotten the look. His style was more like John Belushi in *The Blues Brothers*. He loved that movie, extravagant police chases and all.

He sunk his bottom on the unmade bed and waited for Zachary. Five minutes later, his phone buzzed again. He looked at it, put his hands on his knees, and heaved his weight onto his feet. He walked out and down the narrow stairway. It creaked and strained under his weight, and his head barely cleared the dangling light bulb at the base of the entranceway.

Zachary had the Suburban parked by the curb. Alexei went down the concrete stairs and opened the passenger door. The car sank as he planted himself in the seat.

"How did you sleep?" asked Zachary.

"Peachy," said Alexei. "Did Maxim get the computer stuff?"

"He delivered it last night to the warehouse," said Zachary. "It's going to take some time for our people to get into it. Everything is password protected. Luckily, the hacker left a list of old passwords in a book in the apartment. That should help speed things up."

"Great!" Alexei reached over his shoulder to grab the seatbelt and clicked it in place at the waist. "You tell me Jericho has no people working in the morgue, correct?"

"No one."

"Then how do they figure this was a good place to dump the body? The hacker has been dead for nearly a week, and there are close to thirty stab wounds in his body, including one straight to the heart. By now, the coroner will have examined the body and discovered that the hacker did not jump."

"Yes, boss. An unusual way to get rid of a body. Unless he wanted you to go down for it."

Alexei cracked his knuckles by interlacing his fingers and stretching them out far in front of him. "Jericho wanted to get some stupid program from the hacker," said Alexei. "We argued about it."

"On his computer?"

"Yes and no." Alexei became engrossed in thought, considering everything. "The program was on the computer, but I don't think Jericho took the laptop. He asked the hacker how long to deliver the program. I'm confused by that."

"Think of it like your phone," said Zachary. "It does many things, but when you load an app on the phone, the whole program is not on the phone. The app only allows you to access the information from somewhere else. There must be a big computer somewhere that has the program. That is what Jericho was after. With the hacker dead, he must figure out where that program is stored."

"So there is a good chance Jericho does not have the laptop as he said," said Alexei. "Could he have dumped it with the body?"

"Possibly," said Zachary. "That is what we are going to find out."

"Good," said Alexei. "Now we are getting somewhere. The hacker wrote the username and password for his laptop on a little sticky note. It should still be with the laptop. But wait. If he had the laptop on him when the train hit, it is now in pieces."

"No sweat," said Zachary. "They can do wonders rebuilding a hard drive. Trust me. It will not be a problem if it is in pieces."

"Even better," said Alexei. "Let's go."

It took forty minutes to weave through the busy morning traffic. Alexei was preoccupied with the possibility that he had made an enemy of Jericho Black. He saw no recourse if Jericho was retaliating somehow. Jericho's finances were so entrenched with Russia that the *Vory* would never be permitted to lash out against him. Especially for a lowly hitman like Alexei.

The turnpike connecting New York to New Jersey flowed like a slow stream. They found the Newark exit and arrived at the Essex County morgue just off South Orange Avenue. Zachary drove into the lot and parked near the two-story brick building on the side closest to the employee entrance. He sent a text message to his man on the inside, and they waited by the door.

"Can you trust this guy?" asked Alexei.

"I don't know," said Zachary. "Never met him. He is supposedly doing this for a sizable amount of product. Party drugs. I'm guessing he can be trusted, or else Carlos would not have suggested it."

They were surprised when a petite woman in blue scrubs poked her head outside. Apparently, their inside guy couldn't be trusted.

"Can I help you, gentlemen?" she asked. She looked Indian, maybe Black, possibly Hispanic. Light freckles on her face. Childlike.

"Yes," said Zachary. "I was told someone could help me."

"I'm Dr. Carrie Blake, one of the medical examiners here. I was getting ready to end my shift when I saw you on camera. How can I help you?"

"We're waiting for one of your coworkers," said Zachary.

"No one else is here right now. The Chief Medical Examiner is on vacation this week. Is there anything I can help you with?"

They looked at each other. Plans never go as smoothly as first drawn up, so they were accustomed to improvising. But they had to tread lightly, as they needed a contact on the inside they could control.

"We will return later," said Alexei. "This is a business visit involving a cadaver named Jake Coltrane."

"Jake?" said Carrie.

"Yes," said Zachary. "The man who took his life the other day. He jumped in front of a train."

"Oh... um... yes."

Alexei noticed dark circles under her eyes. He nodded goodbye. They were halfway to the car when he noticed Dr. Blake following them into the parking lot. She waved them down. She looked apprehensive. Nervous. Maybe she was the one they were supposed to meet.

"Are you lawyers?" she asked. "From Jake's family?"

"He is the lawyer," said Zachary, pointing to Alexei. "I am his assistant."

Alexei played along. "We noticed certain inconsistencies, and we want to inspect them for ourselves." He was trying to sound like a lawyer but had no idea why a lawyer would go to the morgue. Why would she ask if they were lawyers? Seems suspicious. Engage her.

"Listen," said Dr. Blake. Her eyes and voice were jittery. "I reported the van with his body as missing, not stolen. I was the one who retrieved the body from the train station yesterday. There's no reason to get authorities involved at this point. My assistant has the van, and he'll be back shortly. Please tell the family this issue will be resolved by tonight, at the latest. This has never happened before, and we're sorry."

Alexei and Zachary traded glances. Perhaps Jericho's people knew what they were doing, after all. It didn't make much sense to throw a body in front of a train to steal it again later, but who knew what amateurs were thinking

"Jake worked for a computer company," said Alexei. "Their lawyers contacted us about an important project he was working on. Just to let you know, his computer was paid for by the business, so technically, it does not belong to Jake. Did he have the laptop on him when he jumped? We need to know if it is still serviceable. Even if we get something like the motherboard or any memory chips, that would be helpful to his employer. This is of utmost importance."

"National security," added Zachary. "He worked for a government contractor. Very sensitive stuff that cannot fall into the wrong hands. Did you collect any computer parts among his possessions?"

"National security?" asked Carrie. She looked them up and down. "Well, I was there to collect the body that morning, and we logged everything. A computer wasn't among the items collected."

"Do you think your assistant had something to hide?" asked Zachary. "Why would he drive off with the body?"

"I told you. He had an emergency. I—I went through this already with my boss." She squinted. "What law firm do you work for again?"

"A small one," said Alexei. "I doubt you have heard of it. We work for the billionaire Jericho Black. Have you heard of Jericho Black?"

She shook her head. "Not really."

"Not really? What does that mean? Do you know of Jericho or not?"

"Not!" Her eyes darted between the two of them. "Listen, I'm swamped. I need to get back to work." She moved to return to the building.

"Just a few more questions," said Alexei. He grabbed her arm. She looked down, startled, and Alexei let go. "I promise it won't be long. It would help us greatly if we had a name for the guy with the missing van."

"For national security," said Carrie, unconvinced.

"Yes," said Alexei. "This worker of yours may try to pawn the computer for money. We want to put out the word at the pawnshops nearby, just in case. That is why we need a name."

"Sorry, I can't give you a name. That's confidential."

"You have no idea where he is," said Alexei, eyes narrowing.

Carrie shook her head firmly. "No laptop at the scene. None recorded into evidence. No body here at the morgue."

"Can we see the record of everything found at the station?"

"That was in the van," said Carrie.

"I see," said Alexei. "There is no record of anything. Except what you can remember."

"There was no laptop! I can remember that! Excuse me, but I have to get back." She hurried away.

"What was the condition of the body?" Alexei blurted before she could leave.

"His condition?" said Carrie, turning back toward Alexei.

Alexei walked closer to her. She was shaken by the question. "Could you tell how long he had been dead? Were any other wounds found on his body?" said Alexei.

Carrie swallowed hard. "What do you mean?"

"I mean, was he already dead when the train hit him," said Alexei.

Dr. Blake's lower lip trembled. "Has he come back from the dead before this?"

"Before?" asked Alexei.

Alexei and Zachary exchanged looks.

"Back from the dead?" asked Zachary.

Carrie opened her mouth, then closed it. Her hands shook, and she balled them into fists at her side. "Sorry, I have no time for this. Your laptop is not here." She spun around, but Alexei cut her off.

"Wait," said Alexei. He plastered a smile on his face. "I did not mean to frustrate you. For this, I am sorry. My English is not so good sometimes. I meant to say, are you sure that he was alive before the train accident. No one had heard from him for several days. He had not come into work. No one could contact him by phone. Then suddenly he jumps in front of a train. When you look at the body, you can tell if something was wrong, right? You are a doctor."

"You mean if he had been dead and was somehow still walking around like a zombie."

"No, no, not like a zombie," said Zachary. "Let's not get cute. You are the one who talked about 'back from the dead.'"

She glared up at Alexei, who was more than a foot taller and three times her weight. Reluctantly, Alexei took several steps back, clearing her path back toward the building. She took a few steps and then stopped to turn around.

"Can I get a business card from you or something?" asked Carrie. "When the police release the evidence, I can give you a call if you like."

Alexei patted his chest. "Sorry, fresh out."

CHAPTER 32

One day into his weeklong hideout and Jake was already stir-crazy. Jericho asked if he could trust Jake to stay hidden just before he shoved him in front of the train. He thought that would put Jake out of commission for a week. But Sly brought him back within hours so Jake was hiding from both Jericho and the Russians. Catalina was constantly on his mind and he knew it was wrong to get her involved. He fought hard against the urge to text her. And if Jericho found out, he might run Jake through a meat grinder next.

Bottom line, stay hidden.

With the entire country his to explore he only got as far as an hour south of his apartment. He thought about going farther, perhaps into Delaware or Maryland, but he was scared of leaving the big city for the south. The thought was uncomfortable. He settled for a cheap hotel room outside Trenton, New Jersey.

The place smelled damp and musty, the carpet worn smooth by the door. The end table by the side of the bed had a leg missing, and the burgundy chair beside it was soiled with something he didn't have the stomach to inspect. But overall, the place served its purpose. He had a roof over his head.

With nothing to do except watch television, Jake tossed the black card Jericho had given him into the air and caught it. He looked at the name on the card. Ernesto Flores etched on the front. With no other form of identification this sleazy hotel was the only thing that fit the criteria. No cameras and no one asked questions.

Jake went into the bathroom and clicked on the lights. He was greeted with mildew between tiles and a toilet with permanent stains in the bowl. The mirror above the sink was large and clean. He stared motionless before turning his back and pulling up the black tee to examine the marks spanning his shoulders. Hell was real. He had the scars to prove it. The patterns were outlined, like a tattoo that hadn't been filled in yet. The next time they caught him, one would get filled in. Those were the rules. Seven chances to get through hell's maze by avoiding Hell's Apostles.

Jake slid the tee shirt back over his head and went to lay down on the bed. The sheets were rough and the bed hard but it was the only thing he was willing to let touch him. Thoughts of the marks on his back lead to the old man from Aruru's dollhouse. *If the eye causes one to sin it is best to pluck it out.*

Adonis Silver was the name the old man gave him. He had never considered saving someone from sin before. That was the job of priests and preachers. Everyone else is responsible for saving their own souls. Besides, this guy could be anywhere in the world. How would he find the right one? Jake gathered he was a young man.

He pulled out his phone and typed *Adonis Silver* into a search engine. There was one person in the tristate area with that name, a student at Pembroke High School in Hempstead, Long Island. Brown hair, brown eyes, fair skin, athletic build, attractive. He looked for other pictures online. Anything that linked him to the old man in hell. An obituary of a Joseph Silver popped up in a search from a local paper in Long Island. He clicked the link. The image was a strong likeness to the old man. He was survived by a grandson and his family. One of the great grandchildren was named Adonis. He was the guy.

Jake's first guess was that Adonis was planning to shoot up the high school. What else would a kid his age be capable of doing that would land him in hell? But he seemed like a stable kid. Honor student. Popular. Physically gifted. Not the ostracized, bullied type easily pushed over the edge. His sins must be deeper. Jake was curious.

He ran the facial recognition app to track Adonis Silver. The program quickly detected his image on a mall security camera. With nothing better to do, Jake checked out of the hotel, early afternoon, and took the Amtrak into Grand Central Station. He took the Long Island Rail into Hempstead, Long Island. Instead of transferring via buses, he called an Uber, taking him right to the mall. Three hours had passed, and Adonis was still there. Jake checked the recognition software on his phone for a current location. The food court.

He stepped into the mall to put eyes on him. The large mall was shiny and new. The directory put the food court at the other end. He passed Nordstrom and North Face. Turned right towards Coach and Michael Kors. Made a left at Crate and Barrel and past the Godiva store. This was an upper-middle-class to upper-class kind of mall. Anytime Jake saw a Godiva chocolate store he was nowhere near the hood.

It was full of consumers, primarily young adults and teens, plastic bags in hand, leisurely strolling from store to store. A weekend afternoon. Most teens were there to hang out. Which is what he assumed Adonis was doing. He was sitting alone in front of a sandwich shop, sipping a milkshake, and writing in a notebook. Jake found a nice spot next to a store selling adjustable comfort mattresses at the edge of the food court. He had a clear view of Adonis Silver. He had on a black tee shirt with an anime character on the front, blue jeans, sneakers, and a backpack in the chair beside him.

Jake tried to look casual. Pretend he was waiting for someone to finish shopping. Then Sly appeared next to Jake and soured his mood. He was fidgeting with the cuffs on his new shirt. Then he began messing with his hair. It was parted in the middle, extended down to his shoulders, and curled upward slightly. His white silk shirt sported a sizable open collar and he wore gray pants with matching alligator shoes.

When he finished making sure every thread was in its proper place he said, "I see you're about to get yourself in trouble again."

"Right," said Jake with a sneer.

"What's this all about?"

"Some recon work, that's all."

"I can see that, fool! Why?"

"Don't you know already? Aren't you a part of me?"

"I'm in your body, not combing through your thoughts. Spill the beans, asswipe."

Jake clenched his teeth. "I was told that if I saved this kid's soul, I'd be free from the tortures of hell for all eternity."

"Hell?" said Sly. "Fantastic. How do we save the kid?"

"By taking his eye."

"Brilliant," said Sly. "Who came up with that plan?"

"It's in the scripture," said Jake. "If your eye causes you to sin, pluck it out, for it's better to enter the Kingdom of God with one eye than have two . . . or something like that."

"Mm-hm, mm-hm," said Sly, nodding. "You do realize that's not meant to be taken literally, right?"

"Piss off."

Sly stepped in front of Jake to get his attention. "I don't like this!"

Jake pushed him away when he noticed Adonis suddenly looked up and followed a woman riding down the escalator with his eyes. She was of average height, with light brown hair tied tight in a bun and a thin jacket over a blouse with slacks and high-heeled shoes. A white plastic bag with a logo dangled from her fingertips. She hit the bottom of the escalator and strolled straight through the food court with a graceful air about her, although she walked with purpose.

Jake could sense something was up when Adonis put the milkshake down on the table and stood. He snatched his notebook, then weaved his way through several tables to get right behind the woman, about three paces behind.

"Is he a thief or something?" said Jake. "Is that his sin?"

"Not quite," said Sly. "This guy is a little more dangerous than that."

Jake turned. "Why would you say that?" asked Jake.

"You'll see," said Sly.

The woman looked to her left at Jake as she passed by. Jake froze, thinking she'd seen him talking to no one like a nutcase. Then she glimpsed Adonis following and turned all the way around to confront him. She spoke. His face widened in surprise, but soon they were smiling at each other and chatting away. He seemed very much at home talking to this woman who was probably in her early thirties and flirtatious toward him. They headed for the exit together.

Jake caught his breath and sighed in relief.

"You need to follow them," said Sly.

"No way! She looked right at me. She will think I'm stalking her."

"You are. She's in danger."

"He's going to do something now? Fuck!"

Jake wasn't prepared for this. Was Adonis a rapist? Did he abduct women and hold them against their will? Was it more like blackmail? Did he have weapons in the backpack?

"Get going Jake," said Sly.

Jake made sure they got at least twenty paces ahead before pretending to check the time and getting behind them. They walked side by side saying very little to each other. They came to the first set of doors, and the woman reached in her purse for her phone. She put it to her ear, then hung up in frustration. Adonis held open the second set of doors leading outside. She walked through. A flock of pigeons took flight, and she disappeared from Jake's view.

There was a scream.

Jake took off running and pushed through the doors. He squinted in the sun. A long stone stairway led from the entrance to the street. A trail of blood marked the stairs about halfway down. Jake ran down the stairs to get a closer look. His heart was racing. What did he do? Adonis held the door open. That was all.

The woman had landed on her back with her eyes open, hair strewn across her face. A bulge at the side of her neck gave Jake the impression that her spine was no longer connected to her skull. She was dead.

How?

He jogged up the stairs as Adonis, carefully avoiding the blood of the woman he'd just met, made his way down. Their eyes met. Jake felt a pang of danger. It was weird. Perhaps he had imagined it.

Adonis got to the bottom of the stairs and walked past the scene at the bottom without looking. He left the mall grounds on foot, seemingly without a care in the world.

CHAPTER 33

M ost of the mall customers were outside viewing the accident involving the woman who tumbled down the stairs. Jake wanted no part of it. Reminded him too much of the spectacle on the train platform when the train cut him in half. He wondered if the woman could see and hear what was going on before dying like he did. He walked back inside to the food court and was hit with intense hunger pains. Ever since he'd returned from hell the first time, he had the belief that he could eat a cow. The entire thing.

There were at least ten different vendors to choose from and Jake hit each one.

Joey Chestnut is going down, Jake thought as he carried his food-laden trays through the mall cafeteria.

Jake sat down at an empty table near a column in the food court center. He had a little of everything: burgers, Chinese food, Mexican food, Thai food, pizza, Peruvian chicken, fried chicken, subs, and for a snack, three soft pretzels. He unwrapped his first sandwich and quickly shoveled the twelve-inch hero into his mouth. Down it went.

Sly appeared next to him. Most of his appearances revolved around eating. He was leaning back with his legs crossed, admiring the scenery.

"I'll go broke if this continues," Jake mumbled through a mouthful. "I can't afford to eat like this every meal."

"You used the credit card Jericho gave you, so hush. And you won't have to eat like this every meal. Just the meals before or after I have to expend a ton of energy."

"Energy you steal from my body because you're a parasite."

"Small price, I'd say."

"I ate like this yesterday after you revived me. Wasn't that enough?"

Sly didn't answer. He sat beside Jake swirling whiskey in a glass, and stared straight ahead.

Jake shrugged and took a bite of tender Peruvian chicken. Damn good. He woofed it down, then picked the bones clean and licked his fingers. He started on the mashed potatoes, finished with fried plantains, and washed it down with about half a liter of Coke. A large, satisfying burp gurgled from his throat. He unwrapped a bacon double cheeseburger.

"In most cases, parasites introduce diseases into their hosts," said Jake. "I'm not going to have a strange disease, am I?"

Sly took a sip of whiskey holding the glass with his fingertips. "My side effect is saving your ass. Regrowing tissues, and such. Be thankful instead of complaining."

Sly's words struck something deep inside Jake's sense of reality, and he put down the cheeseburger. The parasite hadn't only replicated tissue. It had regrown an entire head in less than six hours—skull, bones, and brain. Jake had been decapitated, and his arm severed. Now he had a new arm and a new head.

Jake looked inside his palm as he opened and closed his hand. "How is that possible?" wondered Jake. "I mean, I feel like me. I have my memories. Wasn't all of *me* in my brain—the brain in my other head sitting in the morgue? How can I still recall my life? I shouldn't be conscious of who I was, er, *am*. Why doesn't any of this make sense?"

Sly swirled the alcohol around the glass by rotating his wrist. "Your primitive brain can't comprehend it. Your species seems to take pride in intelligence, yet you only use one gauge to measure intelligence: your species. Other species have all kinds of advanced, complex bits of intelligence, but because it's different from yours—they can't build a computer or a skyscraper or read and write—you think of them as beneath you. You drink and smoke and do drugs and engage in all sorts of destructive behavior, then refer to yourselves as the intelligent ones. Hell, you think a guy is a genius simply because he has a lot of money. How stupid is that?"

"Isn't that a drink in your hand?" asked Jake. "You kind of look like a hypocrite talking about destructive behavior."

"This image of me is forged from your memories, stupid. How many times do I have to tell you that?"

"Well, you didn't answer my question. What does any of that shit have to do with me having a completely different brain with the same memories?"

Sly issued a long-suffering sigh and took a sip, letting the liquor barely touch his lips. "Mice inherit knowledge from one generation to the next. That means that knowledge can be stored in reproductive organs and passed on. Instincts are nothing more than learned knowledge passed on through DNA. Memories and thoughts are not as unique as you think."

Jake bit into a double cheeseburger, deep in thought. Then he unwrapped two burritos and finished one, then another. He spotted some hot sauce packets and squeezed them all over a plate of drunken Thai rice. He ate it all and washed it down with another half-liter of Mountain Dew.

"In your opinion, mice are more advanced than humans?" asked Jake.

Sly shrugged. "Why not? Think of what your species could accomplish if you could pass knowledge and experience on to your young as mice can. Your civilization's advancement came only when written knowledge was shared and used properly. Your species had to create ways to pass on life experience. I wouldn't call that as advanced as a mouse, would you?"

"Yes, I would. Reading and writing is genius. So are rich people. Genius," Jake sputtered, shaking his head. "Comparing us to a fucking mouse. Just tell me how you got my memories from the old brain to the new one."

"Since you weren't paying attention . . . DNA. I'll dumb it down so that a computer geek like you can understand. A backup file from one hard drive can be loaded onto another. You might not store memories in your DNA, but the electrical sequence is still there. Memories are recorded and stored in the brain. It's not fucking magic. Mice and hundreds of other species prove that. Just because your species haven't figured out how memories are stored doesn't mean it's impossible, stupid. That's the arrogance of your kind. Just because you can't comprehend it doesn't mean it's not possible. How do you like them apples? More advanced than you, and I'm just a *fucking parasite*."

"I didn't call you that. The guy who put you inside me, Jericho Black, is the one that said you were a parasite. I was repeating what he said."

"Whatever. I'm over it."

"Nope. I still have questions. Give me a minute."

Jake waggled his fingers at the three slices of pepperoni and sausage pizza topped with plenty of garlic. He folded the first slice in half and devoured it. The other two slices went down just as fast. He squirted mustard on a polish sausage and shoved it in his mouth, thinking again of Joey Chestnut. *I'm coming for ya, Joey!* He started in on his third drink, a large cup of Dr. Pepper, and drained it while barely taking a breath.

"How is eating all this food used to grow back organs and tissue?" he asked Sly.

"Food is what your species uses for energy, is it not?"

Jake burped. "We are talking about whole body parts here."

"A lizard can grow another tail," Sly chirped, curling his lips with disdain.

"Not the same thing, Sly. It takes an incredible amount of time and energy to develop organs and tissue. You did this all," he said, gesturing to himself, "in a couple of hours."

"Accelerating the growth cycle of a complex organism isn't easy. But again, some organisms can split in half, and bam! There are now two of them. Not so special when you think about it. I just happen to have the energy and the skills to do it."

"How can a parasite possess enough energy to grow human tissue? You're a tiny little spec, what—floating around my bloodstream? This massive frame of mine? The energy needed to grow back organs in that short timeframe is unfathomable."

Sly put his glass down on the table, miffed. "How much energy is in an atom? A single hydrogen atom."

Jake moved his tongue around his mouth, trying to wriggle the cheese from his teeth. "Forget it," he said.

"That's right," said Sly, spreading his hands wide. "Don't underestimate size, motherfucker." He shifted in his seat and crossed one pleated pants leg over the other. "Don't underestimate youth, either. I'm all wrapped up in your synapses, and I know you believe you can figure out what makes Adonis Silver such a bad dude."

"I can."

"We need to stay away from him."

"He's kind of a mystery. Don't you think?"

"He's strong," said Sly. "Much stronger than you."

Jake felt heat rise to his cheeks. "The insults never stop with you. I'm trying to save *my* soul by helping him save his. What the fuck does strength have to do with it?" he tipped over the ice cubes in his cup, and they scattered all over the trays. "How can you know how strong another person is, anyway?" Jake demanded.

"Other animals do it all the time," Sly said plainly. "When a lion roars, it's not the roar that scares the other animals away, jackass. It's the strength the roar conveys. Other animals feel it. His roar lets everyone know he's not afraid to use his strength. They don't have to watch him bench press some weight to know the fucker is strong. Most other animals in nature sense the fights they can or cannot win and avoid the ones they can't."

"You're serious," said Jake. "You can sense the strength of others."

"Yes, as I said, most species can. I guess since humans evolved to rely solely on their brain, you've lost this ability as well."

"Oh, yeah?" Jake puffed out his chest. "How strong am I?"

"Not very." Sly rolled his eyes. "About a five."

"On what scale? Out of ten?"

"Not quite." Sly laughed to himself.

"Out of a hundred? A thousand?" Jake looked around at some of the other people inside the food court. "Okay, that kid over there. How strong is he?"

Sly glanced at the adolescent, who looked to be about ten years old. "A two."

"Okay . . . and what about that woman over there." He pointed at a tan, fit woman dressed for office work in a gray skirt, white blouse, and sensible shoes. Her long ponytail swayed as she meandered by the stores, window-shopping.

"She's a seven," said Sly.

"A seven?" said Jake, raising his voice. "You little—and I'm a five?"

"Yep. She's a seven. Those guys getting on the escalator? Twelve. We walked past a fifteen earlier." Sly manifested another bourbon on the rocks and took a sip, shoulders shaking with repressed laughter.

"But I am a five? Bullshit!" He slammed his palm to the table. Sly threw nothing but insults at him every time Jake opened his mouth. Why was he stuck with such an irritating parasite?

He reigned in his anger. Took a deep breath. He had another question that needed to be answered. "What about Jericho Black?" asked Jake. "How strong is he?"

"The guy who pushed you in front of the train?" said Sly. He slid his jaws left and right in thought. "He's in the thousands."

"What did you say?" said Jake. He slumped against his chair, appetite lost.

"Thousands as in, many thousands. Five, maybe even six digits. I can't put an exact number on it, but if all the people here in this mall were to attack him simultaneously, he'd be the only one left standing. Probably without a scratch on him."

CHAPTER 34

T he four of them warmed themselves by a plug-in heater in the back half an old warehouse in Brighton Beach, Brooklyn. Work was about to begin converting the warehouse into a mixed-use residential and commercial complex. Very modern, thought Alexei. The whole block going upscale. Clothing stores, restaurants, coffeehouses, even a gym, and an organic food store chain were said to be part of the venture. *Gentrification*, the kids called it. Construction began in three months. For now, their job was to clean the place out. Flush out the rats and vagrants, and make sure the demolition went off without a hitch. So went the partnership with the oligarchs: they made the deals legally, and the *Vor* operated within their deals illegally.

During construction, Alexei and Zachary would pillage and resell supplies. They'd intimidate and encourage inspectors. They'd make sure permits were issued or revoked to serve their needs. They'd make money for themselves while ensuring the project was completed on schedule. But for now, it was a private space to use as needed. It was musty and smelled unpleasant, but it had power.

Maxim's men had delivered the hardware removed from Jake's apartment, and now Alexei's men, Dima and Vlad, hovered over computer monitors. Alexei trusted them; they were hackers the *Vor* could control. Soft white light lit their faces as their fingers worked the keyboards. Two floor lamps plugged into the power strip behind them. Alexei paced back and forth between the lamps. His shadow grew as it slid across the dusty concrete floor, only to shrink again when he changed directions.

Dima finished first. The typical loner type, he was thin and short and wore glasses. He leaned back in his chair and waited for Vlad. After another minute, Vlad hit the spacebar and shook his head.

"Nothing but bits and pieces of some program," announced Vlad. He was thicker than his partner but not much taller. Alexei guessed by his look that Vlad got out more and was into the bar scene.

Vlad did the talking for them. "Dima has the same thing. The program seems pretty elaborate, but there are no financial transactions. As far as I know, this hardware was never used for anything except writing this program."

Alexei held out his hand for the satellite phone. Zachary dialed the number and gave it to him. Sergei picked up on the second ring. "Nothing we can use on the hard drives," said Alexei.

"What does your gut tell you?" asked Sergei.

Alexei paused. Sergei did not ask that kind of question often. He was a structured, hard-nosed man who played by the rules and only took calculated risks. For him to ask Alexei what his gut told him was beyond the Sergei that Alexei knew. That meant Sergei was desperate to get to Turgenev. It also meant Sergei had the support of someone powerful up the food chain. Another oligarch, or perhaps someone else in the government. Maybe even the Kremlin.

"Julie Shubert was believable," answered Alexei. "Her brother was *Vory*. She would not lie about this. I am certain information regarding Turgenev was in her possession at some point. Turgenev would not have paid the money if he had not received what she had. All of it. This might be a dead end."

The phone hummed with distance. "I have word from the Odessa family that Maxim was offered six figures for retrieving the laptop used to take the money from the accounts. Turgenev himself offered the money."

Alexei realized Maxim's deception had beset him from the beginning. He'd received the hard drives taken from Jake's apartment from Maxim. The laptop could have been there, and Maxim kept it for himself. The repugnant taste of being the goose turned to rage.

"I will get this laptop first," said Alexei.

"I pray that you do," said Sergei. "Everything is riding on this."

Sergei ended the call, and Alexei handed the satellite phone back to Zachary.

"We need to find Maxim," said Alexei. "He was after the laptop all along. He must have taken it from the apartment and given us this shit!" Alexei used his blocky arm to swat the hardware off the table and onto the floor, crashing a monitor with it. Little bits of glass and plastic bounced and scattered across the dusty concrete.

Alexei felt the rising implications of his failure. He was the ninny, the numbskull, the fathead, the ignoramus. A lowly hitman that would never rise any farther in his station. Sergei put his trust in Alexei, and Alexei had failed him.

"I don't think Maxim has the laptop," said Zachary. "I've been having him followed."

"Really?" asked Alexei.

"Something about when he was outside the hacker's apartment bugged me. When I first spotted him, he had an object in his hand. I thought it was a book. By the time he walked over to us, he had nothing. I knew he couldn't be trusted, So I had one of my guys follow one of his guys, and my guy says they are staking out a place in Newark. The girlfriend of the hacker lives there. She was the one that Maxim was talking to when we pulled up in front of the apartment."

Alexei felt his tense neck muscles relax. Optimism warmed his cold body like the sun. The potential of beating Maxim to the punch thrilled him. "If you were not so straight, I would kiss you right now."

CHAPTER 35

The concrete was still wet from the storm the night before. Worms crawled around helplessly, trying to find their way back to the soil before the pigeons spotted them. The damp sidewalk beneath his shoes made a gritty sound as he paced around. He looked down the block at the row houses and small apartments that made up his neighborhood. Trash day had green plastic trashcans lined up on the sidewalk to the corner. He walked between two parked cars as the blue Suburban approached and pulled to a stop. Alexei opened the door and planted himself inside.

The inside was quiet; only the hiss of the heater could be heard. It smelled of cigarette smoke, probably from Zachary's clothing. Zachary had on a pullover with athletic pants and sneakers. He brought the car forward and turned the corner. The engine made a gentle purr as he confidently pulled away from traffic.

"Once again, you impress me, Zachary," said Alexei. "When did you come up with this plan?"

"Before he delivered the hard drives from the apartment. I made it known that someone was following him. I told my men to be careless and let him spot them occasionally, so it looked as if we were incompetent. Oleg drove, and Maxim rode in the back. But Dimitri was a different case. He's new to the crew, and we figured that he'd be the one Maxim gave his orders to once he knew we were not going to stop following him. That is exactly what he did. We were careful while following Dimitri, and he led us to the house in New Jersey."

"You're a fucking genius," said Alexei. "Have they gone inside the place?"

"Not yet."

It was late afternoon, and the sun was still visible through the clouds. Alexei put his head back and looked up through the moonroof at the sky above. He closed his eyes, lulled by the gentle rocking of the car traveling through traffic. It felt as if he had only closed his eyes for an instant when thirty minutes later, the Suburban backed into a parking spot. He opened his eyes and found himself in a residential neighborhood.

"That one," said Zachary, pointing to a red house down the street.

Two stories. Red in color with white trim. Wrought iron bars caged the windows and front door. The narrow driveway extended to the back of the house, leading to a small garage, also red. Alexei surveyed the area. The entire neighborhood had a similar layout: house, driveway, house, all the way down the block. Most had garages in several states of decay. Some yards were immaculate, some unkempt, but in all, just another city neighborhood.

"The woman's name is Catalina," said Zachary. "She works at a hotel near the American football stadium. She shares the home with her mother. I have word that the mother has not been seen in years."

A single woman working at a hotel down the road from the football stadium could not afford a house on her own. Her mother was probably dead, and Catalina hid it to collect her mother's social security and pension. Alexei knew these things happened. He didn't blame her for her survival instinct. If the old woman died prematurely, why not stuff her in a freezer and continue to collect her benefits. Who did it hurt? The government?

Fuck the government.

They walked side by side across the broken concrete of the driveway, peering through the blind slats on their way to the back entrance. A white wrought iron door guarded the back door in a welded iron frame. Alexei pulled on the knob and leaned over to inspect the cylinder that locked the door in place. It served as adequate protection against the amateur and undetermined. Alexei was neither of those things.

They strolled back to the Suburban. Alexei made a phone call. After about twenty minutes, a van pulled up to the front of the house, a Bert's Home Repairs decal on the side. Several ladders were stacked on the roof, and welding equipment could be seen through the back window. A man wearing blue Dickies walked up the driveway with a tool bag in hand to the back of the home. He was gone seven minutes. Then he walked back to his truck and left.

After another half an hour, Alexei and Zachary went back up the driveway behind the house. The wrought iron door stood ajar, its lock and cylinder missing. The back door lock and deadbolt were unlocked. They pushed the door aside and walked in.

Alexei and Zachary made themselves comfortable—a handy trick after many years of breaking and entering. If a neighbor called the police, the officers would be surprised to find the alleged intruders eating sandwiches at the kitchen table. They'd tell the officer they were visiting a friend, and the cop might believe it. And if someone came downstairs to find two people sitting in the living room watching television, they'd be puzzled and wonder what was going on. Both cases caused a moment of confusion in which Alexei and Zachary would take full advantage.

Since they were hungry, they stayed in the tiny kitchen. Painted-over wallpaper bubbled and peeled. The off-white celling had brown stains in several places. The kitchen appliances were a mismatch of colors, green stove, stainless steel dishwasher, and a white refrigerator with a water dispenser. Old Formica countertops reminded Alexei of black pearls. A small, rounded white table stood flush against the wall with three chairs surrounding it. Several pots and plates dried on the counter. The double sink was empty.

Zachary opened the right side of the refrigerator door and took a peek at the inventory. Orange juice and milk occupied the top shelf. The second shelf had an assortment of storage containers, both plastic and glass, filled with food. The third shelf had sandwich meats and cheeses, and the fourth shelf had a couple of packaged steaks.

Alexei found the loaf of bread, twelve-grain, on top of the refrigerator. An abnormal amount of yogurt and berries crowded the door. Under the yogurt was the good stuff—real mayonnaise and mustard. Zachary made two pastrami and cheese sandwiches and poured two glasses of ice-cold milk.

After eating half a sandwich, Zachary said something about finding a bathroom, and he left. Five minutes later, he returned. "There's an old woman in there," he said.

"Where, the bathroom?" asked Alexei between bites.

"In the foyer."

"Did she see you?"

"Yes, but there is nothing to worry about."

Alexei nodded. It hadn't seemed like anyone was home. He had a nose about these things. He paid attention to the signs. Darkened windows. Drawn curtains. No lights or sounds. Obvious stuff. But also, a home with no one inside felt void of life. It was as if the house itself came alive when people roamed within it. And when they didn't, it was dead, like this one.

Alexei stood from the kitchen table with half a sandwich and decided to explore a little. He walked through the tight hallway into the living room. A small blue couch faced a flat-screen television. Old hardwood floors that needed oiling creaked as he poked around. A dusty oriental rug filled the middle of the room. He peeked into a small bedroom over to the right. It smelled funny. He shrugged his shoulder and moved on to the foyer. There was the woman Zachary mentioned, sitting in a wheelchair.

An oxygen tank with wheels sat next to her. The hoses looped around her head and over her ears, leaving the tube openings directly under her nostrils. The skin on her hands looked as thin as paper and covered with age spots. A cloudy gray tinted her eyes, and a light tremor ran through her aging body. Alexei had noticed a similar condition in himself as he neared the fifty-year-old mark. Hands not as steady as they used to be. The body not as flexible.

He took a step closer. The woman was beyond old. She was barely grasping at life. She gave no indication of being startled by him or aware of him at all. The blanket slipped off her lap and was bunched up by her feet. The room had a chill so Alexei went to fix it, then decided not to. He went back into the kitchen to finish his sandwich.

CHAPTER 36

Jake was still sitting in the food court when Catalina texted. Someone had busted the back door of her home while she was at work. She was afraid to go inside but had to check on her mother.

His heart lurched from the bombshell text. Jericho had warned the Russians would scour every facet of his life to find his laptop, and the reality of his words was like a thunderbolt splitting through the darkness. Despite his efforts, trouble still came to Catalina's doorstep.

He wanted to tell her not to go inside, to get as far away as possible, but her mother was inside and barely had the strength to push the toggle on her wheelchair. He could tell her not to go inside but call the police, and they'd take care of her mother. His fingers started typing out the text when Jericho's ominous warning rang like a cacophony of horns: no contact.

Fuck that. Catalina needed him.

Another text popped up on the screen. Her mother was fine, and the only thing missing so far was Jake's laptop. She joked about nothing else in the house being of any value, followed by a laughing emoji. Jake exhaled in surprise and relief. Then he stared at the phone, puzzled.

Why did Catalina have his laptop?

Jake tapped his phone against his teeth. The Russians had what they'd been looking for. Maybe there was nothing else to worry about.

"You got shook there for a moment," said Sly, who'd been downing bourbon after bourbon. "What's going on?"

"Nothing," said Jake, sliding his phone into his jacket pocket. "It's been handled. No need for me to hide anymore. I can go home."

"Are you sure about that? Wouldn't want you to get pushed in front of another train or anything."

"Shut the fuck up, will you?"

A family at the next table stared at him. "Do you mind," said Jake, touching a finger to his ear as if he had earbuds in. "I'm on my phone. This is a private conversation. Go back to your food. And it's not like your kids haven't heard this language before." Once again, Sly had him looking like an imbecile, talking to himself.

"Kids are starving in Africa, you know," said the woman, nodding at his wrapper-filled table. He still had two chicken sandwiches and a large fries, a plate with Mongolian beef and rice, two cheesesteak subs, and two large sodas left to consume.

"They should be happy to hear that I'm going to eat it all, thank you," said Jake, grabbing a chicken sandwich.

"What the fuck does starving kids in Africa have to do with your food?" asked Sly.

"I don't know. It's just something moms say."

"Maybe you need to eat more than that salad, you skinny bitch," shouted Sly. "Don't know how you had three kids as scrawny as you are. Jake, tell this bitch to mind her own business."

"I did, Sly, I did."

"But you didn't do it the right way. Tell her what I said."

"No, the way you say it is rude. You're abrasive, do you know that? I don't even cuss, yet you revealed yourself to me, and I've been foulmouthed ever since. It's best that we treat our relationship as strictly business. In fact, now that I'm healed, you're no longer needed. You can go back in that phial to heal the next person, for all I care. The Russians are off my back, and I can grow old with Catalina. Parasite, you are fucking out of here! I'm calling Jericho to have you removed!"

He pushed the unopened food aside. The pile of sandwich wrappers and french fries slid to the other end of the table. "I'm not feeling so well. I need some air." He looked around. "What the fuck is happening to me?"

"You ate too much," said the woman with the kids. "Go outside if you're going to puke. I rather not see, hear, or smell it."

"Shut up!" said Jake, head spinning. His sense of hearing and smell went haywire, and his eyesight doubled. He looked around for Sly. He was gone. Jake tried to stand but faltered. His hand landed hard on one of the food trays, and it tumbled to the ground, spilling his wrappers like confetti.

He searched for the exit. Concerned faces crowded his periphery. His skin sprouted beads of sweat. He needed air. He took two steps before the darkness overtook him, and he hit the ground with a muffled thud. Just like that, Jake was back in hell.

CHAPTER 37

Scorching darkness enveloped him. He walked with his arms in front of him, using his hands as feelers, slowly sliding his feet across the surface, using his toes to feel for inconsistencies. He started at a snail's pace, then grew more confident and began taking longer steps. He moved faster, spreading his arms out even wider, searching for anything.

An immeasurable amount of time passed. The endless obscurity weighed on him. There was nothing and no one. He occupied his thoughts by remembering how comforting it was to see. How reassuring it was to hear. How soothing it was to feel. Sensory deprivation was crushing him, bit by bit. Alarm overtook Jake and whipped him into a frenzy. He ran haphazardly around in the darkness, then screamed into the nothing, lungs burning with each soundless exhale.

Jake froze in place and slowly stroked his arms, horrified. He couldn't feel himself. He felt the heat, ever-suffocating, but not himself. Suddenly, his feet no longer felt the ground. He had no idea if he was standing or sitting or upside down. Was he floating?

He ran and spun and flew and swam, hoping to crash into a wall or fall off a cliff. Any sensation would be welcome. Nothingness had him scared silly. He clawed at his unfeeling body with his unfeeling fingers; at least, he thought he did. Maybe he didn't exist at all.

Suddenly his feet hit sand. He felt sand! An orange sun floated below the horizon. He could see! Ocean waves crashed along the shore with a thud, casting ocean spray into the air, and the mist was cool. He could hear and feel! He dropped to his knees and cried for a bit. Not sure why he was crying since he was so relieved. Yet the tears continued to stream.

When he was done, he stood, brushed the course sand from his knees, and surveyed the coastline.

Jake spotted a building off to his right in the distance. Closer to the water than all the other structures. Practically jutting up from the sand. He walked along the beach, appreciating the rough grit of sand between his toes. As the structure grew closer, Jake thought it might be a parking garage. Thousands of people lined up inside where the parking spaces would be, one behind the other. All their faces turned outward to gaze at the ocean waves. Cautiously, he made his way toward them, comforted by the sight of so many people.

He stopped several dozen feet from the corner of the multilevel parking garage. A woman with fair skin and a thin build noticed Jake. Her hair was long and straight and came down to her buttocks.

"You made it through the nothingness," she said. "Congratulations."

"You came through as well?" asked Jake. He looked in the direction he had come and saw only beach and water. Mountains and the silhouette of a cityscape loomed on the far horizon.

"Don't bother trying to look for it," she said. "It lets you out just as easily as when you were sucked in, but only when you are worthy. The only thing you need to do now is wait." She turned her gaze back to the waves.

It was almost pleasant—a city by the beach. The orange hue of the sun under the horizon was like predawn or right after sunset. A great time of the day, either one. Jake wouldn't mind staying awhile. Except, something was off, something he couldn't quite put a name to. Then it came to him. Everyone in the garage seemed anxious.

"Wait for what?" said Jake.

"We are waiting for the boat," she said.

"Boat to where?"

"You know," she said with the slightest smile. "This is it! The secret port that leads to paradise. A boat pulls right up to this parking garage at high tide. The ship is large enough to hold nine hundred and ninety souls. It sets out to sea, and the ones who are not ready to enter paradise are eventually brought back here."

"How many people don't make it?" asked Jake.

"About two or three per trip."

"How do you know when the boat is coming?"

"I told you. High tide."

Jake looked out at the beach. The waves crashed ashore about a hundred yards from the parking garage. "The ones that returned told you they saw heaven?" he asked.

She looked upward as if in praise. "They're usually so in awe of what they witnessed that they can no longer speak. Their eyes are wide, their faces frozen in glee."

It sounded suspicious. *More than suspicious,* thought Jake, *it sounds like the same ol' hell.*

"The line starts back there," she said, pointing. "On the other side of the building." She motioned behind her right shoulder with her head.

Jake looked down the side he was facing. No entrance point.

"The other side," she said. "Walk that way and go around the building to the end of the line."

To satisfy his curiosity, Jake walked along the side of the parking garage, toward the corner of the building. A thousand things ran through his mind all at once. He'd been to hell several times and each time, hope turned to tragedy and frustration. He doubted the ship was a means of escape, even though his heart pleaded with him to take a chance.

Jake stepped off the curb and into the street, past the abandoned cars and blinking streetlights. He saw a line of people at the opposite end of the building. It swerved out one way and back, like the lines of an amusement park ride, letting people believe they were close when they were nowhere near the front of the line.

Jake studied the situation with a newfound calm. He suspected the people at the top of the garage would be the only ones to board the ship. Getting to the top would be a battle of attrition. The people on the lower levels, like the woman he'd spoken to, would become immersed entirely underwater and most likely washed out to sea.

The boat to paradise was a cruel joke.

"Jake Coltrane," said a familiar voice.

The searing burn of the first mark on his back filling in had Jake's entire body trembling. He fell to his knees more from the pressure of his presence than the pain. Tartarus approached, and Jake could hear the masses moan as they were crushed to the floor.

"Why is he here?" Jake heard one of them scream.

"This was my chance at salvation," cried another. "I was finally going to leave this place."

They could do nothing except watch as Tartarus approached along the beach line. His tall, black void of a body moved like cheap Claymation. His arms flowed with the waves of the ocean and his gloved fingers played a silent melody.

Tartarus reached Jake and grinned. Jake felt like he was kneeling in front of a flashy neon sign. "Back so soon, Jake Coltrane?" said Tartarus. "What a surprise."

"You brought me here," said Jake, trembling. "I knew it. I was eating in a mall. I wasn't stabbed or pushed in front of a train or shot. No danger. Yet here I am. You did something to me. Those marks are visible on my real body."

Jake strained his head toward the thousands of people lined up to go into the parking garage. It took all his strength to remain on his hands and knees and not crush himself into the sand. "They're not going to paradise, are they?" said Jake.

The smile of Tartarus grew wider.

"Hey!" Jake screamed to the crowd. "You were never going to paradise. It's another trick. Something is waiting for you beyond the horizon. Something terrible. Tartarus just confirmed it. Arrghh!!!" Jake screamed in pain as the second mark filled on his back. "Damn you! That's my second mark!"

"Say what you wish," said Tartarus. "They won't believe you. Spread enough lies, and the truth will never be found. Your words only make them more determined to get on the boat. They'll talk among themselves and cast you as the liar. People believe what they've already convinced themselves to believe, Jake Coltrane. The truth you speak has already drowned and sunk as deep as that ocean." His dancing gloves motioned toward the water.

Jake braced himself with his hands sinking deeper into the sand. The weight on his knees became unbearable. But he wanted to face Tartarus. He needed to confirm what the old man had said. "If your eye causes you to sin, pluck it out and cast it from you. If I save the soul of Adonis Silver, I will be delivered to paradise. Is that a lie too?" asked Jake.

The fierce weight lifted. Jake cried in relief right as a large, gloved hand grasped him around the neck and lifted him into the air, all the way up to the face of Tartarus. The large teeth no longer grinned. The grip upon his neck tightened.

"Jake Coltrane," said Tartarus. "Are you looking to escape hell?" He squeezed harder and pulled Jake's face closer to his mouth. "I guess you figured out that you have a distinct advantage over everyone else. You can save the soul of the living by returning to your body. But you only have five opportunities left."

"Arrgghh!!" Jake screamed again. His legs flailed, and his toes wriggled as another mark was burned into his back.

"Four opportunities left," said Tartarus. "You seem to be repeatedly dying. Interesting. Can you defy hell with the meager opportunities you've been given? Can you avoid dying before you figure it out?"

Tartarus opened his eyes.

Jake instantly felt at ease. Tartarus was gone. The prickling heat on his skin subsided. It was still warm, but a different kind of warmth, not so sweaty. He was back in the world.

Something felt strange about his return.

Jake had on a tee shirt, shorts, and sneakers. He was in the hallway of his childhood home in Queens, between the main bedroom and the mustard-colored kitchen. His mother stood in front of the sink washing dishes. He'd forgotten how beautiful she was, how her brown skin glowed in her favorite yellow A-line dress, the back seams of her stockings ending at a pair of comfy house slippers. Silky black hair flowed down her back.

Jake stood at the entrance to the kitchen admiring her. Every morning she made him pancakes with corn oil because they had the crispy edge and soft, fluffy middle he loved.

Why was he there?

He looked outside the kitchen window and saw the tree out back filled with the pesky green crab apples that the yellow jackets loved so much. Summertime.

Then he remembered. He'd been playing tag when he decided to head inside and get a drink. His father, a tall, dark-skinned man, stormed from the living room and into the kitchen. He still had on the tan khakis of his electrician's uniform, and he was tense, all balled up tight and ready to spring. The energy he gave off was unfamiliar, and it scared Jake. He stepped down the hallway and into the shadows.

"What the fuck is this, Pauline?" asked Jake's dad. He held up a letter. The thin white paper crinkled as he extended it toward her.

She turned to her husband while her hands continued to scrape the crust off the bottom of a pie pan. "It's divorce papers, Ricky. You read them."

"Are you crazy?" he asked. "You're throwing all this away?"

"Yes," she said, still working the pan in the soapy water. "I want to end this lie for you."

"You want to end it for me? What are you ending for me?"

"I cheated on you, Ricky." She took her hands out of the water and faced him, chest held high, looking him right in the eyes. "Some kid around the corner. He used to howl at me all the time when I went to and from the store. He said it was his birthday and he turned eighteen. I thought, what the hell, so I blew him."

Ricky's fist flew up above his right shoulder, big and intimidating. His bicep flexed. His fist shook. He held it there, wavering behind his ear. Pauline never blinked. Never flinched. She was about as relaxed and calm as if she were watching the sunset.

"I thought so, Ricky. I was so sure I was willing to bet my face on it. That's why you need to sign the papers."

He lowered his hand. "You thought what? That I loved you so much I wouldn't hurt you?"

"No. That you were so in love with Chuck that this divorce will be a relief to you."

Ricky's face twisted and distorted in disbelief. He took a step back as if he couldn't believe what he'd heard. "Are you out of your mind, woman?"

"I saw you, Ricky. When we went to the cabin in Pennsylvania last August with Chuck and Jackie. You two went inside to get the fish, and I stumbled in a few minutes later to see if I could help. When I turned the corner, I saw you touching his face. I know how a man touches someone when they're in love with them. That's what I saw."

Ricky started laughing. He walked around the kitchen nervously. Gesturing as he spoke. "At the cabin? I remember you were drunk then. And . . . and Chuck had some fish guts on his face. I wiped it off for him."

He clicked his teeth. "That's what this whole divorce thing is based on? Come on, Pauline."

Pauline's face was void of all emotion. She spoke plainly. Businesslike. "It's you and Chuck's little love shack in Pennsylvania. You guys go up there three times a year. When Jackie and I insisted we go with you guys, I saw how you two reacted. I wanted to go on that trip because I thought we could reconnect away from the kids, but you wouldn't touch me. Said they might hear us. And when we heard Chuck making love to Jackie, I could see how pissed you were. I thought it was because you were embarrassed, but now I know you were jealous."

"Oh, come on, now," scoffed Ricky. "You're making stuff up." He tossed the divorce papers in the sink. "Let's put this nonsense to bed. You are my wife and that's that." He turned to leave the room.

"Jackie knows about you and Chuck," said Pauline.

Ricky stopped dead in his tracks.

Pauline took the divorce papers out of the sink. They were soppy. She plopped them on the counter and pressed it flat with her hands. "Jackie knows your relationship is more than friends," said Pauline. "Jackie knew he was having an affair but thought it was with a woman. When she found out it was you, she decided she could live with it. I tried. For a whole year, I tried to live with it. But I can't." She faced her husband. Her eyes pleading just as much as her voice. "We haven't made love once in over two years, Ricky. You're out who knows where for hours after work. You come home, hop in bed, and while you're sleeping, I'm smelling you, sniffing for perfume, finding no scent of a woman on you, and thinking cool, at least he isn't cheating. Well, the joke's on me, right? Sign the papers, Ricky. I don't want to live a lie. Your world no longer includes me."

His eyes drifted away from his wife's and a calmness came over Ricky Coltrane. His shoulders slumped in deep thought.

"The kids are coming with me," said Pauline. "I won't lie to them, Ricky. You're going to have to tell them who you are."

Jake hid in the corner of the hallway, wondering what he was seeing. It wasn't part of his past. He heard his father say, "I'll go get a pen."

The words triggered something in Jake. His mind convulsed in recognition of what was about to transpire. He tried to move from the corner. He tried to scream. Tried to warn his mother, but he couldn't move or change what was about to happen.

His father marched through the living room and into the bedroom. Jake heard him rummaging around. Then he returned, entering Jake's vision for a moment and then out of sight. Jake heard a pop. So loud it rang his ears. Then another pop.

"I'm not gay, bitch! Don't go around saying I'm gay because I'm not! I'm not fucking gay, you hear me, you stupid fucking cunt? How dare you say that to me? I'm a fucking man. And you want to tell my fucking kids I'm gay just because you can't turn me on, bitch? That's your fault. It's on you!"

Dead silence. Jake couldn't hear his breath, it was so quiet. Heavy footsteps slowly creaked out from the kitchen, and Jake saw a flash of his dad one more time, lumbering back through the living room. The side door opened and slammed shut. He was gone.

It was another five minutes before Jake went to view his mother's body.

"Blocked it all out of your mind, did you?" said Tartarus.

Jake felt the grip on his neck. He swayed, suspended in midair, looking deeply into the rich amber eyes of Tartarus. Then the eyes snapped shut.

"Do you think you can save poor Adonis Silver in time?" asked Tartarus. "I can wait for an eternity," said Tartarus. "When your last chance expires, you'll become a part of me, never to leave again. Only four chances left."

Jake's vision blurred. His skin prickled with heat, and his lungs felt like fire. Rage coursed through his veins. His tears turned to blood and dripped on Tartarus's gloves. He screamed until he'd squeezed every drop of air out of his lungs. Then he screamed more. The darkness turned bright. Blinding.

CHAPTER 38

Jake blinked at the skylight of the mall. A crowd of concerned onlookers surrounded him. His black tee shirt had been cut down the middle, and sensors stuck to his chest and ankles. The paramedic who'd earlier examined the woman with the broken neck stood over Jake's supine body, visibly relieved that Jake had opened his eyes and remained conscious.

"It's okay," said the paramedic. "You'll be okay." His bushy hair bounced as he checked the data on his monitors. "Just relax. Can you tell me your name?"

"Jake Coltrane," he said. "Am I back?"

"Ha! You sure are, buddy. Do you know where you are?"

The crowd of faces unnerved him. Grown men and women. Teenagers. Little kids. All focused on his wellbeing. "I'm in a shopping mall in Long Island," said Jake, feeling a little like he was on stage reciting lines for an audience.

"Fantastic. You're doing great. You gave us quite a scare for about a minute or so, but your vitals are stabilizing. My partner will be coming by any minute. We're going to take good care of you."

"I'm fine," said Jake. "I don't need to go to the hospital."

He tried to stand, and the paramedic placed his hand on Jake's chest.

"I recommend it," said the paramedic. "You collapsed about five minutes ago."

"I have a history of seizures," said Jake. "Happens often."

"This was no seizure. I suggest you relax and let us take care of you. There's a possibility whatever's happening isn't over."

Yeah, no shit, thought Jake grimly. Going to the hospital wasn't going to save him. Tartarus could bring him to hell and keep him there whenever he wanted. Jake pushed the paramedic away and ripped off the cables and tubes hanging from his chest and arm with a swipe of his hand. A collective gasp rose from the crowd. Before the paramedic could restrain him, Jake took off running, parting the crowd like Moses's Red Sea. He exited the mall and scrambled down the stairs, past the dead woman's blood, and out into the street. Gummy residue from the sensors chaffed against his skin, so he peeled off what he could from his chest and arms and flicked the sticky remnants into nearby bushes. *Now, where to go?*

He cut through a restaurant parking lot, then ran onto the street alongside an accelerating bus and pounded on the door with an open palm until the driver slowed and let him in. He paid his fee and turned to see a whole new audience staring at the wide, jagged strips the paramedic's scissors had made of his shirt. He grabbed the frayed fringes of material with one hand and held them together, managing only partially to cover his chest, then wobbled down the center aisle as the bus sped off to the next destination.

He slumped in a seat, knees extending halfway into the aisle, and sulked. He worked at the sticky residue on his ankles, but the sensors had adhered pretty well. Frustrated, he placed his hands on his head. A deep-seated pang of hurt burrowed out of his heart and into his chest.

What had Tartarus done? Jake cringed in pain. He hadn't asked for the truth, but he couldn't unsee what Tartarus had revealed.

Shortly after her murder, the police had questioned his father, who told the cops about how some guy named Greg was constantly harassing his mom. One of the investigators asked if Jake's father ever confronted Greg and his father said no, that he was afraid if he talked to Greg he might do something he'd regret later. Greg was much younger, after all.

The police paid a second visit right after his mother's funeral. Jake and his little sister were rushed out of the house and to a neighbor. His dad told Jake they were too young to hear what the police had found. When Jake got back to the house, everything was torn apart. Clothes and boxes scattered everywhere. His dad told Jake that he'd fought with the police because they were stupid, but he didn't seem angry; he seemed scared. He sat frozen in the kitchen chair as if his entire world had been shattered.

His father's fear and silence made sense to Jake because Jake felt the same way. Fractured. He went and gave his father a hug. His father reached up and touched Jake on the cheek, and Jake winced from the stitches in his face. He'd just confronted Greg two days prior.

The police must have been searching the house for the murder weapon, Jake thought as the bus rumbled over potholed streets. He'd blamed himself all those years for a young boy's cowardice, never considering that he might've repressed an even worse tragedy.

Ricky Coltrane, Jake's father, hung himself from the second floor railing two months later. His best friend Chuck had found him hanging with the phone cord wrapped around his neck, the receiver dangling next to his heart. Ricky called Chuck just before he stepped into air. Later, Chuck had said that before he died, Jake's father told Chuck that he loved Jake's mother so much that he couldn't live without her.

Bullshit, Chuck, thought Jake.

Jake's eyes swept over the tired faces of the crowded bus. Some looked back at him. Salty tears burned his cracked lips. He used a ragged end of his shirt to wipe his face and stood to leave. *Show's over, folks.* He'd had enough of being a spectacle for one day and jumped out the back door when the bus made its stop. A cold breeze hit his chest, but he didn't care. It was time to go home.

Jake arrived at his apartment late in the evening. The door stood wide open. He'd expected something of the sort. His place was trashed. Again, expected. He didn't expect to find Dr. Carrie Blake pacing in his bedroom.

CHAPTER 39

Time was ticking for Dr. Carrie Blake.

Carrie soaked in a white claw-foot tub near the window in her studio apartment bathroom, deep in thought over her next move and waiting to hear from her assistant Lee Barbarossa so they could line up their story about what happened to the body. He needed to confirm her story. She couldn't tell her boss all by herself that the guy who was cut in two grew a new body and head and then asked her to drive him home. They were doctors and scientists, for gosh sakes; they'd want verification and corroboration at the minimum.

She'd taken the van to her parent's house earlier and stashed it in their garage. Carrie went back to the office, making a big fuss about taking an Uber because Lee left prematurely. Then she kept busy and waited for Lee to show up or call. Four hours had passed before the Lead Coroner started making inquiries.

Carrie's self-protection mode kicked in, and she made up a story about a family emergency and Lee storing the body in Trenton while he got the family situation sorted out. The Lead Coroner was none too pleased but expected the van and body to be back the following day.

Luckily, he was off for the next three days and took Carrie's word for it when she said Lee would be back the following day. However, he wasn't. Then came the lawyers of the family looking for the body. The Lead Coroner was due to return in two days, and still no word from Lee despite her sending twenty-seven text messages.

Carrie emerged from the tub and slid on a shiny, teal-colored robe that ended mid-thigh. Her wet feet left footprints across the hardwood floor as she plodded to the couch and sat down. With her feet kicked up on the ottoman, she rubbed lotion on her freshly shaven legs. Her wet hair draped over her left shoulder. For a moment, she thought about doing her nails, thinking it might take her mind off her problems or at least eat up a few more minutes.

Her phone chimed. Social app update. A friend of hers added a link to a video. The title said: *Man severed by train. View now before the video is removed/censored.*

Weren't you there? Her friend asked.

Carrie clicked and watched. She saw the head and arm of Jake Coltrane between the train tracks. He looked up at whoever was taking the video. The fingers on his hand mimicked a spider crawling slowly. Her heart plummeted to her stomach as his mouth began to move. She stopped the video, deleted the message, and dropped the phone on the couch.

What had she thought was going to happen? Of *course* it was all over the internet. Jake asked her not to say anything, and she agreed, but how far did he expect her to go? His family had hired lawyers to find out what was going on at the Coroner's office, for gosh sakes. And his employers wanted his laptop back for national security.

C'mon, Carrie, you don't believe that bullshit, she thought.

Carrie rested her head on the back of the couch and studied the ceiling. As a kid, she watched television shows about forensics and murder mysteries—sixty minutes of total excitement. The line between coroner, detective, and psychologist blurred into one super-investigator. In real life, it was nothing of the sort. All three had their minor boring parts, and no one changed lanes. Putting bad guys behind bars was more procedural than exciting. Her part consisted of lab work, reports, and following painstaking procedure to the letter. If there was a single question regarding her integrity, she'd no longer be able to do her job properly.

Carrie sat up straight, struck by an idea. One person could shed light on this mess: Jake Coltrane. Maybe she could take Jake to the Coroner's office and have him explain what happened. It would make him culpable as well, and she'd no longer be stranded alone on an island. It was her best defense.

She quickly dressed, then jumped in her car and headed over to Jake's. As part of procedure they took pictures of everything, including Jake's identification which had his apartment number. She went up the elevator and to his front door. She knocked on the door, and it swung open. She peeked in. The couch had been flipped over and its underside cut open. Clothes scattered across the floor. Shoeboxes had been opened and emptied.

She tiptoed inside. She passed the kitchen, stepping over pots and pans. All the cabinet doors gaped open. Carrie ventured on down the hall and into the bedroom. More clothes on the floor. The bedframe had been flipped, and a sagging mattress leaned against the wall. Old computer parts lay broken and discarded. Several of the towers had been disassembled. His dresser drawers were stacked under a window. She walked from the drawers to the mattress, then back to the drawers, unsure what she was supposed to do. *What now, Carrie?*

"What the fuck?" yelped Jake.

"Jake!" she cried out. "It's me, uh, Dr. Blake . . . Carrie. From the morgue? I didn't do this! I found it like this! Two guys showed up at the morgue asking about you. Said that they were lawyers. Asked about your laptop."

Jake walked into the bedroom. His sunken eyes scanned the damage. He looked like he'd been crying. The front of his tee shirt was torn in half. "What are you doing here?"

"I came because I need your help," she said awkwardly. She was much braver in her head. Seeing the place ransacked had her feeling extra nervous.

"Get the fuck out of here!" he said and pointed to the door.

Carried noted the unkempt condition of Jake's hair, and he had some white gummy residue on his arms. "Don't worry. I'm gone."

She stepped over the shoes and clothes and squeezed past Jake, who smelled of food and sweat. "I did an autopsy of the head that you left behind," said Carrie, chattering like she always did when scared. "I wanted to know how you could reproduce whole organs."

"I would not repeat stupid talk like that to anyone else," said Jake. His tall frame hulked behind her. "It makes you sound crazy."

She walked outside his apartment and into the hallway. "I found a brain tumor during the examination," she said. "Kinda strange."

"No surprise there," said Jake. "I've had that tumor since I was a kid."

The door closed behind her, and Carrie sighed. That hadn't gone as she'd planned. And she still had no story for the Lead Coroner. The door reopened, and Jake's tired face contemplated hers. Something had changed.

"Wait a minute. You said there was a tumor in that head?"

CHAPTER 40

D r. Blake picked up Jake's clothes and placed them back in the closet. She flipped his furniture upright and set the pots and pans back into the cabinets. She listened to Jake's tale about the parasite who took up residence in his body and manifested as a small pimp and then about his trips to hell. He showed her the marks on his back, which hadn't been on his other body, but he couldn't tell if she believed him.

Jake went to take a shower. He turned the water all the way hot and stood in it until his skin was plump and sore. Thoughts crowded his mind. His father, his mother, the Russians, and whatever he was going to do to save his soul. Then the fucking tumor. All he had done to cure himself, all the shit he had to endure in hell, yet still he had this tumor wedged in his brain. A part of him felt as if being in hell had been a relief compared to what he had to deal with in real life. He was more anxious than ever. He toweled off and retreated to his bedroom, putting on a fresh set of black jeans, a blue crewneck tee, and no socks. He went to the living room to talk more with Dr. Blake—Carrie. Sly sat next to her on the couch, his arm slung casually above her shoulders.

"What the fuck, yo?" shouted Jake.

Carrie startled and straightened. "I waited until you were out. I thought you wanted to talk some more."

"Not you," said Jake. "Him!"

Carried eyed the space next to her.

"Are you still freaking out about that tumor in your head?" asked Sly. "No one here is more disturbed than I. Best I can tell, the problem is in your DNA."

"You're supposed to heal me!" Jake said. "Heal as in, new."

"Ah, well. Yes . . . but all I do is copy, motherfucker! I copy DNA and then reproduce it. I read the code. I duplicate the code. And there you are, good as new."

"But I'm not good," said Jake. "That head that she cut open shouldn't have a tumor. I'd already died a couple of times."

"How many times have you died?" asked Carrie.

"Four times," said Jake. "The last time was at the mall. I was walking toward the exit and then died. I thought it was Tartarus pulling me back to hell, but it was the tumor. It killed me." Jake turned to Carrie. "You said it was so large that I shouldn't have been able to walk, right?"

"Yes," she said. "The tumor is located between the cerebellum and the brain stem. You should have trouble with coordination, balance, breathing, heart rate, and simple motor skills. It's a miracle you survived as long as you have. But . . ." she gulped, incredulous to be saying such things, " . . . when you died at the mall, that was after the train?"

Jake nodded. "My head regrew with another tumor inside! How fucked up is that?"

"*'Do you understand the words coming out of my mooouuuth!'*" said Sly. "You have a genetic defect. The tumor is in your DNA."

"I'm fucked, then," said Jake. "I can die at any minute. Then I go to hell. I revive only to die again until Tartarus traps my soul forever." Jake dropped to the floor, defeated.

"You said the parasite copies your DNA, is that right?" said Carrie. "Why can't that thing search for what causes the tumor and try to correct it?"

"I thought you were the smart one," said Sly, leaning into Carrie's face. "There are trillions of fucking code. If I start fucking around, who knows, he might come back as a lobster or a pterodactyl."

Jake rolled his eyes at Carrie. "He said it's too complicated. Something about dinosaurs or something."

Carrie shook her head. "Small changes wouldn't have such dramatic effects," she said. "Listen, when reproduction begins, copies of the mother and father determines what the DNA for the offspring will be. A copy, just like this, uh, parasite inside of you does, but you get differences— evolution—from generation to generation because out of the trillions of codes it copies, it gets some wrong. This is how you get different skin colors, eye color, hair, and so on. It will be like an experiment of sorts."

"Or a foot growing out of his head," said Sly trying to play with Carries long hair. "How about that, Doc?"

Jake didn't bother repeating the parasite's contribution.

"If this parasite is as intelligent and advanced a lifeform as I believe it is, it should be able to do it." reasoned Carrie. "It doesn't matter how many mistakes it makes along the way. If it keeps a copy of your present DNA, it can always reset you back to your current state. The genetic code between humans and chimpanzees is less than 1 percent. But 1 percent of a trillion is . . ."

"10 billion," said Sly. Sly looked serious. He was silent. His eyes darted around in his head, and he gestured with his hands as if he were calculating. "Let me dwell on this awhile," he said and disappeared.

"What did it say?" asked Carrie.

"He's working on it, I guess," said Jake. He went to the window and peered through the blinds. Nightfall. Lights of the city glistened in the darkness. "It doesn't matter. I'm still hosed. I was so close to putting this whole experience behind me. After the Russians got what they wanted, I thought things would get better."

"Russians?" she said. She shifted around on the couch to where Jake stood. Intrigued.

"Yeah, don't worry about them. They think I'm dead."

"They were the ones who came by the office posing as lawyers."

"Probably in search of my laptop. They won't be back. They have it now."

"Why were they after it?"

Jake removed his finger from the blinds and shut the curtains. "I stole nearly 400 million dollars from the Russian mob," he said casually.

"Is that all?" asked Carrie.

"Yeah. But I don't know why they want my laptop so bad." Jake rubbed the back of his neck in thought.

She laughed nervously. "How about so they can get their money back? Holy crap, how can you be so nonchalant? This gets more interesting by the minute."

Jake took a deep breath. "Long story, but they have the money already. They took it before they killed me the first time."

"Oh," said Carrie. She recalled the uncomfortable exchange between her and the Russians in the parking lot. "So *they* killed you the first time. I see."

The mystery of the computer was troubling. Jake sat on the couch next to Carrie hoping to come up with an explanation that made sense. "This is nuts."

"Ahem . . . speaking of nuts," said Carrie. "I need you for something. Something big!" She shot him a nervous smile.

"Like what?"

"Like saving my job," said Carrie. "I spent four hours at the train station picking you up, sorting you out from the other debris, carefully tagging and identifying everything that was Jake Coltrane. Then you walked out the back of the van. How do I explain this to my boss?"

"What about that guy that jumped out of the driver's door while driving?" said Jake. "That was kind of crazy."

"Crazy?" She did a double take. "Did you say jumping out of a moving vehicle after a severed cadaver grew a new head and sat up from a body bag was crazy?"

"Sorry," said Jake. "I've come back so often it's no longer novel."

Carrie shook it off, as crazy seemed to be the new norm. "I've been trying to reach Lee by cellphone, calling and texting, so that we can in to work together and tell the same story. Now I'm thinking there's a better way. You can walk in there with me."

"Me?" said Jake. You want me to go to your boss and tell him I regrow body parts. No thanks. What's he going to accept as proof? Will he lop off a finger and watch it grow back? No way."

"You're going to leave me high and dry?" asked Carrie. "Thanks a lot. You're going through a lot, but I shouldn't be dragged into it. You need to clean up the mess you left in my life. If it comes down to losing my job or ratting you out, I will rat you out, buddy."

"Okay, fine!" said Jake. "I'm still in trouble with Jericho Black, so I can't exactly make an appearance just yet, but I will help you find your partner. The two of you can talk to him, or I can call someone to help persuade him to let it go."

Carrie studied Jake, biting her lip. "Are you some kind of secret government experiment? Are we going to get our minds erased if we can't sort this out?"

"Who knows?" said Jake. "I have no idea how Jericho will handle it. What's your assistant's name?"

"Lee Barbarossa."

Jake pulled out his phone and searched social media, downloading as many pictures as possible of Lee Barbarossa. Next, he accessed his software. "Got him," said Jake. "Not much activity, but here's an image of him heading to a house in South Jersey about three hours ago. I'll give you the address."

"Wow!" said Carrie. "That's some super-secret, government-spy gadgetry you got there. Are you sure we won't be killed if you contact that other guy with the parasites? I'm a bit worried now. Jake? Jake?"

His eyes rolled to the back of his head, and he felt nauseated. "Sly," slurred Jake as dizziness set in. "Where are you? What's going on?" It was happening. The now-familiar feeling. He was about to die.

"Lie down, Jake," Carrie instructed.

Jake swung his legs around the couch and stretched out, elevating his head on one of the armrests. Carrie hurried to the kitchen and grabbed a handful of ice from the freezer, rolled it up in a hand towel, and pressed it against the back of his neck. A cold sweat formed on his forehead. His eyes glazed over.

"I can't go back. Not now. It's too soon. I can't take it," said Jake.

"Go back where?" asked Carrie.

"To hell!"

Carrie rubbed the ice at the base of his head and checked his pulse. "There must be something triggering the swelling. How often does this happen?"

"All the time now. Ever since I—"

"It's the parasite," said Carrie. Consternation furrowed her brows. "The tests I ran showed elevated levels of histamine, bradykinin, and prostaglandins in your bloodstream, which leak into tissue and cause swelling. Toxins cause the release of those chemicals. Parasites produce toxins."

Carrie popped to her feet and went into the kitchen. She opened the cabinet where Jake kept his drugs and vitamins. She grabbed a handful of ibuprofen. In his spice cabinet, she found turmeric, put a spoonful in a glass of water, and returned to Jake. "Here. Take this." He winced and gagged but got it all down.

"It seems to have passed," said Carrie. "You're fine. For now."

CHAPTER 41

A range of emotions, from elation to failure, swam through Alexei's gut as he made the phone call to Sergei. They had the laptop and had gone through its contents from end to end. They found on Jake's computer files an investigation written in Russian by an ex-KGB officer who worked as a private investigator, and about ninety hours' worth of voice recordings. A lot of fluff to work through. The bottom line was an investigator was looking into the death of Julie Shubert's brother while he was in the *Vor*.

Sergei picked up on the third ring.

"We have the laptop," said Alexei. "Nothing involving Turgenev. She was investigating the death of her brother. That's all."

"Did you comb through it?" asked Sergei. "Turgenev is sweating this. Very nervous. The investigator must've found evidence that connects Turgenev to something big. Major implications, Alexei. A man like Turgenev does not pay hundreds of millions of dollars to a mail-order bride unless his fortune is at stake."

"I understand," said Alexei. "Vlad and Dima are the best."

Alexei glanced in their direction. The two sat side by side in the soft glow of computer monitors. Their throats emitted a collective gulp as the distant focus of their eyes glossed over momentarily. Alexei hadn't meant to intimidate, but they needed to get it right.

"We will take another pass at it," said Alexei. "If we can't find anything else, I will call Jericho Black and ask for his hacker. She is supposed to be a tech hotshot. A prodigy."

"Wait," said Sergei. Alexei could almost hear the gears of Sergei's mind churn through the details. "Was the mail-order bride from Samara?"

Alexei nodded before speaking. "I heard Samara mentioned in the recordings."

"The brother must have been one of the *Vory* slaughtered in Samara during the midnineties." Sergei chuckled, abruptly in good spirits. "Forward the recordings to me. Then call Natalia and tell her we have listened to the recordings. After that, the ball is in your court. You can do what you wish with Turgenev."

Alexei had heard in his youth about the *Vory* incident at Maximillian's Restaurant in Samara. Twenty-seven members of a *Vory* organization killed, some by gunshot, but most by a single strike of a sledgehammer. In the early nineties, the *Vor* essentially took advantage of a destabilized government. The gangsters made obscene money while the average Russian could barely afford a loaf of bread. *Vory* mob wars were common. Under Putin, the *Vor*'s influence had lessened, taking a back seat to politicians and oligarchs who often used tactics as brutal as the *Vor*. Even Putin occasionally used *Vory* slang to show his political opponents what methods he had at his disposal.

Alexei understood Sergei's pressure, and he was happy that he had provided the information they requested. He was simply stumped as to what he had found.

"Good work, Alexei," said Sergei. The call ended.

His cellphone buzzed with a new contact. Natalia Makarova.

CHAPTER 42

---◆◆◆---

Jake had been waylaid on his couch for over a day. It was close to noon, and he'd gone through half a bottle of ibuprofen. The makeshift icepack at the base of his neck had long ago turned to warm water. Carrie had also gone hours ago, most likely to the address of the home where her assistant hid. She'd left him with instructions to take two pills every four hours. Jake thought about calling Catalina several times. With her caring heart, she was sure to come over and keep him company, lift his spirits, and be the friend he needed.

He resisted calling. His situation hadn't changed; he wasn't cured of the tumor. Plus, he had new problems. Jake reached behind him and traced the markings on his back. Three out of seven felt rougher than the others. They were the marks that were filled in. He felt them being burned into his skin, once, twice, and then the third time, all within a few seconds of each other. From what he had gathered, the paramedic was bringing him back to life before Sly had the chance to reset his body.

Suppose Catalina or anyone else was in the room when he died. In that case, they'd call the paramedics, and the same thing would happen, another mark filled without Jake getting the opportunity to use them properly. The next time, all four of his chances could go at once.

Jake sat up on the couch. He'd made a decision.

"Whatcha thinking, brah?" asked Sly from the kitchen, drink in hand, wearing a fuzzy white fedora hat and sunglasses. "I can feel the malice coursing through your veins."

"Then you know it's best you stay away from me right now."

"I can't," said Sly. "You're about to do something stupid. I can't let you go without trying to talk sense into you."

"I'm going to find out about that kid, save his soul, and save mine at the same time," said Jake. "Which is more than what you're doing."

"You think I'm lounging around?" said Sly. "I am searching for the way to alter your DNA to get rid of that tumor."

"Then what's taking so long?"

"There are billions of chains involved. I'm studying the mRNA sequence to see if I can spot the source of the cell defect."

"Good. You do that. Meanwhile, I'll take care of things on my end." He stood, unplugged his phone from the charger, placed it into his pocket, and headed to the door. Sly blocked his way.

"What are you doing?" said Jake.

"I can physically stop you if I wanted to, but I'm not going to do that. I want to explain something to you before you go."

"You have ten seconds."

"Remember when I said those things about sensing strength in others? I was trying to insult you, and I'm sorry. You're not a five, but I wanted to give you a good indication of the uphill battle you're facing if you insist on meeting with Adonis Silver. He's many times stronger than you. The other men in the mall were between twelve and fifteen. Adonis Silver is about two hundred."

"What?" said Jake.

"He's not normal, and he's dangerous. I don't know why he's that strong but until I figure it out, stay far away from him."

"That's insane, Sly," said Jake. But after thinking about it a moment, it made perfect sense. "That means there's something special about the guy, like Samson or Moses. Putting him back on the right path will earn me my place."

"But taking his eyeball? Come on, Jake. Even you can figure out it's a trap."

"I don't take it literally, Sly. I'm not an idiot. I'm going there to talk to the guy. Save his soul."

"He killed that woman yesterday," said Sly. "I don't know how he did it, but he killed her. He'll kill you too. His strength is peculiar. You don't want to end up in hell with another chance wasted."

"Time's up," said Jake. "I'm not convinced."

Jake grabbed the door handle, but Sly pushed his hand so that it struck the door. He willed his muscles to pull, but nothing happened. It was as if the impulses from the brain had been cut off. "Sly . . ." Jake muttered, frustrated.

"If you're going to do this, you need protection," said Sly. "I implore you."

CHAPTER 43

A series of storms were in the forecast for the next few days. Dramatic streaks of gray swirled above him. Sparks of light flashed, rendering everything with eerie illumination. The old man in hell all but promised that taking the eye of Adonis Silver would save Jake's soul. Jake had a valuable eye of his own: the eyes of every camera in the city. He watched Adonis throughout the day, biding his time. When he spotted an opportunity, he'd put his plan into action.

Adonis frequented a synagogue in Manhattan almost every day after school. It must have been a volunteering gig or something, as he had a key. It was the perfect place for a private conversation.

Jake called for an Uber ride into New York. Staten Island to Brooklyn, through Brooklyn to Queens, near where he grew up. He asked the driver to let him out just short of his destination at a small bodega on the corner of Hollis Ave. He stepped inside to grab another bottle of ibuprofen and a bottle of water. The clerk, an Indian man in a light blue collared shirt, stood behind a Plexiglas barrier surrounded by scratch-off tickets and random, brightly packaged performance-enhancing concoctions. Jake slid his card through the opening. The clerk looked at the black card strangely but swiped it across his machine to take $7.48 of Jake's money.

Jake walked back onto the corner and looked across the street at a storage facility, one of those chain places with bright orange doors advertising cheap monthly rates and charging exorbitant service fees. He repeated the security code for the front gate in his head so he wouldn't look a fool trying to recall it in front of the touchpad. Feeling confident, he crossed the street and punched in the code at the gate.

The wrought iron gate rolled to the side, and he walked into the lot. Jake had opted for one of those controlled climate spaces to store his mementos, precious pictures and other belongings once belonging to his mother, father, and sister. To Jake, the place was like a family mausoleum. He visited when he felt lonely. He liked to spend some time with objects that triggered good memories in his life. The monthly rent was killing him, though.

The cold, orange roll-up door rattled as Jake raised it. He looked left and right. No one. Corner cameras pointed down each hallway within view of his unit. He didn't want the management to see what he had stored, so he promptly let the door fall closed behind him. With a click, a four-inch LED flashlight lit up the inside of the storage unit. He moved a few boxes filled with old items and computer parts he wasn't ready to part with and found the black plastic gun case beneath some old shoeboxes. He opened it.

The massive stainless steel gun, a Magnum Research BFR, emanated power and elegance. BFR stood for Big Frame Revolver. It fired 45-70 government rounds—rifle cartridges capable of killing elephants—from a slender ten-inch barrel. Five pounds, five shots, and a kick like a freshly-branded mule.

A low whistle from the corner. "Serious gun for serious shit," said Sly, emerging from the shadows. "I like the idea of having a gun by your side. Just in case."

"I'm not going to have it by my side," said Jake. "It'll be in front of me, pointed right at him. I don't have time to build a relationship with him. A quick, impactful, life-changing event will do the trick. I plan to use the 'scared straight' tactic. You said he killed that woman. I'm going to tell him I know about it and threaten to kill him if he doesn't change his ways."

"That's risky, Jake," said Sly. "I don't know how he killed her. Maybe if I get close to him again I'll sense how he does it. Until then, I suggest you keep that beauty hidden."

Jake reached in deeper and pulled out a box of Underwood Ammo Xtreme Penetrator bullets. A solid copper round with the nose shaped in an X pattern. It delivered 3740 ft. lb. of energy. When fired, flames danced from the barrel. And whatever it hit exploded.

Jake loaded the ammo and spun the cylinder.

"A ten-inch gun with Xtreme Penetrator bullets," said Sly. "You can't make this shit up."

"Stop trying to be funny, asshole," said Jake.

Sly pointed to the weapon in disbelief. "How are you supposed to handle that thing with your flimsy-ass wrists?"

"I can handle it fine," said Jake.

"Use a nine milli like every other brother out there," Sly pleaded. "I'd feel so much more comfortable."

Jake shook his head. "I purposely bought this single-action revolver out of respect for life. Pull the hammer back, hold on with two hands, aim and fire. This gun makes every bone in your hand hurt. It puts a strain on your forearms and elbows. The kick reminds you that you're going to take someone's life." Jake aimed at an empty shoebox. "A nine millimeter you can squeeze all day without flinching. This gun forces you to be steady on your feet, aim properly, and pull the trigger—once! And once I pull the trigger, I want there to be no mistake. No flesh wounds, no through and through. I intend to kill the man on the other end of the barrel. Dead!"

Jake put on a Shamrock Holster with a three-piece Bandito shoulder belt. He checked to make sure everything was concealed. He dug into more boxes to find his father's black leather Jacket. His father was tall, like Jake, and it fit perfectly. Hiding that monster pistol inside a long leather jacket was no easy task. Especially while taking public transportation through the city. But because he was so tall, it was easier for him to conceal than for most people. When he was satisfied that the pistol wouldn't be seen, he looked through his boxes for another item. It was a coin. A 1976 bicentennial quarter his mother said was special because it would be worth something someday. He had always cherished it as a good luck charm.

"Let's go," said Jake.

Jake pulled down the door of his storage unit, locked it behind him and headed outside. He pulled out his phone and triggered his program to locate Adonis Silver, who was leaving school and heading to the synagogue in West Village. Jake hopped on the train from New Jersey and headed there. He stood the entire trip, holding the handrail, regardless of if there were empty seats or not. With the BFR hand cannon under his arm, it was easier if he stood. He played it cool, even walked by police with his coat partially open on the way out of the terminal. He emerged on Christopher

Street and checked his phone to see if there was any movement. The arrow stuck on Adonis's last position.

The synagogue was a hulking brick structure in the middle of a block of attached buildings. It looked like the Catholic church his mother used to drag him to every Sunday morning, with the Star of David over the door instead of a cross. Jake climbed the concrete stairs, ten of them, and tried the brown double doors at the entrance. Open.

The sounds from outside disappeared as the heavy door closed behind him. He stood on a thin red swath of industrial carpet, getting his bearings. It smelled sweet and warm. Before him ran the central aisle with wooden pews on each side. Small chandeliers were suspended over the pews down the length of the synagogue. A velvet curtain, burgundy in color, was past the pulpit, with gold fringes hanging down a foot from the top. His eyes panned down the curtain and stopped. Adonis Silver stood to the right of the pulpit wearing a yellow button-up and tan slacks. His young, fresh face radiated innocence as he placed ivory-colored candles one at a time in a menorah.

Jake pulled his revolver out and cocked the hammer. The sound echoed through the synagogue. Adonis turned his head toward Jake, unfazed. Not even a widening of the eyes or a tensing of the muscles. He was strikingly calm. Self-assured.

Jake raised his massive weapon and looked straight down the barrel, lining up the sights with Adonis's chest. Doubt entered his mind. His throat tightened as he tried to speak.

"I know you killed that woman at the mall yesterday. If you keep this up, I will have to kill you. Stop this madness. Be good, Adonis Silver, or else you will go to hell."

"I don't understand," said Adonis. His hands were by his side. Unshaken. "Why can't I see you?"

"What?" said Jake. The question made no sense. Nothing about who he was or why he was there.

"I can't see you," said Adonis. "It is as if you don't belong here."

Three people, Jake thought it might be Adonis's family, came through the burgundy curtains at the rear. They froze when they saw Jake. The mother put a hand to her trembling mouth. His father stepped forward, but his wife grabbed his arm, holding him back. His sister, about twelve, started to wail. The barrel of Jake's gun swung toward them. He immediately regretted it and aimed again at Adonis Silver. But the young girl's wails turned to shrieks, so he pointed the gun back in her direction. Back and forth, Adonis and then his family. Tiny beadlets of sweat popped up on Jake's forehead.

"Don't anybody move," said Jake weakly. It was the only phrase that came to him. "And shut that damn kid up. I can't think." The mother instantly removed her hand from her mouth and placed it over the child's.

"This is between Adonis and me," Jake continued.

"You're not going to kill my son!" said Adonis's father, breathing heavily. He wasn't a big man, but Jake could tell he wanted to move, could see his body tensing. He swung the gun toward the man.

"Didn't think this through, did you?" asked Adonis.

So calm even in the face of death. As if he knew Jake wouldn't harm him. Jake hated and admired that about him. Admired because if Jake were as calm things would've gone down much smoother. Coincidently, he hated Adonis for the same reason. Jake mentally kicked himself for not tracking the family. Now he was in a dilemma. They were witnesses. His plan was coming apart at the seams.

"What do you want?" asked the mother.

The chance to scare Adonis privately was gone. But perhaps another option had opened before him. Gaining confidence, he spoke freely. "Your son knows the things he has done!" said Jake. "I'm here to let him know that if he continues on the path he's chosen, he will pay the consequences. *If your eye causes you to sin, then pluck it out, for it is better to enter paradise with one eye than to be cast into hell with two!*"

Adonis flinched. He recovered instantly as if it never happened, but Jake noticed.

"Did you see that?" said Sly, sitting in one of the pews to Jake's right. He pointed right at Adonis. "That verse triggered something. His bloodlust is elevated like it was at the mall."

"I see," said Adonis. "You know more about me than I know about you. You have me at a disadvantage."

"His power scares the shit out of me," commented Sly. "Now that I'm close, I can sense his strength. I think . . . I think he can kill people by wishing them dead."

Oh fuck, thought Jake.

"Do it now," shouted Sly. "Shoot him! His bloodlust grows! This motherfucker is bad news. He's trying to kill you. Shoot him!"

Jake snapped his head over to where an animated Sly sat and gestured wildly, urging Jake to pull the trigger. Movement from the corner of his eye revealed Adonis's mother approaching slowly. Showing her hands.

"I see you're conflicted," she said as she crept forward. Her long black hair was tied up wildly in a bun. She eased in closely. Careful not to invade his space. "I understand. Whatever Adonis did to you or someone you love, it was a mistake. An accident. He didn't know what he was doing." Somehow she knew what he could do.

"Mom," said Adonis. "I can handle this."

"It's a mother's job to protect her children. Do you have any children, sir?" she was close enough that he could see her features. Compassionate dark brown eyes looked out from a tender-faced woman. Nothing but concern for her child.

"Don't listen to her!" snapped Sly. "She's weakening your resolve. Squeeze the trigger! The old man in hell told you to do it if you had to. Kill him, Jake!"

"Shut up!" screamed Jake. He looked around, blurry-eyed and confused. Everyone needed to be quiet.

A mother, she'd said. Mothers protected their children. Moms protected through love and forgave their children, no matter what they may have done. Even someone like Adonis, a kid who could be a killer.

"Who was there to show me love?" Jake cried, although he hadn't meant to say it aloud. The confusion of thoughts in his head spilled out and tainted everything. He grew dizzy.

"Is that what this is all about?" said Adonis, smirking. "Mommy didn't love you? I thought you were stronger than that."

His harsh voice was like a pinprick directing Jake's focus. He re-aimed the gun barrel toward the center of Adonis's chest. "What did you say about my momma?"

He waited for any excuse to pull the trigger.

"I'm streaming this whole thing, mister," said a voice.

A young voice. Female. Her phone pointed right at him, the three lenses in the top left corner like the eyes of a hunting spider. "You shoot my brother, and everyone will know what a monster you are."

Me? A monster?

"Give me that phone," Jake said and pointed the gun at the young girl.

The mother stepped in front of the barrel, and the father stepped in front of the girl.

"Give me that fucking phone, or I will shoot you all," said Jake.

"Too late for that," said the girl. "It's going out to all my friends, and they know where we are because they come here too."

"She's right, Jake," said Sly, appearing at his shoulder. "I feel people heading in this direction with the intent to do bodily harm. Must be the pigs! No time to dilly-dally. We have to move."

"Don't worry," said Adonis. "He won't be killing any of us today."

The smug fuck. Jake wanted to shoot him just because Adonis seemed so positive that he wouldn't. He stepped briskly down the red-carpeted aisle and waved the gun at the mother.

"Move," he said.

She stepped aside. Adonis stood tall, not an ounce of fear in his eyes. It reminded Jake of his time in juvie. So many young men pretending to be brave to the point of stupidity. Jake kept his aim firm. Adonis soon lowered his gaze and calmly stepped to the side.

Jake went around the right corner of the pulpit, pointing the cannon at the father, who hesitated at first; a nudge of the barrel got him to move enough for Jake to reach the girl. Her wide eyes looked up at him. A mixture of fear and hatred welled within the mirrors of her soul. Jake snatched the phone from her hand. He placed the gun against the girl's chest just in case anyone wanted to make a move while he checked the phone. She hadn't bluffed. Fifty people and counting viewing the stream.

"Stupid girl," he yelled and flung the phone to the other side of the synagogue. It bounced and clattered against the pews before tumbling to the floor. By the time the phone's broken pieces had settled, he'd escaped through the velvet curtains at the back.

CHAPTER 44

Natalia Makarova marveled at the palace-like setting. Thirty-foot ceilings with windows almost as tall. It was nighttime in St. Petersburg, and the scintillating display of soft blue sparkles of water from the fountain outside the Admiralty building stood out from the background.

Inside, golden statues of Greek gods in various poses of strength and stature lined the wall, one every ten feet. Old World carvings of golems and fairies topped the archway entrance, looking down on those who came and went. Long tables draped in white cloth displayed an abundance of appetizers, fruit, wine, and vodka. A small orchestra at the end of the room played soothing music. Servants stood at attention, ready to cater to the guests.

It was a celebration for Piotr Turgenev. Mr. Turgenev circled the room, talking and shaking hands with his wife by his side. He was anticipating a major award from the government regarding oil production—several billions of dollars' worth. All wealthy and influential power brokers in Russia, friends and enemies alike, lined up to congratulate him.

Natalia played her part for the evening, making rounds among the dignitaries, smiling, laughing, and flexing her power as a key figure within the government. Her longtime friendship with Turgenev had strengthened over the years. She had the Kremlin's ear, and Turgenev was often the beneficiary.

Natalia cherished her role as a high-ranking official. Her sumptuous red gown with ritzy glass beads begged for attention. She extended her delicate hand as a greeting and drank wine with those eager to have an opportunity to be in her presence. Natalia was a conduit of sorts; if her admirer impressed her enough, she'd pass their name on as someone worthy of the Kremlin's time.

She scanned the hall for Mr. Turgenev, lost somewhere among the dense population of guests. She smiled, thinking about later when Piotr would claim an urgency to discuss work with someone of importance at the banquet and that Mariya, his wife, shouldn't wait for him. His driver would whisk Mariya back to their living quarters while another car absconded Piotr to the secluded cabin off in the woods, where Natalia would be waiting. Her heart fluttered. The things men hid from their wives only to seek out from other women.

Being the other woman had its advantages. Indulging in Piotr's special needs made it that much more exciting. The sex was passionate. She was a person who did not need the cuddling and fondling, although she did enjoy when Turgenev showed her those courtesies.

Music and the low murmur of conversation brought her thoughts back to the ballroom. The man in front of her was Kotsky, who seemed to have bribed his way into the banquet by his knockoff suit and cheap footwear. Men with no real wealth always forgot about the shoes.

She kept glancing down at those ordinary brown shoes as he spoke, smiling as if she were interested while secretly laughing at his lame attempt to be accepted as one of them.

"My scientists are urging me to explore the Belukha Mountain for natural gas," he said. "There is strong evidence that what we will find will furnish the entire country for the next fifty years."

"Fifty years? Fascinating," she said.

"The government must be made aware of this incredible resource waiting to be tapped."

Her phone rang from the small clutch under her arm. She pulled it out and glanced at the screen. United States. "Excuse me," she said and left Kotsky with his sad little shoes.

She pressed Accept. Nothing at first, not even a greeting. Finally, she heard Alexei's voice.

"We have Julie Shubert's recordings," said Alexei. "We should meet."

"We will come to you," she said. Her heart pounded. "We will make arrangements. I will be in touch. Good evening, Alexei."

She swallowed the sudden jolt of anxiety and turned her radiant smile up a notch. Natalia was a skilled politician, proficient in pretending everything was positive in the face of disaster. And Alexei's call was unquestionably hell breaking loose. He most definitely knew she tried to have him eradicated, and now he held the evidence that could destroy Turgenev. Breaking the news to Turgenev would not be easy.

Natalia twisted her way through the crowd, ignoring those eager to bend her ear. She retrieved her long, sable fur coat and headed to the balcony for fresh air and some time alone to think in the brisk night air. Her hand fumbled in a pocket for her favorite pack of smokes. She lit one up and sucked the nicotine into her lungs.

As she exhaled, an uneasy chuckle escaped her. That bastard Alexei proved to be smarter than she'd given him credit. She regarded the big oaf as a tool with no mind of his own. Such a description was true for most of the hitmen in the *Vor*, merely instruments used to soothe the worries of those in power and when necessary sacrificed for the greater good. But this Alexei had a few tricks up his sleeve. All she could do now was arrange the meeting and find out what he intended to do.

Natalia looked back into the banquet from the balcony and saw Mr. Turgenev with his wife on his arm. She was a statuesque Russian beauty ten years his junior. Tall and slim with long blonde hair and eyes the color of a tropical ocean. Back in the days when the Soviet Union first collapsed, his wife's family came into prominence and was at the forefront of the economic resurgence during the time of Gorbachev. An influential and well-connected woman, if rather stuck up about her position in society. If she only knew how close to death's touch she stood, joined as she was to Piotr's arm.

Natalia took out her phone and called made a call. "I have an emergency trip to make to the United States. Urgent business that cannot wait. I will be gone for only a few days."

She wanted to say more, how she enjoyed life with him and being with him provided the opportunity to excel within the government. He'd granted her access to things that would've been impossible on her own. She wanted to thank him for his love and understanding. Being married to her wasn't easy with the type of ambitions she sought out in life. She could've gone on and on, but her sudden candidness would only cause him to worry.

In the end, she simply told her husband of twenty-two years, "I will let you know when I have returned."

CHAPTER 45

Jake's spirit was crushed. His chance of a normal life, over. He wandered through the city. No one needed a tracking program as accurate as his to tell him his days were numbered. Video investigators were a common thing. They probably already knew his name and where he lived.

The little girl called me a monster. Jake's sister said the same thing about the person who shot their mother.

He'd only confronted Adonis Silver for a chance to save his soul. Advice given from hell, he reminded himself. He felt stupid and manipulated. Like people sacrificing virgins on an altar or suicide bombing, someone had convinced them it was the only way to save themselves and Jake's willingness to believe ended up no different.

Jake roamed the subway system, riding around Manhattan for hours on end. He transferred trains into New Jersey, the same Penn Station where he'd died several days before. His head swiveled as he emerged from the tunnels, wary of the officers patrolling the platforms.

A fine drizzle of rain turned the streets a hazy gray. He couldn't go to his apartment since officers would be there waiting to question him. Jericho would be no help since he pushed Jake in front of a train for being stubborn. The Russian threat was over. The last chance to raise is spirits was Catalina. So he called her. The wet streets were devoid of activity. He could speak freely.

"Hello?" she said cautiously.

"Hey, this is Jake."

"Yeah," she said bitterly.

"Ah . . . I wanted to talk for a bit. Tell you what's going on with me."

"Okay, explain yourself."

"I, uh . . . screwed up this time and—"

"The police were here, asking if I know where you are. They said you assaulted a family with a weapon. What happened to you, Jake? First you stole money, now you're threatening people?"

"I—I don't know what I was thinking." He couldn't tell her about the old man from hell asking Jake to save Adonis's soul. That would make him sound even crazier. "I recently found out I had some repressed memories involving my father."

"Your father made you hold those people at gunpoint now?"

"No, but it turns out that my father was the one who—"

"Wait," she said. "Stop right there. I've been listening to your sob stories about your family situation for years. Always looking for sympathy about how you ended up in group homes. But look at you. You made something of yourself, Jake. You have a great job, you put yourself through school, and you have the kind of skills that make the privileged jealous." She softened her voice. "You're about to tell me what your father did when I don't even know who my father is, Jake. Lots of us grew up in broken homes. Don't blame your upbringing on what you've done. In case you didn't know, Jake, you made it! Against all odds. But you threw it all away, and why? Because you feel like you've been cheated by life somehow."

"You don't understand," said Jake. "I . . . the tumor . . ."

"We're all going to die someday, Jake. All of us. How you live is what's important, not how long. Don't—" Her voice cracked. "I had something good I wanted to tell you, Jake, but you don't deserve to hear it. Don't call me again." She cursed in Portuguese, and the phone beeped twice.

Jake looked at his phone, stunned. Then he kept moving. The rain had turned cold and heavy. He'd let her cool off a bit before trying again. She'd forgive him. She always did. She had a kind and compassionate soul.

But Jake still had to get what happened off his chest. Explain himself. For the good of his soul, he needed to confess. He wiped raindrops from his phone to look up the medical examiner's office. Carrie was the only other person he could talk to. She'd listen. The office was a half hour from where he was. The rain-darkened streets made it easier for him to walk without notice. He kept his head down and coat buttoned up.

The sloshing sound of wet shoes squished with each step he took.

Some of the drivers passing by took pity on him and swerved, while others splashed him with road water as they drove past. People at stoplights wondered why he was out on such a night; he could see it in their eyes as they sat warm and dry, staring at him while he waited for the light to turn. Rain struck the top of his head and ran down his face. His pants were so drenched they clung to his legs like a second skin.

A half hour later, Jake spotted the Coroner's office. He headed straight for the building, sloshing through a large puddle from a backed up storm drain. The glass entranceway was fogged up from condensation. He peered inside. A reception area. He tried the door. Locked. He banged on the door, sure Carrie was inside.

Fluorescent lights blinked one by one down the hallway. A man hurried toward the door. He was young, slim, and familiar, but practically a blur since Jake was focused down the white hallway, looking for Carrie.

The door opened and he felt the warmth of the inside.

"Dr. Blake?" the man shouted. "He's here."

Jake focused down the hallway that ran the length of the building to an emergency exit at the other end. There were matte gray doors leading to offices, three on the left and two on the right. Carrie poked her head through the middle door on the left.

Jake took a step out of the falling rain and then recognized the man who opened the door. Lee Barbarossa. Up and personal was different than in pictures. The only live glance Jake had was when he jumped from the driver's seat. Black hair, dark eyes, fair skin, wearing light green scrubs. Jake stood next to Lee, dripping with rainwater.

"I screwed up," said Jake. "Everything's screwed up."

Carrie motioned for him to come inside and Jake sopped through the hallway, drenched shoes squishing. Her curly black hair was swept up in a plastic clip, and thin metal-rimmed glasses slipped down toward her forehead. She looked very businesslike, especially with the white lab coat over her blue blouse and black slacks.

Lee walked behind him and closed the door. It was an examination room, large enough to hold four convex stainless steel operating tables designed to keep bodily fluids. Jake strode past the tables and a large bookcase filled with medical books of all sizes. He brushed his hand along the top of a small desk stacked with a couple of laptops. There were microscopes on a table against the wall and other equipment he did not recognize. Lastly, he spotted the cooling lockers where they kept the bodies.

He strolled through the space confirming it was just the three of them in the room. He even clicked open a couple of the cooling lockers to check for bodies. He told them about how he held Adonis Silver and his family at gunpoint. To justify his actions, he stripped down to his underwear and showed them the seven marks—three filled in—and explained his fate given by Tartarus.

Lee left the room and came back with dry green scrubs for Jake to wear, including little hospital booties to go over his feet. It felt good to be warm and dry, even though his confession did nothing to quell the anxiety. Jake sat in an ergonomic computer chair next to one of the monitors, hoping one of them would understand that he was not the monster the little girl accused him of.

"I guess that answers why the police were at your place a few hours ago," said Lee with a sigh.

"What?" said Jake. "You were at my apartment?"

"I asked him to go to your place and see if you were okay," said Carrie. "When I left, you were still on the couch with the icepack, afraid that you were going to die again."

Jake leaned forward, resting his head in his palms. "Then I left and took a gun into the city. That gets me three years mandatory."

"Don't forget the racial aspect of it," said Lee. "Hate crimes. Anti-Semitism. You were in a synagogue. NYPD's going to get off its ass and do everything to put you away for much longer than that."

Jake hung his head even lower.

They sat for a moment and let the gravity of what lay ahead sink in. Jake could only shake his head while contemplating his life choices. No matter how he tried to fix his situation, it only worsened. Not even death offered an escape. Hell in life, hell in death. Nothing but suffering existed in Jake's future.

"Maybe there's a way out of this," said Lee. He scooted his butt onto a stainless steel table near Jake. His sneakers dangled about a foot from the floor. "You're supposed to be dead, remember?"

Jake raised his head. "How does that help? They have video of me. Hard evidence."

"Exactly," said Lee, swinging his feet like an excited teenager. "But Jake Coltrane is logged into the system as deceased. Suicide by train. It couldn't be you who assaulted those folks in the synagogue because there's video all over the internet of your head flying from your body and rolling over the rail tracks."

Jake involuntarily cringed.

"Yes," said Carrie. She rose from her lab stool to come closer to the conversation. "I've seen it. A friend sent it to me. I have it on my phone."

"But the body never made it here," said Jake, expressively with his hands. "To confirm a death, you need a body."

Lee stopped his feet from wiggling. "We have one now," he said, looking at Jake.

Carrie's eyes widened and her mouth dropped open. "Of course. That's the answer!" She slapped the back of her hand into an open palm. "We can all be saved from this." She tapped a finger to her chin, wheels churning, then sprung up from the table excitedly.

"The reason I couldn't tell the truth about what happened was that I would lose credibility. No credibility means no one trusts what you say is true."

"I follow that much," said Jake.

"I told the Lead Coroner that Lee had an emergency and took off with the body," she continued. "He returns from his days off in the morning. We can show him your body. It saves us all."

Jake agitated. "But I am all put together now."

"You grew another head before, right?" said Carrie.

It took him a second. "No freaking way!" Jake yelped. "Are you crazy?" He leaped from his seat and stared them down. "Forget about it."

"Okay, calm down. Let's say you do nothing," said Lee. He pointed to himself and then Carrie. "I'll be fired for negligence, and Carrie will eventually lose her job. But you have much bigger problems," he said pointing to Jake. "If you're caught, you'll go to jail. The video of your decapitation will bring about a flurry of other questions. Someone died with your identification on him. Who was he?" He put a hand to his chin. "Damn, if he doesn't look just like the person whose identification he stole."

Jake furrowed his brow and looked to the ground. They were valid points.

"Do you think no one would compare the two videos as some sort of new mystery?" Lee continued. "If you think your main problem is jail, think again. You've seen those true-crime Netflix mysteries, haven't you? Do you think this will be put to rest after you're in prison? There's a good chance you'll become a lab rat. They'll cut and poke and eventually realize that you can regrow entire organs."

"The price of human survival, Jake," said Carrie, resting her hip against the table Lee sat upon. "The fascination is too great. I wanted to know how you came back to life, and so will everyone else. You won't be able to avoid the world if this gets out. People will be gunning for you. The government, independent investors, and everyone else. This plan is your way out."

"No," said Jake. He turned to both pleading for his empathy. "What part about going to hell do you not understand?"

"It's not a bad idea." Sly appeared. He reclined on one of the empty tables, looking up at the ceiling, wearing a sky-blue silk shirt and matching gabardine twill pants. His hair was in yet another style. Two big afro puffs with a part in the middle. His hands supported the back of his head, with his elbows out wide near the table. "You made a good decision in coming here to get chopped up. If everyone thinks you're dead we are home free."

Did no one hear him when he said he goes to hell? "Forget that noise," said Jake. "I'm out." Jake stood and went to gather his drenched clothing.

Carrie placed a hand on his arm. "NYPD detectives have already asked about viewing your body, Jake. They left a message a few hours ago. They expect an answer in the morning. That's why Lee is here so late. We were discussing what to say when they arrive. We're all out of options. There is no time to second-guess this, Jake."

"Stop being such a bitch," said Sly.

"Fuck you!"

"You don't have to be so rude," said Carrie. "I'm trying to save us."

"Not you," said Jake. "Fuck him!" He pointed to the empty table. "The parasite!"

"Suck a dick, nigga!" said Sly.

"Oh, is it back?" asked Carrie. "Where is it?" her eyes scanned the room.

"Huh?" said Lee. His face was scrunched with confusion while looking around the lab.

"Long story," said Carrie. "I'll fill you in later. What did he say?" she asked Jake.

Sly looked up at the ceiling as if he were watching fluffy clouds in a blue sky. His knees were bent with one folded over the other. "Listen motherfucker," said Sly. "I didn't tell you this before because I didn't know how you'd take it. I haven't done anything about the tumor because I can't change anything while you're alive. You gotta be dead when I alter your DNA. I know how you feel about dying, with this whole hell thing and all, so I didn't bring it up. Now you're in a pickle and her plan will help us out of this situation. Bite the bullet and get cut up. When you come back you won't have to worry about the tumor, going to jail, or anything else."

Carrie crept over to Jake slowly. "You've been quiet a long time, Jake," said Carrie. "Is everything okay?"

Jake looked for the chair and sat back down. "Sly said I have to be dead to fix the tumor."

It was the worst news he could possibly fathom. None of them took him seriously when he said he went to hell. They couldn't have or else they would not dare dream of suggesting this solution. The uncertainty of having to face Tartarus, Aruru and Gaap built slowly, until the fear gripped Jake's heart so tightly he could not breathe.

"No way," said Jake. He could run. Get as far away as he could. He had the black card. He could go anywhere in the United States. He was hard-headed before and would not listen. Now he was willing to go anywhere. Jake tightened his grip on the armrest of the chair with the intention of springing to his feet and escaping out the back exit. The darkened rainfall would aid in his disappearance.

As his fingers squeezed, the tension slipped from his body. His troubles melted away. He felt the chair on his back and legs and the firm floor beneath his feet. The soft fluorescent lighting cast a glow on the walls and tables, like sunshine on a careless day. He stared at the books in the bookcase against the wall filled with all sorts of shapes and colors of different binders. He felt good. Unnaturally good. He glanced at Sly.

"Are you doing this?"

"Yep. No more running. We are going to do this."

CHAPTER 46

They went over the details, with Sly's approval, and put the plan in motion. Lee took Carrie's car with instructions on where to find the van. It was parked at Carrie's family home in East Orange. Her parents had left her the house after they moved to Florida, and she rented the place out for extra cash. When a tree recently fell through the roof, the renters bolted, and her insurance wouldn't cover the damages since she'd failed to have the tree adequately trimmed. That left the home with a five-foot hole in the roof while she saved cash to get it repaired.

And a driveway ending at a garage big enough for a van.

While Lee retrieved the van, Carrie made preparations to put Jake under. Soon she'd use the tools of her trade to cut his body exactly like when the train had slashed him in two. She had several glossies of the body, in the condition she found it when she retrieved him from the subway, hanging from the whiteboard as a reference. She placed all the tools she needed on a roll-around cart next to Jake. A bright light shined down on Jake from above as he lay on the stainless steel operating table. A white sheet covered his nakedness from the waist down. The room was chilly.

"How about getting laid before we go under?" asked Sly. He was in a seat off to the right. Relaxed, looking as casual as ever. Same clothes and afro puff hairstyle. "Carrie is pretty nice. What do you think?"

Carried was preoccupied with her equipment, so she didn't notice Jake's attention. He liked what he saw. Black curly hair. Full pouty lips, natural, not like the injected type. A great smile with bright white teeth. Light brown skin with sparkling big brown eyes. Her eyebrows were trimmed and arched. Eyelashes long and full. She wore just enough makeup to cover the light freckles on her cheeks. Light touches of purple over the eyelids and red brushstrokes accentuating the cheekbones. He could see that she was toned and fit beneath the lab coat.

He shifted under the white sheet. "Not in the mood right now," said Jake. "I have bigger problems."

"That's why I'm pumping you full of more hormones," said Sly. "This will make you feel good. Remove all inhibitions so you can perform properly. I want sex, damn it. You have denied me for far too long. Ask Carrie for some booty!"

Carrie glanced over at him with a smirk. "What is it?" she asked. "Not in the mood for what?"

Jake shook his head. "Talking to Sly," he mumbled, heat rising to his cheeks. "That's all."

"Sly . . . the parasite."

"I hate being called a parasite, Jake! Call me the Intelligent Overseer!"

"Yeah," Jake said to Carrie. "Sly, the parasite!"

"You see him in your head, right?" asked Carrie. "What does he look like?"

"He looks like Katt Williams."

"Interesting," she said, eyebrows raised.

"She likes you, Jake," said Sly. "Why don't you ask her? We can do it right on the table. Right before she chops your fucking head off."

Jake turned his head to face Sly, who was now lying on the table next to him. "What the fuck is this *we*?" he asked Sly. "I'm the one having the . . . you know."

"I have no idea why you don't do that shit all the time," said Sly. "Sex seems to be the bomb! But I wouldn't know since you've denied me the pleasure. All I have are your dreams."

"Dreams?" asked Jake.

"Yep, I see those too. The ones of your ex-girlfriend. I experience them and everything. But those are memories. I want the real deal, asshole. So put your pride aside and beg if you have to."

"If you can see my memories, then you know it's not that easy!" said Jake.

"All that opportunity that you let slip by . . . only to go home and jack off!"

"Fuck you, man . . . aw, shit." Jake rubbed his head in frustration.

Sly laughed. "You're so embarrassed right now. You can't even jerk off in private anymore. I can feel the distressed neurons telling your asshole to pucker. Ha-ha!"

"Shut the fuck up, asshole!"

"Why are you cursing at him?" asked Carrie. She peeked at Jake curiously.

Jake placed his head back down on the table and tried to relax. "Stupid stuff he's saying, that's all. He's *a parasite*. He doesn't know squat!"

"I know how to spank that ass while we're doing it!" said Sly.

"Doing what?" said Jake. "Doing what? You don't even know what *it* is!"

Carrie picked up a syringe and inserted it into a clear phial. She pulled back the plunger, measuring the amount carefully. Then she flicked it a few times and squirted out some liquid to remove air bubbles.

"Here we go," she announced. "I'm going to give you this shot, and you'll be out. I'll give you another injection that will stop your heart. Once I complete the procedure, I'll have the cops and my boss view your body and schedule your body for cremation. After that you can come back to life, home free."

Jake shook his head. "I don't know if I can do this," he said. "No one seems to understand."

"I get it," said Carrie holding the needle upward. "I mean, who in their right mind is going to agree to get their head chopped off to keep from going to prison and save some stranger's job at the same time?"

He was really referring to his trip to hell, but it did not seem like anyone understood. Sly kicked in some more endorphins to calm his nerves and Jake was feeling good. His troubled thoughts melted away.

"Is there anything I can do for you before we get started?" she asked.

"No," said Jake, realizing he could not fight Sly on this. "Let's get this over with."

CHAPTER 47

A lexei could see the lights from a car moving outside the warehouse. He checked his watch. They were right on time. Just over twenty hours since he made that phone call to Natalia. The urgency of their wish to meet meant he had some leverage, although he still didn't understand what he had. Sergei had been vague, so it was a secret only those high enough in the *Vor* would appreciate. He'd also said Alexei could negotiate his terms with them. Alexei needed to keep this secret to himself if he were to reap its benefits.

He walked to the middle of the warehouse floor. A single lamp lent warmth to the cold space. The computer gear was gone, but he wasn't alone. The bodies of Vlad and Dima stretched on the floor beside the lamp. A cloudy blue sheen over their eyes indicated that they'd been dead for nearly a day. In a cool warehouse, enough to keep the bodies from decomposing to the point of being rancid.

Natalia and Turgenev came through the door. "What's this?" said Natalia stopping short of the bodies at Alexei's feet. Anxiety glinted in her eyes.

"Gesture of good faith," said Alexei.

They came closer, to where the lamp could illuminate them properly. Natalia had on a light-colored coat with a fur collar. Her hair was in a bun. She wore a scarf over her shoulders and stood next to Turgenev as if they were a couple. Turgenev was wearing a blue suit with a gray-speckled tie. Dressed for business.

Two other men entered with them. The muscle. Both well over six feet tall and broad at the shoulders, wearing black suits with a black shirt and no tie. Alexei chuckled. Like bouncers at a nightclub.

The two bodyguards reached inside their jacket pockets and pulled out their weapons in unison. Automatic pistols. Rather large. They pointed the barrels at the ground with their fingers beside the guard at the ready. Alexei was not about to raise his hands or agree to be patted down for a search.

Wisely, Turgenev waved his hand for the men to put their pistols away. "Wait outside," said Turgenev. "We won't be needing you for this meeting."

He spoke to the men in English, which triggered a thought for Alexei. They had access to American mercenaries. Like the man who tried to kill him in California. Alexei put the info in his back pocket to be brought up later.

The two men holstered their pistols and glared warnings at Alexei. Cute, he thought. A Russian would've known his reputation and never done something so ill-advised. They left with no idea how close they'd come to having their bodies added to the two at his feet. The large metal door slammed shut in the darkness, and all was still for a moment.

"Does Sergei know about this?" asked Turgenev.

"He does," said Alexei. "He is the one who told me to set up this meeting."

"How much does he know?" asked Natalia.

"Maximillian's Restaurant in Samara," said Alexei. It was really all Alexei knew in response.

Turgenev nodded in acceptance. "What does he want?"

"As far as I know, he doesn't want anything yet," said Alexei. "This is my negotiation. We start with what you were going to pay Julie Shubert to keep her mouth shut."

What was the mention of Samara worth? Going for the full $400 million was just to get the negotiations started. If they weaseled him down to a few hundred thousand, he'd be happy.

"Ten million," said Turgenev.

Alexei fought to maintain composure. He could've jumped high enough to reach the ceiling of the warehouse. He thought Turgenev would laugh at his request. Maybe offer him a few thousand after he figured out Alexei knew nothing. Alexei killed the hackers because they were not *Vory* and Sergei wanted to keep every aspect of this a secret. At the very least,

Turgenev would have to pay for his losses there. Ten million was beyond anything he could imagine.

How high was Turgenev willing to take this?

"Two hundred million," said Alexei.

Turgenev scoffed at the number. "Fifty million, and that is all I am willing to pay you because I have no idea what Sergei will ask. You will never have to steal another penny in your life if you don't want to. I would take the fifty million and be done with it."

Alexei was beaming on the inside, but this was a negotiation. Pushing it further was part of the game. There had to be something he could use to continue negotiating. "What about a penthouse on Fifth Avenue?" asked Alexei. Many of the *Vor* in Russia were given luxury apartments fully paid by oligarchs owing favors.

"Done," said Turgenev, without even thinking about it.

Unbelievable. He resisted smirking. But he wanted to smile and giggle like a schoolgirl. *Don't screw it up*, he thought. All he had to do was continue playing like he knew the dirt on Turgenev until he got paid.

Natalia reached inside her bag for a cigarette. Instinctively, Turgenev pulled a lighter out of his pocket and lit the tip, clicking the lighter shut after she exhaled. The two looked about as satisfied as if they had just had sex. Something about this negotiation was very wrong.

Turgenev stepped forward. Handsome and imposing. He looked great in his suit. And any anxiety he had in the beginning was long gone. The mixture of grey and brown hairs around the ears stood out as he got closer to the lamp. "Let me tell you why I gave you this money," said Turgenev.

Alexei tried to maintain an illusion of control. "What are you talking about?" said Alexei. "I know everything. That is what this is about."

"You know nothing," said Turgenev. "If you did, you would not have settled on fifty million. Nor would you have walked in here to try to negotiate." His eyes sparkled under the light of the lamp.

"Perhaps I did not make myself clear," said Alexei. It was his last attempt at maintaining the rouse. Fearless often backed down the weak.

Unflinchingly, Turgenev said, "Don't be stupid, Alexei. You need to know what this money is buying you. You are old enough to remember the collapse of the Soviet Union. You remember starving as a child and the violence that ensued. But it was also the opportunity many young entrepreneurs used to build massive wealth through Gorbachev reforms and obtaining government assets. Most made their money through arbitrage. The difference between oil and natural gas market prices determined by Russian standards and world markets made several entrepreneurs billionaires overnight. However, I did not start there. I began by simply stealing my money."

He looked down at Alexei as he was several inches taller. He stood close. Close enough for Alexei to count the sexy wrinkles in the corner of his eyes.

"Many outside the nation were eager to obtain Russian assets and capitalize on the wealth," said Turgenev. "I served as the broker, setting up investors in other countries with the promise of investing in Russian oil and other commodities. I stayed behind the scenes, so no one knew who I was. I employed the *Vor* in Samara to pull off the charade since Samara is at the center of oil production in our country. With my plan I made billions.

"Soon many of the investors found out it was nothing but a scam—that they were dealing with the *Vor* and not a reputable investment company. Most wiped their hands clean and moved on. All except one man. A German named Gunther Lange. He came to Samara to talk to the *Vory pakhan*."

Turgenev took a step back, motioning to Natalia. "We thought no one would dare come to Russia and take on the Russian mob, especially at a time when the government lacked stability. But this man came. Alone. He had a sit-down meeting with Vadim Baranov. All Vadim's men were present in the restaurant. We watched the whole thing from the kitchen. We wanted to see who this guy was. I had over seven hundred million of the German's money, and he wanted it all back.

"Gunther Lange spoke to Vadim in precise words. He told Vadim he needed the money to start a new life. He said, 'Give me the name of the true architect of this scam or else your lives will all be forfeit.'

"Vadim laughed in his face and recited the *Vory* code: *Forsake all relatives, Do not have a family of your own, Never work or have a job under any circumstances, Help other thieves, Keep secret information about the whereabouts of accomplices . . .*

"Vadim stopped there with his fingers extended. All five of them. He held them up to Gunther so he could see and cursed at Gunther for being a lousy German. Even without the *Vory* code, Vadim would not tell the German a thing. He thanked Gunther and told him to get the fuck out of his sight.

"Gunther Lange removed his glasses and took off his shoes, then his socks. He placed them carefully under a table. I saw this with my own eyes from a cracked door through the kitchen. There was a boom and a crash, and the shooting began. I immediately took cover under the kitchen counter.

"It went on for about five minutes. Gunfire everywhere. People screaming. The dense thud of bodies hit with heavy impact. I pressed my hand tight against Natalia's mouth trying to keep her from making a sound, praying no one came into the kitchen to find us. Then everything was quiet. The first chance we had to escape, we took. When I looked around the dining room, everyone was dead. Some had gun wounds, but most were beaten severely.

"One person was beaten much worse than all the rest. His body was a pile of mush. He was wearing Gunther Lange's clothing, but I knew something was wrong right away. It was the shoes. They were on his feet and in perfect condition. Not a drop of blood on them.

"Later reports came that the German investor Gunther Lange was killed during a gang war in Russia. I thought nothing of it until nearly eight years later when I saw Gunther Lange on television. Except this person said their name was Jericho Black."

Natalia's hands were shaking as she smoked the cigarette. Turgenev went over to comfort her. He put a hand around her and kissed her forehead.

"Impossible," said Alexei.

He recalled a body had washed ashore in the late eighties. Bloated from the water. Within hours authorities knew exactly who the man was. He was identified by the resume he wore on his skin. *Vory* tattoos. Stealing an identity of a member of the *Vor* was impossible. Just as Alexei concluded that there had to be another explanation, Turgenev backed up his deduction.

"It was Julie Shubert's brother," said Turgenev. "He was new, just starting. With his body a pile of mush and the *Vory* known for our natural hate for Germans, no one bothered to look at Gunther's body closely.

What few tattoos he did have were ripped from his skin. He was quickly cremated.

"Julie used her husband's money to hire an investigator and find out what happened to her brother. Most assumed that after the slaughter in the restaurant, he escaped and was hiding in the US.

"The investigator was able to put together everything I already knew, and then he was killed. Not by me, but by Jericho. I gave her hush money to drop this insanity for the good of both of our lives. But she was stubborn and defiant and used Jericho Black to broker the payment. I don't know what she was thinking. Some people like playing with fire."

Then the hacker stole the money, and it all went to hell, thought Alexei. That's why Jericho had become involved so quickly. It explained why he was more interested in the tracking program than anything else. But how? How did he pull off the slaughter of the *Vor* in that restaurant?

"Did Jericho pay off another group to take out the people in Samara?" asked Alexei.

"Stop thinking along those lines," said Turgenev. Natalia dropped her cigarette on the ground and stomped out the ash beneath her shoes.

Turgenev walked back over to the light. He stood within a foot of Alexei. "He isn't human," said Turgenev. "I don't know what he is. A demon, a vampire, I don't give a shit. I am trying not to get killed by him or kicked so hard that everyone believes I was hit with a sledgehammer."

"No," said Alexei. "This cannot be." The Civil War photo was real? It was actually Jericho Black... or whatever his real name is.

"Not believing will get you killed," said Turgenev. "Trust me. If you mention the name Gunther Lange and he pieces together you received fifty million dollars, he will kill you even if you give me up."

It was making sense now. This was why they were so satisfied. He wasn't extorting Turgenev. Turgenev was buying an accomplice to keep this secret. No double cross or slip of the tongue would implicate Turgenev without Alexei paying the price first. *Clever,* he thought. There was a reason oligarchs were considered as ruthless as the *Vor*.

"I suggest you find yourself another set of hackers to take care of the financial transactions between us," said Turgenev. "Use someone other than Jericho Black to handle the money launder. I wouldn't want another misunderstanding to happen."

Turgenev and Natalia left Alexei standing in disbelief. Turgenev put his hand around her waist and escorted her away. Before vanishing into the darkness of the warehouse, Natalia turned to lock eyes with Alexei. Their secret was now his secret. When the metal door slammed shut, he was alone with the bodies of the two hackers at his feet.

However, Alexei was still in denial. He put the pieces together in his mind to see if they fit. From Julie to Jericho to that goddamn hacker with the program, it all seemed to fall in place. Even sending someone else to make sure Julie Shubert was dead. After witnessing her fiery personality in regards to her brother's killer she was not one to remain quiet. Not about this.

Julie Shubert was on his mind when his phone buzzed and his looked at the screen. Karma. More women who don't understand when it's time to play nice and accept things as they are.

Fucking Tatiana.

CHAPTER 48

———◆———

Arina was in her room when she heard Tatiana singing. It was a song from way back when they were children. She belted out the notes with such melodious clarity that it held Arina's attention, and she smiled in a place where smiles seldom occurred, the house where the escorts and strippers slept during the day. Arina opened the door to her room and instantly saw one of the men, Boris, sitting at the breakfast table. He toted his usual nine millimeter pistol in his shoulder holster and sipped on coffee. He caught Arina poking her head out and yelled at her, spilling some coffee on his lap.

"Close the door," shouted Boris. "It is not time for you yet."

Arina nervously closed it but left a small crack open to peek out. She could see past the kitchen to the small foyer and a door to the bathroom. After that was the living room where the streetwalkers slept. Beyond the living room was another bedroom on the opposite side of the apartment. Her sister Tatiana was singing in that other bedroom.

Boris sat trying to ignore the singing, but he couldn't. He yelled at Tatiana to shut up, but she kept going as if she didn't hear him. Finally, he stood, scraping the chair on the floor. He walked through the foyer and out of sight. There were hisses and shushes as the other girls tried to warn Tatiana of the danger. Despite the warnings, they could not quiet Tatiana. Light from Tatiana's door came through the living room and down the hallway. Arina heard Boris and Tatiana scream, followed by a quick succession of slaps. Boris always hit the girls on their necks to avoid ruining their faces.

The light from the open door went out, and the foyer was dark again.

Boris came back into the kitchen and took his place at the table. He exhaled and opened his magazine to the place he'd left off. He took hold of his coffee cup, but before he could take another sip, Tatiana resumed singing. Arina chuckled. Her sister was happy for some reason. Something lifted her spirits.

Arina pushed her door closed and waited patiently. It was late afternoon, and everyone would soon be getting ready for their work. The first to take their showers were the four girls who walked the streets. Once they were done it would be Tatiana, followed by Arina. She counted the times she heard the hot water popping through the pipes. They popped whenever someone first turned on the spigot. She counted two, three, four, and then the fifth time. Tatiana was in the bathroom.

She pretended it was her turn and walked past Boris, who still read his magazine, hand on his lap. He glanced up but said nothing. Arina went into the foyer and tried the doorknob of the bathroom. It opened about a foot before Tatiana slammed her foot at the base, blocking it from opening farther.

Tatiana had short, straight black hair and light blue eyes. She was shapelier than Arina and, even without makeup, attractive. A towel wrapped around her waist, and her lips pouted from holding the toothbrush in her mouth. She sighed when she saw Arina and moved her foot from the door.

"I thought you were Boris coming for a peek," said Tatiana. She went back to brushing.

Arina shoved herself into the tiny bathroom with her sister and sat down on the toilet. She studied the red marks on her sister's neck and waited for Boris to say something, but he did not. He understood. They were sisters and rarely got the chance to speak to each other even though they lived in the same house.

"I heard you singing this morning," said Arina. She lifted a leg toward the toilet seat and picked at her big toe.

"Mmm . . . something wonderful happened." Tatiana looked at herself in the mirror and made kissy faces, then spit the toothpaste out.

"What is it that has you in such a good mood?" asked Arina.

"It is our freedom, sister, our path out of this hellhole."

"Papa has the money?" asked Arina.

"No. Not Papa." Tatiana stepped over the tub and into the flowing water, closing the frosted sliding glass door. She grabbed the shampoo and washed her hair, working the soap into foaming suds.

Arina and Tatiana lived in the hellhole because of their father. The *Vor* wanted to kill him over debts that he owed from gambling. He fled Russia and went into hiding. Alexei told the family that since the father ran away like a coward, his daughters would have to pay his debt. That was over a year ago. Still, they held out hope that soon their father would return to save them.

"Why are you so sure we're getting out this time?" asked Arina.

"I have made a special friend," said Tatiana. "That's how."

"Who? One of your johns?"

"Don't call him that," said Tatiana with a sneer on her lips. "He's not a john. He is strong and brave and loving and loyal."

Arina sighed in frustration. "Dear Tatiana, how can you be so stupid? You can't believe that this john will save us. He is a man who pays for sex, and most men in that position are sad and stupid. He will say anything to make himself look important to you because he thinks you will not know any better. In the end, to him you are a whore."

"Not so," said Tatiana. "Not this guy. You don't know because you have not met him. But when you do, you will see."

"And what will he do? What will he tell his family? He met a wonderful whore who makes his life complete, and he wants to spend the rest of his life with her?" Arina threw her hands in the air.

"He is willing to pay for our freedom," said Tatiana. "How about that? The both of us!"

Arina's heart filled with hope, if only for a split second. Then the reality of their situation took root, and she steeled her heart once more. "As I said. You are stupid to believe in such things." She flushed the toilet, making Tatiana yelp at the sudden cold, and washed her hands. When she'd heard her sister singing she thought it was good news. No john would ever pay for her freedom, not to mention both.

"Who is this john?" she asked.

"I told you he is not a john," said Tatiana. "He's a Paul." She giggled.

Arina rolled her eyes and said nothing more to her sister. Tatiana finished and left the water running. Arina took her shower and afterward got dressed for the club. Before she left every afternoon, she had a snack at the kitchen table. A hardboiled egg with Havarti cheese and black olives. Tatiana joined her still wearing a robe.

Boris stood near the refrigerator, smoking a cigarette through an open window. He had a dark, thick beard and sleepy eyes with a big nose and lips. He reminded her of the Yugoslavian basketball player Vlade Divac except Boris was nowhere near as tall. He hung around the kitchen, as he was told to do, especially when the two sisters were together. Alexei considered it dangerous for them to be together all the time. The only reason that they shared the same apartment was that the other apartments were full.

Arina began with cordial conversation, speaking to her sister in code. "So how are things?" she asked. "Are you getting enough sleep?" She nodded slightly toward Boris. *Get rid of him.* Tatiana knew how to irritate Boris enough to walk away for a few minutes. They knew he hated his job, having to look after a bunch of women in a cramped apartment, listening to their complaints, and breaking up the daily squabbles between them.

"I slept just fine, sister," said Tatiana. "I look and feel better than ever, except for the red marks on the side of my neck. What do you think, Boris?" She arched her neck to show him. He smirked and exhaled a tendril smoke out of the window.

"Boris here is my friend," Tatiana continued. "Boris, when you get some money, I will show you a good time."

His eyes rolled to the side, away from them. "I prefer my women to not be whores," said Boris. "Clean and pleasant girls for Boris."

"On the other hand, since you have the face of a baboon your opportunities are slim, are they not?" asked Tatiana sweetly. "The ones who would go out with you don't look like me, Boris. Trust me; I will treat you like we are a couple. You already treat me like a girlfriend. See?" Tatiana turned her red neck to him once again.

Boris flicked the cigarette out the window with his fingers. Red sparks of ash sparkled like fireworks then disappeared. He slammed the window shut and sneered. Tatiana looked up at him with bright blue eyes as he walked past her. He went into the living room where the other girls were camped out and sat in a darkened corner, lighting another cigarette.

They leaned in close to speak. Arina cut the hardboiled egg in half with a knife. "What was this nonsense you were speaking about earlier?" asked Arina.

"I am going to see Paul tonight, dear sister," said Tatiana. She stole the other half of the egg off the plate and took a bite. "He called for me again. I am to be dressed nicely, and he will take me to the theater. We will see a movie together. This time, I can see an American movie without reading the subtitles down below in Russian. I can understand enough English to enjoy it as it is originally made. This will be the first time since leaving Russia that I will see a movie with a man."

Arina cut a slice of cheese from the block. "Why is he taking you to the movies?" asked Arina.

Tatiana took the slice from her plate and ate it. "One day we were talking in bed, and I told him about my love of the movies. Then I played something for him on the piano—a classical piece. I played *Moonlight Sonata* for him, and he was in awe. I said, what do you think, that all whores are dumb women who spread their legs for money? Some of us only do these things because of the mistakes of our fathers. Some of us are forced into servitude to repay a debt. This is my situation. I am here, spreading my legs for you, but that does not make me who I am."

"This is what convinced him to pay for you?" asked Arina. "He heard you play the piano and figured out that you are human? Little sister, this will only bring trouble upon us. We have only been here for a year, and you have constantly tried to escape and scheme. They will not care that an American wants you."

"It is too late, older sister," said Tatiana. "He has already been in negotiation with Zachary. We are waiting on the final word from Alexei. Paul is going to pay for us. No matter what the cost, he said that he will pay it."

"Who is this Paul, anyway?" asked Arina. She popped a black olive into her mouth. Maybe Paul's position in the world would give her some hope.

"He is an artist," said Tatiana. "A painter."

Arina stopped chewing. Her appetite ruined. "How does he have money for us?" Her head bit the back of the chair as she looked to the ceiling. "He is playing with you," she insisted. "He does not have the kind of money that Alexei will demand."

"He does, dear sister. He is wealthy. He inherited his money. Enough to pay for whatever Papa owes Alexei. Then Papa can come home, and you can go back to Russia as well. I will stay here and be Paul's new wife." She put her hand on Arina's hand. "Be happy for us. Paul said that the energy we put out in the world will manifest itself. If you think bad things, bad things will happen. You must help me to believe that everything will work out."

Arina pulled her hand away. "So this is why you are singing? Because Paul told you to? Bad things happen because there are bad people out there, Tatiana. In real life the knight in shining armor gets killed by the bad guy, and everyone he is supposed to save suffers for his effort."

She left her sister at the dinner table with half an egg and a slice of cheese.

Working at the club was hard on the knees. She was on hers constantly, crawling across the hard stage, working for tips. Every evening they were sore and red, and they were the first thing she felt when she got up in the morning. Arina was thin at first but had grown toned over the year. When she first got in servitude of the *Vor* she could barely do any stage tricks. The thought of taking off her clothes in front of strangers was the most frightening thing she'd ever faced.

To introduce Arina and the other girls into the life, Alexei had made them take their clothes off in front of his men at the apartment. When someone new arrived, they gathered the four apartments into one living room. Some would sit on the floor, some in chairs, and others stood in the doorway. Nearly twenty people all packed into the small space. The windows were drawn, the lights turned on bright, and each new girl had to strip to nakedness. They played music and the girls were shown how to get on their knees. It was one of the first things Arina learned. When in doubt, go down on your knees and crawl around like a baby. Crawling on all fours always got the men's attention.

They told Arina she was going to be a stripper. They said a pole would be there for her to dance around, but the pole wasn't necessary. Most men did not care about the pole. All they wanted was for girls to take their clothes off and prance around to some music. Just spread your legs and crawl around the stage to collect the money, they said.

Arina viewed the pole differently. It was her escape. A way to get lost, if only six minutes at a time. She started practicing. She watched what some of the other girls were doing. Not the ones brought in by the *Vor*, the other girls, the ones who lived around New York. They had complex routines and were interested in putting on a show because they got paid more if they were good. Not all the time, but enough to make a difference.

Arina wanted to perform, like them. So she watched the good dancers and asked questions whenever she could. She saw them spin and hang upside down. They were graceful and sexual, not crawling around like dogs. She watched, and she emulated.

As she practiced, she grew toned and flexible. She learned how to do a full split, something she could never accomplish before no matter how hard she tried. She learned to climb to the top of the twenty-foot pole, hang upside down, and slide down with no hands, using only the pressure of her thighs to stop her fall, her head only a few inches from the stage. She twirled around the pole, seemingly floating in the air, pretending she was walking on the clouds. Her incredible illusions made men throw money at her for her efforts. For those six minutes once an hour—two songs—she was able to forget who she was and what she was doing there.

Arina worked until the early morning hours. The other girls, the free ones, used their tips to pay security, the bartenders, the DJ and staff, and management. After that, the rest was theirs to keep, usually a decent amount left to pay their bills and live a good life. Arina kept none of her earnings. It all belonged to the *Vor*. No one got a cut of the money Arina made, not even the club. When all the payments were settled, it would typically be somewhere around 4 a.m. The early risers would be out heading to work.

Arina stood outside and waited for the van to pick her up. The driver was one of the men who occupied the basement, usually people in the *Vor* who still had to prove themselves. Their job was to gather up the girls and bring them back to the apartment building in the Bronx. It wasn't prudent to have all the girls working at the same club, so they were scattered throughout the city. The driver also collected the escorts. They were usually picked up first and slept in the back.

The giant passenger van pulled up, and the door slid open. Arina ducked her head down and found a seat in the second row. She looked around for Tatiana but didn't see her. She sighed. Tatiana had probably called for someone to pick her up early.

Going to the movies.

How silly.

CHAPTER 49

Carrie watched a plain-clothed detective enter the reception area of the morgue with what appeared to be a family behind him, a husband, wife, and two kids. The boy was in his late teens, the girl barely a teenager. They huddled inside the reception area while the detective chatted with the receptionist. There were a few nods and then the door buzzed, followed by a click.

The detective, an athletic Black man with a trimmed mustache wearing a blue suit, opened the door and held it open for the family. The man was White, a few inches shorter than the detective, with brown hair and a clean-shaven face. He had his arm around his wife, a fair-skinned woman wearing burgundy Capris and pink Crocs. Their daughter tightly held her mom's hand and followed closely behind. The boy entered last, leaving space between him and his parents. He was a fit kid with brown hair; his adult features just beginning to appear underneath the awkwardness of adolescence. He had a backpack slung over his right shoulder.

It's about time, Carrie thought. Things could finally move forward. She took a deep breath, watching the family from the camera feeds in her office. The detective, Kevin Duval, held his credentials up to the door camera so she could see them. He was from Manhattan. She'd spoken to him a couple of times over the phone. Based on his voice and manner, she'd assumed he was a veteran of the force. Up close, she could see he was a young detective. She opened her door to greet them.

"These are the Silvers," said Detective Duval. "Joe and Sara." He pointed to the boy. "This is Adonis."

"Call me Don," said Adonis.

Duval inclined his head politely as if he had simply forgotten. "The young girl here is Jasmine. Is there somewhere Jasmine can stay?"

"She insisted on coming," explained Sara. "Then she got cold feet after stepping into the building."

Carrie understood. "It happens to a lot of people," she said to the young teen clutching her mother's hand. "This is a scary place. We have another waiting area near the entrance. It's private. You'll like it."

"I'll take her," said Lee from the doorway of his office. He motioned for the girl to follow him and pointed to another door not too far from where he was standing. "Anyone else want to wait? There's a television, and we have Wi-Fi."

Sara stood firm and shook her head. The father, Joe, grimaced and stared straight ahead, determined to see it through to the end. Adonis looked calm, almost bored.

"Are you sure, Don?" asked Carrie.

It was imperative that Don be the one to identify Jake's body for their plan to work. Still, she didn't want to seem overanxious and insist that he be there. It was proper for her to offer the waiting room since he was a minor.

Adonis turned to Carrie, and she suppressed a tiny gasp. She didn't believe in auras, but this kid was imposing. He had a presence. So many people in the room, yet Adonis commanded attention. For a moment, he was the only person she could see.

"I'll be fine," said Adonis.

"Okay," she said, pleased everything was going as planned. "Everyone, follow me."

Sara bent down and kissed her daughter on the forehead before handing her off to Lee for safekeeping. They disappeared through a door on the right, and Jasmine looked pleased with what she could see of the room. She waved to her mother before entering.

Carrie led the procession down an intersecting hallway and into one of the examination rooms. Joe and Sara shivered at the cold temperature. Two large tables, about three feet apart, occupied most of the floor space. The table farthest away was bare. Clean and sanitized. The table closest to them held a body covered by a white sheet. The lights above the table were so bright that the sheet almost glowed. They worked their way around the table and crowded by the head.

Duval signaled with a nod when everyone was ready. Carrie reached over, uncovered the head and laid the sheet down around the body's waist. A jagged line went from its left shoulder to under the right armpit. The two body parts were pushed together like a puzzle.

"Our video analysts say that this is the guy in the stream," said Duval, his smooth voice calm and reassuring. "Is this him?"

The lights reflecting off the table made Sara look pale and disheveled. She reached up and tied her hair back unevenly to see better, then peered down at Jake's brightly lit face. "It looks like him," she said, looking down the length of the body. "What happened to him?"

"He was hit by a train at Penn Station," said Carrie.

"I see," said Sara.

"What about you, Joe?" asked Duval. "Is this the guy? Take your time."

Joe Silver glared down at Jake's face through his glasses. "People look slightly different dead on a slab," he commented. "The size and body type look right. His face is the same. This is the guy."

Duval pressed both palms against the table and shook his head. "Now for the crazy part. This man was hit by a train almost a week before the incident in the synagogue."

Joe flashed a nervous smirk. Like a reflex or a tic. "Is this some sort of joke, Detective?" asked Joe. He adjusted the glasses on his face while looking at Duval. "Then it couldn't be him. So why are we here?"

"To tell you the truth, I don't know," said Duval. "It seemed pretty clear-cut in the beginning. We got leads saying this was the guy. We checked his place, talked to friends, to coworkers. All positively identified him as the person in the blown-up image. The DA keeps asking me, what's the problem. Well, this is the problem." He pointed to Jake on the table. "I'm asking you again: is this the man in the synagogue that day?"

"What are you asking?" asked Joe. His face reddened. "Seriously! This guy's dead, so it can't be him. What a fucking joke!"

"I can't believe this," said Sara, holding her forehead. "We came here for closure. This is unbelievable."

"We need another detective on this case," said Joe. He rubbed his wife's back in support. "Someone with more experience." He looked up and down Duval, like he was preparing to say something more insulting, but held back.

Duval stood upright, chin held high and folded his hands in front of him. "It's essential that you be clear about this guy," said Duval, feeling the heat. "You have to be sure this is not him. All of you. Because everything we have so far says—"

"It's him," said Adonis. He stepped in closer, focusing on the details of Jake's face. The light gleamed off his handsome features as he peered down. "This is the man that held us at gunpoint." His eyes scanned Jake's body, taking in everything.

"Didn't you hear the detective? It can't be this guy," said Joe.

"I heard him," said Adonis. "But this is him."

She stuttered. "He startled you," said Sara. Frustration poured from each word. "He pointed a gun at you. The stress has distorted your memory. I'm sure the evidence will say that this is not the man, honey." She looked to Detective Duval for help. "Isn't there some DNA at the scene? How can your main suspect be a dead guy?"

Duval remained straight-faced. No emotion. His demeanor acted as a kind of calming influence on the crazy scenario. He raised his head high and said, "State of the art science and technology says this is our suspect. First, we got lucky. Someone who went to high school with this guy called in and gave us Jake Coltrane's name. He didn't have a driver's license because of an inoperable tumor that caused seizures, but he did have official identification with New Jersey. After checking the photograph, we could see a strong likeness to our suspect. We fed the synagogue footage into our system to search the internet for any matches. What it found was footage of Jake Coltrane cut in half. We interviewed everyone on the platform that day. This office recovered the body. Dr. Blake took custody of the body to do the autopsy. Dr. Blake? Have you examined this man's skull?"

She popped to attention and nodded. "I have."

"Does he have a tumor?"

"Yes," said Carrie. "Benign and inoperable."

"This is Mr. Jake Coltrane of New Jersey," said Duval. "All evidence suggests this man is the perpetrator." He unfolded his hands and patted the front pocket of his slacks. "So is there something that you wish to tell me?"

"What do you mean, Detective?" asked Sara. Her eyes narrowed.

"That broadcast stream. Was it legit? Or was it a stunt? Tell me the truth." He looked each of them in the eye, waiting for an answer.

Sara's mouth hung open in disgust. "How dare you?" she cried.

"You think we doctored that video?" sputtered Joe. "What kind of . . .? Your supervisor is going to hear about this." His shoulders shook with anger.

"My supervisor is the one who told me to bring you all down here and ask you in front of this body," said Duval. He pointed at the body. "*He* has a solid alibi. The only evidence you have is that video."

Carrie looked back and forth between the heated exchange. Her heart rate increased from guilt as the intensity was building to a crescendo.

"Are you trying to mess with our minds, Detective?" Joe panted. His face had taken on a purplish hue. "I already told you this guy isn't who held us at gunpoint. Get the real guy in front of us, and we'll identify him." He raised a finger in the air and thrusted it downward with authority. "Do your job, Detective!"

"Can you?" asked Duval. He raised his hands plaintively. "Can you really identify him? Not someone who looks like him or could be him. You must be sure it's him. Is there any feature, a club foot, a broken fingernail, anything, that can distinguish this guy from the guy who held you all at gunpoint?"

Joe and Sara looked down at the body simultaneously with a furrowed look of concern on their faces.

"What kind of jewelry was he wearing?" continued Duval. "Was there a ring or watch? Did he have a phone? Was he left-handed or right? Any scars on his face or neck or hands?"

The couple looked at the various bumps and broken bones protruding from his torso. They seemed defeated, as if reality had set in. Joe flexed his jaw muscles, and tears welled in Sara's eyes.

"This is him," said Adonis. "This is definitely the guy. Now we just need to figure out how he does it." Everyone looked up at him, startled.

"How he does what?" said Duval.

"How he was at the synagogue after getting hit by a train," said Adonis as if it were elementary. "Maybe a time distortion? An alternate reality?"

Duval raised his eyebrows. "Excuse me? An alternate reality? Any word of what you just said gets out, and you'll be deemed unreliable as a witness. The case will most likely be thrown out of court if we ever do find the guy."

"What about the gun?" asked Joe hopefully. "The gun had to have been special. I've never seen anything like it. It was huge. You should be able to track the real assailant by following the gun. I'm certain of it."

Duval shook his head slowly, lips pressed tight. "Haven't found the gun yet, but from the video stream we could see what it was. Big Frame Revolver. Not too many people want to own one of those. A novelty item, mainly for collectors."

"How many people own one?" asked Joe. He looked down at Sara and squeezed her shoulders.

"In New York State? A couple hundred. One of them is this guy here on the table."

Joe and Sara were visibly stunned. They held each other close, fresh tears running down Sara's cheeks.

"The gun proves that this is him," said Adonis excitedly. "I'm positive. He was following me before he came to the synagogue."

"He's been dead for over a week, kid," said Duval. "So I guess a ghost was following you and then tried to kill you. Is that what you want to go on record as saying?"

"That's enough, Detective," said Sara. "My son is under a lot of stress. A man stalked him, pointed a giant gun at his head, and threatened to kill him. Don't forget that my husband and I were there too. The closer we look at this man, the more certain we are that this is not him. You have your answer, Detective. This is not the man who held us at gunpoint." She took a moment to wipe the tears from her eyes. Her chest was heaving up and down as if she was going hysterical. "It's your job to keep looking until you find him," she pleaded.

He took a moment to stare into her eyes, feeling her pain, then dropped his gaze to his shoes. "Is that right?" said Duval, turning his attention to Adonis. "Is your memory fuzzy or unclear, Don?"

Adonis had not moved from the table. His attention was on Jake's body and did not turn away from it when he spoke. "His hand bore no scars," said Adonis. "No blemishes or inconsistencies. His face was also smooth like the skin of a newborn. This man has those same features. Perfect skin. Uniform color and texture. The way his eyebrows are shaped and their thickness are the same. This is him."

"Perfect skin?" said Duval. An inconceivable snare. "The guy has been run over by a train and looks it. What do you mean by perfect skin?"

He finally turned away from Jake. "Look beyond the bruises, Detective," said Adonis. "No old scars. No blemishes on his face."

Duval threw up his hands in frustration. "You understand that you're making this impossible to prosecute, right? The man who was cut in half by a train a week ago is the same man who held you at gunpoint two days later."

"Your computer science says the same thing," said Adonis. "Why are you looking at me as if I'm the one who is crazy? I agree with your investigative deduction."

"What?" Duval snapped. He looked around the room at no one in particular. "Well, I tried."

"What do you think, Dr. Blake?" asked Adonis. He stared at her intently.

"About what?" She felt the pressure of his gaze. This handsome kid and his aura was focused upon her. Deep and penetrating. It felt as if he could see her soul.

"About the possibility that this man isn't dead," said Adonis.

She scoffed and tried to play it cool, but her body refused to play along. Her heart rate increased. Her cheeks flushed.

"You think this guy is going to get up off this table?" asked Duval, dumbfounded.

Adonis never took his eyes off Carrie. "I see," he said. "You've seen him awaken from the dead before. You busted him up and cut him in half to fool us."

"Adonis!" shrieked his mother.

"That's it!" said Duval, stepping between Adonis and Carrie. "Let's go. This show is over. Thank you for your time, Doctor. We'll see ourselves out."

The family was speechless. Taken by surprise. He must not be someone who says things that are irrational, so they don't know how to place it.

Carrie knew he was far from crazy. He was dead on. But how? Who is this kid?

"I don't say this often, but I believe this is a cry for help," said Duval to the parents, waving them out. "I suggest a good therapist. He's not speaking like someone sane."

"Oh, I'm sane," said Adonis, snapping his head toward the detective. "I'm not finished here."

Duval said nothing. He lowered his hands but remained as a shield between Adonis and Carrie.

"I'm done now," said Adonis. He blinked twice and turned around, walking around the table, behind his parents and out the door.

Joe and Sara were the next to leave. Silent. Embarrassed, perhaps, at Adonis's behavior. Duval heaved a sigh of relief, throwing apologetic glances in Carrie's direction. "I'm releasing the body from this investigation," he said. He panned across Jake's wounds. To him, Jake was just a troubled soul who ended his life prematurely. "The family of Mr. Coltrane can prepare services if they wish." He nodded as if convincing himself it was the right thing. "Crazy fuckers," he whispered glancing towards the hallway.

He slumped his shoulders and walked out. A flicker of remorse gripped Carrie's heart, guilty about what she had just done. Her master plan worked as advertised but she ignored the other side of it. She hadn't thought about the consequences the family might suffer.

Carrie walked alongside the table to the entrance of the lab. She spied Duval saying a few words with the Silvers and everyone left the building. Her hand was against the doorframe. It was trembling. It was for the best, she thought and quickly returned to Jake.

Carrie leaned down to Jake's lifeless corpse. Slightly pale, cold, and severed in two. "I'm sorry, little guy. I hope you can hear me. You're a champ for waiting until the investigation was over before doing your thing. We're in the clear. You can come back at any time."

She stood upright and looked around the room. It was just her and Jake. "I must be crazy. I'm having a conversation with a parasite inside a corpse, for gosh sakes."

The cold, isolated room seemed to amplify her uneasiness. "Jake will wake up, right?"

CHAPTER 50

Zachary was driving Alexei through the city. He was talking about various things beginning with the women in the Bronx that Alexei could no longer hear since he was deep in thought. Even the sites of downtown Manhattan passed in a blur. Senses continued to fade until he was alone with his thoughts.

Sergei was acting strange. He'd been the one to push Alexei into finding dirt on Turgenev, and now Sergei played ignorant. He interrupted Alexei anytime he tried to bring it up, saying whatever deals were made in that warehouse were between Alexei and Turgenev. He didn't even bat an eye over Alexei's newfound riches. He merely grunted and congratulated Alexei on his new Fifth Avenue apartment.

Alexei had a suspicion Sergei was distancing himself, abandoning Alexei to sit on an island alone with Turgenev's secret. *It's your secret, too, Sergei,* thought Alexei.

Alexei even used a new hacker to look up Gunther Lange. He gave the man specific instructions that the search advance with the utmost security precautions. About ten seconds into the search, he'd detected a trace. Someone was trying to bounce along the servers to find out who was looking into Gunther Lange. Alexei panicked and pulled all the plugs out of the computer. Alexei knew it was the girl, Cardigan Paige, searching for the source of the inquiry. She was the best, Jericho had said. He knew better than to try that again.

Alexei was a believer.

It wasn't Turgenev's story that convinced him. It was Sergei's behavior. Sergei was able to piece the story together so quickly. He had to know the people in the Samara restaurant weren't killed by a gang rival. He probably had a spy watching the restaurant back then. Many of the rival *Vor* had spies throughout the various cities. It was only good business to know what the competition was up to. Sergei might've gathered from his reports that only a single man left the restaurant. Perhaps the heads of all the families knew this.

It still didn't explain Jericho Black. What was he? Alexei mistrusted what he could not understand. He went over the details numerous times, and each time the whole thing sounded ridiculous. Jericho Black, a monster who traveled through time, lived among humans, and changed his identity when it was time to move on.

Alexei entwined his fingers and bent them backwards cracking his knuckles. Sergei had stopped speaking. Maybe he asked Alexei a question and did not get an answer. Maybe he was finished and had nothing else to say. Difficult to tell since Alexei's mind was elsewhere. He looked out the window as they crossed the bridge into the next Borough. Tires gave off the sound of bees while going over the metal bar grating.

Over twenty-seven people tried to kill Jericho that day in Samara. Twenty-seven people. And he killed them all. He was cheated out of hundreds of millions of dollars and he showed no mercy.

That triggered Alexei's mind into panic.

Shit. The hacker's program. Had Jericho forgiven him for wanting the hacker dead? He didn't kill the hacker, Alexei reminded himself. Jericho killed him. Still, there'd been some tense discussions leading up to the hacker's death. Appeasing Jericho was probably in Alexei's best interest. Maybe it was best to start there. If he delivered the software to Jericho, it would serve as a peace offering. He needed to find out more about the hacker and where he worked. He thought about who might know this information without going through Jericho.

He thought of someone.

CHAPTER 51

The sound of rumbling awakened Arina. Scuffling feet and grunting from straining, as if things were being moved. She opened her door and saw Boris standing, arms crossed, jaws clenched tight. He shook his head, telling her not to ask, to go back inside and close the door, but that made her more determined to stay put. The basement men carried boxes of clothing and other items out of the apartment. She recognized one of the blouses as Tatiana's.

The feeling of optimism that had eluded her for the last year seeped inside the barrier she'd erected for her protection. Her sister was so sure that her john would pay for their freedom. Did it finally happen?

"Where is my sister?" she asked Boris.

"She is going to be upstairs from now on."

"Why?"

"Because Alexei thought it was a good idea to separate you two," said Boris.

"What brought this on?"

Her question was a cautious one. She could not just come out and ask. Many girls within earshot of her conversation were victims of human trafficking. The mobsters might not want the other girls to discover that one bought their freedom. Maybe the first step was to separate them, and then, in the middle of the night when no one was watching, they'd be allowed to leave. Then again, the worst could've happened. Alexei asked for a price Paul couldn't afford, and the move was meant to punish Tatiana for her ignorance.

"This is for your own good," said Boris. "Trust me."

"Does this have anything to do with one of her customers?" asked Arina. Boris gave her a strange look. She'd let it slip and hadn't meant to. "What I mean to ask is if she has been rude to one of her customers and is now receiving punishment. You know how my sister can get sometimes."

Boris squinted suspiciously. Probably to guess how much Arina knew. But he was not about to crack her armor. She stood calm. "You need to stay here and behave," said Boris. "As I said, this is for your own good."

The crashing sound of a lamp in the other bedroom startled Arina. Sounds of bodies hitting walls and then the scream of Tatiana, followed by crying. The quarrel caused a stir in the apartment. The girls gasped and pled for the men to be gentle. Arina took a step toward the commotion, and Boris put his hand out to block her. Her sister's screams grew louder as a large man carried her hoisted over his shoulder into the foyer. A brute named Nicholai. He was in the third apartment, the first one at the top of the stairs. A no-nonsense type of person. One who gave no leeway to the girls under his watch. Tatiana and Nicholai had the kind of conflicting personalities that produced constant fireworks. Her sister would most surely get the worst of it.

Tatiana stretched out her arms when she saw Arina at the threshold of her bedroom. Her red, tear-stained face filled with anguish and despair. They were no more than ten feet away from each other.

"Paul paid the money!" said Tatiana, hammering her fists into the brute's back. "The bastard doesn't want to let us go!"

Her words echoed down the hallway and up the stairs as she kept repeating that Alexei doesn't want to let them go, no matter how much Paul offers to pay. "Don't worry," she screamed. "Paul will come for us. He will not take this lying down. He has friends that will help us. This is not over!"

The door slammed shut on apartment number three, but the screaming continued as Nicholai used every molecule in his lungs to scream at Tatiana to shut her mouth. There was a moment of silence, followed by a violent pounding.

Arina withdrew into her room slowly. Her fingers pressed against her lips. She shook her head. This was the worst thing that could happen. She continued to back away. The sudden stop of her back hitting the dresser at the far wall jarred her senses. This was as far as she could retreat. No escape. They were never getting out of there. Not even if their father paid his debt.

Boris lit up another cigarette. "What your sister said will get back to Alexei." He took a long drag and exhaled. "Why couldn't Tatiana behave like you? She is trouble. I don't want you to be near her when word gets out. He will take it out on you. This is Alexei Voznesensky she is threatening!" Boris took another drag of his cigarette and dropped his hand beside his leg. "Especially now," he muttered. "Alexei is more paranoid than ever."

Boris rubbed his head in frustration and closed Arina's door.

CHAPTER 52

After Jake disappeared from hell, Tartarus destroyed the parking garage with one mighty blow. People scattered far enough to escape the damage, but they crept back and hovered around, unwilling to accept their fates. Then the vessel came. An enormous cruise ship. Nearly seventy feet high and no way to board the ship except for one single boat lowered by a wench. High tide came in swiftly and washed the unprepared out to sea. Several hundred thousand more swam out to the vessel. The panic and disorder quickly turned to chaos, and the small boat toppled before anyone could get on board. With the rescue boat broken and sinking, the vessel moved from the shore. People clung to the slippery hull as the ship departed. Thousands of bodies bobbled in the water.

The low tide flowed out just as quickly, and another few thousand souls with it. The survivors slowly made their way to shore, beaten and broken.

Then Jake returned and Tartarus was there to greet him. Tartarus proclaimed to all that there was another way to get to paradise. Tartarus would personally escort them to the ship's final destination if they deliver Jake Coltrane to him.

Jake sensed the desperation in their eyes. They'd been in hell for far too long to leave anything to chance. They were going to beat Jake, and no amount of reasoning would change their minds, so he ran. Like Tartarus had said, create enough lies and truth will be lost forever.

They chased him through the broken and foul remnants of a city until his sides ached. The sky was no longer bright blue. It was black and red and reeked of death. The glowing eyes of rats followed him as he ran. The

253

soles of his feet were blistered and bloody from the heat, glass, and busted concrete. But he refused to slow down. The thought of what would happen if they caught him made it easy to ignore the pain and keep going. People came out of buildings from the left and right to join the chase as Tartarus echoed his shallow promise to everyone within earshot.

Nearly a hundred people chased him, some coming quite close to catching him. His only advantage was the skin-on-skin contact of hell's fury. No one dared tackle him or try to subdue him; they threw objects and tried to trip him up or slow him down. He dodged left and right, barely avoiding the bricks and bottles. Occasionally one would find its mark and hit him in the leg or torso, bad enough that he'd swear, but not enough to slow him down.

Jake turned down an alleyway where the rats were so thick their glowing eyes looked like Christmas lights on a dark December night. They joined the hunt, nipping at his feet and screeching their high-pitched displeasure as he kicked a path through them. At the end of the alley, the landscape changed. Concrete crumbled into hardened soil. He was nearing the edge of the city.

"Hurry and grab him before he reaches the creek," someone shouted.

Jake saw the flowing water ahead of him. He looked to the left and saw that it had no beginning. To the right, he found no end. Jake headed straight toward the creek. He wondered if it was a pool of acid or boiling water. Another brick whizzed past his ear and he decided it did not matter. Whatever was in the next hell, he'd take his chances there.

His feet entered the water, and instantly he had the urge to lay down in it. The creek was shallow, and the flow wasn't strong, nothing more than running water heading for a drain after a torrential rainstorm. But his body buckled at the knees, followed by his elbows. His hands splashed into the water and then his face. The right side of Jake's body was immersed. The left floated above like an island. He inhaled through his nostrils and breathed in the water. Jake was completely docile. Unwilling to move.

Jake felt indifferent to what was about to happen. He watched the angry mob back away from the flowing water. Any moment they'd pull him from the water and beat him. Any moment now. A few turned around and ran back toward the city. It had to be something about the water, except the water felt perfectly fine to Jake. No burning on his skin. No acid on his lips. His flesh was not melting, nor was it dissolving on a molecular level.

Maybe a creature lurked around the water. A creature that could detect movement through the ripples. Perhaps he was about to be swept downstream and carried over a cliff into the mouth of a beast. Whatever the peril, it was a good idea to get out of danger while he still could. He considered standing up. Even wanted to. But standing up seemed unfair when he'd caused so much pain for the people closest to him.

He was so stupid, with no consideration for others.

He'd stolen millions of dollars. So what if the guy was a criminal? Is that any kind of justification? No. It was selfish. He hadn't given any thought to the consequences. Just like the time he poured hot sauce made from ghost peppers in his sister's spaghetti. He thought it was going to be hilarious, and it was. He laughed as she gagged and coughed, her eyes watering a beet-red face. She couldn't even regain her breath to tell her mother what was happening.

What kind of older brother does that?

Something bumped into Jake, burning his skin. Another body drifted in the water next to him, a man in his elder years, with stringy white hair and pale blue eyes. They faced each other, the man's gaze unfocused. Jake spotted another body and another. All caught in the creek not deep enough to sweep them away. Jake thought it strange no one moved. He was sure they could easily stand at any time and walk to the other side. Yet everyone remained perfectly still, just like him.

A foot came out of nowhere and stepped hard on the shoulder of the old man, planting his face further into the water. Jake heard the sizzle of skin-on-skin contact. A young girl winced above him as she used the man as a stepping-stone. *Slick.* Jake listened for her footsteps, thinking she'd run away, but she remained. He couldn't see her from his position. All he could see was the old man's face crunched down in the water.

"You'll remember this trick next time," said the girl. "You landed in the pool of guilt. It is said the creek is made from the tears of everyone who's ever been hurt. As tears fall to the ground in the real world, they funnel here so that our wicked souls can experience the pain we've caused." He heard a long sigh. "First, it siphons your will to move. Then it drags you through your memories of when you were an asshole to someone else."

Ah. That was why he was so preoccupied with all the bad things he'd done and didn't care to stand. Another hell he was unprepared for. And cruel. Almost as cruel as taking away Catalina's choice to love him, even if he were destined for early death. Jake wiggled deeper into the water.

"People say you can get up and leave when you are remorseful for all you have done," said the girl. "Until then, you rot there, experiencing their pain over and over." She paused. "I've never seen anyone walk out of the tears. The only people who get out are the ones dragged out by one of Hell's Apostles."

Or when he was revived, Jake thought. It shouldn't be long, now. Any minute. Carrie had a great plan. He trusted her. She was a doctor. Doctors were trustworthy. Jake once broke the window of a doctor's office while playing baseball. A glass splinter pierced one of his patient's eyes, and they had to be rushed to the hospital. The patient supposedly lost that eye. When the glass had shattered, Jake ran through the hedges and disappeared. A nurse looked out the window, and another kid, a known deviant, was in front of the office building. Everyone assumed he'd thrown the ball. He was forever known as the guy who cost some poor woman her eye.

I should've told the truth, Jake thought.

From the corner of his left eye, Jake spotted movement. Another woman. She also stepped on the bodies of those stuck in the stream and crossed without falling prey to the water's charms.

"Did you get it?" the girl asked.

"Yep. I got two."

"Perfect."

Jake heard a grunt and something hard and fast struck him soundly on the shoulder. Pain registered in his mind, but he did nothing. Not even a grunt.

"Not yet," said the girl. "We're going to have to pull him from the water first. If we start beating on him here and splash the water around too much, we might get wet and fall in ourselves."

"Sorry, I got careless. I wanted to beat the shit out of this asshole and earn my right to paradise."

"I hear that," said the first girl. "The others were too scared to get close to the creek, but we're not afraid to risk this fate for the chance to escape hell forever."

Oh, Jake thought. How silly of them. They hadn't learned anything about hell. Their attitudes probably doomed them to hell forever. They dragged a stick over his skin, hoping to latch onto some part of his naked flesh. They were determined. He didn't think they'd give up anytime soon.

It reminded Jake of Catalina. She did not give up either. He'd been too much of a coward to die in her presence. He'd left her for himself, not to spare her feelings. Jake loved Catalina. He loved her with all his heart. He remembered what she said over the phone. That he didn't appreciate how special his life was. He'd overcome so much, and still, resentment filled his heart. Pathetic.

Sly would fix him for good, and then Jake would be alive for at least 200 years. He could use the time to atone somehow. Become a monk, a priest, a shaman, find what enlightenment he needed to never end up in hell again. So long as he spent his life with Catalina. She was what mattered. The pool of guilt had shown what was precious to him. Catalina.

Wait. Someone was saying her name.

But not in hell. She was there in the room. It was Carrie. Carrie said Catalina's name.

"Jake?" asked Carrie. "Finally. You're back."

The cold storage door opened, and Jake squinted at fluorescent lights. His knuckles were sore from banging against the stainless steel. Carrie stood above him in blue scrubs, peering at him through the bottom half of her glasses.

"You've been gone for so long," she said, eyes wide with concern. "I'm sorry it had to be this way. The investigation took a few days longer than I expected. I asked Sly to help out. Thank goodness it had no adverse effects on you coming back. I was getting worried—Jake? Jake?"

He stepped out of the body storage unit in the nude. His feet touched the cold ground, and Jake froze in fear. He felt the thick grip of tension in his muscles. He knew where to look. Two tables over to his right. One of them had a body. He turned slowly and fell to his knees. His breath escaped his lungs in short bursts. Water sprung to his eyes. He crawled over to the table with the body and pulled himself up, grasping the edge.

"I know her," said Jake. His heart slammed against his ribcage. "My ex-girlfriend. The woman I love."

"I'm sorry, Jake," said Carrie, sickened to the point that she sat down in the closest chair. She pushed her glasses to her forehead and rubbed her eyes. "She drowned. She was . . . she was pregnant."

Every muscle in Jake weakened. It was as if gravity itself had doubled. He collapsed to the floor and wept. Jericho had warned him. He told Jake not to call her, and he did it anyway. His selfishness killed someone else. Someone close to him. Someone he loved.

CHAPTER 53

———— ◆ ————

Jake sat on the cold floor next to the examining table. His back was to Catalina. For a long time he had wished that he was still in hell and this was another trick from Tartarus. Any minute he would return to find that this never happened. But his wish never came true. Not looking at her body was the only way he could deal with it at the time, so Carrie filled him in on the details.

Someone had forcibly drowned Catalina. She was discovered in her bathtub when a coworker checked on her after she did not show up to work for two days. Her mother was in her wheelchair in the foyer, her neck gruesomely snapped. Catalina's mother had ALS. Her motor neurons were in an advanced stage of degeneration, and she didn't have much strength to fight back. The skin and muscles of her neck stretched down from the shoulders, leaving her head practically in her lap.

Collected evidence suggested two assailants. They'd sprayed the house with bleach and scrubbed the beds of Catalina's fingernails. Investigators weren't optimistic they'd find anything pointing to the culprits.

If only he was there. He could have done something. "How long was I out?" asked Jake.

"A little over three weeks," said Carrie.

According to the initial plan, it should have only taken less than two weeks. What took Sly so long? "When did she die?" asked Jake.

"Catalina and her mother were brought in several days ago. I don't know what to say other than I'm sorry for your loss."

Guilt was ever consuming. He knew he should not have agreed with Carrie to get chopped up but did it anyway. His heart grew as cold as his butt cheeks on the white tiled floor. Especially when Carrie told Jake she had put the fetus aside to be disposed of. It was a boy.

According to Carrie's examination, Catalina had been about four months along in her pregnancy. Catalina had said she wanted to tell him something on the morning he returned from the hospital. Another man was in her life and Jake assumed she was talking about a new boyfriend.

Those assholes snuffed out three generations.

Jake tasted rage on his tongue. He wanted blood. Those fucking Russians took things too far. They had their money and his laptop, therefore no reason to kill her. None. He peeled his cold butt cheeks from the floor and stood. Then went to Carrie's office and found the clothes she hid in one of the boxes in the corner. Black tee shirt, jeans and the leather coat he wore on the day he arrived. He put on the Shamrock holster and tucked the Big Frame Revolver under his arm.

"Coffee?" asked Carrie, bleary-eyed. "I know I can use some." She handed Jake a large paper cup with a plastic lid. She studied Jake, her brow furrowed in worry.

Jake took a sip and placed it on the desk with trembling hands. He wanted to think the shakiness was rage, but he never done this before and was wondering if he could.

"I expected you to be out of there sooner," repeated Carrie. "It must be harder to nail down the origin of that tumor than I thought. The little guy must be exhausted by now. Have you seen him?"

"No," said Jake. "And I can't wait for him to show his face either."

"I understand," said Carrie. "Are you going to use that thing?"

Jake glanced down at the gun under his armpit. "I plan on it," he said.

"I'm just thinking. You're not like those guys, Jake. You just got out of trouble with the police. Why don't you let them handle it? I can tell them I found something that leads them to those Russians."

"Are you going to tell them I stole their money?" asked Jake. "That's what will come out. My pesky little name will pop up again on their radar. All the attention will return to me."

"I hadn't thought of that," said Carrie. She pursed her lips.

"I understand why you're worried," said Jake. "I trusted you with my life, and after I awakened it is more fucked up than ever."

Carrie nodded reluctantly. "Please don't blame me for this?" she asked

How could he really blame her? Agreeing to go back to hell to clear his name was really because he thought he could finally have that life with Catalina. He sought a cure and stole money so that he'd have more time with her. Thoughts of Catalina got him through the most grueling trials of hell. Her essence split through the darkness like lightning.

Jake kissed Carrie on the forehead. She'd done a lot for him. He squeezed her shoulder and headed toward the exit. "I don't blame you. I tried to drag you down with me. I'm sorry for that."

Jake headed towards the quiet exit at the back, alone and afraid. But vengeance pushed him forward.

"I guess I don't have to tell you to be careful." Carrie's voice followed him through the hall. "You won't die. That's for sure. What can be worse than that?"

Jake stopped at the door to wave at Carrie one last time. For her, dying was the end, but to Jake, life was seamless. One long and continuous flow from earth to hell and back again. What was worse than dying? Hell, forever and ever. His troubles on earth were minuscule in comparison, now that Catalina was gone. Knowing death was why he was going after the Russians. Those who killed Catalina deserved hell. Carrie wouldn't understand.

Jake walked out into the parking lot and past the gate where employees parked. The heart of downtown Newark was busy. Cars zipping past on the streets. Businesses with their lights on open for customers. The evening was still young. Not quite as dark as he'd hoped. And watchful eyes were all around.

But that wasn't about to stop him. A clear image of the Russian's face sharpened in his mind. Jake pulled out his phone, finger frozen above the screen. He knew nothing about this man. No picture of him, which meant no means of tracking. No name. Jericho Black simply referred to him as the *big guy* or the *Russian*.

Jake looked about the crowded streets and thought about transportation. He hadn't thought it through with the synagogue fiasco. Hop on a train to commit murder and then get back on the train to get away. *Real smart, Jake.* This time, what—call an Uber? He sighed. This was how dumb criminals get their stories immortalized.

Doubt crept in. He wasn't prepared for this. Didn't think things through. He was about to find a hotel and come up with a proper plan when his gut stirred. Someone was watching him. Two people, close by. Jake casually glanced around the dimly lit parking lot. Only a few parked cars. To his left, a four-way stop. A gas station on the corner. Attendants pumped gas and people went in and out of the store. *Not there.* An office building across the street . . . and a black Escalade. Same one from the diner.

With no plan in his head, he operated from pure instinct. Jake headed toward the car, then turned the corner and kept walking to see if they'd follow. The Escalade began to move. He spotted an alley between office buildings. Perfect. It was grimy and trashy, and it smelled. Dumpsters and cheap graffiti littered the walls. Big enough for the Escalade to pass through, but more important, no wandering eyes.

Jake turned sharply and raced down the alleyway until he spotted a slimy green dumpster with boxes sticking out of the top. He ducked down behind it and waited. The lights of the Escalade flitted past him, then went dark. They must've guessed he was hiding somewhere close. It didn't matter. He still had the advantage. He could hear the rubber crunching on the grimy blacktop as the car rolled slowly through the alley. They came closer. He tensed his body like a cat preparing to pounce on its prey. They would soon be in striking distance. He pleaded with himself not to hesitate.

When the front of the car was in his sight, Jake jumped out and pointed the BFR at the driver. The car halted, and the back window rolled down. The person in the back extended his hands out of the window. A sign of good faith. Jake walked up to the window. The passenger inside was a blond guy. Alone.

"My friend in the back wants to talk," said the driver.

"I followed someone who came to find Jake Coltrane at the morgue," said the blond guy in a clipped Russian accent. "I saw you dead in the hotel room many weeks ago. You fooled me once. I figured you also fooled other people."

The Russian accent made Jake's blood boil. Anger rose from his gut to his chest. He had a good mind to blow them both to hell.

"Are you the one responsible for Catalina?" asked Jake through clenched teeth.

"Not me," said the blond. "That was Alexei."

"Who's that? This guy in the driver's seat?" Jake flashed the gun in his direction. "Or someone else?"

"Big guy. Cheat black suit," said the man. "You met him before. In the hotel."

"Where can I find him?" asked Jake.

It was fast. The driver's pistol was in Jake's face before he had a chance to react. The man in the back drew his pistol and pointed it at Jake. A standoff.

"You are not very good at this, my friend," he said. "How are you supposed to kill Alexei when you can't even get past us?"

There was no fear. Two pistols in his face and he thought nothing of dying. He had come a long way from the time he faced death in the hotel room. "You'll be surprised at what I can do," said Jake.

"Surprised is not the word I would use, considering I have seen you dead twice already."

"Drop the gun," said the driver, "or I will blast your brains all over this nice alleyway."

The threat was so empty it was bottomless. "Makes no difference to me," said Jake, steadily aiming his sights on the man.

"How will you fake this death?" he asked. "Will you come back after we unload all these bullets into your body?"

Jake said nothing.

"Oleg," he said. "Put your gun away." He slid his pistol into his waistband and extended a hand. "I am Maxim Fedorov. Get inside. If it is vengeance you seek, I will tell you where to find this asshole named Alexei Voznesensky."

CHAPTER 54

Jake's confidence was growing. He kept the BFR trained on Maxim. Maxim's nine millimeter Glock rested on the black leather seat between them. The driver had his hands full with maneuvering through traffic. Now that Jake was sitting beside the guy, he could see that Maxim was young, with blond fuzz on his chin and a black fedora in his lap. He had on a burgundy shirt, black slacks, no socks, and black-and-white oxfords. Style was his thing. The driver peeked up at the rearview mirror on occasion. He was a stocky. A tough guy.

"Finger off the trigger, please," said Maxim as they drove down the road. "I don't want a sudden bump, and that cannon go off accidentally."

Jake eased his finger off the trigger and placed it beside the guard.

"Thank you," said Maxim.

The timing was bizarre to Jake. Like a setup. He was searching for a man and had no clue about his name or where to find him when Maxim showed up on cue. Seemed fishy. *Alexei Voznesensky*, Jake repeated to himself, *Catalina's killer.*

"Why were you at the morgue?" asked Jake.

"I told you," said Maxim. "I wanted to see if you'd faked your death a second time. I went to the hotel room after Alexei reported you dead. You looked as dead as dead could be. A few hours later I saw you eating breakfast, as spry as ever. I hid that from Alexei. I was unsure about his motives until about a week ago. He came to the morgue three times. He is spooked. Edgy. All because of you."

"Do you work for Alexei?" asked Jake.

"No," he said. "But I have my spies in his organization. Everyone that works for him is terrified. They don't feel safe. They say he is losing it. Becoming increasingly unstable. After he got rich off you."

"Rich off me?"

Maxim clicked his teeth. He was harried. Possibly angry. "No one knows what deal he made, but he got millions from the information on your laptop," said Maxim. "He bought the company you work for. He owns it now."

Life's a bitch. You die and come back to life, and it's even worse.

"Why did he do that?" asked Jake.

"I thought you could tell me." Maxim shifted in his seat. "Now that you've returned from faking your death yet again."

Jake shook his head, dumbfounded. "Your story doesn't add up," he said. He tightened his grip on the pistol. His eyes met with the driver's through the rearview. It had to be a set up. "You've stood watch over a morgue, waiting for me to walk out because you had an idea I may have faked my death?"

"You faked your death once to get away from the man that no one gets away from. I followed you from the hospital the day after I saw you eating breakfast. People say you died in the hospital too. When I heard about you and this train accident, why would it be silly to think you faked your death another time?"

"I was gone for three weeks!" said Jake.

"Yet, here you are, my friend," said Maxim. "I see street magicians make whole person appear from a bag, in a park, out in the open. I see a man push a metal wire through his hand with no blood and no wound. I see another man levitate. His feet came off the fucking ground and gave my heart such a shock. Why can't a man be cut in half and trick me the same way?"

Jake was stumped. He had to laugh a little. The guy's logic was totally irrational yet it made complete sense. Jake Coltrane; the illusionist who specialized in faking his death.

"Alexei now knows that you did not die in that hotel room," Maxim continued. "Do you know why? Because your girlfriend insisted you were alive after he saw you die, that's why. He went to find the footage of you at the train station that day you got ran over. When he returned he went crazy. Word is he was terrified when he drowned your girlfriend. He can no longer be trusted to keep a cool head. That is why he must die."

"Then kill him," said Jake. "Why did you wait for me to return?"

"Because I am no magician when it comes to death," said Maxim. "Besides, I would need permission." He gazed out the window, detached yet serious. Was there a bit of envy in wanting Alexei dead? Sure. But Maxim's stylish clothes and manicured fingers seemed to suggest above all he was interested in money. Killing Alexei would threaten his future.

"You want me to pull this trick one more time," said Jake.

"So long as Alexei stays dead!"

Jake agreed with a single nod. He felt he could trust Maxim, especially since Sly had not made an appearance to warn him against it. Besides, he needed help. Like a means to escape without taking a cab. Jake eased his grip and holstered his revolver. "You must have a plan, or we wouldn't be having this conversation."

Maxim rubbed the hairs on his chin with a sly smirk on his face. "The perfect plan. Kidnap a girl named Tatiana that works for Alexei in the Bronx. When he comes to retrieve her, you will be there to kill him." He got serious and pointed his index finger towards Jake. "The sight of you alive will provide just enough time to do your thing. You can then use that hand cannon to take his head off."

Jake was thinking his program would make it easy to grab her. "Who is this Tatiana?"

"She works for him as an escort."

Jake frowned. "Why would he be so interested in getting back an escort? Does he have feelings for her?"

"No. Alexei is gay."

Jake sighed in frustration.

"Don't worry," said Maxim. He put his left arm along the top of the door as cool as cool can be. "Alexei's brutish nature will be his downfall. No one gets away from him. He cannot stomach anyone escaping his little pug paws. The girl wants to leave. She wants to make a life with her new man. Alexei was offered money to pay for her freedom, but he refused. She threatened Alexei and told him that her man would come for her if he did not let her go. This is where you come in. Grab Tatiana and make it too messy for him to ignore. He will find you. Then you can take your revenge."

Jake felt better about it and relaxed. His confidence renewed. They were cruising through traffic somewhere in Manhattan, heading towards the Bronx. "Where do I find Tatiana?"

"We are heading that way now. A couple of days ago one of the girls required care. That means one of them probably got the clap. You can get in by posing as a doctor. Just use the magical name Alexei, and they will open the doors. Once inside, you are on your own."

"How many other people will be there?" asked Jake.

"Between nine and twelve armed men. Tatiana is in the first apartment by the door. If you flash that hand cannon, you can be in and out of there without anyone else getting hurt. They won't dare risk shooting on the street, so after you clear the door, you are home free."

With all the adrenaline gone, he came to his senses. Stealing money was one thing. This was murder. "How many people do I have to kill?"

"Do you want Alexei dead or not?" said Maxim sharply. He shot Jake a look then looked down at the BFR. "This is how thieves get justice."

Jake swallowed the lump in his throat. He wanted it. The question was would his body respond when the time came to take action.

Maxim handed Jake the information on a slip of paper. Jake took it between his index and thumb and slid it into his jacket pocket. "Don't try to save the world," said Maxim. "Take only Tatiana. She is your main target."

CHAPTER 55

Jake exited the Escalade on a street corner under the cover of nightfall. Uptown, The Bronx, on a road with train tracks running above it, at a hectic intersection. He looked at the slip of paper with the address. Horns blared in the background. The bright flash of a red light camera snapped a pic of another license. He looked up at the street sign. E233rd, just a few blocks away from his target. Maxim said he would be sending a person in a brown Chevy Cavalier for the getaway. The driver will take them to a home upstate. In the meantime, Jake thought it was best he survey the neighborhood to get a pulse.

It was working-class. Respectable.

Early morning would've been a good time for smuggling someone out of the neighborhood, but since he was posing as a doctor, it would have to be done at a more reasonable time for a physician. Not too early in the morning and not too late in the afternoon. Maxim said the women left for the club sometime around 5:30 p.m., so 3:00 p.m. would work. That gave him eighteen hours. Enough time to think over his plan, gain the necessary equipment, and build up the nerve to pull it off. But first, he needed rest.

Jake found a place nearby with a blinking pink neon hotel sign near the top of the building. They rented by the hour. He paid for twenty-four. It was cheap, old, and sleazy, but all he needed was a good night's sleep. Once in bed, he couldn't sleep. The hard mattress had bedsheets that smelled old and musty, and he hadn't mustered the nerve to take off his clothes or even his shoes, as the worn carpet was a suspiciously dark shade of brown.

The will to pull the trigger plagued his mind all evening. As a kid, he wanted to shoot the man he thought killed his mother but he couldn't.

The gun was snatched from his hand. Which is why he bought a bigger gun… the biggest. No one would dare reach forward to take this one. But could he pull the trigger?

Around midnight Jake left the room to try and find something to eat. He found a corner store with hotdogs and beef patties in the warmer. He took a few. He wasn't really hungry, but he thought it would prompt an appearance from Sly. It didn't. Where was the parasite? Sly's absence had him troubled. He'd get annoyed whenever Sly appeared in the past. Now he welcomed the asshole to pop in and tell him his pants were too tight.

Time ticked off the clock. Night turned to day. Jake grabbed a light breakfast at a gas station that allowed you to heat up frozen sandwiches in a microwave. He had three of them, then went back to the room, waiting for the afternoon. At 2:45 p.m. a buzzer went off in the room telling Jake his paid time had expired. He got up, put on his long leather coat and checked out of the hotel.

He walked several blocks and made a call on the number Maxim gave him. The driver of the getaway car said he would be there in ten minutes. He ended the call, just a few blocks from Tatiana's apartment building. His heart raced. Sly slinked up next to him wearing a black turtleneck, bell-bottoms, and lightly tinted shades. A wooden matchstick poked from his mouth. They walked together.

"You're back," said Jake, unable to hide a sigh of relief.

"It was hard work trying to fix you up, brah. I'm sure you can understand that. But I didn't want to miss this shit. You don't seem focused. Not for what you are about to do."

"I'm not feeling so good," said Jake.

"You should be feeling like shit. You were dead for nearly three weeks. Then you screamed for me to bring you back, so I did. I'm not sure I figured out the source of the tumor, but I did learn all kinds of things about the human body and how to manipulate it."

"You heard me screaming?" asked Jake.

"Yes. Damn it. I told you, I'm hooked into your neural networks."

"I thought I was still dead."

"You were."

Interesting. Jake wondered how closely the two of them were now linked. It would come in handy whenever he was in trouble in the future.

"On the car ride over yesterday, I was sweating like crazy," said Jake.

"You should've eaten more food yesterday."

"I was nervous. I worried it wouldn't stay down."

"That doesn't do me any good, now does it?" Sly repositioned his beret. Straightened the top of his turtleneck and brushed imaginary dust of his sleeves.

Jake checked the street sign. E230th. They were close. "What kind of energy do you think you have left to revive me if shit goes sideways?"

"Not much," said Sly. "How about not getting dead. That would be better."

They stopped on the next corner. The place where Tatiana stayed was near the end of the block on a street with a steep decline, much like the streets of San Francisco. Downhill until it leveled off at the intersecting road, down again and another intersection, and down again. He took a good look at the layout of the buildings and homes on the streets adjacent to Tatiana's building. He walked down the front of an apartment building, went around the corner and down a bit, and spotted a small parking area. Tatiana's place was on the other side. It was a fourplex made of brick. A line of them ran down the block. The brown Cavalier was parked halfway down the block, in clear sight of the building.

Jake squinted at the sun, then walked down the street to the address on the slip of paper. He stood at the edge of the concrete stairs before taking a deep breath and going up. At the top of the stairs was a door. He turned the knob, and it opened. It brought him to an entryway, where people had to be buzzed in. A row of mailboxes ran along the wall to his right. They were marked one through four. No names on the boxes. The mailbox for apartment one was the only one with a button and a speaker. Jake pushed it and waited.

A camera blinked in the upper right corner of the entryway. Jake tried not to look at it, as that would make him look suspicious. Then he thought maybe *not* looking made him look suspicious. He smiled at the camera and held up the bag he'd picked up at a shop down the street. It was full of crumpled pieces of paper and cardboard to make it look like he had some type of equipment in there.

The speaker clicked and a voice came through. Thick Russian accent. His heart raced. His forehead glistened with sweat. It was happening.

"Yes," said the voice.

"I'm a doctor," said Jake. "I'm here to check out one of the girls. Alexei sent me."

A conversation crackled through the active mic. A few seconds later he heard movement down the hallway. Someone approached the door. The door had thin curtains and was made of bullet-proof glass. Jake could make out the shape of a man.

The curtains were pulled back quickly. A face peered out, beard, black hair, droopy eyes, and large lips and nose. He pulled the door open but blocked entry with his body.

"Are you a basketball player or a doctor?" he said, voice gruff, looking up at Jake.

"I'm the doctor. Here's my bag." He offered the bag out with one hand, holding it high so the goon couldn't see inside. As expected, the man grabbed the open end and brought it down to eye level. He stared at the crumpled papers and was about to say something when Jake pushed the barrel of the BFR right into the man's abdomen. He put the bag over the gun so the camera wouldn't see it.

"Say nothing," said Jake. "Don't put your hands up. Don't flinch. Don't even blink unless I tell you to. Got it?"

The man nodded.

"I see you came from the first apartment on the right," said Jake. "That's where I want to go. Take me there. Turn around and walk. Don't make any gestures. No squawks. No attempt at small talk. Just walk there, and this hand cannon won't cut you in half."

The man turned around and did as was instructed. The door to the first apartment was where the hallway turned right so Jake couldn't see the door. Straight ahead of him, a brightly lit stairway led to the apartments above. Strange, considering the hallway was so dark. He glanced up as they passed. A small skylight dirtied by dead moths. The path around the right side of the stairway led to a second apartment. Maxim had told Jake that behind the stairwell was another set of stairs leading to the basement, where the bulk of the manpower resided. He needed to be in and out before anyone from the basement surfaced.

When they were about five feet away from apartment one, someone on the second floor peered over the top of the balcony. He looked straight down at Jake, the bag, and Russian instinct kicked in.

"Gun!" he shouted.

Jake went hard right and shoved his escort through the open door of the first apartment. His shoulder hit the door as they passed, and the recoil slammed the door shut with a bang behind them. Jake locked a few of the bolts and latches. Someone shrieked. Three young ladies in the living room huddled in fear; thin arms stretched around each other.

"Which one of you is Tatiana?" Jake yelled. He grabbed the big-nosed man and shoved him against the wall, pressing the ten-inch barrel of the BRF into his chest. "Where is Tatiana?"

The man's eyes flickered over to the right, and Jake followed suit. A young woman. Petite. Strawberry-colored hair, blue eyes, fair skin. A large, noticeable dimple on her chin. She pressed her arms into her side, a dazed look on her face.

Jake gazed at her, taking in her fear and shock. His initial plan of being quick and quiet was dead in the water. He had no idea what to do. No contingency plan to fall back on. All he could think about was how innocent people were probably going to get hurt. His heart jumped when as her eyes grew wide with fear. Something hard hit his head. He lost his grip on the man and tried to pull the trigger in a panic, but the gun didn't fire. It was a single-action revolver. He had to cock the hammer first.

Jake fell to the ground at the young woman's feet. She jumped backward. He attempted to cock the hammer and move the gun into firing position, but a boot stepped on his wrist, pressing down and twisting until Jake released the gun. Jake attempted to move his free hand but the big-nosed guy grabbed his arm. He swung his head up to see his oppressor. A tall, lean man stood above Jake, looking down at him with disgust.

The two goons pummeled Jake. There was little he could do to stop it. Furious fists pounded against his face. They kicked his torso and stomped on his legs. Welts bloomed on his skin. An angry pain pierced his left side. Bloody swelling sealed his eyes shut. They smashed his nose and Jake gagged as blood spilled down his throat. Jake tried to free himself, but they had him pinned down. He clawed and struggled to no avail.

The one kicking the side of his head turned to stomp on his throat.

One stomp grazed his chin and brought it down to his chest so hard it felt like it knocked something loose at the back of his neck. Then came the next stomp to his neck. Straight down on it. His mind drifted. *So much for revenge*, he thought as he waited for his life to fade away.

CHAPTER 56

Jake was about to die. He felt the life draining from his body. He panicked. He hadn't wanted this. Anything but this. He told himself to fight. Fight with all his might. Summon the will to battle. Strength pulsed through his heart. He was gonna do it. He was going to push back his assailant.

He found himself at the feet of Tartarus.

"Forgot about saving your soul already, I see," said Tartarus.

The bright white grin leered down at Jake. He felt the lingering burn of the fifth mark. Jake lowered his head and cried. He cried because he was a failure. Catalina's murderer would go unpunished. When the moment came, he'd let his nerves get the best of him, and he forgot to cock the hammer. Meanwhile, those he sought to threaten reacted without hesitation. They ended his life like it was nothing.

The gloved hand of Tartarus grabbed Jake by the neck and raised him upward until they were face to face. It was like staring into a giant shadow with teeth. A stench reached out from the back of his throat nearly choking Jake. He turned away to spy a whirlpool of blood swirling beneath him.

Tartarus pulled Jake closer. The grip around his neck softened as Tartarus held him over the whirlpool.

"You can't fight, can you?" asked Tartarus. "You make this too easy, Jake Coltrane."

Tartarus dropped Jake at his feet and into the swirling pool of blood. It barely came up to Jake's ankles.

"Anyone who fights this man will not be burned!" boomed Tartarus. "Stomp the shit out of this bastard. Those souls who beat this man to blood, upon conclusion, will also be able to touch whomever they want, without being burned, forever."

A group of people must have been following Tartarus around at a distance. As soon as he made his decree, they emerged from the shadows. The sky darkened to a sickly gold. Shadowy black clouds covered the sky. And Tartarus walked away, leaving Jake in the pool of blood to deal with his new predicament.

Jake estimated there were a few hundred people there, ready to take him on. What greater gift in this repulsive place than to not get burned by another soul's touch? Back when Aruru presented herself as a beautiful woman on the bridge, she had taken his hand and escorted him along the path. He remembered how comforting her touch had felt. Just the thought of someone holding his hand on his way through hell made him feel better instantly.

They surrounded the pool of blood. He could see in their eyes how much they wanted the decree to be trustworthy. They stood close enough to block Jake from any possible path to escape. Working up the nerve to test what Tartarus had told them. The circle squeezed a bit tighter. Those closest stepped into the blood. He felt their courage building within them, spurred on by desperation.

A large hairy man wadded through the pool cautiously. His belly hung down below the waist. He flexed his forearms, extending his fingers, getting loose. Jake took a fighting position. The man lunged awkwardly and struck Jake on the forearms as he blocked the punch. Jake felt the blow and the searing burn of skin contact. The hairy man stood startled. Then he looked at his fist and smiled. No pain. Only Jake had sizzled. Only Jake was burned. The crowd collectively gasped.

Many rushed in and attacked, sloshing through the blood. Jake's heart raced. He was done for. All he could do was cover himself and hope that Sly would get him out of there in time. He ducked, protecting his head as much as possible. There were a few glancing blows along with the burning pain but that was it. They stopped. Jake uncovered his head, surprised that they had backed away. Then he got his answer. They were clumsy and bumped into each other. They burned themselves.

They soon understood the rules in which they had to work. They couldn't conduct a mass attack. A person had to earn their claim to

Tartarus's prize by stepping in and beating Jake properly, one at a time, perhaps even two if they could work together.

He watched them, trying to get a feel for who would step into the pool next. The sloshing sound came from behind. He tried to react in time but was slow. Jake was grabbed from behind and placed in a chokehold. Jake's eyes rolled to the back of his head. Never had so much of his flesh been in contact with someone else for so long while in hell. It must have been this guy's plan. Turn Jake into one of the Contretemps and he would be in no condition to put up a fight.

All the assailant had to do was hold on tight, and time would take care of the rest. Jake did everything he could. He scratched and clawed, burning his fingers in the process. He kicked and screamed, trying to break free. The pain motivated him, helped him reach deep down and summon strength he didn't know he had.

The assailant wrenched his upper body left and right to get Jake under control, twisting Jake off balance. The momentum worked against the assailant, and he brushed against someone in the circle, causing him to wince and buckle. His muscles twitched and a light bulb illuminated in Jake's mind. Jake wrenched his body again, shifting them off balance. When they got near the edge, Jake reached out and grabbed a woman who stood unsuspectingly close. It burned like hell, but he wasn't about to let go. He pulled the woman toward him and pushed her into the attacker, who shrieked in pain and lost control. Jake crawled through the pool of blood on his knees trying to catch his breath.

But the next wave came quickly. Another man at the circle's edge made his move to grapple Jake as he rested on his hands and knees. Jake saw him and kicked him before he could gain momentum. His foot landed at the center of his attacker's chest, and he hurled the man back into the crowd, causing screams as those in the crowd were burned by his falling body.

Jake had realized the beauty of pain. Pain is effective at intimidating prey. Fear of pain was a weapon, and it was about time he learned how to use it. Like when Jake first arrived in hell and Zee had slapped him with an open palm, knowing both would get burned. A plan emerged. It was time to see who had the strongest of wills.

A renewed clarity infused Jake's intentions. Who among them was willing to risk everything? Beat him and be free of burning forever. Fail and become one of the Contretemps. He'd use this to send his attackers into each other. Who would sacrifice themselves to achieve their goal?

Jake realized he had power. Before he could deliver pain to another, he had to be willing to suffer that pain himself. And the chokehold had shown him he could suffer the pain. He knew that with his fear of pain under control, he now had the mental fortitude to wield the threat of pain toward others.

Jake immediately went on the offensive. He dove into the crowd of people, burning himself in the process. He climbed on the man who'd choked him and punched him with all his might, searing his fists with each strike. It was like sitting naked on hot coals, but Jake pressed down so the guy couldn't move. Another man attacked, and Jake kicked him in the gut, burning himself again. The man tumbled into the crowd, burning everyone around him.

Jake clambered his feet and dove into the crowd, latching on to anyone he could. His fists flew left and right. The raucous battle of wills went on until Jake had expended his energy to the point of exhaustion. Yet he pushed on, slapping, kicking, and biting. Catalina was his painkiller. Alexei was his fuel. Pain was his wrath.

And Jake found himself back in the apartment in the Bronx.

CHAPTER 57

Jake's mind felt clear. His body felt stronger. Solid. He awoke to find himself on his back in the kitchen, near the entrance to the apartment. One of the men who'd beaten him to death had his back to Jake. He talked animatedly with the other one, the one who'd let him inside, discussing how Jake had gotten that far into the apartment.

"He said Alexei sent him," said the big-nosed guy.

Jake slowly stood. The big-nosed guy reacted as if cold water had been splashed on him. Before he could say anything, Jake grabbed the other guy by the side of the head and smashed it into the wall to his left. Jake knew that the man's core muscles could easily resist such a move, so he destabilized the man's source of balance by stomping on the back of his left calf. At the same time, Jake grabbed his left wrist as he put his other hand on the right side of the man's head. Jake rotated his hips and drove his weight toward the wall as the guy's knee buckled. Plaster of Paris wasn't as forgiving as sheetrock, and Jake felt the man's skull change shape beneath his right palm.

The guy was down and out with one quick move.

Jake towered over the big-nosed man by about a foot. He raised a weapon. It was Jake's. The BFR. He pointed it at Jake and tried to pull the trigger, but it wouldn't budge. Same mistake Jake had made earlier.

As he moved his thumb toward the hammer, Jake kicked him between the legs so hard that it lifted the big-nosed man off his feet. In one swift motion, Jake grabbed the back of the man's head and brought it down while thrusting his knee upward. The head and knee connected with the

278

kind of force that broke jaws and nose cartilage. He wouldn't be getting up from the ground to cause trouble.

With both of his attackers on the ground, Jake took a moment to survey his surroundings. He saw the thin young woman with strawberry blonde hair from earlier. Her pale blue eyes were as large and wide as they could get.

"Are you Tatiana?" asked Jake.

"What do you want with my sister?" she asked.

Right. This must be her sister, Arina. "Where is she?"

"Not here. What do you want with her?"

"Someone told me to take her."

"Was it Paul?" she asked. Her voice held a tinge of hope. "My sister's friend?"

"No," said Jake. He made a move for the door, and Arina grabbed his hand. It was soft and delicate.

"I will show you where she is," said Arina. "But you must take us both. That was always the deal, all the way from when we were back in Mother Russia. We sisters stay together."

Maxim had warned him about this.

"No deal," said Jake. "Too much for me to handle."

Jake looked over to his side to find Sly standing next to him. He wore a black turtleneck, black pants, and a black beret on his head, a fist button was pinned to the beret.

"So you came back," said Jake.

"No time for small talk. Forces are mobilizing, brah!" said Sly. "Guys downstairs are moving fast. They heard the commotion."

"Shouldn't they be here by now?" said Jake. "How long was I out?"

"Maybe ten seconds, tops. I got your genome sequence down. I can put you together pretty fast, especially when you're in one piece. But that's when you're dead. When you're alive, it's much slower. Then I have to work in a specific area and be careful not to work willy-nilly. It might risk wiping out critical memories and shit."

"Amazing," said Jake.

"Who are you talking to?" asked Arina. She stared at him strangely.

"An invisible friend," said Jake. He looked at the group of women behind Arina, cowering in the dark. He counted four of them in the living room. Could one of them be Tatiana?

"She is upstairs in another apartment," said Arina.

Up the stairs. From the layout, it was the worst place he could be if he wanted to escape. The staircase was in the middle of the building. The bottom of the stairs led to the hallway, about twenty feet long. Parallel to the stairs was ten feet of hallway leading to another apartment door. The top of the stairs had a balcony leading to another apartment with one more at the top. So essentially, going up and down the stairs was like a shooting gallery for anyone with a pistol.

The windows of the apartments at ground level had wrought iron bars which meant that no one could escape the first floor through the windows. If he went to the apartments upstairs, chances were good he wouldn't be able to get out the front without going through a massive shoot-out below.

He paused to examine Arina. Jake wasn't there to cause her further duress. He needed her to remain calm. She wouldn't be if he left her there. Besides, he had no idea what Tatiana looked like. He needed Arina upstairs with him if he were to take the right person.

"Let's get your sister," said Jake.

A pounding on the door. "Hey, what's going on in there? Open the door, Boris. Boris?"

Jake picked up the BFR from the floor and crept to the other side of the door. He cocked the hammer and braced himself. Firm stance. Two hands on the gun. Arms straight. He tightened the muscles in his back and pulled the trigger. The blast was incredible. The crunching of splintered wood and flames shooting out of the barrel was quite a show. He hadn't anticipated the deafening sound, or the ringing in his eardrums, or the screaming that followed.

Jake quickly unlocked the door and opened it. He looked down. Jake recognized the guy who had screamed *gun*. He clutched at where his hand should be, shaking and muttering. Blood spurted everywhere.

Arina came out of the apartment behind Jake and saw the man lying there. "Which apartment is my sister in?" she demanded.

Jake stood in direct line of sight to apartment number two. The door was open, and a man hung back against the doorframe with his pistol drawn. Jake raised the massive BFR in his direction. Stalemate.

"No intention to shoot, brah," said Sly. "Just move away."

"Come, let's go upstairs," said Arina. She jumped over the man on the floor.

Moving toward the stairs meant being in the line of sight for anyone waiting upstairs. And they were. They shouted down the stairs in Russian. Jake thought it sounded like four men in total. Arina yelled back up at them. From his angle, he couldn't see anyone. He didn't want to take his eyes off the guy with the pistol.

Arina screamed something in Russian at the top of her lungs, inspiring a wave of anger that prompted the men to fire. The ricocheting bullets and splintering wood and concrete from the Plaster of Paris meant they were aiming their pistols at where the sound had come from, next to apartment number one.

Arina took cover behind Jake at the base of the apartment door. But Jake didn't move. He remained focused on the guy from apartment two with his gun drawn. The man with the freshly amputated hand must've been a friend of his. He seemed less interested in firing and more interested in stopping the bleeding. Even the hail of gunfire hadn't prompted him to start squeezing his trigger.

Jake shook his head no and put his hand up as a warning. Then he moved. He swung his body over to the far wall in the direct path of the stairs. There he could see someone in the apartment at the top of the stairs firing a handgun. Jake could tell he startled the guy by the way his gun dipped. He'd been shooting blindly until a large figure swooped into the scene. Jake wasn't afraid of dying, and it made a big difference with bullets flying everywhere. Tension and fear wouldn't affect his aim.

Jake pointed the pistol up at the door and pulled the trigger. The boom, the blast, the fire, the carnage. A momentary look of astonishment overcame the man's face, and then his face was gone. The sequence of bullets stopped. It was like a split-second moment of shock that took everyone's breath away.

With a pause in the action, Arina swept past Jake, screaming more obscenities in Russian. She ran up carelessly. Jake ran up behind her. Jake reached out to Arina, who was already halfway up the stairs and pulled her down by her ankle. The blast of a shotgun bore a hole into the stairs where her head had just been. Jake slid her down the stairs and out of the direct line of fire. The blast had come from the apartment on the other side of the top of the stairs. Overhead from where he was standing. The fourth apartment.

He was lining up the shot when he saw the guy from apartment two creeping down the hallway. Jake directed his gun to the guy, and he froze.

"No murderous intent," said Sly. "He's going to check on his buddy with the missing hand. He was about to shoot through the door. Great shot, by the way. You beat him to it."

"You could sense that?" asked Jake.

"Yep. It was perfect timing. I thought you were getting your instincts back or tapping into mine. Then pulled a boneheaded move and jumped up the stairs after that girl. She would've provided the perfect cover."

"Not here to watch an innocent person get splattered," said Jake.

"Whatever."

"What do you think about those guys up top?" asked Jake.

"I think you should shoot the one with the shotgun up through the floor."

"Where?" asked Jake.

"Point the gun upward and to the right, and I'll tell you when to stop," said Sly. "A little more. A little more. Okay. Squeeze."

Jake released another boom, sending sparks flying in the air. He heard two thuds, the shotgun hitting the floor, then a human body.

"Move," said Sly.

A series of automatic fire flashed through the ceiling by the stairs as the last guy in apartment four unloaded through the floor. Jake grabbed Arina by the arm, ushering her up the stairs and straight toward the partially open door of apartment three. The guy with the missing head was slumped between the door and the frame.

Jake jumped over the dead body and into the apartment. He stood inside the kitchen, looking for someone to shoot.

"Behind the door, stupid," said Sly.

Jake pulled Arina into the apartment and shoved her into the bedroom on the right. He turned around and shot through the open door. Two more muffled thuds. The gun and the body. The man he'd just shot buckled on the floor, a trail of blood on the wall behind him. Dead before his buttocks hit the ground. Jake dragged the guy who lost his head out of the way and slammed the door shut.

Jake went to the bedroom to retrieve Arina. She sat quietly on the bed. A woman huddled in the corner. Jake motioned to Arina, asking if this was the sister he was looking for. She shook her head no.

Arina spoke to the woman in Russian. The woman needed some persuasion before answering. Arina grabbed her by the arms and delivered a firm slap across the cheeks to get her attention. A maneuver Jake was familiar with.

She said something in Russian and Arina stepped away from her, shocked and confused.

"What is it?" asked Jake.

"She said they took my sister away. I asked if her clothes were taken, and she said there were no clothes. She said that Tatiana was here in the other bedroom for one day, and then she was gone."

"She's not in the building at all?" *Great.*

Sly spoke up once more. "Got about five motherfuckers coming up through the basement. Our escape through the front door has officially been cut off."

Jake had initiated a bloodbath for someone who wasn't there and had also made his escape more difficult. Too late to mope over it now. Survival mode kicked in. Jake locked the door.

The guy in the apartment across the way had an automatic weapon. Five more headed up the stairs. They shouted in Russian. The other women in the living room heard it too. They began fussing and crying, making it more difficult to think.

"They know we are trapped in this apartment," said Arina. "They are plotting how to bust in and kill us all. I'm sorry."

Jake walked through the living room to the windows. He pulled back the curtains. No wrought iron bars. They were about thirty feet above a small backyard. A van was parked in the middle. To left was a concrete wall that ran to the end of the yard. It was twenty feet below and ten feet to the left of the window. The fence on top of the wall ran the length and was eight feet high. On the other side of the fence was a parking lot. It was unlikely that someone could jump twelve feet up and ten feet to the left to reach the window. Probably why it did not have any bars on them. But to jump over the fence from the window would be possible. Not easy, but it could be done. He checked the BFR. One round left.

"Time to go," said Jake.

Arina shook her head with tears in her eyes. "I am sorry," she said. "But I can't go without knowing what happened to my sister."

"If we can get to that parking lot in one piece, I will find her. But we have to go now!"

"Is your car there?"

"I can't drive."

"What kind of plan is that? You come in to kidnap my sister and take her on a bus ride?"

"I can't drive because of my . . . never mind!" said Jake.

Arina ran back into the kitchen area and returned a few seconds later. She held up the key fob. "I took this from the guy you shot in the head. I know where he parks."

"I have a ride out... never mind!" said Jake.

Jake kicked the window with a mighty thrust, aiming at the wooden windowpane and breaking it with a single kick, causing an explosion of shattering glass. The women in the living room yelped and scattered. Jake used the BFR to break off the remaining glass and stuck his head out the window to take a good look. He felt confident.

Jake grabbed Arina and before she could object, pushed her out the window. She dangled by one arm. He swung her back and forth, then thrust her toward the fence. She flew straight at it and had no other choice but to grab onto the fence with her fingers. Her feet landed on the concrete ledge. A perfect throw.

Arina cursed, then climbed the fence. Jake waited for her to make it to the top before he jumped. He flew over her head and the fence, landing with a hard thud and tumbling several times before coming to a stop. He pulled the BFR from his waist and checked to see if it was damaged. Not even a scuff on the piece. Unfortunately, he could not say the same for his torso. Jake had taken a round to the midsection.

Jake got to his feet quickly and caught sight of the brown Cavalier making a getaway amidst the blaring sounds of sirens. So much for that. Good thing Arina thought of a plan B.

He took Arina by the hand. "Let's get out of here."

From the parking lot, they ran toward a small unpaved space between the two apartment buildings. Jake and Arina pushed through the scattered weeds and scaled a short fence before coming onto the sidewalk. Police sirens blared as the cars shot past the intersection on the right.

"The car is over there," said Arina. She pointed to the dark blue Suburban twenty feet from the corner. "The one you shot in the head also drives the boss around. His name is Zachary."

"Zachary is the boss?" asked Jake.

"Zachary was the one you shot. The boss is named Alexei."

CHAPTER 58

Arina chirped the key fob and unlocked the doors. She got into the front while Jake crawled into the back. Police cars were flying down the hill toward the apartment building. Soon they'd block off the intersecting streets. They had to move.

"Drive," he said to Arina. She pushed the button to start the car and put it into drive. She jerked the wheel, spun the tires, and pulled out into traffic, then stopped abruptly at the corner. Two more police cruisers whizzed past them at the stop sign. She kept going straight. She peeled off down the road far enough away from the action to where she could turn up the main road without being stopped.

"I assumed you could drive," said Jake.

"I watched people drive, so that is good enough," she said. Her pale blue eyes looked at him through the mirror. "What was I supposed to do? I can't drive and you can't drive. You have a gaping hole in your stomach. Our chances are better if I drive."

Jake left it alone. He looked down at his wound. It didn't hurt much but he was bleeding pretty good. "Where are we going?" he asked. "Do you know your way around?"

"I know how to get to the club in Manhattan. That is where we go to work every day. So that is where we are heading."

She looked at him in the mirror as she drove. "What happened to your hair?" she said. "When you first came inside, you had hair on your head."

Jake maneuvered his head around to see himself in the rearview mirror. She was right. He was bald.

"What the—?"

"Sorry. I took the liberty of making some minor modifications," said Sly. He sat in the passenger's seat, wearing his usual silk shirt and bell-bottoms, rolling a toothpick around the corner of his mouth. He smiled. "Like it?"

"I thought I felt different," said Jake, rubbing his head. "Like when I smashed that guy's head through the wall. I feel stronger." He ran his hands over his body. He was ripped. Shredded. Not big and bulky, but firm and athletic. All fast-twitch muscles.

"Yep," said Sly. "Improvements I made to your body when you were out screaming for vengeance. I thought you'd need a boost. As I was trying to get rid of that tumor, I came across how to boost muscle growth and add strength and volume to your frame. You're kind of jacked now, thanks to me."

He'd thrown a grown woman ten feet with one hand. She was small and probably weighed no more than 105 pounds, but still, he threw a person with one arm while dangling her out a window. And he'd been sure he wouldn't drop her. Then he'd jumped ten feet. Granted, he was also ten feet higher than the fence, but still, it was a hell of a leap. He cleared it and landed without breaking anything.

"Nice work," said Jake. "Now you need to work on this gunshot wound because it's starting to hurt."

"Yes, I learn quickly," said Arina. "My driving is improving, but I know nothing about fixing a gunshot wound. You seem surprised about your hair and body. The beating you took is affecting your thinking. Gunshots are supposed to hurt!"

"Your adrenaline is winding down, brah," said Sly. "Let me see this thing. Damn. You took a good hit. It's going to take me a moment to repair. Probably a few hours. Hopefully you don't die before that."

"A few hours? You can bring me back from the dead in seconds, but it takes hours to fix a wound?"

"Different algorithms altogether, brah. Different symmetry. Rebuilding you while you're dead gives me full reign to do all things at once. When you're alive, I'm limited. Think of it as working on the computer, replacing chips and metering out circuits with the power on. Not a good idea, is it? It's better to remove power, change what you've got to change, put power back on and check it out. Got it, amigo?"

"Bring you back from the dead?" asked Arina, wide-eyed. "No. I can't do that. I do pole tricks. You are not going to die, are you? You are talking crazy. Like you see things."

"I'm fine," said Jake. "Just talking to my invisible friend. Like talking to the little demon on my shoulder."

"So now I'm a demon?" asked Sly. "Cute, asshole."

"Something talks to you inside your head," said Arina, nodding. "They say that it's okay to talk to yourself, but if you answer, then you are crazy."

"How is that supposed to work?" asked Sly. "Your brain tells you something, and you don't question it?"

"Talking inside your head is normal," said Jake. "If you ask yourself, 'where are my keys?' You answer by saying, 'maybe I left them on the counter.'"

She moved her head as if he'd made a point.

"See there?" said Jake. "I'm saying it aloud so that you can hear it. Shit!" A sharp pain shot through his side. It throbbed like a son of a bitch, then subsided.

"Are you going to be okay?" she asked. "Do we need to look for a hospital?"

Jake reached around to feel his back. Warm blood soaked through his shirt. He felt around with his fingers until he found the puncture wound. "It's a through and through," said Jake. "I should be fine."

Sly spun around in his seat with his mouth agape. "What the fuck are you talking about?" asked Sly.

"The bullet went in and out. Through and through. No bullet in my body, so I'm not going to die."

"You're bleeding the fuck out, dumbass. How is that fine? How are two holes in your body better than one?"

"The bullet is not inside my body," said Jake. "That's how people die."

"Sorry," said Sly. "My bad. I thought people died because of blood spilling out of bullet holes. Punk gets shot up like swiss cheese, but he's fine so long as there're no bullets stuck in there. Now I'm enlightened. People die because the bullet can't escape. I wonder if you swallowed a slug if you would die before you shit it out."

"Why are you acting like that, Sly? Just fix it. Fast. And turn on the adrenaline or something so that the pain isn't so bad."

"Got it, Mr. Through-and-through."

"Who is this 'Sly?'" asked Arina, tires screeching as she weaves in and out of traffic. "You have named the demon in your head?" She hit the brakes hard and Jake nearly slid off the seat.

"I'm not a fucking demon," snapped Sly, perfectly still in his seat. "I don't know which is worse, being called a parasite or a demon. They both piss me off."

Horns blared as Arina cut someone off in traffic. "Yes! Sly is the demon on my shoulder," said Jake.

"I will leave your ass to the demons the next time you die, asshole!"

"But I'm not going to die," said Jake, pointing to his midsection. "Through and through."

"Okay, dummy," said Sly. "I'm sure Hollywood knows what a fatal wound looks like."

"I'm feeling good because I did it," said Jake. "I accomplished the mission. Mostly. Let me have my moment. Besides, I'm not worried because you can bring me back."

"Not so fast," said Sly. "You haven't eaten like you should've. It could take longer to siphon the energy needed to bring you back yet again."

Jake looked around as they drove through the Bronx to the interstate. He saw a sign up ahead. "I need food," he said. "A shit ton of food. There! Pull into the drive-thru and order something."

It was a fast-food place. Mexican.

"We can't do that," said Arina, swerving to keep the car steady. "You look like you are dying. Someone will see you."

"The windows are tinted back here. They can't see in. I'll sit up when we get to the window so it doesn't look bad. But I need something to eat right away."

"What do you want?"

"Three of everything on the menu. Their portions are kind of small."

"You must be joking."

"Another skinny bitch paying attention to what someone else is eating," said Sly. "Are all skinny bitches like this?"

"Three of everything," Jake reiterated. "Here's my card." He handed the black card to Arina. "If there are ten meals, get them all. If there are fourteen, order fourteen. The entire meal. Drinks and all."

"Would you like dessert with that?" she asked.

"Ha, ha, very funny!" said Sly.

"Yes!" said Jake. "Desserts and all."

"Okay, you freak," said Arina. "I will do that."

Arina chirped tires and spun the Suburban into the drive-thru, amidst honks and angry gestures. Jake rummaged around the back and found a microfiber towel used for cleaning the car. It would have to do. He wiped the blood off his face the best he could. Then he sat upright and kept as still as he could manage. Sly kicked up the adrenaline, which helped, but it still hurt like hell.

She got to the speaker and asked for three of everything, as Jake instructed. They made her pull off to the side so that the flow of the drive-thru wouldn't clog. After twenty minutes, employees came out to the vehicle, three people carrying bags of food and trays filled with soft drinks. Arina released the trunk and they piled everything in. Jake was easily able to reach the food himself from the backseat. The trunk clicked closed, and she put the vehicle in reverse and backed out without incident. They headed out of the parking lot and into traffic.

Arina's eyes glanced into the mirror as the car swayed unsteadily in the lane. "Are you sure you don't work for Paul?" asked Arina. "It would answer a lot."

"No," said Jake, munching down a burrito. "I'm doing this on my own. For other reasons."

"Paul is the man that wants to marry my sister," said Arina.

"I know," said Jake.

"Classic case of someone wanting to turn a ho into a housewife," said Sly from the passenger's seat.

Jake shook his head at Sly. He didn't feel like it was time for that type of humor.

"Fuck you then. I'm out," said Sly. "Eat up, motherfucker. Let's not die anytime soon." He flipped Jake off and disappeared with a pout.

"Who would want to marry a prostitute, right?" said Arina, looking at him through the mirror. "That is why you are shaking your head. Foolish, I know. Tatiana is not known to tell tales. If she said that this Paul wants to marry her and pay for our debt, then that is what he wants to do. The problem is Alexei. He would be insulted, a pride thing. He would retaliate.

290

That is why they took her from the apartment. I first believed it was because Paul offered to pay, but she was taken away completely. I don't know what that means."

Jake could tell she was distraught. The way her pale blue eyes shifted as she thought, her insides screamed something dreadful had happened. Her unsteady hands on the wheel was more than just inexperience. He kept eating.

"Why did you ask for Tatiana specifically?" asked Arina.

He didn't want to talk about it. Didn't want to share his plan. But the way she kept looking at him in the mirror. She needed to know. "I needed her to draw Alexei out of hiding so that I could kill him. He killed a friend of mine."

They came to a stoplight. The car lurched forward abruptly as she pressed too hard on the brakes, then settled. "Friend?" she asked.

"Ex-girlfriend," said Jake, before gulping down the first of his drinks.

She fell silent for a moment, thinking. "When most relationships fail, people are enemies for life," she shared. "I would feel honored to be your ex-girlfriend, knowing you would kill for me." A single tear ran down her cheek, and she quickly wiped it away. "Where did you come up with this idea to take Tatiana?" she asked.

"Maxim," said Jake. "He was the one who came up with the plan. Do you know him?"

"Maxim? Are you fucking kidding?"

"He wants Alexei out of the way. He explained that Alexei is out of control so killing him is for the best."

Arina tapped on the steering wheel anxiously. Her eyes glossed over in worry. "Maxim wanting to get rid of Alexei . . . I don't trust it. Something is very wrong here."

Jake agreed. He crunched on a series of tacos. "When was the last time you saw your sister?" he asked.

"A few days ago when they moved her to the apartment upstairs. The bastard upstairs, who you shot through the door, beat her for a long time. I'm worried about her."

Jake reached into his pocket to pull out his phone. The screen was cracked, but it still worked. The slip of paper Maxim gave him with the number of the driver was the last person he called. Couldn't trust it though.

"Do you know Paul's last name?" said Jake.

She thought about it for a moment. "Paul Smith."

"Paul Smith? Are you sure that's not a fake name?"

"This is the name Tatiana told me," said Arina.

Sounded fishy. Made up. He didn't know what to think of Arina or her sister. They were foreign and victims of human trafficking. But Sly told him to start trusting his instincts. Strangely, he trusted Arina's judgement. "Anything else about him that stands out from other Paul Smiths?"

She thought about it. "Wait! He has money. My sister said he was an artist. I said the two things don't go together, but she said that he inherited the money."

Paul Smith. Artist. Rich. Inheritance. Somewhere in New York. With no facial recognition, Jake did what everyone else did in the internet era. He did a search. More than three hundred Paul Smiths in New York City alone. Twice as many if you threw in the tristate area.

He plugged in the search criteria. Wealth. Family members with money, preferably mother and father. Artist. Not famous, but with money to pretend like he was. He searched the galleries and events in the area and found someone who might fit. The problem was the age. He had no idea how old Paul was.

Jake guessed the kind of man he was looking for. An older man wouldn't confuse lust with love, and if he bought a woman, he'd be more inclined to set clear boundaries within his heart. The same went with younger guys who were extremely good-looking. Having the pick of the litter tended to harden emotions of love. Younger, less attractive men who grew up isolated by their wealth would be the ones most likely controlled by their hearts.

It had to be the Paul Smith on his phone. Twenty-nine years old. Shy, reclusive-looking guy, not the type who hung out at clubs and partied. Conservative with his inheritance. Someone who needed to get laid occasionally without attachments but still had a vulnerable heart. He made Arina pull over to the curb and talked her through how to load the address into the GPS. The computerized voice gave commands, and bright arrows showed her where to turn.

With that taken care of, Jake ate. He shoved the food down as fast as he could. The hunger was insatiable. He topped off every meal with a drink. Large Cokes, Sprites, and fruit punch. While he ate, he worried. The way the tall guy went straight to killing Jake struck him as the rage of someone stomping out a threat. Those men in the apartment had all been on high alert. If Arina thought Paul sent Jake, then something else must have happened. Especially with Tatiana being taken.

CHAPTER 59

Jake pushed the assortment of Mexican American food wrappers, along with all the empty cups, to the floor of the car. If only he had a day to recuperate. Jake had the impression he'd be heading right back into action soon. The drive to Paul Smith's place would take roughly an hour. He stretched out on the backseat, crossed his arms over his chest, and tucked his hands into his armpits. He hoped he'd be ready to move around by then. Jake dozed off.

His eyes opened. It was an hour later and they were in New Castle, New York, a town much different from the concrete and congestion of the city. Lush landscapes spread far and wide, providing privacy for properties. Private parks maintained by private landscapers dotted the neighborhood, along with several manicured golf courses. The people who lived there had enough money to buy whatever they wanted. They were the one-percenters.

Not the typical place you'd find a man willing to purchase the freedom of a Russian prostitute. Or maybe it was exactly the place. Tatiana was a victim of human trafficking. For all he knew, Paul may have been the type of person to keep Tatiana much the same way as Alexei did. He pushed those thoughts from his head.

Arina came upon some open gates, and the GPS told her to turn right. It was after five in the evening and with the cloud cover, darker than usual. Arina turned down the well-lit brick driveway leading to the front of the house. Trimmed grass edged the brick and spread out like an ocean to the left and right of the road. A white house loomed ahead, with large, old-world columns. It reminded Jake of a southern plantation. They entered the roundabout and pulled up to the front.

Arina parked the car and sat rigidly in her seat, breathing deeply. Jake sensed the anxiety coming off her. He had jitters of his own. Wandering into a strange place, afraid of what he might find, was unnerving. He hoped Sly would appear and straighten him out. The vibes emanating from the house were bad. Don't go in there bad.

Arina got out of the car. He grabbed the door handle to follow, then stopped. He rechecked the cylinder on the BFR. One bullet. A large Black man in a black leather coat with blood all over his shirt wasn't someone a person expected to see knocking on their door at night. He didn't want to incite panic if he was wrong about the vibes he was getting.

He looked at Arina standing outside and inspected her clothing. Blue jeans and a snug black tee. The bulk of her strawberry blonde hair hung down her back while bangs framed her eyebrows. She looked presentable. Harmless. Not a drop of blood on her.

"Go knock on the door and speak to him," said Jake. "If this is the right place, give me a thumbs-up. Don't go inside, and don't mention that Tatiana is missing. I'll be watching from here."

She nodded, quickly ran up the three steps, and nervously wiggled her fingers before ringing the doorbell. The door opened after a beat. Arina ducked inside. The door closed swiftly behind her.

What the hell? She'd gone right inside like it was nothing. Was he being set up? Anxiety rippled from his throat to his gut. Where was Sly? Jake felt abandoned right when he needed Sly the most.

"Sly, where the fuck are you?" said Jake. Nothing.

He gave it a few minutes. Maybe she saw her sister and rushed in. Maybe they were rejoicing at that very moment. No, that didn't feel right to him, either. He grew antsy. Maxim could be behind it. Or Maxim and Alexei were working together.

Jake couldn't shake the sick feeling that Arina was in trouble. He exited the car and trotted up the three stairs to the front door, BFR in his right hand. Fuck what it looked like. Jake tried the door handle. Unlocked.

The door slowly glided open, revealing the deep shine of polished wooden floors within a large foyer. A large staircase led upstairs and flat archways were to the left and right side of the entry. The left were bookshelves, a study or den. The right led to a living room with a tan couch and a chair in the corner. Pictures and artwork hung on the wall leading up the staircase and in several places in the foyer. Another opening led to the hallway at the far end of the entrance. From there, the floor changed from wood to tile.

Jake stepped inside carefully. People were talking over on his right. He crept in farther, careful not to make a sound. The talking grew louder. Hostile. He heard Arina pleading. He went through the living room and entered the dining room. He circled past the elegant mahogany table and through the kitchen, then the pantry, and then the laundry room. He found a door and turned the handle.

He stopped. Alexei's voice. He opened the door and found himself in a garage the size of a showroom. At least ten cars were parked. Ridiculously expensive cars. Jake laid eyes on the man for the first time since the hotel meeting. Now he knew his name. Alexei Voznesensky.

He stood over Arina, who was tied to a chair. Two men flanked Alexei's right, and another three flanked his left, near the wall next to a small stand-alone freezer. The lid was propped open, a woman inside. She was young. Frozen. Above the freezer, a man swung from a cord tied to the rafters. Paul Smith.

"A whore does not get to live like this!" Alexei screamed. "I worked hard to get this life, and a slut does not deserve the same thing for opening her fucking legs!" He slapped Arina across the face. She winced and cried. Her body shook all over.

"I told him to forget it," said Alexei, sputtering into her face. "I would give him a price, and he continued to tell me he would pay. I asked for more, and he offered to pay it. I tried to give him a number so outrageous that he would give up, but no. The stupid man said he would pay. He brought me the money, just as I asked. Two million dollars!"

He struck Arina a second time. Harder. Deep reds and purples blossomed on her cheeks.

"Her story would not be some *Pretty Woman* bullshit," said Alexei. "You should have seen his face when I opened the freezer to show him his new bride." Some of the others chuckled along with Alexei. "Then I get a call about some shit going down in the Bronx, and I think, this asshole must have some big balls to attack me. Now you show up here, driving Zachary's car."

Jake wasn't sure if Paul hung himself or if they'd killed him, but it probably didn't matter. He wouldn't have been able to live with himself anyway. Not with Tatiana's death on his hands. He'd thought he'd found his storybook ending, but that was when true evil showed its face.

Jake had been to hell enough times to know what that felt like. His thoughts drifted to Catalina, seeing her body on the slab. Paul's lifeless body twisted over the freezer holding the frozen body of the woman he loved. He glanced at Alexei laughing it up with his goons. Alexei, destroyer of lives. Jake felt a switch flip off in his mind. All fear vanished.

He looked into the face of Alexei and felt for the first time in his life murderous intent. He thought he'd felt it before, when he was a kid and took his father's gun. But that was just anger. Murderous intent is on a whole different level. Empathy and compassion do not exist. What happens to you afterwards is not a concern. The only thought is the target must die.

Alexei Voznesensky.

Jake screamed and ran toward Alexei with the BFR extended in front of him. He had one shot and didn't want to miss. His field of vision narrowed and focused on his target. People were moving and reacting, but he barely noticed. He kept his feet going, barrel pointed straight ahead, vision fixed on Alexei.

Bullets ripped through his body. He laughed. Through and through. Sly appeared behind Alexei, screaming at Jake to stop. Words of reason would not stop Jake. There was no rational thought occurring in his brain.

Only rage.

Alexei's face was frozen. He couldn't move. Jake laughed harder. Alexei was probably thinking: *You are supposed to be dead.*

Soon you'll be in hell, Jake thought. *I'll take you there myself.*

He wanted to see the life leave Alexei's eyes. Nothing else would do. He had to deliver Alexei to hell.

Jake did not make it.

CHAPTER 60

Death took Jake by surprise. He entered hell in a running rage of fury. He went from fixating on Alexei to finding himself face to face with a creature that was practically all mouth. It was the size of a small truck, a big round ball with thick, stubby legs. Tiny tyrannosaurus arms wiggled on either side of its torso, too tiny to reach far but close enough to Jake to grab him. It pulled Jake toward its maw, beady little forehead eyes leaning down to get a closer look. Then up and into the mouth Jake went.

Jake's bones crunched and his flesh squirted blood as he was ground into shreds between its molars. His skull popped like a grape, and his eyeballs dripped onto the tongue of the beast. Every cell burned. Acid ate away at his mass, dissolving it, but not into nothing—into smaller bits even more sensitive to pain.

In the midst of suffering, Jake heard Arina scream, and he opened his eyes. He was face down on the floor. The BFR was still in his hand. He felt the vibration of people running toward him. Alexei yelled at Arina to shut her mouth. Jake gathered himself and sprang to his feet.

"What the fuck?" A cascade of curses flooded the room.

Jake was about twenty feet away. Close enough that he was sure he wouldn't miss, but he wanted to be even closer. He charged forward with the gun straight ahead. Alexei froze, dumbfounded. His eyes widened in fear. Jake wanted those eyes terror-stricken.

Bullets struck Jake like an army of punching fists. Big fists. Hard punches. He ignored them, eyes on Alexei, almost close enough to pull the trigger. His heart was black with hatred. His rage was like an anchor on his soul.

Cockroaches. He sat in a pit of cockroaches up to his chest. Others sat with him, grabbing big handfuls of cockroaches, shoving them into their mouths and chewing. Jake did as they did, taking as many of the twitchy, wiggling bugs as he could grab in one fist and stuffing them into his mouth. The nasty critters oozed bitter juices as he crunched away. The nutty paste in his mouth churned a horrible hunger he couldn't satisfy. He took another handful and shoved them in. They fluttered on his tongue, crawling to break free. Jake couldn't let them escape. He had to satiate the craving in his belly. He ate with mindless gluttony, slurping and swallowing the bits and pieces of carapaces, mandibles, and limbs. He licked his fingers and wiped his lips, and still, he was famished.

Jake's face was on the polished concrete floor of the garage. Alexei screamed in Russian and everyone began shooting. He couldn't tell what was happening, but he knew he had to calm himself if he wanted to figure it out. He mentally collected his rage and bottled it. Tucked it away, somewhere he could find it again. He'd unleash it when the time was right. He breathed in deeply, then out. *Settle, Jake, settle,* he told himself.

The darkness cleared. Jake found himself strapped into the chair Arina had been in earlier. Thick plastic ties, two per appendage, bound his wrists and ankles. He couldn't wriggle himself loose. Five men stood over him with looks of excitement and confusion on their faces.

"The fucker is back!" said one of them in English.

Another shook his head and spat something in Russian. Alexei circled behind them. Jake took in his surroundings. Blood pooled at his feet. Spent shells all over the floor. Empty magazine clips. Body parts. Blood, and more blood. Like a shooting gallery and a slaughterhouse rolled into one. The men were covered in blood, splattered all over their clothing, their faces, their hands.

"What the fuck are you?" asked Alexei, visibly shaken.

Jake resisted the urge to reach inside and unleash the bottle of rage he'd so pragmatically locked away. He wanted to bite Alexei's nose clean from his face. He wanted to take his thumbs and push Alexei's eyeballs back into his brain. He wanted to break the man's fingers, shove a pencil into his ear canal, and smash his toes with a ball-peen hammer.

But now was not the time. Jake smiled. "Remember the magic potion in the hotel room? What was that you called me?"

"Mudak," said Alexei.

Sly appeared behind Alexei, wearing the all-black outfit with the fist pin on the black beret.

"You changed faces," said Alexei. "Changing bodies as if you were becoming other people. It was the most incredible thing I have ever seen."

"They keep killing you, brah," said Sly. "Like a game. It was sickening. That one over there with the machete kept hacking at your jugular without taking your head off. But most of them loaded you up with bullets. Head shot. Head shot. Head shot."

"You knew what they were doing," said Jake. "Why did you keep bringing me back?"

"I could hear you screaming, brah. From the inside. Weird shit. I had to bring you back even though I knew you wouldn't be much better off here than there."

"What's this about me changing?" asked Jake. "He said I changed bodies."

"I tried to fine-tune your body. Strengthen your bones to withstand the bullets. Or speed up your ability to heal. Or at least make you strong enough to break those restraints."

"That must be where the hell of hunger and eating came in," mused Jake. A glimmer of a plan began to form.

"What is going on?" asked one of the Russians. "Who is he talking to?"

"Maybe dying so often is killing brain cells," said the one with the machete.

"The big guy is scared shitless," said Sly. "I don't think he's going to give up until you die. And if I use up all my energy reviving you, you will be dead. Permanently."

"Don't worry," said Jake. "I'm figuring this shit out."

Alexei leaned down to look into Jake's eyes. "Who or what are you talking to?" he asked.

When I die, listen for my cue, Jake thought to Sly. *Bring back my vision first before anything else.*

Sly answered Jake in his mind. *Sure thing.*

"I'm talking to my fellow demons in death," said Jake as ominously as he could. "Do you not know who I am? I am the skull-faced motherfucker with the sickle. I am the rider of the Pale Horse, and I am here for Alexei

Voznesensky. The rest of you, I am willing to let go. I suggest you all make a fresh start. Run now. When I come back from death this time, I am bringing the fury of hell with me."

"They're shitting in their pants," said Sly. "Not enough to run, but enough to make sure that when they kill you this time, you won't come back."

Alexei took the chainsaw from one of his associates and stood before Jake. "Damn you, Turgenev!" he shouted.

Jake had no time to wonder what Alexei was referring to. The chainsaw entered Jake's chest. It flung blood and guts everywhere. Alexei's blood-splattered face was a mask of determination. He cut through Jake's chest cavity and ribs, through the heart to the spine, and then through the back of the chair. Alexei shut the chainsaw off and left it wedged in Jake's chest. A foul smoke filled the room.

Jake's eyes blinked and his fingers twitched. Blood and spit dribbled down his chin.

"Jericho only gave you a potion," said Alexei. "Something like that might wear off. All I have to do is outlast you. This chainsaw in your chest should keep you from reviving." He took the shotgun from one of the men. "If you come back after this, I will cut you into little pieces."

"Goo . . .blk . . . thwac . . ." said Jake. He'd wanted to say *good luck with that*, but the gurgling blood in his lungs prevented him from speaking properly.

Alexei pointed the barrel at Jake, and Jake felt the life fading from his body. He was cold, and then the heat increased. A gag-inducing stench rolled in. It was unbearable. Darkness engulfed him and he heard the rattle and clank of a railcar. Brakes screeched, and Jake stood in the doorway of the train with rats and people running past him. A large hand swooped past him and snatched a naked body. The breeze from its hand felt like a furnace. He slowly walked from the platform and out into the open void.

Only one thing could save him. Tartarus.

He walked until the horizon lightened some, and he could see he was in the desert. He heard the shrill creatures and saw the schoolhouse off in the distance. He trudged on blistered feet around to the side of the building. Tartarus appeared off in the distance. The weight of his presence was intense. It threatened to crush Jake where he stood, yet he remained upright, waiting. He heard no other sound. He saw no other person. It was just them. The two of them. After an eternity, Tartarus was close enough for Jake to see his giant grin. His gloved fingers danced like spider's legs, slow and rhythmic.

Then it came. Just as he thought it would. The sixth mark was filled in, burned into his back. Jake was confident his plan would work.

"What is this?" boomed Tartarus. His teeth were large and bright. "What are you up to?"

"You helped me back there," said Jake. "The last time."

"I called in an army to trounce your body to grit and grime."

"That was your way of helping me," said Jake. "You wouldn't admit it, but that's what you did. I didn't understand then, but now I do."

"Hell warps the brain but never has one shown me such arrogance," said Tartarus. "Do you think we are friends? Do you think you can question me?"

"You gave me seven chances to wander through hell when others get thousands. You said it was because I can return from the dead, but that can't be true. Other people have died and been resuscitated. When the paramedic revived me, it revealed something. What happened to me is nothing new. But you knew I was different because you looked into my past. You saw the moment I first died. Which means you saw who was responsible for bringing me back. Jericho Black."

The dancing gloves of Tartarus stopped in midair.

Jake continued. "The marks on my back don't trigger when I return to hell. They denote the times I encounter you. When I am calm and clear, I can enter your realm. When I am hateful and angry, I go directly to hells of suffering. There is a system here. I am beginning to figure it out . . . and your motives.

"Somehow, you figured out the beating I took would flip the switch in my brain. That's why you turned those people against me. You knew it would release my inhibitions so I could kill without question. You helped me on my path." Jake paced in front of Tartarus. His blistered feet screamed in protest, but movement helped him think. "Yet what path am I on? How far back have you been manipulating my actions? When I thought about it, the old man in Aruru's dollhouse was what stood out as strange. *If an eye causes you to sin, then pluck it out*, he said."

The grin of Tartarus shrank into a smirk.

"When I faced Adonis Silver in the synagogue, he said something strange. He asked why he couldn't see me. I was right in front of him. Why did he say that? Then Sly told me that the kid could wish people dead. Would that be like a form of manipulating?"

Jake stopped pacing. He felt the sand burning his soles.

"Adonis Silver has your other eye, doesn't he?" Jake stated plainly.

The void of Tartarus stood motionless.

"You need me to get the eye back for you," said Jake. He pointed at the outline of Tartarus's body. "This void is your punishment. Your hell. They took your body and soul and cut them into pieces, scattered to where you could not find them." He pointed at Tartarus. "I need you to look at me. Open your eyes and look at me. Before, the pain was so intense I couldn't pay attention. Once I calmed myself, I could see your eyes or lack of one."

Tartarus disappeared.

"Show me, and I will deliver this eye to you!" shouted Jake. "My word is bond."

Tartarus opened his eyes.

Jake fought against the intense pressure pounding his skull. The pain subsided, and he caught a glimpse of Tartarus's single, beautiful eye. Jake cried in awe, but his resolve was at its breaking point. All manner of despair engulfed his soul. What happened when the pain was never-ending? When there was no way to avoid the suffering? How did one escape from oneself? Death. Jake wanted to kill himself over and over again. But there was no relief if one couldn't die. It was as if his soul was fighting against itself.

Jake called out to Sly to bring him back. He called out a second and a third time.

He was back inside the garage. He could hear himself screaming even though the pain had stopped. He closed his mouth and tried to catch his breath as he looked around. Bodies and fresh blood scattered on the floor in front of him. Five bodies, all dead. The Russian with the machete had tried to cut off his own head. The blade stuck three-quarters of the way through his neck. Another Russian slumped against the wall, half his head missing and a shotgun cradled between his legs.

One henchman had slit both wrists and deep cuts on both sides of the neck before thrusting the blade of his assault knife into his heart. He still held onto the hilt with an index finger inserted in the metal ring. Next to him lay a man with a face like mulch. He'd turned the MAC-10 on himself and discharged about half of its thirty-round magazine at point-blank range. The other goon must've run out of bullets because he'd pulled the chainsaw out of Jake's chest and thrust it into his abdomen. The motor was still running even though the cutting chain had stopped turning.

"Sly," said Jake, over the sputtering sound of the chainsaw. "Sly!"

Was Arina okay? He didn't see her. The gaze of Tartarus was not meant for her eyes. He wasn't thinking at that moment. He should've warned her. Jake gathered his strength to tip the chair over. Possibly the motion would weaken some of the straps or finish breaking the chair enough that he could escape. As he moved the chair he heard a sound. A gasp or a whimper. He cringed. It must be Arina, terrified at what she had seen. He twisted his neck to console her and felt the cold steel of a gun behind his left ear.

"Stop calling out to your demon, you monster!" screamed Alexei. He heard the hammer being cocked back. Distinct. His BFR. A pop exploded in Jake's ear, and his life ended once more.

CHAPTER 61

Alexei grabbed the sputtering chainsaw and squeezed the handle, making it roar and crackle. He knew it was a matter of time before Jake came back to life, and he was going to make it impossible for him to do so. The chainsaw whirred with white smoke pouring steadily from the exhaust. He swung the blade like a frantic madman, cutting muscle, bone, and sinew. His arms tired from the pressure and weight. Guttural screams spilled from his throat as he slashed.

He separated the head from the torso, then the arms and legs. The legs he cut into three parts, the arms two, and the torso just kind of broke apart after the blade gouged the ribcage. Alexei cut until he had tidy little pieces, nearly thirty in all. His chest heaved up and down when he was done.

He dropped the chainsaw, went over to the storage shed and rummaged through its contents until he found what he was looking for: black plastic bags and shop towels. He went to the wall with the key fobs and took the key for the gray Maybach parked on the other side of the garage; the only car he could be sure wasn't splattered with blood. He snapped open a plastic bag, shoved one of Jake's appendages inside, along with several shop towels, and tossed it inside the trunk of the Maybach.

He repeated the process until he had every last piece. Then he slammed the trunk, wiped off as much blood as he could from his face and hands, and scanned the room for the girl. She sat next to the freezer motionless. He shouted for her to get into the car. Sharp and direct. She walked over like a zombie. He sat down in the soft leather seat and pushed the button to start the car. The engine purred. He fumbled with a few buttons near the rearview mirror until one of the garage bay doors opened.

The passenger's door was opened and the girl sat down. He looked her over. The girl was clearly broken. He sighed as it was another problem he had to deal with. Alexei put the car into drive and peeled out, heading toward the city.

The next hour went by in silence. He occasionally peeked over at the girl, waiting for her to scream or cry or throw a tantrum, or even jump from the vehicle, but she just sat and looked straight out the window. As they approached the city, she tuned the radio to a station that played the latest dance music. She mentioned something about being late for the club and would he stop by the apartment to get her clothes.

He blinked a few times in disbelief. She was worse than he initially thought. He wouldn't let it go on for much longer. Something quick and painless to send her off with her sister. Since she hadn't gone for the steering wheel and run them off the bridge, it could wait until they were somewhere private.

With his final destination in sight, Alexei turned a corner and drove halfway down the block of residential homes in Brooklyn. He made a right down a driveway that was just wide enough for the Maybach. He drove to the back, where a garage built from cinderblocks and painted white stood. A large parking area was on the garage's left side to turn a car around. Alexei parked in that space and flung the door open.

The home was made of bricks and mortar. The back had concrete stairs that led to the basement. He banged on the door until it was cracked open by the old man that lived there. He yelled instructions and returned to the car. He opened the passenger side and told the girl to get out and help him. Then he went to the trunk and opened it. When the girl came around, he shoved a black plastic bag into her arms.

"Follow me," he said, grabbing a few more bags. Then proceeded to the garage.

The garage had two bays with red roll-up doors. One of the doors opened from the inside by the old man. He had white hair and a thick white mustache that hid his upper lip. His eyes drooped and he walked slightly hunched over, although he wasn't slow. The garage was mostly empty except for a furnace. The fire had been kindled, and Alexei could see through the small inspection glass that it quickly intensified, growing higher and brighter. The *Vor* often used the furnace to dispose of bodies in a pinch. The smokestack went up through a hole in the top of the garage and looked like a regular chimney.

Alexei dropped the bags on the floor and then said, "Girl. Put it here and come help me get the rest."

She did as instructed. They went to the trunk. As they brought the bags in, the old man took them to the furnace and placed them in a metal holding container. Once it was all loaded, the steel door was pulled down and latched in place. The old man turned up the heat and Alexei felt a moment of ease. The hacker's body would be reduced to ash within the next three hours. His bones would be the last thing that turned to dust. The glow of the fire reflected in Alexei's eyes. *Was it enough?*

Why had the hacker come after him in the first place? It wasn't in his nature. Alexei could tell what kind of man Jake Coltrane was when they'd first met. Some men, when pushed, would not push back. Most would push back only when pushed into a corner. Then some wouldn't allow themselves to be cornered. Those were the exceptional few, the ones he knew better than to challenge. He'd see it in their eyes; they were prepared to die.

Jericho Black was one of the exceptional few. He didn't need to hear Turgenev's tale to know that. But the hacker was different. He was supposed to be the guy who pushed back only when pushed into a corner. What set him off like that? The girlfriend?

Shit. Jericho and that fucking program. He'd almost forgotten. Alexei's people were working on it. He wanted to buy out the hacker's employer since it was the most likely where the software was located. A peace offering for Jericho. One that showed Jericho he wasn't an enemy. But the bastard who owned it, Ryan Compton, refused to sell, not even for seven million dollars. He hadn't worried because the *Vor* had their ways. Ryan's father, Chad, was the weak link. He'd unknowingly worked with the *Vor,* and all they had to do was point out they could incriminate him— enough leverage to convince his son to sell. The paperwork should've been completed already.

Alexei pulled out his phone to send a text when he sensed movement out of the corner of his eye. It was fast. An object headed for the side of his neck. He sidestepped it and caught it with his hand. The girl had swung a fire poker at him. Alexei threw a right hook that caught her on the side of her face. She wilted to the floor, still gripping the poker.

Perhaps the girl was not so broken after all.

"Get in the car," he yelled at her. She peered at him from the floor, pale blue eyes burning as hot as the flames of the furnace behind him. She let go of the iron poker and went to the car. Her eyes remained straight ahead, even after Alexei got into the car.

"Don't ever try anything like that again," warned Alexei. He turned the car around and drove back down the tight opening between the buildings.

CHAPTER 62

A lexei drove the girl to his new apartment in Manhattan. He thought about returning her to the Bronx, but the cops were still investigating the five murders in the area, so that wouldn't be a good idea. Besides, she was as useless as a horse with a broken leg. The only thing left for her was to be put out of her misery. But not now. There'd been too many deaths. Even when she'd tried to ram the poker into his neck, he had no desire to kill her. *Going soft, Alexei*, he thought.

Turgenev had purchased an Empire State Penthouse Suite at The Langham for Alexei as part of their deal. It had a doorman at front. When he opened the door to his apartment, the first thing he saw was the view of Fifth Avenue from sixty-one floors up, through the floor-to-ceiling tempered glass in the living room. The other walls were natural wood with decorative trim and adorned by many modern paintings. Hardwood floors throughout the common areas and white slate tile on the kitchen floor. He had a gray leather couch and loveseat, a blue chair for contrast, and glass end tables. The dining table was mahogany with four matching chairs. There was a small office off to the side, and the primary bedroom had a bathroom attached.

There were no roaches, no cracks in the ceilings, no holes in the floor, and no appliances with missing knobs.

Yet he was unable to get comfortable.

He needed a drink.

He took gray duct tape and bound the girl's wrists together so there'd be no more attempts on his life. Then he walked over to the bar and poured himself a glass of vodka. One turned to two, then three, then more. He lost count. The vodka couldn't quell his nerves over what he'd seen in Paul's garage. His mind wandered back to it, over and over. He tried to think of something else, but his mind was determined to make sense of it. Not even vodka could drown out the screams.

Jake had been dead for nearly thirty seconds. The girl screamed and cried, calling Alexei every deprecating word she could muster in two languages. Then the air thickened and grew heavy like gravity had doubled or tripled. A hint of amber flickered in Jake's eyes. All five of his men caught the flicker and stared deep into his dead pupils, mesmerized. Then all five of his men began to kill themselves. They were shaking and screaming as if what they'd seen was so horrifying that they had to kill themselves to get away from it. Alexei had felt their terror in those last moments.

He snapped out of it and took another swig of vodka. His phone buzzed. He read the text and called Jericho Black. Then he passed out in a drunken haze.

CHAPTER 63

There was someone at the door. Knocking. The pounding persisted, and slowly Alexei roused himself. He was on the floor. That was not like him, even when he drank. Sobering memories was like a shot of caffeine. His body stiffened. He looked to the leather couch and saw the girl sitting there, looking at him. Calm with no emotion, strawberry hair disheveled. Duct tape still bound her hands. Why didn't she try anything?

The knocking continued. Alexei lumbered to his feet and made his way to the entrance. He placed both palms on the door and leaned down to the peephole. It was the old man who worked the furnace. How did he even know where Alexei lived? He looked past the old man to see if there was anyone else in the shadows. His left hand slid down to the deadbolt unlatched it, then to the doorknob.

He opened the door. Puzzled. The old man with the thick white mustache had on a red-and-black-checkered flannel shirt and tan slacks. He sported a derby-style hat and wore black work boots. It was his way of dressing up to go out. In his hand, he held a shoebox. He handed it to Alexei.

"What is this?" asked Alexei, refusing to take the box.

"It is the ashes from earlier," said the man.

"Why the fuck did you bring them here?" Alexei looked around the hallway. Doors were all closed. Nothing but decorative wallpaper and carpet.

"I thought it was a friend of yours," said the old man. "You were acting as if you were troubled by his death. I thought it was someone you cared about. A comrade."

Not troubled by his death, thought Alexei, *scared*. The asshole running the furnace couldn't tell grief from fear? Alexei peered into the old man's clouded eyes and got the answer. Yes, he could. The old man knew the difference. He wanted to see if his suspicions were true, that the heartless Alexei hadn't killed this man and chopped him to pieces because of his malevolence, but because he was scared shitless. The asshole just wanted to see his fear again up close. He stood there like a man watching his favorite TV show. Completely engulfed in the program. He couldn't take his eyes off Alexei.

"How the fuck do you even know where I live, old—" The elevator *tinged*, and the doors opened.

Jericho Black and his bodyguard Ronaldo walked out. It was a set up. The old man was in on it. No. His memories returned. He got a text saying the sale of the software company was complete and he sent a text to Jericho for a meeting. He checked the time. After 6:00 pm. He slept the entire day. The girl sat on the couch for over twelve hours. Did she even use the bathroom? Alexei looked back down at the old man with the thick mane of white hair.

"I will come to visit you at your home tonight," said Alexei.

"Is that a date?" asked Jericho. He looked down at the old man and motioned his head like it was time to leave. The old man handed the shoebox to Jericho, who then passed it to Alexei. "He wants you to have this," said Jericho.

Alexei said nothing. He took the box.

"Are you going to let us inside?" asked Jericho.

He backed away, giving Jericho and Ronaldo plenty of room to enter. Jericho entered first, went to the couch facing the door, and sat next to the girl. Ronaldo walked inside next, and stood by the entrance.

Alexei closed the door, then latched it. The shoebox was heavy in his hand. He turned around and worked up his nerve. On the couch was Jericho Black, solid and well-dressed, not a hair nor a thread out of place. Next to him, the girl, pale and battered, slumped over her taped hands. Two completely different sides of the spectrum, yet her presence hadn't thrown Jericho off at all.

Jericho unbuttoned his jacket and crossed his legs while looking around the apartment. "Seems like you've done well for yourself, Alexei," said Jericho. "No more shithole room in Brighton Beach for you, huh?"

Alexei gulped. His purpose for the meeting was to apologize for his impudence and offer Jericho the software company as a token. Talking about how he got the money to do so would only lead to more questions.

"I wanted to give you something," said Alexei, quickly getting on track. "A gift to strengthen our relationship. We left the last time on bad terms. You know. The hacker. I bought the software company he worked for. I was given assurances that the program you are interested in is contained in their mainframe. I offer this to you in friendship."

Jericho was quiet. Only a slight nod from his relaxed demeanor. "You know I could have bought that company myself," said Jericho finally. "Unfortunately it is worthless without the hacker. You know. Jake Coltrane. Tall black guy. I need him to make it work."

The girl's eyes widened. Her body stiffened. Her eyes traveled to the shoebox Alexei was holding. The nervousness must have triggered something in Jericho. He was perceptive. Jericho was staring at Alexei suspiciously and then at the box.

"What's inside there?" said Jericho. "Something I need to know about? What does she know?" He nudged his head towards the girl on the couch.

Alexei searched for words. He gripped the shoebox tightly. Jericho noticed the tension. His gaze returned to the shoebox.

"My father loved to gamble," said the girl, piping up.

She hadn't said anything in hours. Alexei eyed her warily. Willing her to keep quiet.

"He owed more money than Tatiana and I will ever make in a lifetime," she said. "Not even the money that her love offered was enough to buy our freedom from Alexei. But at least our father is safe. He will have to hide for the rest of his life." Her jaws tightened. "I can live with that."

"Is that what he told you?" said Jericho. He looked at Alexei sideways. "If I remember correctly. He told me your story while we were having lunch a month ago."

Shit. Alexei recalled the conversation. Braggadocio exploits of his ruthlessness. Trying to impress the billionaire. But why was Jericho speaking about it? He sensed something.

"Your father is dead," said Jericho. "He died more than a year ago."

Jericho was trying to get her to talk about the shoebox. That had to be it. The girl looked at Jericho, puzzled. Alexei stared her down trying to intimidate her. Trying to shut her mouth.

"Why were we—"

"Taken?" said Jericho. He paused to see if Alexei would interject. Alexei kept his jaws shut. "Your father killed himself before Alexei could kill him," said Jericho. "With his dying breath, he taunted Alexei. Said he was the first person ever to get away from him. That's why he'll never let you go. Your father's debt has nothing to do with money. His mistake was to rob Alexei of the joy of killing him."

The girl turned her head. She looked at Alexei with her pale blue eyes looking as portentous as the eyes of a shark. "The person you are looking for is in that box," said the girl. "Alexei had him reduced to ash."

His knees were weak. Alexei backed up to the sofa and sat down. There was a table next to him. He placed the shoebox on top and waited.

"What's your name?" said Jericho to the girl.

"Arina," she said. Fresh tears welled in her eyes.

"Arina, go get yourself cleaned up," said Jericho. "Go take a bath. Get some of that filth off you, and we'll see if we can lower the swelling on that fragile little face of yours. Let me show you an article that will tell you how to get the swelling down fast."

This didn't look good. Jericho was getting her out of the room. Tears welled in her eyes but he was the one in trouble. She gave him up. He should've put a bullet in her when he'd had the chance.

"Here, look at this," said Jericho, holding the phone up in front of her. She shifted her eyes to Alexei, and Jericho put the phone closer. "Pay attention to this. See what it says. Here, something else that will help with the swelling." Jericho swiped at the screen. "See this. You have to do this too. Got it? Do you understand? Is your English good enough?"

"My English is just fine," she said.

Jericho ripped the tape from her wrists, balled it up and dropped it on the couch behind him. "Get going," said Jericho. "Do you know where the bathroom is?"

She nodded then stood. The girl put her head down and slid her feet across the floor. She went past the sofa Alexei was sitting, took a few steps, and stopped. The shoebox with Jake's ashes sat on the end table. She scooped the box up under her arm and walked toward the bathroom.

"Where are you going with that?" said Alexei. "Put it back!"

"I wish to keep him. You don't want him." Her feet dragged down the hallway and out of sight. There was the faint sound of a door clicking shut.

"Now let's talk about where you got the money from," said Jericho.

CHAPTER 64

A lexei felt the heat rising in his face. It was tense. Every so often, he spied to see where Jericho's bodyguard was. Ronaldo remained by the door like a statue. His arms folded. But Jericho was the bigger threat and he knew it. His head was on a swivel, from Jericho to Ronaldo.

Jericho placed his phone on the cushion next to him. He crossed his legs and got comfortable. He unbuttoned another button on his shirt and put his hands on his thighs. He was waiting for Alexei to answer the question about the money. Alexei thought of something.

"I stole the money from that john the girl was talking about," said Alexei, who knew it was not entirely false. "I got rich from him. He was a fool. He wanted to marry Tatiana and free this other girl here. I used the money to buy the company for you. I knew you would be angry about…"

Damn. How would he explain how he got the hacker's body?

Jericho nodded. "Makes sense," said Jericho. "You are a shrewd negotiator. Getting all this from a john." Jericho waved his hand around the apartment. "You must have fleeced him for about twenty million. Brilliant."

Alexei's tightness in his chest loosened.

"But I bet you are wondering how the hacker survived the stabbing," said Jericho.

Stabbing? How about countless gunshot wounds and being cut in half by a train? "It crossed my mind," said Alexei hesitantly.

"He was revived by a parasite," said Jericho.

"A parasite?"

Jericho clicked his teeth and folded his arms. His slick black hair glistened with the lights of the city in the background. "Many years ago, a battle waged among immortals," said Jericho. "Angels. One, in particular, was very good. I was able to obtain a bit of blood from the victor. Whenever I get such things, I analyze them. Run tests. I did what I could, trying to keep it hydrated while studying its properties, but the inevitable happened, and the blood dried up.

"We kept it between glass slides to study its rate of decomposition. I'd put it under the microscope once every six months to monitor for changes. About two years ago, something extraordinary happened. I introduced a drop of water to the blood slides, and within seconds a parasite formed. This parasite exhibited amazing properties. It was incredible." He shifted in his seat. "I gave Jake Coltrane the parasite because I need him to help me find the angel with the blood that spawned that parasite. That's how he came back to life."

"Interesting," said Alexei.

"But with his body in an incinerator I doubt anything could survive that," he said. Jericho looked toward the ground, mulling it over. "I guess Cardigan will have to go to the company and find the software on their mainframe… now that the company is mine."

The girl came back into the living room. Her hair was wet and she had on the same clothes. Tee shirt and jeans.

"The girl is coming with me," said Jericho. "She had been through enough. Call it compensation for burning up my asset."

Alexei thought to object but came to his senses. It was easier to let her go.

"Did you get in the bath?" Jericho asked the girl.

She shook her head. "I only washed the blood out of my hair. Not in the mood to make myself pretty." She peered at Alexei, and he swallowed painfully.

Jericho checked his watch. "I'm about ready to go. Put your hair over your face to cover that swollen face up."

The girl shook her head like a dog would shake its body trying to get dry. Her strawberry blonde hair swept over her shoulders, and she used her fingers to comb it out, covering her cheeks and eyes.

"Much better," said Jericho. He stood and walked over to Alexei, extending his hand. "Nice doing business with you."

Alexei reluctantly extended his hand. Was Jericho going to kill him? Their hands clasped and they shook. Jericho's grip was firm, not too hard.

"Great," said Jericho. He released Alexei's hand, returned to the couch and retrieved his coat. Then he ushered the girl out the door. She turned back to look at Alexei one last time. It was hard to read her expression through the strands of hair covering her face. Hate and hope. The end of one life. The beginning of another. She mouthed something silently. Under her breath. Without sound, he could not tell if it was in Russian or English. But it was something familiar. On the tip of his tongue.

Jericho stepped between them and broke contact. Jericho steered her through the door and into the hallway. Ronaldo followed behind. The door clicked shut, and the room was quiet. It was over. Alexei gasped in relief. The only thing left now was to ensure Jericho had everything he needed. He wanted to leave no questions Jericho's mind.

He panned down to the couch and saw that Jericho left his phone behind. Puzzling.

Then something else struck him as odd. The girl said she wanted the hacker's ashes but she forgot to take them with her. She'd taken them to the bathroom in his bedroom. She could've done something vile like spread the ashes all over his bed or rubbed his toothbrush in them.

Alexei went to check. He pulled both of the bedroom doors open at once. On the king-sized bed was the shoebox. Empty. He scanned the room. No ashes.

He walked over to the bathroom and placed his hand on the knob, leaning his ear against the door. He could hear something like the ventilation fan was on, but different. Alexei pushed the door open, and steam billowed out. The little bitch had run a hot bath even though she didn't use it. He flipped on the lights and switched the vent fan off. The other sound was still there, a bubbling coming from the large tub in the corner. He crept closer until he could see inside. The tub was filled with boiling water.

What the hell was going on?

Alexei walked quickly through his luxury apartment to the living room to grab his phone. He'd thought to call Jericho and then remembered— Jericho didn't have his phone on him. Jericho's phone was on the couch. Alexei picked it up and the screen lit up, illuminated with the last thing he'd searched. A Wiki-page. Alexei scanned the information. It said simply that the standard tub held approximately forty-two gallons of water.

He didn't get it. Why did he show her that? Alexei swiped one direction, then the other. Another page popped up. A Wiki-page. It said the human body comprised up to 75 percent water. He shook his head in disbelief. It made no sense.

Then it did.

Impossible, thought Alexei. Even Jericho said so.

He ran back into the bathroom, heart racing in panic, and right away spotted the empty plastic bag in the tiny trashcan next to the toilet. He peered into the boiling water. Steam rolled across his face, stinging. Things were floating around, forming. He saw a spine and ribcage, along with the skull. The hips formed right before his eyes. Intestines spun in lazy circles, collecting and assembling with other organs. Alexei tried to reach in and pull out what was in the tub, but the water scorched his hand, turning it beet red.

"He is returning from hell," Alexei screamed. He had to reach for the drain plug. But he'd have to put his whole arm past his elbow into the water. He'd never make it that far, he knew.

Alexei ran out of the bathroom, stumbling on his way into the bedroom. He made it to the living room and dove to the floor for his weapon. The gun felt light in his hand, and he hoped it had at least one round left. He knocked a small table over running back to the bathroom. Then he stood over the tub and squeezed the trigger frantically, only to hear a series of clicks. Empty. Alexei took the butt of the gun and slammed it against the tub. He hit it again and again, near the top edge, hoping it would crack. A hole opened near the top corner, but no cracks.

Alexei looked for something harmful to pour into the water. Ammonia, Drano, and toilet bowl cleaner came to mind, but he lived in the penthouse of a hotel. Others came to clean the rooms. That didn't stop him from looking. He stumbled over to the sink cabinet and nearly pulled the doors off the hinges. The shelves were bare. He slammed the cabinet shut in frustration.

Run, just run, thought Alexei. Put some distance between Jake and himself. Alexei hurried to the entrance of his decadent Fifth Avenue suite, a pang of regret in his side, and twisted the handle of the front door. It wouldn't budge. He twisted again. It would not unlock. He yanked and kicked and tried to peek at the lock mechanism to see why it wasn't moving when a chill shot through his body. Alexei looked out the peephole and saw Jericho Black standing outside in the center of the hallway, facing the door. Alexei started to call out to Jericho when something told him not to. Jericho wasn't there to offer help. He was standing guard.

He was waiting for the hacker.

Alexei turned and slid down the length of his ornate front door to the polished, hardwood floors. He stared wistfully out of his state-of-the-art, floor-to-ceiling windows. It really was a beautiful place, he thought. Then a naked and steamy Jake Coltrane emerged from the bathroom. He looked larger than Alexei remembered, not in height, but stature. More muscular. More defined. His eyes no longer contained the fear of uncertainty or the fire of pure rage. Neither was he intimidated by Alexei. He appeared clear and focused. Calm, yet ready to kill.

The girl mouthed something to him before she left with Jericho. It was Russian. He remembered. *Smert's chernota*. The reason it did not make immediate sense in his brain is because no one says it like that. Smert's means *death from*. Chernota means *black*. If she was saying Black Death it would be chernaya smert' but she said it exactly as she meant it. *Death from black*.

He was the most frightening presence Alexei had ever experienced.

CHAPTER 65

Jake had no idea what it looked like to Alexei, but it took every ounce of willpower he could muster to stand. He was shaking all over, not from anger, but from trying to remain conscious. Breathing was difficult. He'd coughed a lot of fluid out of his lungs before exiting the tub, but the oxygen exchange wasn't happening as fast as it should've. The surface of his skin tingled from the intense heat of the water. His stomach swirled like eels were swimming around his inner workings, and if he tried to speak, he had no idea if words or guts would come out.

Sly stood right beside him in a purple suit with a gold shirt. His permed hair fell to his shoulders and curled up at the end. On his head was a purple Bellissimo fedora with gold trim. He looked like the usual Sly, but Jake knew something was wrong. Sly was barely hanging on.

Alexei was slumped with his back against the door, cringing like a rat trapped in a corner. "Fuck you, asshole," he said, visibly shaken. "In a fair contest you don't stand a chance against me. All of a sudden you are brave, when before you were shitting in your pants."

He rose to move away from the door, legs wobbling in fear, trying to distance himself from Jake. Or trying to buy time. "I did nothing I was not ordered to do. It was just business. I was sent to take care of things. You stole money! Remember that? You stole from us! What about your sins? You can't blame that on me."

He crept along the edge of the wall, squeezing between an end table and passing in front of the flat-screen television hanging on the wall. "Is it your girlfriend?" Alexei asked, sneering. "She knew I was at her house before. She had fingerprints on a glass that she kept. Threatened to turn it over to the police if anything happened to you. You were already dead at the morgue, and I was afraid she would find out and turn the glass over to the police." He pointed at Jake. "It's your fault I had to kill her, not mine."

Jake clenched his teeth. "She was pregnant with my child," he said, sounding like a monster from a cheap movie.

"I did not know that!" Alexei whined. "She never told me."

"Would you have spared her if she did?"

The pause told Jake all he needed to know.

"You're going to die tonight," said Jake.

"You are only talking tough because Jericho gave you that parasite!"

Jake stepped toward Alexei, but his body wasn't ready for combat. His knees buckled and he lurched forward. He felt like all his energy was in a cup balancing on a ledge, and when he moved it tipped over and fell inside his torso. He felt like he was falling off a cliff on the inside. His body screamed at him to sit and relax. Lay on the floor. Breathe. Rest. Recuperate.

But Jake would not. He straightened himself out.

"Why can't I move?" Jake asked Sly.

"I did the best I could," said Sly. He went down on one knee and collapsed on the floor, convulsing.

"Sly," said Jake. "What's wrong?"

"Your body is still healing. If you can stall him awhile, you'll be fine."

"How long?" asked Jake.

"About three minutes. Uh oh. He knows something's wrong. His bloodlust just spiked."

"Talking to your demon again?" asked Alexei. "You said you can't move. Is this a trick to get me to come over there? Come to think of it, you have not moved at all. I am right here, big guy. Come and get me."

"What's wrong with you?" asked Jake.

"I used up all my energy," said Sly. "He tried to burn us up, Jake. You were nothing but ashes. I brought you back because I could still hear you. You were pleading with me to get you back into the action. I didn't have the heart to leave you there. I used half of my energy to resist the flames, then the other half to bring you back. But I got nothing left. The tumor . . . it's gone. I fixed it. But now . . . there's nothing left in my tank."

Alexei watched Jake quizzically. He circled the room, inching closer.

With each step, he grew more brazen. He walked behind Jake, keeping his distance, sizing him up. "Without your gun you don't seem so tough," said Alexei. "There was that eye trick where you got everyone to kill themselves, but that was a onetime thing. I think you blew your load there."

"I'm waiting for you to get closer," Jake said. *Five minutes.* If he could bluff his way out of fighting, he might have a chance. "I want you on your knees before I summon the demon eyes of death." He spoke without gagging, a good sign. His body was healing.

"I don't think so," said Alexei. "You could not wait to kill me before. You ran carelessly through a barrage of bullets just to get close enough to kill me."

"Jake," said Sly, lying on his stomach. "Normally I would go retreat and get things ready to bring you back in case you die. Not this time. There is no bringing you back from this one. I'll stay with you and help you out as best I can."

"Take the energy from my body to rejuvenate yourself," said Jake. "Take as much as you need."

Sly had a solemn look about him. "I wish I could do that, brah, but no. Each time energy is converted it loses efficiency. The compounds . . . it's too complicated to explain. Bottom line is you gotta win this battle, Jake. No do-overs."

Jake summoned all the energy in his body to move but still couldn't. He screamed inside his mind, begged and strained, but nothing moved. It was like being stuck in a dream he couldn't wake from. He felt Alexei inching closer from behind, getting ready to strike. His heart raced as he felt Alexei breathing on his neck. In one swift move Alexei's big arm came around his throat from the back and put Jake in a sleeper hold.

"Damn it! This isn't good," said Sly.

Jake lost his balance and fell forward. Alexei crashed on top of him. Jake's limbs twitched and flexed. He grabbed at Alexei's arm and tried to free some room up around his throat.

"Throw an elbow, Jake. An elbow," said Sly.

He flung his arm back as hard as he could, delivering only a glancing blow to the ribcage.

"Pathetic," said Alexei. "What a joke. You are still the same frail creature you have always been. Do you know what kind of person I am? I love torturing my victims. When they are dead, that is when the fun ends, so I make sure I take my time and enjoy every minute of it. Just like I did with your woman."

Alexei shifted his weight to apply more pressure to Jake's throat. Jake fought back but couldn't gain leverage. His legs kicked along the rug to stand and break free, scuffing his knees and elbows with rug burns. Alexei spoke harshly in his ear. "Killing your woman friend was fun. I told her to tell the truth and I would end it, yet she stuck to her story, never once wavering. I have to admit, it was the most fun I've had in a long time. Most people say anything to save themselves, but she never changed her story. After a while, I knew she didn't know anything, but I was having such a good time that I kept at it until her body finally quit on her."

Jake listened to the bastard talk about torturing Catalina and felt his muscles responding. He twisted his body around on his side. Alexei still had a grip on him, but now Jake had some wriggle room. He used his heel to dig into the rug and gained enough leverage to pull himself toward a chair. He considered taking a chance by removing the arm that kept Alexei from fully choking him and grabbing the chair to swing at Alexei . . . if he could hit him in the head without hitting himself. And not get choked out in the process. It was a gamble he had to take.

Alexei sensed Jake's intentions and stretched his leg out to wrap around Jake's. He kicked at the inside of Jake's knee, preventing him from anchoring himself, and poured more vileness into Jake's ear. "A computer guy who works for me found information on my computer that made me rich. You'd think that would make me happy, but it doesn't. I never knew how depressing life would be without this, my work. I was depressed. Really. Now, here you are. The ultimate gift to me."

Jake's hand finally slipped, right out from under Alexei's forearm. Alexei wasted no time securing the space under Jake's chin, taking his other arm and applying pressure to the back of Jake's neck, wrenching down on as hard as he could.

"You think you are some kind of demon?" said Alexei. "Ha! You are a gift from God. Someone that no one will be looking for. I can kill you over and over again. I can try new and different methods, and you will come back to life. Then I can do it again." He laughed. "I don't know what I was afraid of. You are everything I dreamed of. Now go to sleep. Let Alexei make you his bitch."

"You're about to lose consciousness," said Sly.

"No shit," he screeched.

Jake clawed at Alexei's arm. Alexei's muscles shook as he grunted and applied as much pressure as he could to put Jake to sleep. Jake felt as if the lights were turning out. His head dipped, and all went black.

He expected hell to envelop him. Jake was prepared for it. But hell never came.

Sly said he needed three minutes, and those three minutes had passed.

Jake's eyes popped open. A burst of energy zapped into his legs. He grabbed Alexei's forearm and propped himself up on his knees. Another burst of power shot through his body. He spotted the window with a picturesque view of the Empire State Building. Jake smiled. He was going to kill this asshole and pay whatever price he needed to pay to do it. With a final war cry, Jake thrust himself to his feet.

Alexei was on Jake's back, both arms locked around his neck, weight off the ground. He leaned backward, trying to knock Jake off balance and back on the floor. Jake went with it, using the momentum to his advantage. He stumbled backward, keeping his feet moving so they wouldn't fall to the ground. Alexei held on helplessly, his eyes enlarging when he realized they were approaching the window. He yanked at Jake's head furiously, which only propelled them faster to the window. An explosion of glass followed them out into the cold air of the city and downward from the sixty-first floor of the Lanham penthouse.

The wind whistled past Jake's ears, but he only heard the sweet sound of Alexei's screams as they fell. His fists balled up into Alexei's shirt, making sure they didn't get separated. Jake was riding this puppy straight to hell.

"Sly!" shouted Jake.

Sly appeared by Jake's side. "I'm right here with you, buddy."

The ground approached quickly.

"Sorry," said Jake. "I wish I could've killed him without sacrificing the both of us."

"It's okay. I'm worried about you when you get back to hell. You made

Tartarus a promise to get his eye back if he let you go. He won't like that you're there for good this time."

"You know about the contract I made with Tartarus?"

"I heard every word of it," said Sly.

Jake sighed. "Don't worry about it," he said. "I'm happy knowing I took this bastard with me." He pulled Alexei closer. "Thanks for all that you have done for me, Sly."

"Don't sweat it. Let's ride this asshole to hell!"

Faster and faster the ground reached up to meet them. Then all went black.

Jake stood up.

Alexei stood next to him, trying to hide his naked body with his hands. "What happened to my clothes? Where are we?"

A hazy blackness surrounded them in all directions for many miles. Jake's heart thumped, growing so loud over the dense silence that it sounded like a locomotive. Something was about to happen. Jake had been to hell too many times not to know what was going on.

"What is that?" Alexei cried, cowering in fear. "What is that?"

"Demons."

They came from all directions. All manner of beasts. Creatures that defied imagination. Critters with horns and fangs and tails and bulging eyes. Monsters with scales and slime and grit and grime. Faces inside of mouths. Teeth all twisted and jagged. Some shaped like men and others like aliens, and still others in shapes beyond comprehension. They all descended from the vast reaches of hell, attracted to the filth emanating from one soul in particular.

"No," said Alexei. "This can't be. This isn't real. I'm dreaming. Wake up. I must wake up now!" His eyes grew so wide they looked like they might pop out of his skull.

Tartarus separated from hell's menagerie and stepped forward, his tall, shadowy frame and long limbs cutting through the creatures surrounding him with ease. He came toward Alexei and displayed his neon grin for all to see.

"Show the pale one a good time," said Tartarus.

The creatures roared. They grabbed and tugged at Alexei like sharks in a feeding frenzy, tearing him to pieces and then running off to fight for the scraps.

Tartarus stood before Jake. His fingers doing the dance as it always does. He said nothing about Jake returning so soon. Nothing about the pact they made in order for Jake to travel back to earth after his marks were filled. He turned and walked away. Heading back to his realm.

Jake watched him disappear. The screams of the Contretemps always present in the background.

"Mother fucker, this is where you've been going?" exclaimed Sly, appearing at Jake's side. He wore the same purple pimp suit he had on when Jake died.

"What the hell are you doing here?" said Jake, shocked. "Does this mean you're dead?"

"I guess so. You pushed me to the limit."

"Sorry," said Jake.

"I guess I best get accustomed to this shit," said Sly. A toothpick popped in his mouth, and he rolled it around his tongue.

"I think so," said Jake.

Sly looked around the darkness. "What the fuck is there to do around here?"

"Stay out of harm's way and find a way to paradise."

Jake and Sly headed toward a golden hue of light at the edge of the horizon. The same direction Tartarus had headed. In the midst of his stride, a large hand pressed down on Jake's shoulder. It didn't burn but startled him nonetheless. Jake looked down at the thick purple fingers applying a firm grip. He was spun around. A giant cleaver glinted over Gaap's head. The large bull tong in Gaap's nose seesawed upward as his lips puckered. He prepared to sever Jake from his member when his eyes took on a look of disgust.

"What happened?" said Gaap with a screech.

Jake looked down. His penis wasn't as grand as it had been in life. It hung from Jake's body like a sad little nugget.

"What the fuck?" said Jake. "What's going on here?"

"Listen," said Sly, holding his hands up. "Hear me out. Remember when I brought you back all buffed and shit? Certain things had to be sacrificed to make you stronger."

"Like my *Johnson*?" shouted Jake.

"Motherfucker, have you ever seen the musclemen in those magazines with the speedos? What do you see? Big muscles, no dick, okay? You can't have everything, nigga. It's one or the other. You ever heard of John Holmes? That motherfucker was big-dick famous. But what was he? A scrawny motherfucker, that's what. Everybody wants everything without sacrifices. Tall, muscular, handsome, and a big dick. Shit doesn't work that way, motherfucker."

"Is it ever going to be big again?" asked Gaap. "The little guy can make it big when you get back, right?"

"I don't know if I'll be going back," said Jake.

Gaap drooped his shoulders. He hunched over, fists dragging on the ground. "Nobody wants me to have a big penis," Gaap whined. "God didn't even give me a penis. How fucked up is that?" He kicked at the ground like a kid who lost a baseball game. "This sucks."

Jake shook his head, watching Gaap's wistful jaunt as he faded from sight. "Can you believe that guy?" he asked Sly.

Jake looked around the emptiness. "Sly?"

"Sly?"

PREVIEW OF PART TWO:

A Butterfly's Karma

CHAPTER 1

$\longleftarrow\!\!\!-\!\!\diamond\!-\!\!\!\longrightarrow$

Joseph Silver III stood on the front porch of his grandfather's home near the beach. His nostrils flared, taking in the sharp saltwater air and staring at the sky as if he were reminiscing. Behind Joe stood Sara, his wife. Sara was short but well-proportioned, with shiny, long black hair and a bright, cheery smile. Her eyes sparkled. She had a happy-go-lucky disposition protected by a solid layer of toughness. She often bragged about her time in the Israeli army beating the men at sharpshooting and hand-to-hand combat. At their wedding she'd been spotted by guests smoking a cigar with the groomsmen. It had embarrassed her mother to no end.

Behind Sara was Jasmine, their youngest at age twelve. Jasmine preferred her light brown hair long and combed to glossiness. She had faint freckles scattered about her nose and cheeks. Jasmine was thin and petite and didn't seem to be taking after her mother in any way other than her developing attitude. She always kept a handbag over her shoulder or nearby, filled with nail polish, hair clips, and lip gloss—everything a young girl might need. She was sighing because her parents made her dress in old, ratty hand-me-downs for the day.

Adonis Silver, last in line and their oldest child at seventeen, took a deep breath, not liking what the day had in store. They always lined up like this when they came for a visit, but no one would be there to open the door this time. After ninety-eight years on earth, Joseph Silver, his great-grandfather, had passed on. They were there to clean out his belongings, collect mementos, and divvy out what possessions other family members might like to keep.

Don, as he preferred to be called, used to visit the place regularly before his great-grandfather became sick. His great-grandfather loved the water and always wanted to be close to it, so he'd built his home by the beach. The rickety deck was worn and grayish and needed a new paint job, but its bones were solid. The ocean wasn't visible from the house, but the salty-pungent scent of the sea was ever-present. In the distance, Don could faintly hear the crash of the ocean and the squawks of hungry seagulls.

They'd visited Grandpa Joseph's home in Montauk, New York, many times when Don was younger. Don loved it best during the summer months when the island came alive with tourists. Long ago the founders of Montauk envisioned their little piece of Long Island as the Miami Beach of the north. A place where the people of Manhattan could enjoy a bit of sand between their toes. Grandpa Joseph bought into that dream and purchased the house to stake his claim. Even though the town had remained a small tourist town known for fishing and summer homes, that was fine with Joseph Silver III.

Don's father put his hands on his back, stretched, and exhaled. It was time. He rattled the keys and opened the front door of the modest house. One by one, they walked inside. The house smelled like old people, which was strange when Don thought about it. How would one describe it? Skin cells dying off at an accelerated rate? Internal organs not working properly? Was it the smell of adult diapers mixed with Efferdent?

Perhaps it was the smell of death.

"It smells funny in here," said Jasmine, always the first to complain.

"Shut your mouth," chided Sara. "Show a little respect. Ninety-eight years on this earth, survived World War II, and without his sacrifice you wouldn't be here!"

Jasmine hated getting scolded and retreated to the dining room area. She slammed her butt down on an old wooden chair at the dining table, about twenty feet from the rest of the family. The table was covered with magazines piled three feet high. Mainly tabloids purchased at the checkout aisle of the supermarket. Joseph never missed a week in nearly forty years.

The house was a mess. Very little wall space had escaped a proliferation of junk. Piles of old newspapers since the 1940s were stacked in a corner next to the twenty-one-inch console television. Old shoeboxes filled with bills and letters, at least two hundred of them, gathered dust on top of each other and stretched along the walls. An old brown couch and chair, worn so thin their material was see-through, claimed a space on the hardwood floor, as well as a matted and stained tan rug. A lamp with a torn lampshade stood bent and forlorn next to a lone window with curtains so old they looked like they'd turn to dust if touched.

Sara pulled up the shades to let some light into the living room. The shades rolled up on a spring that she had to tug to unlock and was then tricky to get it to stay once she set it. Just when she'd thought she'd gotten the shades to keep in place, they snapped and unfurled, making quite a racket. Dust particles floated in the air as light greeted the room, undeterred by the accumulated grime of many decades.

Joe drifted off in a daze at the sight of the disaster before him. There was no keeping the place as a summer home. Renting it out as an Airbnb was also ruled out. The stained ceiling and cracks in the walls called for a pretty penny just to get it presentable. He'd already had to pay back taxes to take possession of the property. The best option was to sell as-is. Everything had to go.

Don started by pushing aside the television, knocking over a stack of newspapers in the process. The heavy wooden console looked more like a piece of furniture than a television. It sat on the floor and had intricate carvings etched along its sides. The screen itself was tiny compared to the LCDs at their house. He remembered how Grandpa Joseph never wanted anyone to touch or go near that part of the living room. Sentimental value, he'd called his hoard. With him gone, it struck Don as nothing more than junk that nobody wanted. Funny how things of value to one person were considered trash to another. People held on to their stuff, and after they died, someone else sold it or threw it away.

Don wondered what made people spend their whole lives acquiring and coveting possessions. Pointless, when death was inevitable and value was in the eye of the beholder.

"Remember when Grandpa Joseph was alive?" asked Joe. His classic Jewish New York accent got thicker when he grew nostalgic. "He'd throw a fit if anyone went near his newspapers. I mean, he would get livid. I went through them one time as a kid, and when he caught me, he tore me a new asshole." He smiled at the memory. Joe went over the shoeboxes, reached up to grab one near the top, and the whole stack collapsed. A family of mice jumped from the box midair and scattered in all directions. Joe yelped and brushed mouse feces from his tee shirt.

Sara laughed. Jasmine called him a wuss.

Don grabbed a stack of newspapers, carrying as many as he could at one time over to the window where he could toss them directly into a dumpster at the side of the house. After several trips he picked up a stack of papers, and a small box fell from inside the pile. The box had the word *Timex* embossed on its lid. It was black and worn and dusty like everything else. He picked it up and flinched. Something moved inside. He shook it. It had some weight to it.

"I found an old watch," said Don to his father, who was collecting shoeboxes from the wall and tossing them.

"A Timex," said Joe. "I would like to think that that would be worth something, but I doubt it. Unless it's new. Is it?"

Don took the cover off the box. Inside was a charm. It was gold with two hearts joined side by side and overlapping. Cute. But it was the other object that carried weight: an eye. A complete eyeball with an amber iris rolling around in a Timex box. Don touched it and withdrew his hand quickly. Not only was it real, but it was also fresh. Impossible.

"Let me see it," said Joe. His father held out his hand. "Let me take a look."

Don handed over the box, and his father opened it. "It's empty," said Joe. "By the way you were looking at it, I thought that there was something incredible inside."

"Uh, no, Dad. It was just a box."

"Okay. Well, get back to throwing out those papers. It's been nothing but a fire hazard for fifty years."

Don turned and went to grab another stack of newspapers. The eye was safe in the front pocket of his jeans. He'd slipped it in quietly when his father wasn't looking.

Printed in the United States
by Baker & Taylor Publisher Services